Best Wishes

BIN LADEN'S
NEMESIS

RwKay

BIN LADEN'S
NEMESIS

R.W.KAY

Matador
9 Priory Business Park,
Wistow Road, Kibworth Beauchamp,
Leicestershire. LE8 0RX
Tel: (+44) 116 279 2299
Fax: (+44) 116 279 2277
Email: books@troubador.co.uk
Web: www.troubador.co.uk/matador

ISBN 978 1780881 836

British Library Cataloguing in Publication Data.
A catalogue record for this book is available from the British Library.

Typeset in 12pt Minion Pro by Troubador Publishing Ltd, Leicester, UK
Printed and bound in the UK by TJ International, Padstow, Cornwall

Matador is an imprint of Troubador Publishing Ltd

To all who died as a result of the attacks on 9/11, not only those in New York, Pennsylvania and Washington, but also the subsequent tens of thousands of innocent men, women and children in Afghanistan and Iraq.

Author's Acknowledgment

The author wishes to thank the following for helping him with early drafts: Jean Barlow, Bob Fisher, Tim Gresty, Salwa Jones, John Knewstubb, Angie and Mick Salt, and especially Paul Watson.

C H A P T E R   1

Tuesday 3rd July 1990

'Are you telling me there's no one in our department or MI6 who can speak all these languages?'

'Yes, Sir,' replied the Head of the Irish desk. 'We have Gaelic linguists, of course, but none who can also speak Arabic and Spanish. MI6 has many fluent in Arabic and Spanish but not with Gaelic.'

The Director of MI5 sighed audibly. 'How long would it take to train someone?'

'Eighteen months on the Arabic course and a year in the field – two and a half years.'

'Too long. We haven't got that sort of time. There must be someone, somewhere, surely? Have you tried the Armed Forces?'

'Yes. They can offer similar skilled linguists like us, but not with Gaelic. There was one who filled the job description, but he retired several years ago.'

'A shame; this will not be a job for a geriatric.'

'He's just turned forty. He retired from the Army Intelligence Corps after sixteen years service. He is currently teaching Spanish and French at a school in Cumbria. He also teaches Japanese to managers working in the nearby nuclear plant at Sellafield.'

'It sounds as if he's gifted linguistically.'

'Yes, the only problem is that his Gaelic is Manx, not Irish.'

'Would that matter?' asked the Director, Sir Charles Gray.

'Probably not. Scottish, Irish and Manx are all derived from the same ancient language. He should be able to understand what is being said.'

'Have you got his details? I'd like to have a look.'

His deputy passed over a pink file marked *Staff-in-Confidence*.

Sir Charles opened the file. On the inside cover was a black and white, head-and-shoulders photo of a handsome-looking man, probably in his mid-thirties. A head of wiry black hair, dark eyes, high cheek bones, swarthy skin and a strong chin suggested a man who kept himself fit. He read the frontispiece of the file, line by line:

Major Juan Hasani Quayle

Born:	Bride, Isle of Man, 2 April 1950
Education:	Ramsey Grammar School, Isle of Man 1961-1968, 'A' Levels: English, French, German, and Latin
University:	Durham 1968-71: Joint Honours German and Spanish (2:1 awarded) Leeds 1971-72: PGCE
Commissioned:	Sandhurst 1973, Intelligence Corps. Retired July 1988
Marital Status:	Single
Hobbies:	Sailing, swimming (Member British Long Distance Swimming Association), golf (handicap – 7).

Sir Charles stopped and looked at his colleague. 'I see he's Manx, that could be a bonus, but there's no mention of his ability to speak either Gaelic or Arabic.'

'If you turn over, sir, you'll find his mother was Egyptian, hence his unusual middle name. She met his father when he was serving with the Army in the Canal Zone at the end of the Second World War. Quayle senior married her and brought her back to the Isle of Man where Quayle junior was born several years later. Quayle's father was a farmer in the north of the island and spoke Manx. The boy, who was an only child, was brought up in their home multi-lingual. Both his parents died ten or twelve years ago, leaving him the farm; which I understand he has leased locally. As you say, being Manx could be a plus as he should know the local geography.'

Seemingly satisfied, Sir Charles nodded and turned over the page. He glanced down the summary:

Career History: 1973-76 Asst Mil Attaché, Baghdad
1976-79 HQ BAOR (Int Directorate)
1979-81 Joint Sch of Languages, Beaconsfield, 18 month Russian Course
1981-84 British Commander's in Chief Mission, Berlin (BRIXMIS)
1984-86 Falkland Islands, Interpreter
1986-88 RAF Chicksands Instructor

'I see he never served in Northern Ireland,' remarked the Director.

'No. That may be a good thing?'

'Yes, definitely.'

He began turning over the annual reports that had accrued during Major Quayle's 16-year career. A life-long civil servant, Sir Charles could skim-read quickly and accurately. However, even he had to stop in disbelief periodically. After almost a quarter of an hour of silence, he put down the file, and looked at his Head of the Irish Desk, Sean Doran.

'Well,' he exclaimed, 'this Quayle is something of a Don Juan, if you excuse the pun! Using him might be a risk?'

'Juan is pronounced *Jew-ann* in the Isle of Man, sir. It's quite a common boy's name. However, his annual reports all agree on one thing: he was good at his job,' replied Doran.

'They also agree he has a weakness for the two *W*s: Wine and Women.'

Sir Charles then began listing the occasions that had resulted in Quayle being reprimanded. 'He gets drunk at a dining-in night and is found the next morning in bed with a civilian member of the mess staff who just happens to be the wife of a sergeant on the base. Then there was the incident in the bar when he told the Colonel's wife that she looked better when she had been a peroxide blonde – in front of junior officers. Unbelievable! Finally, there was the incident which resulted in him being slung out of BRIXMIS.'

'That was never proved, sir. My contacts tell me he was set up by the Russians.'

'Nevertheless, a German seventeen year old schoolgirl.'

'I am led to believe she was a young-looking, twenty-two year old East German member of Stasi. He was sent to the Falklands with a black mark. It's probably the reason he decided to leave at his optional mid-career retirement point.'

'The question is,' asked Sir Charles, 'dare we use him? And will he come back?'

'The terms of his Army commission are that he is currently serving six years on the reserve list. We could always recall him if necessary.'

'One volunteer is worth two pressed men, Sean. What else do you know about his present circumstances?'

'I've done some background research. Quayle teaches at St Bees School in Cumbria. The Head is the Rev Reginald Hargreaves who was, formerly, a Royal Navy padre for seven years. He might, therefore, be sympathetic to our cause. Can I suggest you make contact and give him a visit?'

***

A few days later, on Thursday 5th July, Sir Charles was sitting in the Principal's study sipping a mid-morning sherry. 'I was intrigued by your phone call, Sir Charles. How can I be of help?' asked the Rev Hargreaves.

'I'll come to the point, Reggie. You have a teacher on your staff – a Major Quayle?'

'Yes, he takes Spanish to 'A' level, lower forms for French, and helps run the Combined Cadet Force. Why?'

'We desperately need him to work for us for a year or two.'

'You haven't told me what you do, Sir Charles.'

'It's rather sensitive work, I'm afraid, but from your time in the Navy I'm sure you'll understand. Even Padres have to sign the Official Secrets Act.'

4

The mention of the Royal Navy and the Official Secrets Act, which, once signed, lasts for life, made the Head's eyebrows rise. *How did he know I was in the Navy?* he wondered.

Sir Charles continued, 'Let's just say I manage one of the Government's security services.' He paused and took a sip of his Amontillado.

The Principal looked at the dapper, grey-haired man in his late fifties, and thought: *Do I take his word at face value?* 'You'll forgive me, Sir Charles, but that is quite a claim to make. I don't wish to be rude, but have you any proof?'

'You served on *HMS Liverpool*, I believe?'

'Yes, I did.'

'And your Commanding Officer was Captain Trevor Norman?'

'He was.'

'If you ring this number, you'll get him in the Ministry of Defence; he's now a rear-admiral. Have a chat with him, ask him some questions to convince yourself he is your former CO, and he will confirm that I am who I say I am.'

A phone call, some catching up on the good old days, and several minutes later the Principal was convinced. 'What do you want with Quayle?' he asked.

'Quayle is rather unique,' replied the Head of MI5. 'Did you know he can speak Arabic and Gaelic as well as German, French, Spanish, Russian and Japanese?'

'No, I didn't.'

'I would like to meet him, and invite him to join my department on what is an essential mission. Rest assured I wouldn't come all this way if there had been any alternative.'

'Without being self-centred, if he leaves my school where will I get a replacement?'

'We thought about that, and have found you a volunteer who is currently a lieutenant commander in the Royal Navy's Instructor Branch. We have given his details to the agents Gabbitas-Thring. If you contact them, he can be with you next term.'

5

'You seem to have thought of everything, but what if Quayle won't play ball?'

'Then we might have to resort to plan B.'

The Rev Hargreaves decided not to ask what plan B was, but replied, 'I'll get Juan to join us for a private lunch in the Governors' Board Room. Meanwhile, you might like me to show you around the school?'

Sir Charles found the lunch difficult. Firstly, the lack of choice reminded him of his time at Prep School: *Meat, potatoes and gravy followed by sponge and custard.* His two co-diners seemed to find the meal acceptable. Secondly, he wanted to explain his presence to Quayle but without giving too much information away in front of the Principal. Fortunately, Rev Hargreaves sensed this and offered to take Juan's first class that afternoon – 4B French – as, 'You two have much to discuss.'

The pair strolled out of the school grounds and down the lane leading to the beach, half a mile away.

'Let me explain my being here,' began the Head of MI5. 'However, I must remind you that what we are going to discuss is subject to the Official Secrets Act. I am sure you understand the implications.'

Juan nodded.

'It's no big secret the British Government is having discussions with Sinn Fein, the Irish Government and the Ulster Unionists to create some sort of power sharing arrangement for Northern Ireland. It's officially denied, of course. However, this so-called Northern Ireland Peace Process is in danger of grinding to a halt. The problem is the Unionists demand a total scrapping of all the Provisional IRA's weapons. The successful supervision of the decommissioning of arms is going to be crucial. The matter is further complicated by the Provos being organised in brigades, each semi-independent. Some are more inclined towards giving up their arms than others and no one knows what stocks the brigades have as, over the years, there have been several sources of supply. The Derry Brigade, for example, has received weapons originating from Yugoslavia slipped through Donegal, whereas the South Armagh and South Belfast Brigades have been supplied from Libya by a chain involving Spain and the Isle of Man.'

Juan stopped, looking puzzled.

'Yes, I thought that might make you take notice. The Libyans have been using Spanish registered trawlers that legally fish for scallops off the Manx coast. We believe they have transferred arms to Irish fishing boats in harbours such as Port St Mary and Peel, but despite Manx Customs officers regularly inspecting the boats, nothing has ever been found.'

'Why use the island? Surely Spanish boats can enter Irish waters?'

'True, but they don't trust each other. The Spanish boats are crewed by Libyans, posing as Moroccans from the Spanish enclave of Ceuta. They speak Arabic. The Irish crews speak Gaelic among themselves. The Isle of Man is seen as neutral territory and with two Spanish banks in the same Douglas street as three Irish ones, transferring Irish punts to pesetas is easily supervised by both sides.'

'I'm not sure what this has got to do with me.'

'I'm coming to that. The Provisional IRA bought its weapons by undertaking bank robberies, both in the North and the South of Ireland, by raising money from sympathetic groups in the USA, by trafficking drugs on a gigantic scale from places such as Colombia and Afghanistan, and by running prostitution rings in Dublin, Cork, Edinburgh, and even London. We estimate the total value of their stocks to be in excess of thirty million dollars.'

'That's quite an industry,' exclaimed the retired intelligence officer.

'Indeed, and the Provos aren't going to throw that sort of money away for nothing. Have you heard of an Islamic organisation called al-Qaeda?'

'No. Should I?'

'No, it was only formed about two years ago. You may have heard of it by its former name: al-Khidamat.'

Juan nodded slowly, 'They were a faction of the Mujahideen in Afghanistan who fought the Russians, if I remember rightly?'

'Yes, and they were a big factor in getting the Russians to withdraw. The Russians lost over 10,000 men. Al-Qaeda wants to overthrow the

Saudi Royal Family, drive Israel into the sea and create a new Palestine. They see America as their main stumbling block, and are not afraid to take on the US in any way possible. I fear we may be entering a new phase of terrorism that will make the IRA appear to be Dad's Army. Al-Qaeda has wealthy sponsors; we think Saddam Hussein may be giving them money as their aims are broadly the same as his. He sees al-Qaeda as a bunch of mercenaries doing his dirty work. Al-Qaeda has its head screwed on financially and see the IRA weapons as a cheap source of supply. The most likely route for them to receive stocks will be the reverse of the Armagh one; namely back through the Isle of Man, Spanish fishing boats, and Libya. Colonel Gadhafi is sympathetic to their cause. We need you to infiltrate the Islamic fundamentalists: find out how they work, how they recruit, where they train, that sort of thing. It needs someone who can understand the languages – Irish Gaelic, Arabic, and Spanish.'

'I'm not sure it's for me. I like St Bees. It's a friendly school; the kids are happy, I'm happy.'

'The trouble is Juan, we haven't got time to train someone. I haven't told you this, because if it ever became public knowledge then all hell could break loose. We believe the Armagh Brigade acquired a dirty uranium bomb from Libya four years ago. If this falls into the wrong hands...' he stopped, never completing the sentence.

'I assume it was a small tactical one?'

'Yes, probably equivalent to 3,000 tons of TNT.'

'I witnessed the Russians fire one, about that size, against a hardened aircraft shelter in East Germany when I was in BRIXMIS. I was about five miles away. It left a big hole. But why didn't the IRA ever use it?'

'They took fright after their attack killed eleven people at the Enniskillen War Memorial in 1987. The public outrage as a result, even among their own supporters, has probably been the driving force for them to come to the negotiating table. The bomb's existence and location has been secret ever since they acquired it, but it is too valuable for them to bury in a bog. We think it's a simple device and not very efficient. Two sub-critical pieces of Uranium-235 are fired into each other to make them critical and start the fission. We believe it was Colonel Gadaffi's prototype atomic bomb and, rather than test it himself, he thought the IRA would do it for him. The Provos are now looking to sell it to the highest bidder. God only knows what al-Qaeda would do with it: London, New York, Tel Aviv? We must intercept it, somehow.'

'OK. So, if I agree, what do you want me to do?'

'Good man! Let's walk back and I'll tell you what we've got in mind.'

Two weeks later, on 20th July, the IRA attacked the London Stock Exchange, setting off a 10lb bomb. Although no one was killed, it made Juan realise, listening to the report on the radio, that his future was about to become less secure than it had been since his arrival at St Bees two years previously. However, the thought excited him. Although he'd never admitted it to anyone, he was missing the cut and thrust – the adrenalin that flowed through the veins when you're not sure what lies around the corner. He'd wondered if he could survive another twenty years of teaching languages to youngsters, who seemed less motivated than when he'd been at school. Before meeting Sir Charles he'd even considered getting a dog.

He'd turned forty; his flow of testosterone was slowing down. Women had always been an enigma for Juan. Having been brought up an only child in a small village by church-going parents, he had been led to believe that getting a hand inside a girl's bra or up her skirt constituted an agreement to marry them. If he buried his head inside their blouse, he expected to find her father's shotgun waiting for him when he withdrew. His best pal in the sixth form had had to undergo a shotgun wedding. Juan didn't want the same thing to happen to him. Consequently, progress with girls could only be made by promising them everything; letting them take over his life for a short period, and then running away. For Juan, the love bug was something of a hang-up. He'd noticed he hadn't been catching the virus as frequently lately; he was slowing down, golf was taking over. There'd been the PT mistress, usually fondled in the showers after she'd walloped him at squash; it had lasted a few months until the rumour had spread around the school staff and was in danger of getting out to her husband who ran a taxi firm in nearby Whitehaven. Otherwise, the odd glance at the school secretary's backside, as she had given him an invitational wiggle whilst walking past, was all that had happened. Perhaps the adventure waiting ahead of him would pull him out of the comfortable rut.

CHAPTER 2

Monday 27th August 1990

Juan Quayle found himself undertaking training at an isolated country house in North Devon. Woodside reminded him of the National Police College at Bramshill, where he had undertaken some short courses while in the Army, but on a smaller scale. Originally purchased for the Army at the outbreak of WW2 as a staff HQ, it sat in its own wooded grounds of some twenty acres, surrounded by a six-foot-high wall. At its only entrance, on a quiet 'B' road, was the former mansion's original gate-house; now used as a reception and security office. A sign at the electrically controlled gate announced: *Woodside College – visitors report to reception.* There was no indication of the college's function; nor any welcome. *Trespassers Keep Out* was, however, implied. Totally self-contained, there were some thirty newly-built en-suite rooms in an annex at the rear of the old house. The kitchens, the communal dining room, various ante-rooms and the library were in the original building. With locally recruited domestic staff, it was to all intents a small officers' mess. He noted the security staff were MoD Police. *Strange,* he thought, *a Home Office college guarded by Ministry of Defence personnel.*

His training was a one-off: a mix of private study and one-to-one tutorials with specialists brought in from outside. It was a strange experience; at school, university and in the Army he'd always been in a class with others. Consequently, there had always been a rapport; someone to talk to about the course and criticise its teachers, people to get to know and go out with for a drink, lifelong friendships to be made. The first week was particularly lonely as other students were in small groups; usually younger than himself, he had little in common with them. He wanted to tell them about his background in the Army and how he'd spent time in East Germany watching the Russians. He knew, however, that secrecy was the name of the game. He would have to find relief from his pent-up frustration at the weekend. He decided to ask the college secretary if there were any arrangements to play at any of the local golf clubs. Perhaps taking pity on him, the secretary agreed to play with him each Sunday morning at Westward Ho!

His conversational brush-up in Arabic with a native Libyan gave him little trouble. His mother's Egyptian and three years in Baghdad had prepared him well. His intense Irish Gaelic lessons were more difficult as the instructor, an agent operating under cover in Southern Ireland, spoke Connacht Gaelic, the least similar of the four variations of Irish to Juan's Manx.

A new identity had to be learnt. He would get quizzed periodically by several permanent staff – at odd hours when his guard might be down. He assumed the alias of Alan Quine, a common Manx surname. He grew a beard and lengthened his hair. Grey strands appeared; they hadn't been there before. It reminded him he was past forty.

Juan found the most difficult part of *Operation Third Leg* was learning his new CV; he had to become Alan Quine. Born and educated in New Zealand, he had gone away to sea when sixteen years of age and spent much of his life on oil tankers plying routes between Australasia, Japan and the Persian Gulf. He had worked hard, taken exams, and acquired a master's ticket. He had learned to speak Japanese competently. He was, for several years, Shell's representative in Al Faw – Iraq's only deep sea oil terminal. It accounted for Alan's ability to speak Arabic with an Iraqi accent. However, his Gaelic ability was not explained and he would have to remember to use it only for eavesdropping.

A speech therapist taught him to speak English with an antipodean accent. After a week, she remarked that he would fool everyone except an Australian or a Kiwi. He spent several weeks learning the skills of a deck hand on a trawler working out of Ilfracombe. A similar period was spent on an oil tanker at Milford Haven.

Prime Minister Margaret Thatcher's resignation that November had passed without him noticing.

The Christmas and New Year holiday period was spent quietly at a hotel in Cornwall. On Monday 7th January, a specialist came from the Atomic Energy Research and Development Establishment at Harwell to instruct Juan on how to recognise crude atomic devices.

'The Libyan bomb will be gun-fired,' he said. 'An explosive charge, probably TNT, will fire a chunk of Uranium-235 into another chunk.'

Juan was amused at the boffin's use of the word 'chunk'.

'When forced into each other, the two chunks become critical and nuclear fission begins. It may take several minutes before the explosion, depending on the purity of the Uranium. If the device is, as suspected, equivalent to somewhere around 3,000 tons of TNT, then it will be roughly the size of a large suitcase. It could weigh as much as four sacks of coal: nearly a quarter of a ton. So, it's not the sort of thing you can sling onto the back seat of your car.'

'I thought these things were much smaller,' remarked Juan.

'These days they are,' replied the scientist, 'but remember this was built five or six years ago and Libya has never been at the forefront of nuclear research. Much of the space of the device will be taken-up by the detonator, the timing device, the anti de-arming circuits and so on. The two pieces of uranium will be encased in a metallic sphere, probably a titanium-lead alloy, about as big as a medium-sized Easter egg. It will almost certainly be strengthened by a wickerwork net of wrapped steel cord so that if the detonator went off accidentally it would not affect the uranium pieces inside.'

Self-defence, firearms practice, interrogation techniques, methods of communication with MI5 and MI6 and physical training kept him busy.

∗∗∗

In late-January, Alan Quine was deemed ready to leave for the Isle of Man with a New Zealand passport, driving licence and bank account, together with a purported family tree of the Quines. Monthly sums of money would be transferred from his account in Auckland to the Isle of Man Bank in Athol Street, Douglas. On Saturday 2nd February, he booked into *The Sefton*, an updated Victorian hotel popular with travelling salesmen on Douglas promenade.

Infiltrating the IRA gun runners was not going to be straight forward and although a strategic plan had been agreed at Woodside with his course supervisor, day-to-day tactics would be left to Juan. Watching the entire Manx coastline of some 100 miles for suspect Irish boats could not be undertaken by one man. The Island's Chief Constable, a former colonel in the Royal Military Police, had agreed to help by providing a part-time detective constable as an extra pair of eyes. The following Tuesday, he met the Chief Constable, Colonel Madoc, and the DC, George Costain, in *The Glen May*, a quiet pub on the west coast. Colonel Madoc struck Juan as being a well educated but rather pompous Welshman, who had been reluctantly coerced into the subterfuge by MI5. Lunching with a member of one of his lower ranks was not something he took to easily.

'My Force consists of about one hundred men and women. DC Costain is one of my Special Branch officers; I only have three – a sergeant and two DCs. They have, however, done the necessary courses and been given top security clearances by Scotland Yard.'

It was agreed that their method of communication would be to telephone the Chief Constable on his private line at specific times. The CC would then contact Sir Charles Gray directly, as required. The three would use coded names based on Manx promontories: Colonel Madoc would be Douglas Head, George – Maughold Head, and Alan – Bradda Head. The use of any other promontories, such as Scarlett, or Langness, would signal trouble and, normally, would only be used outside the agreed times.

'If DC Costain were put full-time on this job, it would attract too much attention from his colleagues,' explained Colonel Madoc. 'Therefore, it will make sense if he watches the north of the island from

Peel, around the Point of Ayre, to Douglas. There are far fewer places where a boat could land in the north and I can't see the IRA trying anything at Douglas; it's too busy and our only permanent Customs and Excise officers are based there.'

'You said permanent. Are there any part-time Customs Officers?'

'No, but my constables based in the smaller ports, such as Port Erin and Ramsey, have delegated powers from the Excise people to search any vessels they suspect of carrying contraband.'

'And do they?'

'Often, but they have never found anything untoward in the Irish or Spanish boats that land regularly at Peel or Port St Mary.'

'I was thinking of renting a one bedroom apartment in Port St Mary, so it would tie-in if I took responsibility for the south of the Island. The village seems the most likely harbour after Douglas for illicit activities.'

'Fine. If you watch the south then everywhere should be covered. You will get a holiday-let easily at this time of the year. However, Port St Mary is small and everyone knows everyone else. Have you thought of a good reason for your arrival in the middle of February?' asked the Chief Constable.

'I'm a Kiwi taking a couple of years out to do Europe. My father, Fred Quine, a joiner, emigrated to New Zealand from the island after the war. I am here to research the family tree and, possibly, trace distant relatives. I'll buy a small car to run around the island looking at gravestones. It will be my cover for looking out for the gun-runners. I'll take casual work, if I can get it, on the local fishing boats. I have sailed deep-sea extensively – mostly in tankers to the Gulf. My mother was half-Maori, which explains my suntan.' He smiled as he thought of his late-mother. He had decided to keep his real identity confidential – even from the Chief Constable. Having been brought up on an isolated farm in the north of the island, there would be little chance of anyone knowing him in the south.

The following day he bought a Ford Escort for cash from a dealer on the quay in Douglas and began his search for a suitable flat in Port St

Mary. The two estate agents in nearby Port Erin, there being none in Port St Mary, were keen to offer him a four month lease but made it clear that in June the rent would rise substantially owing to the influx of summer visitors for the high season. He decided to look further and, whilst strolling through the main street of Port St Mary, he looked at the small ads in a newsagent's window.

Self-contained one bedroom apartment to let – long-term preferred. Kitchen, shower/toilet, sitting room with colour TV and own phone. Fully furnished. Own key. £40 per week. Apply: Mrs Molly Kelly – PSM 2855.

'Can I come and have a look? Where are you?' he asked from the public phone box.

'Well, where are you ringing from?' a soft voice, with a Manx lilt, asked.

'I'm in a phone box on the corner of The Promenade and Bay View Road.'

'Walk towards the Quay and turn first right up Victoria Road. At the top, look diagonally to your left, and I'm in *Eastview*, Cronk Road.'

Five minutes later, he was pressing the doorbell. An attractive, fair-haired, blue-eyed woman in her late-twenties opened the door. She wore a pinny and had a three-year old toddler at her side.

'Mrs Kelly?' he asked. 'I'm Alan Quine. I rang a few minutes ago.'

She smiled, a rather sad smile, and stood to one side, ushering him to enter. The youngster, who Alan suspected was a boy but couldn't be certain, clung to his mother's thigh. He entered the dimly-lit corridor hallway with steep stairs in front of him.

'I'm Molly Kelly. The apartment is at the top of the house,' she said. 'Let me show you the way.' She picked up the infant with one hand, tucking it under her arm. Alan followed them slowly up the stairs to the second floor. The child never took its eyes off Alan as they climbed; the face expressionless even when Alan, trying to break the ice, pulled a funny face. Molly's skirt was knee length; he noticed she had long, slender, strong legs, with firm buttocks beneath a slim waist.

She unlocked the door at the top of the stairs and entered. 'We had the loft converted into an apartment a year ago to accommodate my father when he agreed to come and live with us,' she said. 'However, he passed away before he could move in. It's completely self-contained.'

'I'm sorry to hear about your father,' sympathised Juan.

She shrugged, looking paler. She clearly remembered him with fondness.

He looked around. He liked what he saw; everywhere was spotlessly clean, the furniture unused, and the bed comfortable. The small kitchen had an electric cooker, a microwave, and fridge. 'I notice there is no electricity meter.'

'No. I was hoping you would pay a contribution towards heating and lighting; perhaps, another ten pounds per week?'

Juan looked at his prospective landlady. She was about 5ft 7in tall; *weighing ten stone? A size ten/twelve,* he thought. Her fair hair was neat, combed and shoulder length, but hadn't seen a professional stylist for some time.

She looks hard-up. I wonder what her husband does.

She was smiling, hopefully, at him. However, there was sadness in her eyes, as if there had been a recent tragedy in her life. The toddler was still staring at him impassively.

'What's your name?' Juan asked.

'He's shy of strangers. His name is Mikey,' Molly replied, as the boy turned and buried his face in his mother's hair.

'Well, Mikey, we're going to get to know each other better,' Alan replied. 'Fifty pounds per week is very reasonable. Will a month's rent in advance be OK?'

For the first time, her face lit up. When she beamed, she had irresistible dimples that Juan wanted to kiss.

'Would you like a cup of tea?'

CHAPTER 3

Thursday 7th February 1991

Thursday 7th February began with a bang. John Major's cabinet meeting at 10 Downing Street was interrupted when the IRA fired three mortar shells from a parked van in Whitehall. Fortunately, no one was injured when the rounds exploded in the back garden. The Prime Minister later that afternoon told the House of Commons that it had been a deliberate attempt to interfere with a democratically elected government. The Provisionals issued a statement claiming responsibility. The incident heightened Juan's awareness of the danger of the game he was now playing. A thought passed through his mind: *a dull life at St Bees might not have been so bad after all*, but he knew there could be no turning back. The old tingle that he used to have as a BRIXMIS operative behind the Iron Curtain had returned.

He divided his time between buying a wardrobe, particularly bad weather clothing, and studying his patch. After poring over the Ordnance Survey map, he would travel to remote bays, discovering nooks and crannies where small fishing boats could unload light freight. The south of the Island was a smugglers paradise, though access to most of the inlets would require a high tide and a smooth sea. Fleshwick Bay was an example. It was reached from the village of Ballafesson by a narrow, two mile track. The lane was a steady incline for the first mile, and then dropped to the sea, passing a farm that appeared to be unoccupied. The sides of the valley were steep; reaching a height of 300 ft. The dilapidated jetty could accommodate a small boat.

Derby Haven was similar. There, an unusual, if not unique, 80-yard long island-pier straddled the bay. It could accommodate two trawlers tying up astern of each other. Transfer from one to the other would be easy. If moored on the seaward side, they would not be seen from the shore. However, bringing equipment to dry land would require a small boat.

The days were short, the nights long, and the weather generally damp, cold and miserable. Leaving the comfort of *The Sefton* would be a wrench. He realised he would have to rely, in future, on pub lunches, microwaved meals and the local Chinese takeaway to sustain him.

He moved into Cronk Road on Monday 11th February, spending most of the morning buying essentials to stock his fridge. Molly had volunteered to help, and with Mikey in tow, they went to the nearest supermarket in Port Erin, two miles away. Afterwards, he offered to buy her lunch; he was delighted when she somewhat coyly accepted. She directed him to *The Colby Inn*. 'It will be quiet there,' she said, 'not too many prying eyes.'

Presumably, he thought, *she does not want her neighbours to find out.*

Over lunch, he discovered Molly was a widow. Her husband, Tommy, had been killed in a motorcycle accident the previous summer. She explained her husband's death in a distant, matter-of-fact way.

'What did Tommy do?'

'He part-owned a fishing boat with his brother. They mostly caught scallops off the Calf of Man in season but sometimes would go as far as Kinsale in Southern Ireland for herring.'

She showed little emotion. However, despite her brave exterior, he believed that below the surface she had not recovered from the double loss of her husband and father.

She has learnt to be calm and pretend she is coping, but with difficulty.

She had taken a part-time, three days per week, job as a classroom assistant at the nearby Primary School where her eldest son, Peter, aged five, attended. In the summer months she planned to work as a cleaner in one of the village's boarding houses. The jobs would allow her to have the children with her.

As she slowly relaxed, Molly began to reveal her background. The co-owner of the fishing boat was Tommy's elder brother, Mark, who lived near the quay with his wife, Pam. They were always happy to have their two nephews for an odd evening; giving Molly the opportunity once a week to attend night school.

'What are you studying?'

'Spanish,' she replied.

'Why do you want to learn Spanish?'

'Mark and Tommy used to sell most of their scallops to the Spanish boats that came into the port regularly. However, negotiations over the prices were difficult as no one spoke their lingo. I thought I could help them get a fairer price.'

Money is obviously tight, and times hard.

'I can speak Spanish,' he said. *'Quieres otra copa?'*

'Gracias. Seria bonito.'

'Hey, that's good,' he remarked enthusiastically.

She blushed slightly, embarrassed at the praise. 'No, it just happened to be one of the phrases I've been taught.'

Throughout their meal, Mikey had been well behaved, sitting in his high-chair. His fish fingers, chips and tomato ketchup had gone. The ice cream was being spread around his bowl to a creamy constituency before disappearing. He hadn't said much, but when they came to leave, having been prompted by his mother, he thanked Juan, 'Thank you, Alan,' he said. His shyness was beginning to evaporate.

That evening, Molly invited Juan downstairs for dinner after she had put the boys to bed. 'After all, catering for two is as easy as one.'

They ate informally, sitting on the floor with plates on their knees. Conversation was not as one-way as it had been at lunch. Juan gave her a brief summary of his official background, including stressing his experience as a seaman.

'I didn't want to ask whether you were from Australia,' she said at one point in their conversation, 'in case I was wrong.'

Juan smiled. 'That's OK,' he replied, 'most people can't tell the difference between a New Zealand accent and an Australian one.' *Thank goodness.*

Molly was interested in Juan's quest to find his father's relatives. 'There are a large number of Quines in Port Erin,' she said. 'I went to school with some of them.'

'I think my father's family came from Ballaugh,' he replied. He hoped mentioning the small northern village might throw Molly off the scent. He continued, trying to change the subject, 'I am thinking of staying on the island for about a year before I go back to New Zealand. Much will depend on whether I can get a job.'

'I am sure Mark is looking for a deckhand. If you like, I'll take you to meet him in the morning.'

'That would be great.'

If I can get some time under my belt on a Manx boat, I should be able to meet the Spaniards she's been talking about.

'Do Irish boats ever come into the port?' he asked.

'All the time,' she answered. 'There is one in now. I saw it yesterday when I took the boys for a walk to see their Aunty Pam.'

'What do the deckhands do in the evenings?'

'They spend most of their money in *The Old Vic*.'

'A Pub?'

'Yes.'

'Perhaps, we can go down there for a drink when we've washed up the dishes?'

'No way.' Her face was a picture of horror at the thought. *How dare he make such a suggestion?* '*The Old Vic* is a spit-and-sawdust establishment. The women who go there, well...' she stopped before finishing. 'Anyway, I can't leave Peter and Mikey alone. You can go on your own if you want.' She said it in a way that implied she didn't want him to go.

Enjoying Molly's company, he had forgotten the boys were upstairs. He apologised and changed the conversation.

He dried the dishes whilst she washed-up. Standing behind her, and admiring her slim athletic figure, he desperately wanted to put his arms around her, give her a hug and cup his hands under her firm breasts. His love bug was stirring his loins, but his hang-up was constraining him. He didn't know what to do. He hadn't felt this way since his fling with the PT mistress.

It's a funny thing about women bending over a sink, he thought. *Why does it turn me on? I've only known her for a few hours, and yet I know I must have this woman. Perhaps this time I won't run away afterwards. Whatever you do, don't rush and spoil your chances. Play it cool.*

She had looked at him all evening with a light in her eyes; albeit a very distant light. Nevertheless, it was a bright light – a lighthouse flashing on the horizon over a clear sparkling sea.

Is she signalling hope? Has she the same feelings? I mustn't let my imagination get the better of me.

Having thanked her for supper, he ascended the stairs confused about his feelings, wondering where they may lead. He lay in bed, unable to get her out of his mind. *Don't be daft,* he thought, *you've only known her for five minutes and you're behaving like a seventeen year old on his first date. Bide your time and the initial fascination will wear off. I'm only going to be on the island for a few months – at the most. I can't afford to get involved with her. Be sensible! Anyway, I'll have to get DC Costain to check her background.*

The following morning he made himself breakfast and found Molly waiting for him when he went downstairs. She had already taken Peter to school.

'I promised I'd take you to meet Mark,' she reminded him.

'Do we walk or take the car?'

'The walk will do us good. You may meet some of the villagers. They'll want to give you the once-over. Port St Mary is that sort of place.'

Mark and his wife Pam lived in a three-storey terraced house in Lime Street, at the rear of the quay. Mark was a giant: six feet three inches, weighing seventeen stone. Thick black curly hair, he was round-faced with a ruddy complexion and a broad smile that displayed a gap between his two front teeth. He had a handshake like a vice.

'Nice to meet you, Alan,' he greeted. 'Molly said she'd found a tenant for her flat. We were puzzled, however, as to why you would want to take a long-term lease at this time of the year.'

He has the best interests of his sister-in-law at heart, and is probing.

Juan reassured him that there was nothing sinister about a Kiwi taking a few years out to do Europe. 'I thought I'd find a part-time job over here while I research my family. Molly tells me there are a lot of Quines in Port Erin; perhaps I'll start there.'

'What sort of work do you do?' asked Mark.

'Anything really. I've spent most of my life sailing deep-sea on tankers between Australia, New Zealand, Japan and the Gulf. I have a master's ticket. During much of the time, Iraq was at war with Iran so it could get exciting. I spent last summer in Devon, and did a month on a trawler sailing out of Ilfracombe.'

'Then you've a job. We need another pair of hands. Would you like to come down to the quay and have a look at the *Manx Rose*?'

The quay was less than 100 yards away and, as the two men walked, Alan remarked, 'I'm sorry to hear about your brother.'

'Half-brother,' corrected Mark, 'My father died when I was Mikey's age, and our mother remarried some years later.'

'So, your surname isn't Kelly?'

'No, I'm a Killip – another Manx name.'

The *Manx Rose*, named after Mark and Tommy's mother, Rosemary, was a 60ft trawler with a 20ft beam, weighing 35 tons. Mark showed Juan around the cabin with sleeping accommodation for six. 'We can stay at sea for up to a week, but rarely do,' explained Mark. 'The hull, as you can see, is oak, reinforced with two layers of fibre plastic. The engine is a 250HP Volvo diesel, giving us ten knots. We have an echo-sounder, surface radar with a six-mile range, and a VHF radio. The hold is refrigerated.'

'I'm impressed,' said Juan. 'When are you next planning to go out?'

'The weather looks set for the weekend. We're fishing for mackerel, and will leave on the high tide on Thursday afternoon. We should be back on Sunday morning. You'll need to get yourself geared-up. I suggest you go across to Cooil's shop in Port Erin. His clothes are not the cheapest, but tell him you're working for me and he'll give you a discount for cash.'

Walking back to Lime Street, Juan saw the Irish trawler mentioned by Molly. 'Do you have much to do with the Irish?' he asked, nodding towards their boat.

'Not really,' replied Mark. 'They're a funny lot. They speak to each other in Gaelic, so you never know what they're saying. Molly can speak Manx Gaelic and can catch their drift, but she won't come into *The Old Vic* to overhear their conversations.'

I must be careful not to let Molly know I can speak Manx.

'How did she learn Manx?' asked Juan. 'I thought it was a dead language.'

'To all intents and purposes, it is. Molly was brought up on a small isolated sheep farm up there at Ronague.' He stopped, turned, and pointed to the distant hills. 'Her father was one of the last native Manx speakers, Ned Qualtrough.'

So, her maiden name was Molly Qualtrough – a nice ring to it.

'How often do the Irish come into the port?'

'They tend to be fair-weather fishermen,' laughed Mark. 'Then again, I sometimes wonder if they fish at all.'

'What do you mean?'

'Well, ten years ago they would come over from Ireland, go pair-trawling with the Spaniards, and disappear back home, apparently fully laden. I'd have sworn they'd never caught anything because the Spaniards would come into the port afterwards and buy our stocks to return home.'

'By pair-trawling you mean two boats sharing the same net, spread out between them?'

'Yes. It's strictly illegal in Manx waters, but who is to stop them?'

'And now?'

'It's the other way. The Irish come in here to buy some fish and the Spanish don't buy as much, unless it's scallops.'

'But they still go pair-trawling together?'

'Yes, if the weather is fine.'

'Is it possible for the net to be brought-in by the boat that didn't lower it?'

'Of course. Sharing the catch alternatively is the usual method. Two boats working together can catch almost twice as much when they pair-up, but the catch is always shared. That's what makes their behaviour so puzzling.'

C H A P T E R 4

Tuesday 12th February 1991

Tuesday was Molly's class at night school. The two boys stayed at their Aunt's. Juan prepared his first meal in the flat. He had thought about pair-trawling, and had made further enquiries at Port Erin when buying his oil skins and sea boots at Cooil's shop.

The proprietor, Eddy Cooil – 'Everyone calls me *Tinny*' – was about Alan's age and his shock of bright red hair, from which he got his nickname, triggered Alan's memory.

I played cricket against this fellow when I was at school. I wonder if he'll recognise me.

'So, you're sailing with Mark on the *Manx Rose*,' he asked when parcelling-up the clothes. 'I used to fish the same waters. There's always been a friendly rivalry between people from Port Erin and those from Port St Mary. You're going out for mackerel?'

Juan nodded.

'Give Mark my regards. Is there anything else I can get for you?' he asked. Clearly, he hadn't recognised Juan; almost twenty-five years later, the beard, and the antipodean accent had done their work.

'Have you ever seen boats pair-trawling?'

'Only the Irish and Spanish. It's supposed to be illegal in Manx waters, as they can catch nearly twice as many fish as they would otherwise.'

'Were they bottom-trawling or midwater-trawling?' asked Juan.

'Midwater, definitely. Probably for mackerel or cod.'

∗∗∗

Sometime after 2130 hours, within the agreed time-frame for regular reports, Juan rang the Chief Constable.

'Yes,' answered the educated Welsh voice.

'Bradda Head is clear of fog.'

'So is Douglas Head.'

He gave the Chief Constable the details of his address, the job on the *Manx Rose* and the fact he would be at sea over the forthcoming weekend. 'I have identified two possible sites for transferring arms: Fleshwick Bay and Derbyhaven. Can you check out who owns the farm near the beach at Fleshwick and whether the gate across the track with *Private – Keep Out* is legal? Finally, contact Dover Castle and get him to find out if it is feasible for the gun-running to be conducted at sea by a technique called midwater pair-trawling.'

'OK. Anything else?'

'No, that's all sir. I'll make contact when I get back next Monday.'

'Fine,' replied Colonel Madoc. 'Maughold Head has scoured the north of the island for possible sites. He has ruled out Peel, Ramsey and Laxey as being too busy. Port-e-Vullen is a possibility. Cornaa and Groudle are outside possibilities but unlikely as the access to them is poor. I'll give you more details next week and the answers to your questions. Good Luck.' He put the phone down abruptly. Juan was taken by surprise and, with the phone still to his ear, thought he heard a second click.

It must be my imagination.

He turned on the TV. The news was all about the liberation of Kuwait by the coalition forces: Operation Desert Storm. The ground invasion of Iraq would begin within days according to the pundits. It took his mind back to the happy days in Baghdad when, as an assistant military attaché, he had made several good friends in the Iraqi Army.

I wonder whatever happened to them. They probably died in the war with Iran. If they didn't, they will in this one.

27

The senselessness of both Iraq's wars sunk him into a depression, and gave him an excuse to finish his bottle of wine.

***

In the 1950s, the number of Jewish families living on the Isle of Man was fewer than the number of fingers on your left hand. However, with the rapid expansion of the international off-shore banking and the insurance industries in the 1980s, the number of Jewish families increased dramatically. By 1987, there was a small synagogue in Douglas. Unlike his father, Ben Mannion had not entered the banking profession but, having acquired a degree in Electrical and Electronic Engineering at Liverpool University, had returned to the island and joined the staff of Manx-Telecom. Unknown to his parents, he had been heavily influenced while at Liverpool by Zealots in the university's Jewish Society. He had spent two of his long vacations on a Kibbutz in Israel, and become a resolute Zionist. He had tried to join Mossad in his final year at university but had been persuaded there was a need for an agent on the Isle of Man where, he was told, it was suspected a fundamental Islamic group was making contact with the IRA. Consequently, he became a member of the *sayanim* – a secret worldwide brotherhood of amateur spies that were the eyes and ears of Mossad.

In Manx-Telecom his career had mushroomed. Still only 27 years of age, he was already the senior engineer of the telephone division. The recently introduced digitised exchange in Douglas was his baby. Tapping phones had been simple; an undetectable software operation. Apart from the private line to the Chief Constable, he was able to record conversations on the phones of the Governor of the Isle of Man and the senior politicians in the House of Keys – the Manx Parliament. Most of what he heard was tittle-tattle; of no use to Mossad. However, the conversation from 'Port St Mary 2855' that evening struck a cord.

Why had the Chief Constable called himself Douglas Head? Who were Bradda Head, Maughold Head and Dover Castle? What was the link between transferring arms and pair-trawling? Indeed, what was pair-trawling?

A few keys were tapped on his keyboard. Seconds later he had the details of the subscriber to PSM 2855 – a Mrs Kelly.

An odd place to ring from, he thought. *Who would be there undertaking an undercover operation? Could the man's voice be Mr Kelly?*

He excitedly rang an 020 number. A voice simply said, 'Yes?'

He announced his code name, 'King Orry here.'

There was a pause at the other end; presumably the Mossad Duty Officer for the night was making checks. After nearly a minute, the voice asked, 'When was she launched?'

Ben replied, '22nd November 1947 – exactly sixteen years before Kennedy was shot.'

Seemingly satisfied with the reply, the voice asked, 'What have you to report?'

***

Juan had decided he must discuss with the Chief Constable the likelihood that his private phone was being tapped. Accordingly, he woke early and drove to the police HQ on the outskirts of Douglas. The portly sergeant at the reception desk showed some surprise when Juan asked to see Colonel Madoc personally.

'He's not in yet, sir. He always arrives punctually at nine. Who shall I say wishes to see him?'

'Tell him Major Quine from Langness is here. Remind him that we knew each other at Dover Castle.'

Juan was asked to sit and wait in reception. The sergeant went into his office behind the reception desk. Some twenty minutes passed. At 0901 hours exactly, Juan watched the overweight sergeant pick up the phone through the glass partition. A few minutes later he was being ushered into Colonel Madoc's office.

'What's the panic?' asked the Chief of Manx Police.

'Have you made contact with Dover Castle yet?'

'No. It was the first thing on my plate this morning. Why?'

'I suspect your phone is being tapped. Last night, after you put the phone down, I heard a second click. Someone was listening to our conversation.'

'Are you sure?'

'Certain.'

Colonel Madoc stared at Juan, saying nothing.

I don't think he believes me.

After a few moments, 'If you don't mind, I'd like to call in my Deputy, Superintendent Bob Crellin. He's been positively vetted and I'll keep our business out of it as much as possible. However, he's a local lad and, if anyone knows who we can trust in Manx-Telecom, he will.' He paused, waiting for Juan to nod approval.

An old-fashioned policeman, thought Juan when the Superintendent arrived. He was well over six ft tall, had a 48 inch chest, and must have weighed at least 16 stone. *I bet the criminals don't argue with him.*

'Bob,' began the Chief, 'this is Major Alan Quine of the Army Intelligence Corps. He has reason to believe our phones are being tapped. Do you know anyone in Manx-Telecom who can be trusted one hundred per cent?'

The Deputy never queried the tapping assertion.

'Arthur Kewley is my point of contact. He's their Managing Director, and I've known him all my life. I went to school with him,' answered the Superintendent.

'Go and see him. Tell him this must be kept strictly between us. We must find out who has been fiddling with our phones. He is not to trust any of his staff – no one. Understood?'

Crellin nodded, and asked, 'If we discover who is doing it, do we arrest him?'

'NO! Definitely not!' It was Juan who interrupted the dialogue.

Both men stared at him; neither was used to having someone yell an order at them.

'I'm sorry,' apologised Juan, 'but we may be able to use this to our advantage.'

30

'I don't see how,' began Colonel Madoc, then realising he would have to give too much away about Alan's role, dismissed his Deputy. After he had left, he repeated his question.

'Whoever overheard our conversation last night knows something's afoot. He will have traced the call to my flat, he's learnt our codenames, and he knows we're watching landing places for the transfer of arms. He will have guessed we were talking about IRA weapons. He knows I'm sailing on the *Manx Rose* in two days' time, and that I'm interested in the technicalities of pair-trawling. He won't know who Dover Castle is. The question we need to ask ourselves is what organisations would find all that interesting?'

'The Provos, obviously,' suggested the Chief Constable.

'Possibly. Could they have planted an operative in Manx-Telecom?'

'There are a lot of Irish people working over here,' sighed the Chief.

'Who else?'

'The CIA?'

'Hardly!'

They both paused, apparently stumped. After a short silence, Alan asked, 'Who would be excited at discovering a link between Arabs and the IRA?'

Instantly, the Colonel exclaimed, 'Mossad!'

'Exactly. I'll bet there is a high-grade technician in Manx-Telecom who has contacts with Israel.'

'In that case,' replied Colonel Madoc, 'until we have decided what we are going to do with our Jewish friend, the only secure line I have with Whitehall is our military crypto telegraph link. I will have to get my Special Branch Sergeant to send everything to Dover Castle via New Scotland Yard – far from ideal.'

'One other thing, if I may?'

'Yes?'

'Can you get DC Costain to check out my landlady: birth certificate, wedding licence, that sort of thing? I'm sure she is OK, but we should be careful after this telephone business.'

31

***

Meanwhile, in a detached house in Bushey, a northern suburb of London, the previous evening's report by the Duty Officer was being discussed by two fulltime Mossad agents: David Mestel, one of five agents with geographical responsibility for activities in Britain – his patch being Northern England and North Wales, and Simon Rosenberg – his boss and the Head of Mossad Britain.

'Do you know this King Orry?' asked the Head.

'He's a bright spark – first class honours in Electrical and Electronic Engineering – he's been our sayanim on the Isle of Man for about five years. This is the first time he's submitted a report with some substance. The island is hardly a hotbed of activity.'

'Yet, if I remember rightly, there have been rumours of the Provisionals smuggling weapons through the island from Libya for years.'

'True, but that's all they have been – rumours. We know the Manx Police have inspected Irish and Spanish fishing boats regularly, but have never found anything. This is the first time we've ever had any evidence that some under-cover operation is ongoing,' answered David.

'Let's analyse this carefully,' said Simon. 'We know the Chief Constable is Douglas Head. Right?'

His subordinate nodded.

'We know Bradda Head and, possibly, Maughold Head are MI5 agents.'

'Do we? How?'

'Because Dover Castle is Sir Charles Gray; who else could it be, except possibly Scotland Yard's Head of Special Branch?' smiled Simon. 'Either way, something big is brewing. I've no idea what pair-trawling is, but you can find out. The two possible landing bays suggest to me that arms transfers, in future, may be conducted there. Tell your operative to survey the sites, tail Bradda Head, and see what he is up to. Why is he going fishing on a Manx boat? If you feel he needs help, go over there yourself.'

32

CHAPTER 5

Thursday 14th February 1991

It was a fine day. Juan decided to scout the island's southern peninsula for further possible landing sites. He walked the coastal path from Port St Mary to The Sound, the most southerly tip of the Island. There was nowhere suitable. The path continued north towards Port Erin; again nowhere suitable. He made a mental note to ask Mark if there were any landing places on the Calf of Man, other than the small pier that was visible when looking across the straits between the two islands. His map suggested there may be landing places invisible from the mainland. It needed checking out.

When he returned to Cronk Road, Molly handed him an envelope. 'I found it on the floor when I returned from school with Peter,' she said. 'It wasn't there when I left.'

Briefly, they touched. Her hands were warm, his cold. He felt something passed between them, something special, something unsaid, something… *Did her face glow as she withdrew her hand? Did she experience it too?* He was thrilled at the thought. *Maybe there's a future…*

He excused himself, his reaction made him feel awkward. Upstairs he opened the envelope addressed:

By Hand: Alan Quine.

There were but a few lines:

To Bradda Head

From Maughold Head

Please meet me 2000 hours in The Old Vic

Have answers re Billy Tote.

Who the hell is Billy Tote?

He had a shower and changed from his hiking clothes. He made himself a meal, watched TV: more bombing in Iraq.

He gave himself ten minutes to walk down Cronk Road and reach *The Old Vic*. It took only five. *The Old Vic* was, as Molly had said, a spit-and-sawdust establishment. To the left of the central entrance was the saloon, to the right – the public bar. Alan looked through the door on the right. There were several drinkers supporting the bar. The atmosphere was smoky, the floorboards bare except for occasional cigarette ends; it was uninviting. He decided to tackle the saloon. There, the furniture was less spartan, a coal fire blazed, the dark red carpet needed attention from a Hoover, but gave the illusion of some sophistication. The room was empty. He approached the bar, behind which an opening allowed one barmaid to serve both rooms. A buxom brunette came from the other side. She wore too much make-up, but smiled. Her face asked: *What would you like?* But she never spoke a word. She had a nametag on her blouse – Sylvia.

'I'd like a pint of Okells, please,' he said, 'and a packet of crisps.'

'Plain or Cheese and Onion?'

'Plain, please.'

She nodded and without saying a word disappeared into the other bar.

When she returned, he gave her a £5 note and said, 'Take something for yourself.'

She looked surprised; clearly this was unusual, even in the saloon. She thanked him, saying she would have a half. He sat by the fire. It was inviting on a cold St Valentine's night. He had almost finished his pint when George Costain entered.

'I'm sorry to be late, but it's taken longer to get down from Douglas than I expected.'

Juan nodded, 'What will you have?'

'The same as you would be fine.'

Juan approached the bar and called through the gap, 'Sylvia.'

She appeared in double-quick time, smiling, 'What would you like?'

Ah, the success of simple bribery.

Again he proffered a tip. This time he was rewarded with a look that suggested: *I get off at eleven o'clock.*

The two men drew up closer to the fire. Juan took the coal tongs and stoked it.

George began, 'I was called in to see the Chief Constable early this afternoon and ordered to make contact with you. When you weren't at your digs, I left the note. I hope you don't mind.'

'No, I'm glad of an excuse to come here. It's where most of the fishermen come, and I need to get my face known. What's the news from the Chief?'

'Firstly, they think they know who has been tampering with the phones. The engineer in charge of the Douglas telephone exchange is a guy called Ben Mannion. He studied Electronics at Liverpool University and is something of software genius. Our Deputy Chief used his contacts with the Merseyside Police to discover that Mannion was the Treasurer of the University Jewish Society and has been to Israel at least twice. The Merseyside Police believe he is a sayanim.'

'Ah, that makes sense – the brotherhood of amateur Zionists who act as eyes and ears for Mossad. What else did Colonel Madoc say?'

'The farm at Fleshwick Bay was sold quite recently to a company called Cushag Holdings. It has a small office in Douglas. Apparently it's a wholly owned subsidiary of a Dublin company called the Trefoil Group. The Chief asked Dover Castle to find out more about them. They own several properties around the Irish coast, from Cork in the south to Larne in the north. The *Private – Keep Out* notice is new and illegal. The track down to the bay is a public right-of-way. I did some delving and Cushag Holdings also own *The Golf Course Hotel* at Derbyhaven.'

'That's interesting,' remarked Juan. 'Trefoil is near enough Latin for three leaves, in other words, a clover. And the Manx national flower is a cushag.'

George looked blank, as if wondering what relevance the connection may have. He continued, 'Finally, Dover Castle contacted the Ministry of Agriculture and Fisheries on the feasibility of transferring arms by pair-trawling. The answer is that it would be possible providing the packages were sufficiently light and hermetically sealed in something like a strong plastic. However, anything weighing more than a couple of hundredweight would create too much drag, even for powerful trawlers. I was told to tell you that Billy Tote will probably weigh at least three to five hundredweight.'

'What's this Billy Tote you're talking about?'

'I'm sorry, I thought you knew. It means nothing to me.'

They had another pint. They discussed how they could keep in touch, now their phones were not secure. George gave Juan his home number. 'It should be safe if you ring from a public phone. I live alone; if you need me at any time I will come. And, by the way, your landlady is as Manx as the hills. Her father, grandfather, and great grandfather all farmed at Ronague.'

Alan nodded his thanks; his ambitions for Molly clicking up a notch. 'How much do you know about this operation?'

'Not a lot, I have been wondering what a New Zealander is doing in the British Army.'

'It's a long story, and I won't bore you with it. Did the Chief Constable tell you that we have intelligence that the Provisional IRA is beginning to disarm in order to get a peace deal in Northern Ireland and, rather than give up their arms, they are selling them to the highest bidder?'

'No, I was only told that there might be a large parcel slipped into the Island that must be intercepted.'

'It's a nice way of putting it. The parcel could be a very big bomb. I can only assume some idiot has decided to give it the code name Billy Tote. At the moment I'm inclined to think it will be landed at Fleshwick or Derbyhaven. Either way, I will need you as an extra pair of eyes.'

'Count me in – at any time.'

As they left the pub, Sylvia showed interest when Juan mentioned she might see more of him in the forthcoming weeks, as he had taken a job on the *Manx Rose*.

'Ah, so you're Molly Kelly's Australian lodger. Lucky old her!' Clearly, word had got around the locals in the village that there was a stranger in town – even if no one could tell a pseudo kiwi accent from a real one.

He walked back up the hill, trying to think, *why call a bomb Billy Tote? It must be an anagram of something, but what?*

He thought about his lessons on atomic bombs.

What were the first two American ones called that were dropped on Japan?

Then the penny dropped.

Little Boy and Fat Man! Billy Tote is an anagram of Little Boy, the first bomb dropped on Hiroshima, made of Uranium-235 and detonated by the gun method – the probable way the Libyan-IRA bomb will be fired. Fat Man, the second bomb, dropped on Nagasaki, was more sophisticated and made of Plutonium-239 and used the implosion method of detonation.

Did Sir Charles use an anagram because he wanted the Manx Police kept in the dark? He doesn't want them to know there might be an atomic bomb coming to the island.

★★★

The *Manx Rose* left port at noon the next day, shortly before high tide. The weather was wet and cold, but, fortunately, not windy. Visibility was good, perhaps three miles, and the sea relatively calm. They headed south-west, hugging the precipitous cliff coast that Alan had walked the previous day. As they passed between the mainland and the Calf of Man, the sea suddenly became much rougher: five foot waves crashing over the sides. The *Manx Rose* was swept south as the tidal rip through The Sound was running at ten knots.

'Don't worry,' shouted Mark to Juan over the roar, 'it's always like this here except at low ebb. The current can sometimes reach twice this speed.'

The trawler continued to head west towards the Chicken Rock lighthouse, skirting the south-side of the Calf.

'I walked to The Sound yesterday,' Juan said to Mark, 'and noticed on the Ordnance Survey map there might be a landing place over there.'

'There used to be, perhaps one hundred years ago when the old lighthouses were built on the Calf. The small pier disappeared ages ago, and the track down the cliff was washed away. Look through the binoculars. You'll see what I mean.'

Juan scoured the cliffs but could see nothing that would allow a landing. 'So the only way onto the Calf is directly across The Sound?'

'Yes, but only when the tide is changing. There is a window of an hour, if you're lucky.'

Juan's other two colleagues were Alec Kennaugh and John Maddrell. Both had worked with Mark for many years. They knew their way around the boat, and at times Juan felt like the twelfth man in a cricket team. Nevertheless, by the time they were south west of Chickens, Juan was too busy helping cast the nets to worry about Billy Tote, or possible places where it could be landed. Alec was the cook. Although their galley was impossibly small, he kept their appetites satisfied. His perennial and only joke as he served-up was, 'This might not fatten but it will fill.'

The fishing was good. The nets rapidly overflowed. By Saturday mid-morning, Mark had decided they could catch the evening tide. It would allow them to land at Port St Mary's inner harbour. 'You've brought us luck,' he said to Juan. 'The mackerel are not always as plentiful as this.'

They landed shortly before 7 pm. 'This calls for a celebration,' said Mark. Juan found himself being led up the short hill from the quay to *The Old Vic*. This time, it was a right-turn into the smoke-filled public bar, heaving with men in their working clothes. 'Four pints, Sylvia,' shouted Mark as he approached the bar. Juan noticed others making a path for him. He was obviously a regular, judging by the way he was greeted by so many. The four crewmen found a table in the corner. 'It's a pity the Irish boat has sailed,' said Mark. 'They usually pay over the odds for our catch. Now I'll have to get the wholesaler down from Douglas tomorrow morning to buy the fish. He'll haggle.'

'What about the Spanish? Do they pay well, too?'

'Yes, if it's for scallops. It's something to do with them believing the shell is the symbol of Saint James. Usually, we can't catch enough for them. But of late their demand has dropped off. The wholesale price for scallops is still good, mind you. The season for fishing scallops starts on 1st March, so that's when we get busy.'

'Are there any restrictions on catching scallops?'

'Yes. When we started up, the code of practice was voluntary. However, it became law about five years ago. It determines all sorts of things such as the size of nets, the number of days at sea, when and where you can fish. However, in this game experience is everything. I know where the best beds are and make sure neither the Irish nor the Spanish find out. In two weeks, the Spanish will turn up. It's rare to see them around here in the winter. They will come to buy our scallops.' He paused, and then shouted, 'Sylvia, same again, love!'

CHAPTER 6

Saturday 16th February 1991

At closing time, Juan staggered up the road feeling decidedly the worse for wear, his senses diminished. Had he been fully *compos mentis,* he would have noticed someone tailing him. As an operative in BRIXMIS, he had developed a sixth sense for when he was being followed. The British Commanders'-in-Chief Mission to the Soviet Forces in Germany was the reciprocal exchange of liaison teams set up in 1946 to foster good relations between the British and Soviets in their respective Zones. His job, to gather intelligence on the Warsaw Pact forces stationed in the Soviet Zone, had taught him to smell a tail at 100 yards.

He tip-toed into his digs; there were no lights. *Molly must have gone to bed.* He was glad. He would not have wanted her to see him in this state. He managed to undress and lay down on his bed. The room began to spin.

I haven't felt like this since I was at Sandhurst.

He didn't get the best night's sleep and the following morning lay-in late. When he crawled downstairs, the house was empty. Molly had, presumably, gone to church and taken the boys to Sunday school.

He walked towards the beach; the main street in the village was deserted. He saw no one; just an odd cat taking itself for a stroll. He went to the public phone box he had used previously when initially contacting Molly. He rang George. 'I thought we should get together and inspect our two possible landing sites.'

'Why don't we meet at Ballasalla? *The White Hart* serves good lunches. If we meet there in half an hour, we should get a table even though we haven't booked.

Over their meal, they decided to go to Derbyhaven first. They drove separately towards Castletown, turned left at the first roundabout, passed Hango Hill, and parked their cars at *The Golf Links Hotel*. They walked towards St Michael's Island, a small isle off the northern tip of the peninsula. Reached by a short causeway, the island accommodated a ruined fort that was built by Henry VIII in 1540 to protect what was then the Island's main harbour. To George's astonishment, the track was blocked and a notice declared: *Private. Keep Out.*

'That's illegal,' he declared. 'This is a public right of way.' He ripped the wooden notice from its support and threw it, discus style, into the sea. 'I have brought you here to show you that this is the best vantage point to observe the pier.'

As they returned towards their cars, they were met by a burly man blocking the causeway. 'What the hell do you think you're doing? Can't you read?' he yelled in an Irish accent.

George took control. 'What do you mean?' he replied as politely as he could. Juan noticed the veins on George's 16 inch neck were bulging as his blood pressure rose.

'You're trespassing,' the man replied. 'I saw you damage that notice. You'll have to pay for a new one.'

'I'm Detective Constable Costain,' retorted George. 'I am going to charge you, or your boss, with obstructing a public right of way under the Isle of Man Road Traffic Act of 1985, section 4, sub-para 3b. What are YOU going to do about it?'

The Irishman's face dropped, it was a picture. He squirmed, 'I'm going to get my boss to talk to the Chief Constable.'

'A fat lot of good it will do him,' replied George. 'If you want, tell him my number is PC49.'

George turned to look at Juan, winking. He was finding it difficult not to burst out laughing at the reference to Juan Stranks' one time radio

41

character. Clearly, the Irishman was unfamiliar with the fictional character, PC Archibald Berkeley-Willoughby of 'Q' Division, Metropolitan Police.

'Oh, and tell your boss the maximum fine under The Act is £2,000.' With that they passed the deflated hotel worker, got into their cars, and drove towards Fleshwick Bay.

They passed through Ballafesson, driving up the narrow road that climbed steadily for a mile, before dropping towards the sea. They passed the farm house on their right and parked near the stony beach. They agreed that establishing a suitable observation post would be difficult. The bay faced due north, with precipitous exposed cliffs guarding the entrance. There was a small copse on the west side of the road, half a mile from the beach. It could offer some cover. They walked to it; agreeing it was their best vantage point for a look-out.

'Shall we check the farm house while we're here?' suggested Juan. It was empty. However, there were some signs of recent life. They could see unwashed coffee cups on a draining board in the kitchen. 'They weren't there last week,' said Juan. As they turned to walk back to their cars, it was beginning to get dark. Juan picked up a small pebble, placing it in the centre of the step to the front door. 'It looks insignificant, but if anyone uses the door they will dislodge it. It will prove people are coming and going.'

They decided to go to *The Colby Inn* and discuss their findings over a pint.

'I think that we may have established a possible link between Cushag Holdings, the Trefoil Group and the IRA today,' began Juan. 'The clod we met at Derbyhaven will have alerted his bosses that the police have been sniffing around. I think we can discount them using Derbyhaven to transfer any goods, don't you?'

George nodded.

Juan continued, 'Have you noticed we have been followed since lunch?'

George looked surprised. Obviously, he had not noticed anything suspicious.

'There was a grey Astra in the car park at *The White Hart* when we came out from lunch. It was in the car park at *The Golf Links Hotel* when we returned from meeting your gorilla. I could see no one in it on either occasion, but it was parked outside the Methodist Chapel at Ballafesson when we came back from Fleshwick. Again, I could see no one in it. It drove past us as we were crossing the road to come into the pub. Can you check it out? Its registration was BMN 101.'

George made a note of the number and commented, 'With a personalised number plate like that it must be our friend the phone tapper. He must be tapping my home number too.'

'It looks like it,' Juan replied. 'But there's another thing I want you to do. In a week or two, I am going to try to get pally with the Spanish fishermen and gain their confidence. To do that, I will need you and the PC from the Port St Mary station to trump up a charge against several of the Spaniards. This is what I have in mind...'

✳✳✳

Pushing in time when you have nothing to do is difficult; especially in February in the Isle of Man when the weather is wet and windy. Mark had been keen to go out for more mackerel on Monday morning, but decided that the forecast was too bad and postponed the trip until the end of the week. Consequently, with little to do, Juan decided to begin researching his mythical relatives at the Manx museum in Douglas. Although the building was warm and there was plenty to read, time passed slowly. He found himself day-dreaming more and more of Molly. Since meeting her, he had watched how she coped with the two boys. He had begun to realise what a treasure she was: a worker not a shirker, a hoper not a moper. He could imagine her telling her boys, *There's always someone worse off than yourself; learn to grin and bear it.*

On the second Monday of lodging with her, she again invited him to have supper.

They sat and chatted socially. Lying about his background to someone with whom he wanted to have a real relationship was difficult. As a teenager he would meet girls he fancied at a dance and tell them he was an airline pilot. He suspected they didn't swallow his story, but it was part of the grand game to get a fumble afterwards on the park bench. It was different now. The bug he'd caught for Molly felt different. It was lodged deep inside. He knew he wasn't going to be able to shrug it off. He felt guilty and wondered how much he could tell her of his true circumstances. The dilemma was unbearable.

Molly, on the other hand, was totally open with him. She had been brought up on a small hill farm, the only child. Her mother had died when she was fifteen. Consequently, she not only had to attend to the domestic chores, but had to look after her father and study for her 'O' levels at the same time. Although the school wanted her to stay on and study for 'A' levels, times were hard. She left with eight good GCEs. She had known Tommy at school; he had been a few years older than her. He had a motorbike and was able to ride up to the isolated farm regularly to see her. He had been her only boyfriend. She had been just nineteen when they married. Their early life together had been bliss. To a young Molly, Port St Mary was a big place – streetlights, shops, and cafés. In the summer, it was full of visitors. There was work in the boarding houses. Now aged 28, she was at her peak of womanhood, but didn't complain that time may be passing her by.

He listened intently. Their two worlds were miles apart but he had also been brought up on an isolated farm; albeit a more prosperous one. It was one of their common bonds; the other – they could both speak a language that few understood. His was longing to tell her who he really was.

God, Molly. I'd love to put my arms around you and give you a big hug. I'd love to be able to articulate how I feel.

***

Juan went out on the *Manx Rose* twice before the end of February. Their catches were good on both occasions; Mark was happy. The drinking sessions afterwards were boisterous. Sylvia grew evermore come hither and Juan's hang-up with women was testing him. He fancied her raunchy style but knew Port St Mary was the sort of place where a passionate fling could not be kept secret and would be broadcast widely. He didn't want Molly to be given any reason for spurning his advances. It was bad enough her not approving of his drinking in *The Old Vic* with her brother-in-law.

'Next Monday is the 4th of March,' Mark had said one evening. 'We'll rig the *Manx Rose* up for scallops that day and sail on Tuesday. The weather is looking good.'

He left his fishing comrades shortly before eleven o'clock and called into the fish and chip shop on his way back to Molly's. To his surprise, George was waiting for him outside his digs.

'The car that followed us a week last Sunday did belong to Mannion. I have been watching him and he met a fellow off the London plane on Monday evening. His ticket was in the name of David Mestel. He's staying in *The Sefton* and currently booked in for two weeks. I asked The Met's Special Branch to run a check on him. He's supposedly an administrator in the Israeli Tourist Board but they told me he is Mossad's co-ordinator for the North West.'

'Then we must assume they know everything including the identity of Dover Castle. They will know that Billy Tote cannot be transferred at sea and that it will most likely come ashore at Fleshwick. Like us, they don't know when, nor its final destination.'

'One other thing,' George continued, 'I asked Superintendent Crellin about you creating a fracas with the Spaniards. He raised some queries, but came up with a few good ideas.'

CHAPTER 7

Tuesday 5th March 1991

Trawling for scallops proved to be more strenuous than midwater trawling for mackerel. Bottom-trawling involved dragging the nets along the sea bed with weights and special floats to keep the mouth of the nets open. The maximum speed of operation was much slower – three knots as opposed to seven or eight. Pulling the nets in after a run was backbreaking despite the help of the *Manx Rose's* machinery. Mark had been fishing for scallops for nigh on 20 years and knew where to look. As the beds had been lying dormant for four or five months, the catch was high.

'We'll make a pretty packet with this lot,' he shouted, as they began their fourth run along the beds.

There were no other boats to be seen.

'I was not expecting to be alone,' remarked Juan to Alec, as they hauled together.

'No, nor was I,' he replied. 'I'm surprised there's no one here from Port Erin.'

'What about the Irish or Spanish?'

'They'll be another two or three weeks yet.'

***

On Monday 18th March, a Spanish trawler, the *Dom Pedro*, tied up at

Port St Mary inner pier. It was in immaculate condition; no evidence of it ever having fished at all. Mark made contact with the captain, Carlos Marcial, who seemed, initially, to be the only one of the crew who could speak English. An evil looking fellow with dark eyes that were too close together, a broken nose and a twisted mouth, he made it clear that he wanted to buy as many scallops as Mark could provide. His price was generous. 'I will stay in port for at least a week while you catch them,' he said.

There's something fishy going on, thought Juan, excusing himself the pun. *Billy Tote will probably be getting transferred next week.* That evening he rang Colonel Madoc, knowing full-well that the message would be overheard by Mossad's agent.

Juan spent as much time in *The Old Vic* as possible, hoping to befriend the crew and gain as much information as possible. When he initially spoke to the four-man crew, it was a simple greeting in hesitating Spanish. They barely acknowledged his greeting.

Subsequently, however, the conversation increased as he misled them into believing his Spanish was rusty through lack of practice. By Wednesday, they were accepting him as the friendly local, and allowed him to sit with them. They were surprised to discover he was a New Zealander, taking several years out to see Europe and that he was researching his Manx family roots. They lied too, claiming to be Moroccan fishermen but, from their reluctance to talk about fishing, it was obvious that they knew little about trawling.

The skipper's mate called himself Anibal – very tall, perhaps 6ft 3in, with black eyes that pierced you. The other three deferred to him. Eduardo, the engineer, was the antithesis. A round chubby face on a round chubby body, he stood no more than 5 ft tall. There was strength in his arms and oil under his fingernails. *He probably uses a spanner to eat his breakfast.* Felipe was thin: an athletic-looking weasel. His nickname was *El Raton* – the mouse. He may have looked mousey, but Juan suspected he was the type who could be useful in an emergency. The fourth member, Rodrigo, was the handsome one: dark hair, swarthy-skinned, a shaved moustache, an Adonis figure with a sparkle in his eyes. He was the epitome of what Juan thought women would fall for. By chance, it was Rodrigo who mentioned that they expected to return to Spain the following week.

Juan pressed, 'Why so soon?'

Anibal coughed, and changed the subject; glaring at Rodrigo not to answer.

On Thursday, Juan sailed with the *Manx Rose*. They trawled through two consecutive nights using lights. Their catch was excellent and, on returning to harbour on Saturday morning, they tied up alongside the *Dom Pedro*. The scallops were transferred to the Spanish ship's refrigerated hold. Mark was paid in cash.

Tradition demanded both crews adjourn to *The Old Vic*. A long liquid lunch ensued. Carlos, the captain, kept himself distant from his crew; there appeared to be little love lost between them. He only mixed with Mark at one side of the bar. Juan assumed he had made contact with the Irish during their absence.

If something is going to happen next week, then I must warn Molly I may have to disappear suddenly.

Later that evening, knowing she would have put the boys to bed, he knocked on the door to her lounge.

'Can I come in and have a chat?'

She smiled warmly, and seemed to welcome the interruption. 'I am only watching the TV while doing the ironing,' she replied. 'Come in. Would you like a cup of tea? I was about to make myself one.'

He sat in the warm back-parlour while she disappeared into the kitchen to put on the kettle. Her coal fire was burning brightly; nearby a clothes-airer was displaying the efforts of her labour: the boys' shirts and vests – looking and smelling clean. The room was cosy and tranquil; the furnishings and décor reflected Molly. On the mantelpiece was a framed photograph of Molly with the two boys and, he assumed, Tommy, her late husband.

It's Saturday night, he thought, *a woman like her should be out enjoying herself; not ironing.* He stretched out so that his slippered-feet could toast by the fire. *I could settle down here, but how am I going to tell her I may have to leave next week, and be away for some time?*

She returned with a tray, carrying cups, a teapot and some chocolate biscuits. She moved the ironing board to one side, placed a small table in front of the fire between them and sat down opposite. She beamed at him – a distant, shy, attractive smile that lit up her face. She poured the tea, offering him the biscuits. 'It's nice having you here,' she said. 'The boys seem to have taken to you, and Mark is pleased with your work on the *Manx Rose*.'

'Ah, so you have been talking about me?' he asked, laughing.

She blushed and looked away at the fire.

'I'm only pulling your leg,' he added quickly. He knew he had made her feel uncomfortable. There was an awkward silence as they both sipped their tea, looking at each other.

'Molly…' he began, but then faltered.

She looked at him quizzically. *She knows what I am going to say.*

'There's something I must tell you. I may have to go away next week at very short notice.'

Her face dropped. Her look of dejection gave away her disappointment. He continued quickly, 'What I am going to tell you is secret; you mustn't tell a soul. I am an undercover policeman,' he lied.

Her eyes widened; her expression – a mix of puzzlement and fear. She didn't say anything but nodded, as if accepting the inevitable.

'I was chosen to come here because I can speak Arabic, Spanish, and understand Gaelic – all languages that may come in useful when I deal with the Spanish and Irish crews.' He paused to let her catch up on what he had said.

To his surprise, she asked in her native tongue, 'Do you speak Manx?'

She was testing him to see if he really could understand Gaelic – in her case spoken in a Southern-Manx accent.

He replied, 'Yes, a little.'

'What is your real name?'

He noticed she had asked him the question in the informal mode – like the use of *tu* in French, as opposed to the formal *vous*.

A hopeful sign, he thought.

'Juan.'

She smiled.

'Where are you from?'

He was torn between telling her the whole truth or the minimum necessary to protect her. He chose the latter.

'New Zealand.'

She visibly relaxed, sitting back in her chair, but continuing in Manx, 'And I thought that accent was false,' she laughed. 'How come you speak Gaelic with a Northern Manx accent?'

'It's a long story, but my father was from Ayr.'

'And how do you speak Arabic?'

'My mother was Egyptian.'

She nodded, satisfied with his answers, and resumed speaking English.

'I thought from the beginning there was something different about you. Somehow your story of seeking-out your family history didn't ring true. However, the boys and I shall miss you; you told me you would stay here for up to a year.' The last phrase had a hint of annoyance in her voice. She paused, as if thinking how she might demand compensation for his breaking their unwritten long-term lease agreement.

'No, don't misunderstand me. I intend to come back. It's just that I have no idea how long this job might take. The monthly Standing Order from my bank will continue to pay the full rent. I want you to keep my flat available while I am away. It could be as long as a year.'

She looks relieved. Is it because she'll continue getting the rent or because she wants me to return?

'A year?' she gasped.

'The problem I am having is playing everything by ear. Whatever happens in the next few weeks, please trust me. Don't believe what people say about me. I am going to have to let Mark down, but it will be for the greater good. Just remember me fondly. Someday I will return and tell you everything.'

She responded by smiling at him, but said nothing; her eyes were shining brighter than ever. He wanted her to take the initiative. He felt awkward, not daring to rush.

She arose from her easy-chair and went to the ironing board to continue with her chores. She asked innocently, 'I don't suppose you're going to tell me what your plans are?'

'I don't know myself, and the less you know, the safer you'll be. All I can do is to repeat – please trust me, my motives are for the best. There will be occasions when you may have doubts. I have a gut-feeling something might blow-up next week. There may not even be time to say goodbye.'

She ironed steadily without saying anything. Then, she pulled a large sheet from her washing bag and asked him to help her fold it. It was a task he had undertaken countless times with his late-mother. They folded it in quarters. As he approached to give her his ends of the sheet, their fingers touched and he held them firm, not letting go. He looked into her eyes; she smiled awkwardly but didn't attempt to release her grip. He brought her hands to his mouth and kissed them gently. She still made no effort to withdraw.

'I love you,' he whispered in Manx whilst still kissing the back of her hands.

'I don't understand you,' she replied.

'Molly, you do. You just won't accept the fact.'

She sat down, burying her face in her hands and said nothing. Minutes passed in silence. When she looked up there was moisture in her eyes. Juan didn't know how to react.

'I didn't want this to happen.'

'What?'

'This,' she repeated quietly.

He remained silent.

'Tommy hasn't been dead a year yet. I promised myself that I would honour his memory.'

'Molly, you have done nothing wrong. Tommy would want you to be happy. You will always have him at your side as long as you have Peter and Mikey. They are his sons and you are their wonderful mother, but time moves on and you must also. Trust me I am not some gigolo; what I said, I meant.'

She remained seated opposite him reflecting on his words, looking into the fire; her distant smile looked miles away. She was the most openly sincere woman he had ever met. She sat in front of him, saying nothing and gazing into the embers. A long time passed, as she daydreamed in her own world.

Then, suddenly sitting up, she asked, 'Would you like a drink?'

Juan nodded.

'I have no idea what's in the cupboard. Tommy was the drinker. I know there is some sherry left over from Christmas. I like it with some ice.'

'That sounds good to me.'

She made her way across the room, disappearing into the kitchen, allowing Juan further time to admire her slim figure, and reflect. *Have I told her too much?* While she was preparing the drinks, he wondered if his declaration of love had been premature or immature.

She returned with two large tumblers of iced sherry. She pushed the coffee table to one side and sat on the rug in front of the fire, facing him. Her skirt had risen to accommodate her squatting position and he could see her thighs. She didn't seem to notice him looking. They sipped their drinks quietly for some time before Juan said quietly, 'I am going to see the Chief Constable tomorrow and will be away all day.'

'You will come back, won't you?' There was a trace of urgency in her voice.

'Of course. I should be back before it gets dark.'

'No. I meant after you have been away for a year.'

'It might not be that long. With a bit of luck, it may only be for a few months.'

'Where are you going?'

'I'm not sure. I have somehow got to gain the trust of the Spaniards, and go with them when they return to Spain or wherever. I have a suspicion that something dramatic might happen, and I could be in the thick of it. Whatever happens, you must believe me and not the local gossip or even the newspapers.'

They finished their sherry and Molly stood, moved towards Juan, stretched up and, putting her hands around his neck, closed her eyes and kissed him. It was a delicate kiss; not passionate. She was saying *Thank-you.* There was no heavy breathing but he could feel her firm body against his shirt. He was excited and began to tighten his grip around her waist. However, she resisted his premature advance. Smiling, she blushed, whispering, 'Not tonight.'

She rested her head on his shoulder. They stood motionless for several minutes holding each other before Juan whispered, 'I'll see you tomorrow evening when I get back from Douglas.'

CHAPTER 8

Sunday 24th March 1991

The following morning, Juan used the phone to signal George. Two rings and hang-up, thirty seconds pause, two rings and hang-up, indicated that Juan wanted a meeting with the Chief Constable present. A pub midway between Douglas and Laxey, *The Halfway House,* had been previously agreed as suitably private. An hour later, George rang back, 'Twelve-thirty,' and put the phone down. Juan arrived first and found a corner table.

When George arrived, not only was he accompanied by Colonel Madoc, but also by Superintendent Crellin.

They ordered drinks and the Chief explained he wanted his deputy present, 'Dover Castle has instructed me most precisely what part he wants my Force to play in this affair. If we are to be successful then my Superintendent here will have to coordinate the troops.'

'It looks as if something is going to happen this week,' replied Juan, 'so we are going to have to decide our plans today.'

'Fine,' exclaimed the Welshman, 'but Dover Castle has moved the goal posts. I was initially led to believe that all we had to do was keep a lookout for Billy Tote arriving, then intercept it and catch the scoundrels red-handed.'

Juan felt distinctly uncomfortable. All along he knew that any agent from MI5 could have been used to achieve such a simple goal. Now the cat had been put among the pigeons. He tried hard to act as if this was

54

what he, too, had understood the task to have been. He nodded, trying to look blank.

'However, I now believe that he wants you to gain the confidence of the Spanish crew and for you to leave with them, taking the bomb. He wants us to pretend we are stupid and incompetent and let them go. Did you know this all along?'

Juan drew breath, not quite knowing where to start.

'I was chosen for this job because I speak Spanish, Arabic and Gaelic, amongst other languages.'

He noticed their faces drop.

'Arabic?' asked the Chief Constable.

'The four crewmen on the *Dom Pedro* are probably Libyans posing as Moroccan-Spaniards. I'm not sure about their captain.'

'Libyans!' exclaimed the Deputy. 'The bastards who blew up Pan Am Flight 103?'

'Yes,' replied Juan.

The three Manx policemen were lost for words.

'Dover Castle believes they are al-Qaeda terrorists, an extreme group planning a bombing campaign aimed at the heart of Western society,' continued Juan.

'I've never heard of them,' scoffed the Colonel.

'No, until last year neither had I. They were formed in Afghanistan a few years ago from groups who fought against the occupying Russians. Ironically, they were then equipped with American weapons. Now they are determined to create havoc in Israel and the West in order to set up a Palestinian state. They see Britain and the United States, in cahoots with the Saudis, as the bad guys. Unfortunately, we don't know much about them. If I can help them escape with the bomb, after you have impounded it, then they may accept me. My job will be to learn as much as possible about their organisation.'

He stopped and noticed the big deputy staring through him.

Juan continued quickly, 'One problem we have is that we don't know exactly when the Irish will pitch-up. I came here this morning via

Fleshwick Bay. There has been someone there since George and I were there a month ago.' He looked at George, explaining that the pebble on the step had gone and the coffee cups had been washed. George nodded understanding.

It was the strong, silent man's turn to speak. 'If I was bringing a valuable item across from Ireland to sell to the Spaniards then I would create a diversion,' he said authoritatively. They looked at him for an explanation.

'I gather you and DC Costain had a spot of bother when you were at *The Golf Links Hotel*?'

Juan nodded.

'And you were followed to Fleshwick?'

Juan nodded again.

'I would use two boats; one bringing a lookalike bomb.'

They stared at the Superintendent.

He continued, 'They'll mislead us to believe the transfer will take place at Fleshwick, but conduct it elsewhere.'

'Where, Bob?' asked the Colonel; his tone implying admiration for his deputy's hypothesis.

'Possibly Derby Haven, but my money would be on Castletown.'

'Why?' asked Juan. He was all-ears. *This big fellow has brains as well as brawn.*

'Firstly, Castletown's outer pier is practically tidal independent. They could swap the bomb quickly at almost any time – day or night – and make a quick getaway. Secondly, it's not far from Port St Mary; no more than half an hour sailing at ten knots.'

'But wouldn't they be seen, and arouse suspicion?' asked Juan.

'I doubt it. Hardly anyone goes down that pier. Most of the boats in Castletown are berthed at the inner harbour.'

'I agree with Bob,' said the Chief Constable. 'It makes sense to try and divert attention from the real handover. However, we still have the problem: when will it occur, where will it occur, and how are we going to persuade them to accept help?'

'The key to your question, sir,' said the Superintendent, 'is to watch for when the money is transferred. The banks concerned are in Victoria Street. As soon as we know the transaction is complete, we swoop, find and impound the boats whilst Customs undertake a search. We imprison the skippers in Douglas police station pending further investigation. We release the crews on bail.'

'What good will that do?' asked Colonel Madoc.

'Alan meets the Spanish crew and persuades them that he knows how to get the two leaders out of the cells. He takes two or three with him. They break into Castletown station that evening, where they, mistakenly, think the skippers are located. He shoots the two PCs on duty when they try to resist, they panic when they find no one and they leave. If he times it right, the two boats, the Spanish and the Irish, should be safely across the sea and in Irish waters before daybreak.'

'I presume you intend that I use blanks when I shoot your men?'

'Of course. I have a loaded point three-eight revolver in the car. I will give it to you when we leave. I suggest you keep it hidden under the spare wheel in your car. It is loaded with three blanks and three live bullets.'

'Why three live ones?'

'In case they take it off you to check. Whatever you do, don't fire more than the first three shots at my men. The press will get to hear of the escape the next day and I will make sure it gets in the national papers and on TV. The PCs will appear with arms in slings, or whatever.'

'There's only one snag,' said Juan regretfully.

'What?'

'The Libyans are going to ask me why I should help them escape.'

'We are going to have to give you a reason for hating us,' smiled the big man.

'I don't follow,' puzzled Juan.

As they ate their lunch, swilled down with a second, and then a third pint – no one seemed too concerned about drinking and driving – the Deputy outlined his plan.

'Tomorrow evening we'll arrest you and a couple of the Spaniards in

The Old Vic on cooked up drug offences. You will take the lead in resisting arrest, and the local PCs will call for help from Castletown, the Southern Division's HQ. I will ensure that PC Corlett attends, among others. He was the Northern Command's heavyweight boxing champion when he was in the Army. He has a reputation for being heavy-handed on occasions like this – useful in the summer when we have trouble with Glaswegian holiday makers. It might mean he will have to draw blood to convince you and the others to go quietly. We will lock you up for the night in the cells in Castletown. On Tuesday morning you will appear before the High Bailiff. I know him well through playing chess. He will order the three of you to be birched. The only occasion it can now be administered is for assaulting a policeman. Corlett will volunteer to undertake the task.'

'Birched?' gasped Juan. 'That's a bit OTT, isn't it?'

'Not if you really want to convince these bastards you're on their side.'

By now the Chief Constable had stopped eating. His eyes were wide open; his face full of admiration for his Deputy's plan. George Costain, by contrast, was sitting quietly with a grin on his face. He knew PC Corlett. He was imagining the brawl in *The Old Vic* and the subsequent shenanigans. Juan's reaction was, despite the potential pain of being birched, one of high regard for the Superintendent. *He has clearly given this some thought.*

'When you come to escape later in the week, Corlett will be one of the PCs on duty. You will get revenge and make a great play of shooting him.' Superintendent Crellin looked to his boss for any signs of disagreement. There were none and he continued, 'We will, of course, sir, have to give the two shot PCs time off to recover from their artificial wounds.'

Colonel Madoc coughed, 'Yes, Bob, it's an excellent plan, excellent.'

'When Corlett beats me up in the pub, will you ask him not to break my nose?'

Everyone laughed, especially George who said, 'You haven't seen Corlett – he makes the Super look small.'

Superintendent Crellin chuckled at the reference to his size. 'We have a weakness, however,' he said, 'communications. I have brought some short wave, hand-held radios with me. George, go and bring them in from the boot of the car, will you?'

George returned and gave out the radios; each was the size of a building brick, albeit much lighter.

'You will see there are nine channels. The inspectors in charge of our four divisions use channels one to four.' The Super looked at Juan and for his benefit explained, 'The inspector of the southern division in Castletown has channel four. If you want him, use that channel. Your code name is *Scarlett Point*. I have told him anyone using that code name is to be given all possible assistance. The Chief Constable has exclusive use of five, I have six. Channel nine is to be unique between us. If you turn the dial to nine,' he paused as they flicked the knob, 'and now on the keypad enter the same unique four-digit code, shall we say 5082.' He waited while they obeyed his instructions. 'We now can have a secure four-way conversation at any time.' He looked pleased. Juan nodded, impressed. The other two, being familiar with the system, appeared less so.

***

Juan drove back to Port St Mary wondering where the subterfuge would lead. *Tonight might be the last time I will be in the house with Molly.* He didn't know whether to tell her or not.

She heard him entering through the front door and came out of the kitchen to greet him. 'I thought you might be interested: I was at Mark and Pam's for lunch today. Mark said that there are two Irish boats fishing for scallops south-east of the Chicken Rock lighthouse.'

Then things might develop soon. I'd better tell her what might happen.

'Look, Molly. Perhaps when you've got the boys to bed I can come downstairs for a drink. I have a bottle of wine in the fridge. There is something I want to tell you.'

'OK. Come down after seven o'clock.'

He went to his apartment, sat down, and tried to think what he should do if things were to go awry. He wrote a long letter to Molly explaining who he really was, what he had done and for why. He tried to describe his feelings for her as best he could. He concluded by telling her why he was making her the sole beneficiary in his will. He sealed the letter in an envelope and addressed it to her. He then wrote a second letter to the manager of the Isle of Man Bank, Athol Street, Douglas. He made it clear that the letter to Molly was only to be sent if his death was confirmed by the Chief Constable. He enclosed a further page entitled *The Last Will and Testament of Juan Hasani Quayle (alias Alan Quine)*. He left the house, walked to the Post Office at the bottom of Victoria Road, and posted it Recorded Delivery.

He walked down Bay View Road to where he could clearly see boats tied up in the inner harbour. The *Dom Pedro* was where she had been since arriving. He smiled to himself and turned around.

When he later entered Molly's lounge, he saw that she had made an effort to entertain him. She had baked some sausage rolls. The fire was roaring. She had changed from her usual drab working clothes and was wearing a dark green smock dress over a cream blouse. She had back-combed her strong hair. There was a faint whiff of perfume.

He poured two glasses of his Sancerre wine, and they sat on the rug smiling at each other. *She seems more relaxed this evening.* She offered him the product of her efforts in the kitchen. The sausage rolls were good and were soon finished.

'Molly,' he said. 'Tomorrow evening I will get arrested for fighting with the police and be put in gaol.'

It was a bolt from the blue, and Molly choked on the wine she was sipping. She coughed and he moved quickly to pat her on the back.

'I didn't mean to alarm you. Don't worry. It is all being staged in order for me to inveigle my way into the confidence of the Spanish crew of the *Dom Pedro.*'

He still had his hand on her back and was standing above her; she was looking up at him. He knelt down and kissed her cheek. He was encouraged by her positive response. She put her arms around his neck and pulled him closer. Her eyes were closed tight as she pulled herself up. He cupped her left breast with his right hand. She didn't object. Her breathing became heavier. He lowered himself to the floor as she leant backwards. They were both gasping noisily as everything went out of control. His head told him not to rush, but his heart was in a hurry; he couldn't stop the feverish haste. Her eyes were still closed as he lifted her skirt. She tried to undo his trousers, but was inexperienced. He helped her. With her smock pulled over her waist, she groaned loudly and within a few moments she was climaxing. He kept a tight hold of her panting body. He looked at her as he hugged her; her eyes were still closed as she pressed herself against him. She had the most exquisite face: high cheek bones, broad forehead, wide lips, the hint of a widow's peak and strong flaxen hair. He was mesmerised by her. They lay motionless, bound together, for a considerable time; only the crackling of the fire disturbed the peace. 'I'm sorry,' she said. 'I must have disappointed. You're only the second man I've ever known.'

'I know,' he replied. 'I love you the more for it.'

She wept silently.

He said nothing, continuing to hold her as close as he could. Time passed in silence.

'Would you like to come upstairs,' he said. 'It might be the last time for quite a while.'

They went to his room, undressed, and got into bed.

He was totally drained when he whispered, 'You were wonderful; you are the loveliest, warmest woman I've ever known.'

Her eyes were already closed; she was sound asleep.

CHAPTER 9

Monday 25th March 1991

When Juan woke after the best night's sleep since leaving St Bees, the house was empty. Molly had been up, given the boys breakfast, washed the dishes and gone to work. He knew she would not be home until after 3 pm.

How does she do it? Week after week, month after month.

He walked down Bay View Road and looked at the boats in the harbour. The *Dom Pedro* hadn't moved. Neither were there any newly arrived vessels. Satisfied that *today will be the day*, he returned to his digs, sat down, and with a heavy heart wrote:

Dearest Molly

Whatever happens today, you must believe in me. What you will hear in the forthcoming days may be correct factually, but the consequent conclusions people reach will be wrong. Our friendship will lead to speculation of the worst type. You are going to have to be very strong and resolute. You will find out who your true friends are. Whatever happens, however, DO NOT be tempted to reveal what I told you about my being an undercover policeman. Doing so will endanger me, even possibly yourself and the boys. It could even cause the death of thousands of lives (I am not exaggerating). Ignore the jibes and the snide comments at street corners. Hold your head high – I promise I will return.

I have tripled my monthly standing order for the rent while I am away. It should ensure that you will have few financial worries; I fear there will be plenty of other problems for you to overcome. I have also asked a colleague in the Manx Police, whom I have been working with, DC Costain, to arrange for you to become the owner of my car. Take the boys out as much as you can, enjoy yourselves!

Yours always and forever,

Juan.

He left the envelope on the small table in Molly's hall, and decided to try out the Superintendent's radio. George was the first to respond.

'George, I am going over to Fleshwick this morning to see if there is any activity there. Do you think you could cover Derby Haven? If you like, we could meet for lunch at *The White Hart* afterwards.'

'It's the Super here,' butted in the Deputy Chief Constable, who must have been listening. 'Is the *Dom Pedro* still in port?'

'Yes,' replied Juan. 'The tide is nearly out too, so she's stuck there for at least the next seven or eight hours.'

'Fine, then we'll raid her this evening.'

✱✱✱

As Juan drove through the village of Ballafesson, he noticed a car parked in front of the Methodist Church. *Odd,* he thought, *a car parked there on a Monday morning.* He slowed down to take a closer look. He could see a sticker in the rear window: *Another car rented from Mylchreest Motors.* A warning bell rang: *Why there?*

He proceeded cautiously up the narrow lane towards Fleshwick Bay. Cresting the hill, before the road dropped towards the sea, he saw, a mile away, a fishing boat alongside the small jetty. He stopped then reversed 100 yards back down the slight gradient to where a gate led into a field. Opening the gate, and reversing through the gap, he took out his binoculars. After closing the gate, and walking back to the top of the hill, he could see six men struggling to carry a wooden box, perhaps measuring four feet by three by two. It reminded him of a short, fat

63

coffin. They were loading it from the boat onto a trailer attached to a tractor. He scanned around the scene but could see no one else watching. However, the hairs on the back of his neck told him he was not alone. The tractor driver left his seat to give the others a hand. Once loaded, it took less than two minutes to drive the tractor into the barn next to the farm where the seven men disappeared.

Is that the Super's decoy or the real thing?

Its apparent weight made him wonder if the Deputy Chief may have incorrectly guessed the Irish plan. He decided to leave.

George was waiting for Juan when he arrived at *The White Hart*. 'I used my influence to get access to the edge of the airport in order to watch the outward facing pier,' he said. 'And guess what?'

'There was a fishing boat tied up,' replied Juan.

'How did you know?'

'There's one at Fleshwick too.'

'So it's really happening like the Super predicted,' exclaimed George.

'It looks like it.'

'What you don't know, however, is that BMN 101 was parked in the car park of *The Golf Links Hotel*.'

'That's interesting. Could you see Mannion anywhere?'

'No, and I looked. I suspect he may have been well hidden in the old fort.'

'I suspected there was someone watching at Fleshwick, too – possibly Mestel – but I couldn't see him either.'

'So, Mossad are definitely active.'

Juan nodded and fell silent for a while. Then he asked, 'Was there any activity on the boat?'

'No, nothing. In fact, I wondered if they had gone ashore into the hotel.'

'Then all we can do is wait.' They ate their meal in relative silence. As they were finishing, Juan said, 'George, there is a favour I have to ask.'

'What?'

'You know my landlady?'

'Molly Kelly?'

'Yes. I've grown fond of her and her boys. By tomorrow I could be seen as the devil incarnate in Port St Mary and I'd like you to arrange for my car to be transferred to her name – you'll find all the documents in the flat.'

'Yes, of course. By the way, did you find out why the bomb is called Billy Tote?'

Juan sighed. He knew he should keep it a secret, but after getting George's assurance, replied, 'It's an anagram for Little Boy – the name of the atomic bomb dropped on Hiroshima. I'm afraid Billy Tote is a small atomic bomb; perhaps the equivalent to 3,000 tons of TNT.'

His friend whistled, 'Jesus. I'd no idea.'

'Don't worry; it is safe enough as long as no one starts trying to disarm it without knowing the six-digit codes that protect each of the many circuits.'

'And if they do fiddle?'

'There would be a big bang.'

***

Juan arrived back at Cronk Road before Molly and the boys had returned from school. He arranged everything as neatly as possible so that if the police should search his apartment for evidence, they would find things easily, and not leave a mess for Molly.

He left and decided to return to Fleshwick to see if there had been any developments. The hire car was no longer in front of the Methodist Chapel. He parked as previously, and carefully approached the brow of the hill. The fishing boat had gone. Everything appeared quiet. He chanced approaching the farm; there was no one there. He peered through a broken window into the barn and could see the edge of the box that had been transferred earlier in the day.

He drove into Port Erin, found a café opposite the bus station and ordered a substantial all day breakfast. Midway through his eggs, bacon and chips the police radio came to life.

It was the Super, 'They've transferred the monies this afternoon – $1,000,000. What's so special about this Billy Tote, Quine?'

'I can't say, sir, but if I tell you its name is an anagram, you will be able to work it out for yourself. Does this early transfer affect our plans for this evening?'

'No. The Customs people, supported by four of my men, are on their way now to impound the *Dom Pedro* on the pretext that we have received information that there are class 'A' substances on board. They will tell whoever is in charge that the boat will not be allowed to sail until given Customs clearance. We will confiscate the sailors' passports but allow the crew to leave their trawler and walk into the village, if they wish. You know what to do when we raid *The Old Vic* later.'

'I have just returned from Fleshwick and the boat that unloaded what we think is the decoy has sailed.'

'The boat at Derby Haven is still there, and the crew are drinking in the bar of the hotel. Presumably, they are spending some of their ill-gotten gains.'

***

It was dark by the time Juan had returned to Cronk Road from Port Erin. He parked the car, leaving the keys and the police radio and revolver hidden in the boot, as agreed with George. He desperately wanted to see Molly for the last time, but knew she would be busy with the boys. Walking slowly towards the port, his heart was pounding, his mind racing as he wondered what the future would bring. His only certainty was, come hell or high water, he was coming back to live with Molly, *if she will have me*. Nearing *The Old Vic*, he could see, across the inner harbour, three police cars, their blue lights flashing, parked on the quay above the *Dom Pedro*. Entering the pub, he turned left into the empty saloon. Sylvia greeted him civilly; she had long realised that she was getting nowhere with her advances.

'Molly let you out early this evening, then?'

He ignored her sarcastic question, smiled and requested, 'A pint of the usual please, Sylvia, and a bag of crisps. Get one for yourself too.'

She momentarily disappeared into the public room, came back with his order and asked, 'You look a bit down. Is everything all right?'

Not answering the question, he asked, 'There looks to be a bit of bother down on the quay. Do you know what is going on?'

'The police raid? They do that from time to time when they've got nothing better to do. Sergeant Curphey from Castletown has probably had a tip off. He raids this place sometimes. He's never found anything. He doesn't know where to look.'

'Why? What might he find?'

'The boss gets most of his spirits from the Irish boats. The stuff is much cheaper over there.'

'So what you sell here is contraband?'

'It's the same in most of the pubs around here.'

It occurred to Juan that what he had seen earlier in the day might not be a decoy bomb.

Is the box illicit whisky?

He smiled to himself, tickled at the idea that all the subterfuge could be for nothing more than a few bottles of Scotch.

'What's so funny?' asked Sylvia.

'I'm just trying to imagine someone's face when they open a certain box.'

There was a noise from the other bar. Juan could hear several of the Spaniards talking. Sylvia left him alone as she went to tender their orders. He sat in front of the fire. It reminded him of the previous evening with Molly on her rug. He relived the fleeting moment when she climaxed and hung on to him as if her life depended on it.

Molly, my dear Molly. My maiden, my dear Molly…

He remained alone in the saloon for some time, staring at the flames as they wound their way upwards, gazing at the colours in the coals: blue, green and red. When he came out of his trance, he knew what he had to do. He pulled himself up to his full height, breathed in, tightened his belt, and thought: *Come on, Juan, let's go for it.*

C H A P T E R   1 0

Monday 25th March 1991

Juan entered the public bar, and saw three of the *Dom Pedro* crew looking glum.

'Cheer up,' he greeted in Spanish.

Anibal, his long face and shaved-beard making him look more miserable than ever, replied, 'The bloody fuzz have raided the boat; accusing us of having drugs.' He made the motion of spitting on the floor as he mentioned the local constabulary. He slurped the last drops of his pint.

'Let me get you a round,' insisted Juan. No one objected. Eduardo and Felipe quickly emptied their glasses. Rodrigo, the fourth member of the crew, was missing. Juan didn't ask why. 'I'll tell you what, I know what'll cheer you up – some specially imported whisky.'

Sylvia scowled when Juan requested, 'Four illegals and four pints, please.'

An hour of heavy drinking passed. The four men were in high spirits. Anibal had begun talking about himself. 'My name is Anibal Esmando, I am the mate. My father named me after Hannibal the Great,' he proudly declared.

It was time, Juan thought, to tell them he could understand Arabic. He picked up on the topic and said in Arabic, 'Ah, Hannibal, the leader of the Carthaginians with his army of elephants. How he ever got them across the Alps is still something of a mystery.'

The three sat up, their faces registering surprise.

'How come you speak such good Arabic?' asked Anibal. His cold, piercing stare demanded a truthful answer.

'I used to sail deep sea on tankers between Australia, Japan and the Gulf. When I won my master's ticket, BP asked me to manage their terminal at Al Faw.'

'Iraq?'

'Yes. I was there for several years and made many Iraqi friends.'

'Shias?'

'Some Sunnis, but they were all friendly and got on well together. I feel strongly about this invasion business.'

'It is unfortunate, but Saddam brought it on himself. He should have realised the Yankees would liberate Kuwait. Now they will get cheap Kuwaiti oil and Saddam will be doubly shafted.' Anibal chuckled to himself, as if he knew a private joke.

'In that job, I picked up some Japanese as well. We often had to spend weeks in their harbours. They're not as efficient at turning round ships as you might expect.'

'Ah, but their car and electronic industries are second to none. Some day all cars and TVs will be Japanese.'

Sadly, you're probably right, thought Juan before revealing he spoke other languages. 'I have been in Europe travelling round. I spent a year in Germany and met a beautiful Russian girl. She would make your heart stop; long, fair hair, pale blue eyes, a figure to crave for – she taught me Russian.'

'And other things too, by the sound of it,' replied Anibal, his deep laughter sounded as if it came from the bottom of a well.

Anibal was slowly unwinding and getting friendlier when the door burst open. Two giant policemen wearing heavy great coats entered. The sergeant shouted at the three crew members, 'You lot stand up. You're under arrest.' He was a big man: six feet, 16 stone, aged about 45 with a large head and staring, steely-blue eyes. Juan assumed he must be Sylvia's not-too-bright Sergeant Curphey. Behind him was Goliath: at least four inches taller, much the same weight, early-thirties, black hair, dark brown eyes. *He must be Corlett,* thought Juan. *George was right, he does make their Deputy look small.*

The three sailors, not understanding the sergeant's command, turned to look at him but remained motionless in their seats. The Sergeant, clearly impatient, moved forward, grabbed Felipe, the lightest of the three, by the collar and lifted him off the floor.

'Hang on a minute,' shouted Juan, standing up and facing Curphey. 'What's the charge?'

'You stay out of this,' ordered the Sergeant. With Felipe still hanging in the air, the PC advanced and grabbed Eduardo's arm, yanking him out of his chair. Their table overturned in the melee, their drinks flying across the floor. The locals looked on passively. Tomorrow this was going to be the only topic of conversation in the village.

'Leave him alone. He's done nothing wrong,' protested Juan as he moved forward, grabbing the PC's arm to unlock Corlett's grip on Eduardo.

Corlett turned, looked at Juan, sneered, and unleashed a punch into Juan's solar plexus that left him winded as he doubled up in pain. As he tried to straighten up, the second punch was a perfectly executed uppercut that sent Juan backwards across the room. He felt the back of his head hitting something hard. He saw stars and never remembered anything else, until coming round in the back of a van – handcuffed. Sitting on the floor with him were his three drinking partners, looking frightened. He felt the back of his head. There was a huge bump and semi-dried blood.

'What happened?' he asked.

It was Felipe who replied, 'The bastards banged us about a bit. We think they've cracked Anibal's ribs.'

He could see Anibal was doubled up, in considerable pain.

'And Eduardo's nose is broken.'

His face was covered in blood.

'Where are the rest of the crew?'

Felipe shrugged, as if he didn't care. 'These Manx pigs are as bad as ours at home. It's the same the world over,' he grumbled.

They arrived in Castletown. Sergeant Curphey, Constable Corlett and two other PCs bundled them down some stone stairs into a cellar at the rear of the police station. Their handcuffs were removed. No one spoke to them. When Juan pleaded that a doctor should see his three friends, Corlett smiled and said nothing as he pushed Juan backwards into the cell. The oak door, through which they had entered the large, cold, stone-floored room, was slammed shut. Juan was bunked up with Anibal in a two man room. The lights went out; there was just a dull, red glow in one corner. He knew they were locked up for the night. He looked at his luminous watch, it was just ten o'clock. Surprisingly, possibly in their eagerness to lock the four up, the police had forgotten to make them empty their pockets. There were two blankets on the hard benches, but no pillows. Anibal allowed Juan to examine his bruised ribs; touching them made him wince. Juan took off his shirt and vest, and ripped his vest into strips. He bandaged Anibal's chest as best he could, firmly but gently. In one corner of their cage there was a stainless steel toilet and a wash basin with a roller towel. They attempted to clean themselves up but it was going to be a long, uncomfortable night.

It was past 9 am before anyone entered their cell. A woman brought in stainless steel trays each bearing a small packet of cereal, some milk, two rounds of cold buttered toast and a mug of tepid coffee. She neither looked at them nor spoke.

Nothing happened until 10.15 am when Sergeant Curphey, PC Corlett and two other PCs entered. Juan and Anibal were handcuffed together. Felipe and Eduardo followed. The four were frogmarched out of the station, across the road and into Castle Rushen. No one spoke. There, they were locked in a small room, presumably, thought Juan, to await their fate. The walls were solid stone: cold, dark and damp. Juan was shivering by the time the solid door was opened; the light flooded in, temporarily blinding him.

They were ushered up some narrow stairs and the four colleagues found themselves in Castletown's court house, located in the middle of the medieval castle. Opposite sat the High Bailiff; to their left stood a police inspector who read out the charges.

'The three Spaniards, if that is what they are, are accused of possessing class 'A' illegal substances, having false passports, and resisting arrest.' In each case he referred to the appropriate Act that had been broken. Juan never caught the details.

'The fourth member of the gang is accused of organising their resistance, disturbing the peace, and assaulting PC Corlett in the execution of his duty.'

The judge asked, 'What about his passport?'

'It appears genuine, unlike the others. He's a New Zealander.'

They must have searched my apartment. I remember leaving it at Molly's. I wonder what lies they told her. I hope she read my letter.

Evidence was given by a civil servant from the Passport Office in Liverpool, who had been flown into Ronaldsway on the first plane that morning. 'The Spanish passports are fake,' he declared, 'but cleverly done.'

Sergeant Curphey and PC Corlett then described how, acting on intelligence received, they had raided the *Dom Pedro*, found drugs in the bunks of the three accused, and confiscated their passports. Later, having made checks with the Immigration Authorities, they realised the passports were fakes. They then had to resort to force to apprehend the miscreants who were found drunk in *The Old Vic*. Both emphasised how Quine, '…heavily under the influence…' had led the resistance and assaulted PC Corlett.

'Anything to say before I pronounce judgement?' asked the High Bailiff.

It occurred to Juan that his three colleagues had hardly understood a word of the proceedings and decided to point this out. 'My Lord,' he began.

'Don't call me that!' yelled the black-gowned, rotund, owlish, chief magistrate.

72

'Sir, these three men are simple fishermen trying to earn a living. They understand very little English. They are a long way from their home and families. The drugs found have not been produced in court, and cannot possibly have my friends' fingerprints on them. You must dismiss the charge. I admit I know nothing about their passports. As for resisting arrest, I admit the charges on their behalf but would draw your attention to the fact that the Police were overly heavy-handed; our injuries bear witness to this. Had we known what they wanted, then we would have given them all possible assistance.'

'Is that it?' asked the High Bailiff.

Juan never had the chance to reply, before the latter-day Judge Jeffreys, as Juan perceived him, boomed, 'Quine – four strokes of the birch for assaulting a policeman and being the ringleader. Your passport will be returned to you and you are to leave the Island on the first boat tomorrow morning. Six months' imprisonment if you don't. The others – two strokes each. You are to remain on the *Dom Pedro* until we have sorted out your passports with whatever consulate is appropriate. You will then be deported from the Island. Take them away.'

Still handcuffed in pairs, the four were taken into the bowels of the castle. In a dark dismal room their hands were individually tied to a horizontal bar, facing a wall. The height of the bar, about knee height, ensured that they were bent in two. Corlett stood to one side smiling as he swung, in a circular motion, the cat-o'-nine-tails.

He's enjoying this. I wonder if his Super has filled him in with the background.

Also present was a second PC and a civilian, who Juan assumed was a doctor although he never spoke a word. The PC unceremoniously undid their trousers so all four were baring themselves. Corlett started with Eduardo. He yelled in pain at the first blow, but bit his tongue at the second. This set an example to Felipe and Anibal who remained silent as the birch struck. Juan winced; his four lashes hurt beyond his imagination. As the third hit him, he knew blood had been drawn.

When finished, the two policemen withdrew. The civilian bathed

Juan's bleeding weals. The others watched, amazed at the barbarity of the punishment; their two lashings had not broken their skin.

Juan talked to the medical practitioner who turned out to be a nurse. Juan asked him to look at Anibal's chest. He gasped at his bruises and immediately bandaged him professionally, asking Juan not to tell anyone before ringing a bell; a warden entered. Juan signed some forms, and received his passport. As they left the castle, two press cameramen were taking their photographs from across the street. The battered four turned away and walked painfully up the rise to the town square. They saw the bus stop and Juan looked to see when the next bus was due for Port St Mary.

'There's a bus in ten minutes,' he said. 'We won't have long to wait.'

A mid-thirty, auburn haired, freckled-faced man, whom Juan had noticed following them from the castle, and dressed in a grubby Arran sweater with faded jeans approached, 'I'd like you to come with me,' he said to Juan in a thick Ulster accent.

'What for?'

'Trust me,' he replied, turning away and beginning to walk towards the church, situated at one end of the square.

Juan motioned to the others, and they followed obediently. The three were in no shape to disagree.

Nearing the church, Juan noticed a narrow lane to the left side of the building. It took them to a small, stony beach; 100 yards to the left was the outer pier.

'Are you going to tell me what this is all about?' asked Juan as they approached the jetty.

'My name is Con O'Leary; I am the mate on the *Ballyglen*.'

'The *Ballyglen*?'

'Our trawler.' He kicked a pebble before continuing, 'Yesterday afternoon my skipper, Tom Murphy, was arrested at the same time as the *Dom Pedro's* captain, Carlos Marcial, in Douglas.'

'I didn't know that.'

'Hardly surprising with you and these,' he paused and turned around to look at the three stragglers, 'in jail. Did you hear the explosion last night?'

'No. What explosion?'

'Our diversionary bomb at Fleshwick. Some idiot must have tried to defuse it. We heard the noise at Derby Haven. That must be five or six miles away.'

'What time did it happen?'

'Around midnight.'

'We were in the dungeons. The walls are thick and there are no windows.'

'I'm still surprised you didn't hear it. It must have been heard all over the south of the island. It was a 500 lb bomb, so there won't be much left of the farm house.' He chuckled at the thought. 'However, it has upset the apple cart and the local police are running around all over the place, like headless chickens. The two skippers, I gather, are going to be charged with conspiracy to cause an explosion as well as money laundering. They'll get a long stretch. Currently, they're in prison in Douglas. Anyway, we've got the big one in our hold and I want to get rid of it as soon as possible. Then we are buggering off back to Warrenpoint as quickly as we can. Tom Murphy will have to fend for himself.'

The five men had reached the *Ballyglen*.

Con continued, 'We'll take you back to Port St Mary, and help you transfer the cargo. My advice is you leave the Island straight away before the fuzz impound the *Dom Pedro*.'

Juan spoke to his colleagues in Arabic, 'The Irish boys are taking us back to the *Dom Pedro*. Carlos has been arrested and is facing serious charges. He's in Douglas prison and there's no way we can help him now. If he's found guilty then he'll be locked up for some time. I suggest we load the boat with what you came for, and leave at once. We're lucky – the tide will be in.'

It was Eduardo who spoke first. Juan was surprised by what he said, 'Good riddance. The bastard should be incarcerated for ever.'

'Why?'

'When we left Ceuta, there were five of us. Arturo had a row one night with Carlos. He disappeared. Need I say more?'

Forty minutes after leaving Castletown, the *Ballyglen* was tying-up alongside the *Dom Pedro*. Rodrigo was almost in tears as he greeted them. Before the raid, he had gone for a walk on his own. Having found no one on his return, he had been alone and, not speaking English, was unable to communicate with anyone.

It had occurred to Juan as they had sailed across Carrick Bay that no one was going to interfere with their acquiring Billy Tote. After all, Sir Charles Gray's big plan was to follow the bomb's movements and for Juan to infiltrate al-Qaeda.

If we sail the Dom Pedro *back to Spain unhindered, then Anibal might smell a rat. I'm going to have to make our escape from the British authorities look real.*

No doubt the explosion at Fleshwick was caused by Mannion trying to defuse the decoy bomb. I'll bet the arrest of the two captains and their incarceration in Douglas prison on the explosive charges was a master plan dreamt up by the Superintendent at the eleventh hour.

Thankfully, I'll no longer have to organise Marcial's escape and shoot PC Corlett.

However, I'm going to have to convince Anibal and the others I can navigate them back to North Africa. I wonder if the Dom Pedro *has the range to sail from the Island non-stop to Spain. If we have to refuel on the west coast of France, then there is the problem of passports.*

The bomb in the *Ballyglen's* hold turned out to be identical-looking to the one he had seen transferred at Fleshwick. The Irish sailors had it loaded onto the *Dom Pedro's* deck in minutes and hidden it under a tarpaulin. It appeared to be lighter than the one that had caused so much struggling previously.

'That's it,' said Con. 'We've kept our side of the bargain. We're not staying here any longer than we have to. I wish you the best of luck on your way back to Spain.' He jumped across onto his own deck. His crew released their ropes, their engines fired up and they sailed slowly out of the harbour.

'Look, I think we should sit down for a few minutes and think this through,' said Juan to the others.

Anibal, as mate, spoke first. 'We're full of fuel, but it's over 2,000 kilometres back to Ceuta. That's a week's sailing at our cruising speed of eight knots. On the way up here we stopped at Corunna to refuel, replenish stocks and have a break. We could get back there easily enough, but we'd be pushing it to get to Ceuta non-stop.'

'I've got one big worry,' Juan began. 'How long do you think it will be before the police realise we have slipped away? A few hours, if we're lucky? Then what? They will begin a search for us. RAF Nimrods will patrol the Irish Sea and when we're spotted they will direct the Royal Navy to intercept us. We'll be lucky if we get as far as Caernarfon Bay. Caught red-handed with that,' he stopped, pointing to their cargo, 'we'll be locked up and they will throw away the key.'

'What do you suggest?' asked Eduardo.

'I think there are three alternatives,' began Juan.

CHAPTER 11

Tuesday 26th March 1991

'We could make a run for it; head south and hope for the best. That's what the authorities will expect us to do and where they will concentrate their search. Alternatively, we could set sail now and follow the *Ballyglen* to Ireland, and try to find somewhere to hide. We would be relatively safe in Eire from the British police – at least for a short while. We wait for the fuss to die down; get the Irish boys to help us, perhaps disguise the *Dom Pedro* – paint her a different colour; scuttle her even, and get a different boat.' Juan paused to see their reactions.

'You said three possibilities,' commented Anibal.

'The third idea I have is to leave at once, hide in a cove I know, not far from here, until dark. Then we head due east for England.'

'Are you mad?' asked Anibal.

'No, I don't think so,' replied Juan. 'In three hours sailing, we could be in Whitehaven. We buy a cheap transit van, transfer the bomb, scuttle the *Dom Pedro*, and drive to Spain via Dover.'

'It would never work.'

'Why?'

'You're forgetting we've no passports. We'll never be allowed out of Dover or into France.'

Anibal added, as an afterthought, 'And anyway, we've no money.'

'There's money in the ship's safe,' corrected Rodrigo. 'I carefully watched Carlos open it several times and know the combination.'

'I have my credit card too,' added Juan, 'but I agree we are going to have to get passports. The answer I think would be to stop in London and get them from the Moroccan embassy.'

'That would be no good,' replied Anibal. 'We're Libyans.'

'Well, the Libyan embassy then,' said Juan, trying hard not to give away the fact that he already knew.

The four crewmen sat looking at each other, saying nothing, knowing they were between a rock and a hard place. Each was weighing up the pros and cons of the alternatives – all were risky.

'Another possibility may be to sail to Ireland, get a van, then drive to Dublin, go to the Libyan embassy, get your passports, then take a ferry from Cork to Roscoff,' offered Juan as an afterthought.

All nodded agreement. Their best chances of getting to Spain lay through the Irish Republic.

Thirty minutes after the *Ballyglen* had left; the bigger, faster *Dom Pedro* slipped her moorings and left Port St Mary for the last time.

'The tide is still on the ebb, but only just,' said Juan to Anibal, as they rounded Port St Mary Point. Anibal nodded as if to ask: *so what?*

'It will mean the tidal flow between the Calf of Man and the main island should be to our advantage, not too fast and relatively safe. It will knock an hour off our journey time if we cut through The Sound. We should make Irish waters in less than four hours.'

'Have you ever sailed through the straits before?'

'No, but the skipper on the *Manx Rose* told me the safest way through is to stick to the Calf side of the Kitterland Rocks. If the *Ballyglen* went through and we don't, then we'll never catch them up. There's no choice. We must chance it.'

Twenty minutes later the ebbing tide was pushing the *Dom Pedro* through the narrow gap between the two islands, increasing her speed by some three or four knots. Juan was surprised how much smoother the sea was compared to the ripping current on the *Manx Rose* a month previously. They were through the narrows in minutes and heading due west, full speed ahead, for Ireland. The radar system was showing a small boat four miles ahead of them, travelling in the same direction. An hour later and Juan could see it was the *Ballyglen*. He called up their mate on the radio telephone.

'What are you doing following us?' asked a seemingly annoyed Con.

'We realised that if we had headed due south for Spain then the Royal Navy would have intercepted us before we reached the St George's Channel. Our only hope to get back safely is to hide up somewhere and let the dust settle. We thought you might be able to show us a place where we could bed down for a week.'

He could overhear Con talking to one of his crew in Gaelic. He couldn't hear everything but there was an animated discussion, and something about 'Martin won't be happy.'

'Are you there?' asked Juan, pretending he had been cut off.

'Yes,' replied Con. 'I was asking where the best place might be for you to lie low. There's a small village called Carlingford, we'll take you there. At this speed we should be there in about two hours.'

'That's great, we'll follow you. We have been wondering about our future in the longer term. We thought...'

'Stop there. There's no knowing who could be eavesdropping on this frequency. I suggest we keep RT silence.'

Juan, of course, wanted to be overheard; hoping anything picked up by GCHQ's eavesdroppers would eventually get back to Sir Charles. Two and a half hours later the *Dom Pedro* was mooring next to the *Ballyglen* in a small Irish harbour that reminded him of Port St Mary.

★★★

At the same time, Sean Doran was briefing Sir Charles Gray in Whitehall. 'GCHQ has picked up the *Dom Pedro* talking to the *Ballyglen*. Quayle is in charge and they have Billy Tote on board. They're planning to lie low in Eire for a week or two.'

'Excellent. Up to now we have been in control thanks to Madoc and his men; apart from that explosion near Port Erin. What's going on there, by the way?'

'The Manx Police have cordoned off all access to the site – the road and several coastal footpaths. We have sent an RAF bomb disposal expert across from RAF Wittering. He will pronounce authoritatively that the bomb was an unexploded World War 2 German bomb that must have been dropped on the Island when a Luftwaffe plane was heading back from bombing Belfast. Apparently it is quite common; there have been at least half a dozen such bombs discovered on the Island since the war.'

'And the dead man?'

'Blown to bits and definitely the local Mossad agent. If his family stir the waters, someone will ask why he was there in the first place. Mossad will keep their heads down, that's for sure.'

'Maybe, Sean, but they're not fools. They will soon realise that if the Fleshwick bomb was not atomic, then Billy Tote has slipped away. Their Irish Sayanims will be looking out for the *Dom Pedro*. They won't have any scruples about trying to disarm the bomb a second time.'

***

When both boats were tied up on the quay at Carlingford, Con came aboard the *Dom Pedro*. 'Look,' he said, 'we're leaving you here. You'll be relatively safe. The Irish are fiercely republican around here, and the British authorities over there,' he paused and nodded across the loch towards Warrenpoint in Northern Ireland, barely two miles away, 'will not cross the border. However, they watch everything that comes into the loch from Cranfield Point lighthouse. They will know you're here. I'll get Martin McNeil to come over and see you tomorrow. He's our brigade leader and will know what to do with you.'

Before Juan could ask any questions, he had jumped off the deck and returned to the *Ballyglen*.

What the hell am I doing here? thought Juan as he watched the trawler disappear, heading north to the British side of the loch. For a moment he was lost in his own world, thinking of the possible next move in this game of hide and seek.

'What do we do now?' It was Anibal who asked the question.

'I wish I knew, Anibal, I wish I knew,' sighed Juan.

'I've been talking with the others,' said Anibal. 'We've agreed that you owe us no loyalty and that we've got ourselves into this mess. If you want to leave us we will understand. The worst that can happen to us, now that we are in Eire, is to spend some time in jail and then be deported. What will happen when we get back to Libya is a different matter, however.'

'Perhaps it's time to tell me what you have got in that bloody crate.'

'We don't know exactly ourselves,' replied Anibal. Juan knew he was lying. 'All we know is it's some sort of bomb. Carlos called it a spectacular – whatever that meant.'

'A spectacular?'

'Yes, that's the word he used. I assume it's big – perhaps 2,000 lbs or more. He said it was vital to the success of our cause.'

'What cause is that?'

Anibal hesitated. He took some time to answer.

'We are members of al-Qaeda, a group of radicals determined to regain Palestine for the Palestinians. Israel would not and could not exist without the financial and military aid given to it by the Americans. We are trying to even things up for the Palestinians who have been displaced since Israel was set up illegally in 1948.'

'You've given yourselves a big task – taking on America.'

'Our strategic, long-term plan is to hit them where it hurts most.'

'And where is that?'

'In their pockets.' He laughed; a deep roar that came from his very soul.

'So, you think this bomb will do that in a spectacular way.'

'I don't know. We are lowly foot soldiers and don't know what goes on. Even Carlos wouldn't know what the plan was. Everything is kept in watertight compartments. Our job is to get the ruddy thing back to Ceuta, then take it overland to Libya.'

82

'I've always fancied seeing the Sahara,' grinned Juan. 'It's on my way home to New Zealand.'

Anibal laughed, offered his hand, and they shook warmly.

✱✱✱

In Bushey that Tuesday evening, David Mestel found himself sitting in front of a not-too-pleased boss.

'What happened?' demanded Simon Rosenberg.

'Mannion and I had been keeping a discreet watch on the unfolding events. There were two Irish fishing boats that could have been landing the atomic weapon at either Derby Haven or Fleshwick Bay. Yesterday, Mannion watched the boat at Derby Haven and saw nothing unloaded. Rather, the crew left the trawler unguarded and spent the day drinking in the hotel. Their skipper took a taxi to Douglas after lunch according to Mannion. Meanwhile, I watched a crew unload what appeared to be a heavy rectangular box from their boat at Fleshwick and manhandle it onto a trailer. They drove it into a barn next to the farmhouse – a distance of a few hundred yards. I saw Bradda Head, the man calling himself Quine, watching too. He didn't see me. He left when the bomb was safely in the barn. The men drank coffee for half an hour, and then the crew set sail in the boat. The man I took to be the farmer watched the boat disappear, locked the place up, and drove away. I waited for ten minutes, checking no one was around, and broke into the barn. With some tools I found lying around, I carefully opened the lid of the wooden chest. It was a bomb alright – I've no doubt about it. I replaced the lid and met up with Mannion later that afternoon.'

'Then what?'

'Mannion insisted he should take a look at the bomb. I warned him not to touch it and to wait until the Brits could get a specialist to disarm it. He appeared to listen but I wasn't sure. I knew he had a degree in electronics and was something of a software wizzo. He said he would be all right and only wanted to check whether it was atomic or not. We had tea together, and he left. This morning the only topic of conversation in the hotel was the explosion. I knew then what Mannion had done. I rang his office; his secretary said he hadn't arrived for work – unusual as he was always punctual. I caught the first plane back to London.' Mestel shrugged his shoulders as if to say, *The rest you know.*

'When you looked at the bomb,' began Rosenberg.

'Yes?'

'Did you see two hemispheres that may have been screwed together with connections at each end? The sphere would, probably, have been made from stainless steel, strengthened by a lattice, perhaps coated in lead.'

'I'm not sure. There were a lot of coloured wires.' He was pausing between his sentences, as he realised the significance of the question. 'There were three digital keypads, I remember'.

Simon Rosenberg was silent. He was staring through his colleague into space; almost as if he wasn't there. 'It's possible,' he began, and then paused. 'It's just possible that Mannion disabled the atomic cartridge before the booby circuits blew him to bits.'

'But wouldn't the explosion have triggered the nuclear reaction?'

'No. It's known as the chicken conundrum.'

'I'm sorry?'

'A newly born chicken with no strength can peck its way out of its shell in a few seconds. It couldn't peck its way in; even if it went to the end of time.'

Mestel was thinking about this when Simon continued, 'The hemispheres would be strong enough for the two pieces of uranium-235 inside to be unaffected by the booby trap explosion and remain sub-critical. The sphere would be shot away like a sixteenth century cannon ball. The trouble is, we've no idea in which direction.'

'So we can relax; no more Billy Tote.'

'We can never relax in this profession, David. The Fleshwick bomb was probably the dummy. I will send one of our Liverpool sayanims to the island to do some more snooping. I want to know what happened to the Derby Haven boat, the *Dom Pedro* and Bradda Head.'

CHAPTER 12

Tuesday 26th March 1991

Juan, having been given Carlos' cabin, tidied up his bunk and helped to secure the *Dom Pedro*. The crew wandered into Carlingford as it began to get dark. Juan had expected the local Garda to make an appearance to inspect the foreign trawler tied-up on their quay. No one seemed to take any notice.

Less than a hundred yards from the jetty was *The Swan Hotel*, similar externally in appearance to *The Old Vic*. The interior, however, was much superior – *a three-star establishment*, thought Juan.

Food was served in an elevated section at the back of the saloon. It was scrupulously clean and the locals friendly. No one asked them their business, until towards the end of their meal when a policeman approached.

'I'm Garda Brian Walsh,' he said. 'Welcome to Ireland. How long are you planning to stay?'

The attitude of the local bobby must have seemed to the four Spaniards the antithesis to the punishment handed out by PC Corlett and the Manx Police.

'We were fishing in the Irish Sea when our engines began to play up. I asked a nearby vessel, the *Ballyglen*, for assistance and they escorted us here. Their skipper has promised he'll send someone over from Warrenpoint tomorrow to look at the problem for us. With a bit of luck, we'll be away in a day or two.'

Garda Walsh smiled.

His gut feeling told Juan, *he knows I'm lying*.

'Well, if you want any help give me a shout. I've a lot of contacts. However, what is an Australian doing captaining a Spanish trawler?'

'I'm a New Zealander actually, and it's a long story. I was working on a Manx boat until last week and then received an offer that I couldn't refuse. Going to Spain is the first leg of my journey home. I will buy a motorbike there and complete the journey overland.'

Before ten o'clock the following morning, Martin McNeil, accompanied by Con, arrived in a white transit van. 'We're not happy with you guys being here,' he said to Juan. 'We thought we'd seen the back of that thing.' He nodded towards the tarpaulin-covered trunk. 'It's been a thorn in our flesh ever since we got it from Libya. The British Army and the RUC were forever turning the place over trying to find it – God knows how they knew we had it. There must be a leak in Gadhafi's organisation. We had to keep shifting it from one hiding place to another. I was always terrified it would deteriorate in some way and self-detonate. You do know what it is?'

'Yes,' replied Juan, 'but if it was such a worry, why did you get it initially?'

'It was a big idea of the Derry brigade. The trouble was they'd no idea what they wanted it for; status probably. Now their leader is a big wheel in the so-called peace process, he's trying to wash his hands of the whole affair.'

'Look Martin, can I explain our predicament?' asked Juan. He called for Anibal to come and join them.

Juan outlined possible plans to get back to Ceuta. Martin and Con listened intently; Anibal occasionally filling in details.

'I can't help you with passports for your colleagues, but my brother in Dundalk works in the car trade. He could get you a couple of reliable Volvo estates. They would attract less attention going through customs at Cobh than a van. Leave me to handle the problem of the *Dom Pedro*. How does that sound?'

Juan looked at Anibal. 'It's your boat,' he said.

'I think we should go for it,' replied Anibal. 'After all, the cargo is more valuable than the *Dom Pedro*.'

'If you gather what you want to take with you, we'll transfer the container to my van, and you can be driving into Dublin late this afternoon. I know where you can stay safely for one or two nights while you get the passports from the Libyan embassy. There's no reason why you can't be in France by Sunday. When we get to Dundalk, we'll check the location of the Libyan embassy in Dublin.'

∗∗∗

Sir Charles Gray's personal secretary buzzed the intercom from his outer office. 'Sir, Mr Doran wishes to see you.'

'Send him in, Nigel.'

Sean Doran entered the inner office. 'You asked me to keep you informed about any Manx developments.'

'Yes, Sean. What's happening?'

'Three things. Firstly, Quayle has left Carlingford in a transit van heading for Dundalk with his crew. They loaded Billy Tote in the back and don't look as if they are coming back.'

'Fine, keep your tail on them. What else?'

'Secondly, the RAF bomb disposal experts have confirmed that the Fleshwick explosive device was not, nor ever had been, nuclear. Although there is evidence that there may have been several booby trap circuits, scraps recovered at the scene have no nuclear contamination whatsoever.'

'So we can assume Quayle has got the real one.'

'Yes, and thirdly, the Manx decoy was definitely set off by human interference; whoever did it was blown to smithereens.'

'One less sayanim to worry about, then.'

∗∗∗

87

'We've a problem,' said Juan to Anibal while they were waiting at Martin's brother's garage for the Volvo paperwork to be completed.

'What? Don't tell me the parts they'll strip from the *Dom Pedro* won't cover the cost of the two Volvos.'

'No, it isn't that. I asked Martin to get us the phone number and address of your embassy.'

'And?'

'There isn't one.'

'Are you sure?'

'Yes. He's positive. He even had his lawyer check.'

'So, we're buggered in Ireland.' Anibal laughed a hollow laugh. 'We'll have to go back and sail the *Dom Pedro*, after all.'

'Not necessarily. Martin says he could get you four British Passports. Apparently, the IRA has plenty of spares. The other possibility is to see if they'll swap the *Dom Pedro* for one of their own boats.'

∗∗∗

'Yes?'

'St George's Hall here.'

'What about it?'

'It was completed in 1854 and is one of the finest neo-Grecian buildings in the world.'

There was a long pause before the voice ordered, 'Report.'

'I have just been to a public press conference given by the Interior Minister of the Isle of Man. With an RAF bomb disposal expert standing next to him to take questions, he announced that the explosion on Monday night was caused by a World War 2 bomb self-detonating. They claimed no one was killed but the police are keeping the area cordoned off and are continuing the search in case further bombs are discovered. One of the reporters asked whether the rumour was true that the bomb may have been nuclear. Both laughed and emphatically denied it. The RAF Officer said he estimated the bomb to have been the equivalent of

88

500 lbs of TNT. A second reporter asked how a German WW2 bomb could have been inside a barn.'

'What was the answer?'

'The RAF officer replied that the explosion occurred adjacent to the barn in a disused slurry pit. Everyone laughed when another reporter joked, "So, there has been a lot of shit flying about."'

'He was lying. We know the bomb was inside the barn.'

After a brief pause, the Liverpudlian sayanim continued, 'I have tried to find the whereabouts of Ben Mannion, but he is missing. Do you want me to go around to his parents' house?'

There was a sharp reply, 'No. Do you know where the *Dom Pedro* is?'

'I have been to Port St Mary. It's not there. An old boy on the quay told me it sailed on Tuesday afternoon, soon after an Irish boat left. The village is full of gossip about three of the Spanish crew being birched, along with an Australian for fighting with the police. What do you want me to do next?'

'You can return to Liverpool. That's all we wanted to know.'

Simon Rosenberg replaced the receiver, turned in his swivel chair, and said to David Mestel, 'Contact our embassy in Dublin. Tell our man there to find the location of the *Dom Pedro*. I'll bet my bottom dollar it's holed up somewhere in an eastern Irish port; probably not too far from the Ulster border. I've a feeling the nuclear weapon still exists.'

***

'We'll never be able to pass ourselves off as English,' said Eduardo.

'There are a lot of immigrants in England with British passports who can't speak much English,' assured Juan.

'Even so,' replied Eduardo, 'the Irish Customs people will have been alerted to look out for four North Africans leaving Eire. We would never get past the starting line.'

He was right, and Juan knew it. The five friends fell silent again.

'I think our best bet is to make a run for it in the *Dom Pedro*,' said Rodrigo.

'No, definitely not,' said Anibal emphatically. 'We might as well give ourselves up here and now if we did that.'

'Shall I see if the Irish are prepared to give us a boat in exchange for the *Dom Pedro*?' asked Juan. They agreed; Eduardo more reluctantly than others, after all it was his baby.

Juan took Martin aside and they found an empty room. They sat opposite each other.

'Martin,' Juan began, 'we're buggered without your help. If you want to get rid of this bloody thing, then you're going to have to persuade someone to exchange our trawler for a suitable boat to get us to Spain. The *Dom Pedro* must be worth $100,000 at least. What do you say?'

'And if we don't help you?'

'Then we'll leave in the *Dom Pedro*. We'll either be boarded by the Royal Navy or they'll sink us with a torpedo. Al-Qaeda will have handed over – what, a million dollars for nothing and lost a ship? They won't be too pleased with the IRA. It may mean they will look elsewhere for their arms – your organisation will lose a lot of money, and all for the sake of not swapping a boat.'

'I'm going to have to discuss this with my council. It's too big a decision for me to take on my own.'

'OK. We'll return to the *Dom Pedro* and wait for you to come up with your answer.'

The paperwork for the cars was stopped. Juan and the four deflated Libyans piled back into Martin's van and drove back to Carlingford in silence. The second night was similar to the first.

Garda Walsh approached Juan in *The Swan*. 'Still here then?'

'Yes, it may take a day or two to get the parts needed. We couldn't get them in Dundalk. They'll have to come from Dublin or Belfast.'

The next two days passed slowly; there's only so much cleaning and polishing to be done on a sixty-foot trawler.

On Friday evening while the crew were dining in *The Swan*, Martin appeared with a stranger.

'This is Michael Brady. He's our legal expert. He wants you to sign some documents to transfer the ownership of the *Dom Pedro* in exchange for the sum you mentioned earlier. Then we'll take you and the crew to where you can buy a suitable boat. It'll take us about five or six hours. Tomorrow you can buy a vessel and be gone.'

'What? Travel overnight?'

'If we go as soon as you have finished your meal, there will be less chance of our being followed in the dark. Have the local Garda been in here watching you?'

'Yes, this is the first night Garda Walsh hasn't been in.'

'Good. Perhaps, it's his night off.'

They finished their meal and returned to the *Dom Pedro*. Anibal signed the ownership document – its legality baffled Juan as Anibal couldn't possibly have been the legal owner – but Brady didn't seem too concerned; he handed over $100,000 in a small suitcase and disappeared. They packed their kit, for the second time in as many days. The bomb was loaded into the back of a minibus, driven by a shady-looking friend of Martin who had been introduced simply as Nash. Juan and Anibal sat immediately behind the two Irishmen and the others were in the third row.

'We're heading for the yachting marina at Kinsale. I've been told there are dozens of sea-going launches for sale at this time of the year. You might as well get your heads down. It will be a long night,' said Martin.

It's never easy to see where you are going in the dark, but Juan watched carefully. After Dundalk they picked up the motorway for Dublin and the minibus settled down to a constant speed. Juan's eyes gradually closed; he found himself nodding on and off. He knew they had bypassed Dublin when he saw signs for Cashel. Martin was speaking to Nash in Gaelic. He couldn't catch much of what they were saying over the engine noise, as they were talking quietly. However, what he caught worried him.

'When are we going to do it?' asked Nash.

'Not for another hour. There are suitable cliffs south of Knockadoon Head. No one will ever find the bus there; the currents are vicious and will sweep them and the bloody bomb out to sea.'

CHAPTER 13

Saturday 30th March 1991

Juan carefully nudged Anibal who was asleep next to him.

'Wake up,' he whispered in Arabic. 'I think there may be a problem.'

A dozy Anibal stared at Juan, 'What? What?' he repeated.

'Our two friends are planning to kill us; dispose of our bodies and the minibus in order to keep the money.'

A befuddled Anibal opened his eyes wide, 'Are you sure?'

'Yes – I suspect they've got guns in their jackets and have been planning this all along.'

'How do you know?'

'I understand a little Irish Gaelic – it's similar to Manx and I told you my father originally came from the Isle of Man.'

'What are we going to do?'

'Tell the others to take their shoe laces from their shoes. We toughen them by twisting them and tie them together to make two nooses. When they stop the bus at the next set of traffic lights we lean across, ask them to let us out for a piss to distract them. We throttle them before they can reach in their pockets.'

'It's a bit risky.'

'Have you a better idea?'

From five pairs of laces, they carefully entwined them, effectively doubling their strength. Their two would-be assassins were unaware of the preparations quietly going on behind their backs as the minibus trundled south. When they entered the small town of Youghal, it was approaching 5.30 am. Juan nodded to Anibal to be ready. A traffic light ahead was on red; the bus slowed.

'Is there any chance we could stop for a piss? I'm bursting,' asked Juan.

Nash pulled the bus to the side of the deserted street and applied the handbrake. He and Martin turned around. It was a fatal error; they were too slow to escape their destiny. Juan and Anibal had the fine ropes around their necks; within two seconds they were choking. Their instinctive reaction was to try and use their hands to loosen the nooses, their fingers desperately attempting to scramble beneath the cords. Anibal's victim, Nash, was the first to expire as blood oozed from the cuts inflicted by the strangling string. Martin was still struggling. Juan's muscles were bursting as he attempted to apply maximum pressure on the garrotting laces. He needn't have worried, however, for the speed with which Anibal reached over the back of the driver's seat in front of him, found Nash's automatic, and shot Martin in the forehead was instant.

Juan collapsed with the exertion; catching his breath.

Anibal, by comparison, was charged-up. 'What do we do with these bastards?' he asked.

'You've done this before, haven't you?'

'Once or twice,' he smiled. It was occurring to Juan that Anibal might not be the simple foot soldier that he claimed.

'Just give me a minute to recover, will you? If you pass me the map, we'll drive to the site where they were going to dump us and do it to them. It can't be far.'

They drove out of the town and a few miles later turned off the main road for Ballymacoda and Knockadoon Head. A path led from the minor road to the edge of the cliffs. Perhaps 200 feet below, the sea beckoned their victims. The deed took but a few minutes.

An hour later, the five were tucking into a breakfast of grilled kippers on the quay at Kinsale.

'It's now obvious why they were happy to give us the $100,000. They had no intention of letting us keep it,' said Anibal.

'My worry is what their colleagues will do when they realise they aren't coming back,' replied Juan. 'We've got to get a suitable boat today and leave.'

'Eduardo will be the best judge,' replied Anibal and asked his friend, 'What do you think we need?'

'For the kind of money we're talking about, we should be able to buy a twin-diesel, ten metre cruiser. With auxiliary fuel tanks it should get us around Gibraltar in about three days at 20-25 knots.'

The local boatyard owner was bemused by the motley gang. What he thought of Juan's four North African colleagues will never be known. However, business was always quiet on a Saturday and the sight of cash in a holdall with the prospect of a quick deal dispelled any doubts he may have had that morning about getting out of bed. His customers inspected several boats but settled for an 11 metre Fairline – the *Glengarriff* – with twin 200hp Volvo diesel engines. 'A very good choice,' he reassured them.

Eduardo tested the engines and electrical systems; everything was in good order. 'Her top speed is nearly 30 knots, but she'll cruise all day at 20 knots,' he declared. He was looking forward to his adventure in the new boat. He had already forgotten the *Dom Pedro*.

The vendor found several spare 10 gallon fuel drums. They were filled together with the in-board 600 litre fuel tank. The 500 litre water tank was filled while Juan and Rodrigo shopped for food and other essentials for the week ahead.

By three o'clock the *Glengarriff* was sailing past The Old Head of Kinsale, flying the Irish tricolour, and heading south. Only the notorious Bay of Biscay lay between them and Ceuta, or so the crew thought. Elsewhere, a storm was brewing.

✳✳✳

Sean Doran, awoken by a phone call that morning from Carlingford at

0700 hours, had had no hesitation in calling his boss before breakfast. 'Can we meet in an hour's time at Franco's café for breakfast? We have a problem on our hands.'

The café, situated diagonally opposite Charing Cross Station, was no greasy spoon. Kept clean and tidy by its Italian proprietor, it was popular with those Whitehall civil servants on flexitime who frequented it before starting work; sometimes as early as 6.00 am. Being a Saturday, it was quiet when the two senior members of MI5 met. 'I'm afraid Quayle and his troops have given us the slip,' said Doran.

Sir Charles looked up from his bacon and eggs, 'What do you mean?' he asked the Head of his Irish Section.

'Our man in Carlingford was off duty last night and although the *Dom Pedro* is still moored at the quay, it is empty. Apparently they sold it to some dodgy dealer from Northern Ireland, and left in a minibus heading for God knows where.'

'So how much did they get for the boat? Do we know?'

'No, but our man thinks it may have raised as much as £80,000.'

'In that case they're planning to buy a yacht or a cruiser to leave Ireland. Alert the RAF and the Royal Navy. They have to be found and watched.'

'You do realise that it will be like trying to find the proverbial needle in a haystack?'

'Sean, they've got an atomic bomb, we must know where it is at all times. Tell the RAF to begin looking south of Cobh.' There was a trace of panic in his voice.

'Sir,' a worried Head of Section began, 'if Quayle is moving a nuclear weapon out of our area then we are going to have to alert MI6, and get the Home Secretary and the Foreign Secretary involved; not to mention the Secretary of State for Defence. The Service Chiefs are not going to begin a search with Nimrods just because I ask them – especially at a weekend.'

'Yes, that's true, Sean.' Sir Charles Gray sighed. He knew his number two was right; he so often was! 'The PM will have to know too. I had hoped to avoid this becoming political. It's going to be a fine balancing act: how far do we let Quayle go before we call a stop?'

'Sir, I have a horrible feeling that the PM may want to halt it at once.'

'If we do that, Sean, then we will be blowing away the best chance we are ever likely to have of getting someone inside al-Qaeda. You are quite right, of course, I shall ask Kenneth to call an extraordinary meeting of COBRA as soon as possible – possibly this afternoon.'

COBRA, an acronym for Cabinet Office Briefing Room A, is the Civil Contingencies Committee that allows the Prime Minister, senior Ministers, and other key personnel, as required, to discuss critical situations that can arise across all branches of government. The chairman varies according to the nature of the crisis. Sir Charles knew that his boss, the Home Secretary, Kenneth Baker, would take the lead. After finishing his breakfast, he used the emergency encrypted systems from his office to contact him. They had been at Magdalen College, Oxford, together and were on first-name terms.

Fortunately, Sir Kenneth Baker was spending the weekend in his grace and favour apartment in London. By eleven o'clock, Sir Charles was giving him the background. Kenneth Baker listened silently. Sir Charles concluded, 'We have two alternatives: either let Quayle carry on and hope that he will keep in touch with us through our foreign embassies using the code words we taught him when he was trained in Devon, or we find his cruiser and sink it.'

Kenneth Baker looked at his old friend and said nothing. He was deep in thought, weighing-up the consequences of letting an atomic bomb fall into the hands of terrorists. 'I'm inclined to let you run with this one, Charles, but I very much doubt if Douglas will agree. He always tends to play these things by the book.'

Douglas Hurd, the Foreign Secretary, was a former Minister for Northern Ireland and generally considered to be the safest pair of hands in the Government. The Head of MI5 knew that Douglas Hurd would have been briefed fully, when in his previous post, about the IRA's possible possession of a nuclear device.

'Then we will have to hope that the PM and Tom King will back us,' replied Sir Charles.

'I'll get on to it at once,' said the Home Secretary, 'and give the meeting Priority One. If anyone can't attend this afternoon, then it must be no later than tomorrow morning.'

CHAPTER 14

Saturday 30th March 1991

The COBRA meeting began promptly at 1600 hours; barely an hour after the *Glengarriff* had slipped out of Kinsale harbour. John Major had flown by helicopter from the RAF station at Wyton, adjacent to his constituency home in Huntingdon. Douglas Hurd had been in his office in the Foreign Office. Working Saturday mornings was his usual practice. Not for nothing was he nicknamed by his senior civil servants as *the refrigerator – he's switched on all the time.* He was accompanied by Sir Charles Gray's opposite number, the Head of MI6, Sir Peter Stacey.

Only Tom King, the Secretary of State for Defence, was absent. A meeting of his constituency party in Somerset demanded his presence.

'If it's all right, I'll make sure the Chief of the Defence Staff attends on my behalf,' he had told the Home Secretary. 'I'll go along with whatever he recommends – I can trust him to make the right decision.'

CDS, the Chief of the Defence Staff, was Marshal of the Royal Air Force, Sir David Craig. Sir Kenneth knew him well and also respected his judgement; after all, he was a fellow *alma mater* from Oxford University. With a first class honours degree in mathematics, he was probably the most intelligent CDS of the 20th century.

With Kenneth Baker in the chair, the meeting was briefed by Sir Charles on the background to their dilemma. He concluded by recommending that a search be mounted for Quayle's yacht and, when found, the resources of MI6 be used to tail the nuclear device until such time as they could be certain of al-Qaeda's intentions; thereby allowing Quayle time to infiltrate their organisation.

After what seemed an interminable length of time, the Prime Minister looked at his Foreign Secretary and asked, 'Douglas, what are your views?'

'I'm not happy. I know about the Libyan links with the Provisionals, of course, from my previous position as Secretary of State for Northern Ireland. There have been several radical groups supplying the IRA with weapons for years. Now it looks as if the trade is in reverse. The successful decommissioning of the Provos' weapons will be critical to the peace process. It looks as if the IRA is getting what it can for its stocks before having to destroy them. I also believe Sir Charles. The danger these Islamic groups pose in the future will be far worse than anything we have dealt with in the past. The IRA's terror has been confined to Britain; al-Qaeda's will be worldwide. There were rumours of the Gadhafi atomic weapon years ago, and although the Army and the Royal Ulster Constabulary tried their damnedest to locate it, the story remained a rumour. Had we found it then, we would have disposed of it safely. Now we know where it is, I see no reason for not nullifying it.'

The Prime Minister nodded, apparently in agreement, but said nothing.

Kenneth Baker, seeing John Major's reaction, felt obliged to reinforce Sir Charles' recommendations. 'The main problem is that we know very little about al-Qaeda,' he began. 'They are a Sunni Islamist terrorist group who, we believe, are being financed by Iraq and have set up training camps in the Afghan border region with Pakistan. Radical mullahs are brainwashing youngsters in Pakistan, Iraq, Palestine, even possibly here in Britain, to believe they are fighting a holy jihad against the West; especially the US and Israel. As yet, we have not had to deal with suicide bombers, but they are going to be the scourge of the future. We must infiltrate al-Qaeda and gather more intelligence, find out who their leaders are, and destroy them before they destroy us. Quayle is our best bet.'

'I don't disagree, Kenneth, but this a matter of balance. How many lives would this bomb kill if detonated in a large city, such as Tel Aviv?' asked the PM to no one in particular.

Kenneth Baker looked at Sir David Craig for an accurate answer. Up to now, the Service Chief had said nothing.

'At Hiroshima a similar bomb killed about 150,000 people,' he replied.

'So,' said the PM, drawing himself up to his full height, 'we either destroy Quayle, his four companions, the bomb, and his boat, or risk 150,000 dead. As far as I am concerned, gentlemen, it's a no-brainer. There will be future chances to infiltrate al-Qaeda, but if we were to lose track of Quayle, and the bomb was detonated, then the civilised world would never forgive us.'

'We've got to find Quayle first,' interjected the Foreign Secretary.

'Yes,' agreed the PM. 'What ideas have you got, David?'

'It's almost five o'clock and getting dark. However, I can have a Nimrod Maritime Reconnaissance aircraft from RAF St Mawgan in Cornwall on patrol within the hour. All it can do, however, is to search for likely vessels,' he paused, 'say, anything between thirty and forty feet in length heading south during the night from eastern Ireland. The Nimrod's radar is sophisticated, but to make a positive ID we will need more details of Quayle's craft – its size, make, better still its name. By first light tomorrow I can have a pair of Nimrods from RAF Kinloss in Scotland take over the surveillance equipped with Sting Ray torpedoes. However, we must be certain we are sinking the right yacht.'

'What about the Navy? Couldn't we get them to intercept the launch? Do we have to blow them out of the water?' It was Sir Charles who asked the question.

'I suppose the Nimrods could follow them discreetly and we could send a frigate from Gibraltar to meet them west of Portugal,' replied the Air Marshal. 'We'd still have to positively identify the motor launch, and anyway they may still be in Ireland. We don't know for certain they've left.'

'That's a job for my men in Dublin,' interrupted Sir Peter, who up to this point had said little. He continued, 'I have three operatives in Dublin and will send them down to the Cork area at once. They can make inquiries at the most likely boat yards tomorrow morning.'

'But tomorrow is Sunday,' interrupted the PM.

'That will make little difference, sir. My men will find out who owns the yards and where they live. We will then know what likely vessels have been sold in the past twenty-four hours. A mix of bribery and coercion works wonders.' He smiled to himself.

'Then, assuming your men are able to find out exactly what craft is being used to transport the bomb, we have to decide what we are going to do: use Nimrod torpedoes to sink it or send in the Navy,' said the PM.

'Can I clear up one point, sir?' It was the Defence Chief who had interposed. 'The torpedoes don't necessarily have to be armed like Sir Charles imagines.'

Everyone turned to look at Sir David. By the looks on their faces they had all imagined the yacht being blown sky-high.

'The usual armament on the Sting Ray torpedo is a shaped charge, the equivalent of 100 lbs of TNT. It is designed to blow a hole in a double-hulled submarine. However, in training we fill the warhead with concrete.' He added almost apologetically, 'It saves money.'

There were smiles around the table.

He then continued, 'If the two Nimrods each fired a training torpedo from opposite sides of Quayle's ship, they could be pre-programmed by the Nimrods' Tactical Navigators to hit simultaneously. The launch would sink in less than a minute. It should give the crew time to get away in an inflatable. They would think they had hit a submerged object.'

'But wouldn't they see the torpedoes being fired and take evasive action?' asked the PM.

'No. We would release the torpedoes at a range of about three miles from an altitude of 300 ft. Occupants on a small boat, relatively low in the water, would not see the aircraft at that range.'

'How are the torpedoes guided to their target?' The PM was showing interest.

'The latest model can travel about eighteen inches below the surface at up to forty knots. Before release, the Tac Nav would program the integrated circuits with the signature of the engine noises made by the cruiser, probably some type of diesel engine, as well as the shape and size of the hull. Once launched, the torpedo operates automatically using its own active sonar. The Tac Nav in the Nimrod watches the attack on a large scope and will know when it's all over.'

'I like this idea, sir.' It was Sir Charles who showed enthusiasm. 'It gives Quayle a chance to remain with the al-Qaeda crew; assuming, of course, they get rescued by a ship nearby. The atomic weapon goes to the bottom of the Atlantic. If we were to intercept them with a Navy frigate, we would lose the chance of Quayle remaining inside al-Qaeda's pockets.'

'A modern motor launch has to have a lifeboat with rescue flares and an SOS transmitter. They will be safe enough if they get off in time.' It was Sir Douglas Hurd, an amateur weekend yachtsman, who made the remark in a manner indicating that he, too, agreed this course of action.

'Then, we're all in agreement,' concluded the PM. 'Sir Peter – get your men down to the South of Ireland, and you, David, know what to do. Have a nice weekend, gentlemen; what's left of it!'

✶✶✶

As the PM was calling the COBRA meeting to a close, in North London, David Mestel had entered Simon Rosenberg's office. 'Simon, our man from the Dublin embassy is on the line.'

'Put him through.'

A moment later: 'Yes, Ben, it's Simon here. What have you found out?'

'I'm up country at a small village called Carlingford. I'm looking at the *Dom Pedro* tied up on the quay as I speak to you from a public phone box. There is no one here, all the crew have gone.'

'Where to?'

'Hard to say. I slipped on board the *Dom Pedro*, but it's empty. There's nothing there. Whatever the crew had, they've taken it with them.'

Simon Rosenberg turned to his colleague, 'If you wanted to get an atomic weapon back to Libya, how would you do it?'

'I'd either have to sail it back or fly it back. Either way would involve stealing a yacht or a small aircraft.'

'I think the odds are heavily on the former, don't you? Especially as we know they are sailors and they may have raised money by selling the *Dom Pedro*.'

He asked down the phone, 'Ben, have you any feel for what the *Dom Pedro* may be worth?'

'No real idea – it's a fine modern trawler. It must have cost a packet. I wouldn't be surprised if they got $100,000 for it.'

'Ben, get your team to check out motor launch sales in the last couple of days. My bet is our friends have slipped out of Eire; probably from a south-east port. Concentrate your search there.' He put down the phone and looked at David.

'I think we may have to get our friends in Langley involved in this one, don't you?'

'Do you think they'll be willing to help?'

'Yes, especially when I tell them that al-Qaeda has a nuclear weapon and is intending to use it against them.'

✳✳✳

After the COBRA meeting, Sir David Craig returned to his office on the seventh floor of the MoD Main Building. His Personal Staff Officer, Colonel Mike Harrington, who had been waiting patiently for him to return, greeted him. 'I've forewarned the tri-Service duty officers to be standing by, sir. The comms staffs are geared up too.'

'Good man, Mike. First of all get me the Station Commander at RAF St Mawgan; then OC RAF Kinloss.'

By 1900 hours a Nimrod MR2, *The Mighty Hunter,* from No 120

Squadron had taken off from RAF St Mawgan and was, with a crew of eleven, heading due west across the southern reaches of the St Georges Channel. On reaching longitude 8 degrees 25 minutes west, it headed south at 8,000 feet. Its forward-looking radar, with a cone search pattern of approximately 100 miles diameter, was seeking plausible targets.

Simultaneously, the Ops centre at RAF Kinloss was being manned. 'Operation Little Boy' had begun. Two Nimrods, from No 201 Squadron, were being prepared: armed with training torpedoes, the galleys filled with rations, the crews alerted for an 0600 hours take-off. Nimrod *alpha* would be captained by Squadron Leader Eddie Ledsom – the most experienced pilot in the Nimrod fleet, having begun his career as an NCO pilot on Shackletons almost 40 years previously. His Tac Nav, arguably the most important member of the crew, was Squadron Leader Tim Clarke. He would be responsible for the handling of the computer equipment that would direct the weapons to their target. The success of the mission would ultimately be on his shoulders. Nimrod *beta* would be the supporting aircraft; a belt and braces approach was standard practice. The second string would take minute-by-minute operational instructions from Nimrod *alpha*.

Finally, a secure communications link was set up from Kinloss to the Number One Briefing Room in the MoD Main Building. David Craig, Charles Gray and Peter Stacey had agreed to meet there at 1000 hours the following morning.

It was almost 2000 hours when Mike Harrington asked, 'Is there anything else we need to do this evening, sir?'

The Service Chief looked at his PSO, his eyes narrowed, his lips tightened, his mind raced. 'I think,' he said deliberately, 'you'd better get me OC 51 Squadron on the blower immediately.'

CHAPTER 15

Sunday 31st March 1991

In the early hours of Sunday morning, three cars left the Dublin suburbs. They travelled in convoy as far as the outskirts of Cork, where one turned east for Cobh. The remaining two passed Cork airport and, shortly afterwards, one turned left for Kinsale; the third would continue to Clonakilty.

Sunday mornings in Kinsale are quiet affairs; the population roughly split between those lying in bed getting over their Guinness-induced boisterous Saturday night or rising to go to Mass.

Bill Dale had been an overseas operative for MI6 all his life. Now aged 57, he was on his last tour of duty and looking forward to retiring to his native Norfolk. A final tour in Dublin had, at one time, been seen as a sinecure – a place where people were put out to grass. However, since 1969 when the troubles had flared-up, the three MI6 staff stationed in Britain's Dublin embassy were kept busy. Bill had seen active service in Malaya, Israel and Germany; at various times all hotbeds of unrest. He had, therefore, developed a keen nose for sniffing out signs that most people would miss. He quickly discovered there were three boat yards in Kinsale selling the type of vessel that may have been used to attempt a journey to North Africa. By ten o'clock he had walked around the periphery of two, had grabbed a bacon sandwich and a coffee on the quay, and was carefully inspecting the third. At the back of the yard he noticed a small minibus, the size of a typical transit van. What struck him immediately was it had a Northern Ireland registration. Vehicles registered in Ulster used the letter 'I'; those in the south a letter 'Z'.

He remembered being briefed: *They left Carlingford in a minibus.*

Bill Dale was experienced enough to know he need look no further. He also knew that, assuming a cash transaction had occurred, the shipyard owner would probably have had the bender of all benders the previous evening. There would be little point in trying to find him in church.

A few inquiries on the quay, saying that he had seen a yacht he fancied, produced the address of the owner, Tom O'Connor. 'And, yes, he had spent a lot of money the previous night in Seamus's Bar.'

Purporting to be the Chief Superintendent of the Cork Division of the Garda, with a false ID card bearing the name Eamon Armstrong, Bill quickly gained entry into the O'Connor home. A bleary-eyed, unshaven, overweight man in his fifties sat in front of him and was in no state to either closely inspect Bill's credentials or question why he had been visited by the Garda at such an unearthly hour as eleven o'clock. O'Connor's wife, an attractive thirty-something, presumably a second marriage, showed no surprise at Bill's call. She knew her husband had done dodgy deals many times and wanted no part of the ensuing conversation. She disappeared into the kitchen mumbling something about 'getting the lunch ready.'

'I'll cut to the quick,' began Bill. 'I'm not here from the Inspector of Taxes. I don't want to know about your financial dealings. However, I must know the type of vessel you sold to those five drug dealers from the north: the make, the dimensions, the name of the boat and whether it had any distinguishing features.'

'I haven't sold anything for weeks.' O'Connor slurred his words, barely intelligible.

'Don't piss me about, Tom. I haven't the time to play games. They left you their minibus. What are you going to do with it?'

'I don't know what you're talking about.'

'Tom, you have a choice. Come clean with me or I'll charge you with dealing in cocaine. I know those buggers yesterday had a trunk full of the stuff; perhaps as much as 1,000 lbs. You'll get ten years for dealing in that quantity. What's it to be?'

O'Connor sat upright. He was sobering up rapidly. He'd helped the four middle-eastern looking men and the Aussie load the *Glengarriff* with their large covered trunk and knew what a weight it had been. He shuddered at the thought that it could have been full of cocaine. His brain wasn't clear enough to ask himself where such a load could have come from, although he was sufficiently worldly-wise to know the Provisionals were dealers in illegal substances. He sat wondering what to say to the Garda superintendent.

Bill pressed on. He knew he was about to get a confession.

Kick the man when he's down.

He had learnt the old adage to be a good guideline in such circumstances.

'How much did they pay you, Tom? $100,000? What were you going to do with a minibus without its registration documents?'

'$80,000 – that's all I got,' he gasped, 'plus the bus.'

'What was the boat you sold them? Hurry man, I haven't got much time. Our Navy has to catch them before they get away. Our fastest Peacock Class vessel, LE Ciara, left Haulbowline at first light, but we must know who we're after. I don't give a shite about your dodgy dealings.' And grabbing his arm, shouted, 'Just tell me man!'

Tom O'Connor was sufficiently aware about ships to know that the fastest ship in the Irish fleet was LE Ciara and was based at the nearby main naval base of Haulbowline. He also knew he was getting in over his head.

He blurted out, 'It was an eleven metre Fairline with twin 200hp Volvo diesel engines, called the *Glengarriff.*'

'Speed? Range?'

'Capable of 30 knots, cruise all day at 24 knots. They took on extra fuel tanks. They will get to southern Spain easily. They stocked up with food and water too.'

'It had a lifeboat?'

'Yes – an auto-inflatable hardshelled yellow canister – at the stern. You won't miss it. It is fitted with an emergency radio beacon, flares and several days of supplies. The *Glengarriff* has all the mod-cons: radar, depth sounder and so on.'

'When did they leave?'

'About three o'clock yesterday.'

God, that's twenty hours ago. They'll have covered 400 miles.

Bill Dale stood up, about to leave. 'Two things: firstly, a word to no one about this. If I hear you have blabbered, I'll inform the tax authorities about your dealings. Secondly, get rid of that minibus; it belongs to the Provos and they'll want to know how you got it and what happened to their cache of drugs.'

O'Connor, already sweating with worry, turned puce; his eyes bulged from his head and his jaw dropped.

'If they catch up with you, you're a dead man,' and with that, Bill was gone.

Seated in his car outside O'Connor's house, Bill Dale rang the British embassy. The special phone encrypted his message before transmitting it, via Britain's Skynet space satellite, to Dublin. Minutes later, the information was relayed to the duty officer at the RAF Kinloss Ops Centre. At precisely 1114 hours, the coded data was received by the Tac Navs on-board the Nimrods and in the MoD briefing room.

However, for an experienced operator, Bill Dale was unusually careless. He was so engrossed that he failed to notice a car parked 50 yards away with three men observing him. Bill wanted to get home to his wife and when he finished his message, he drove rapidly away.

Having watched Dale, whom they knew to be a British SIS officer, the three men drove into O'Connor's driveway. They pulled three identical Ronald Reagan rubber masks over their faces, took out three shotguns from their boot and kicked the front door open.

O'Connor was still sitting in his lounge wondering how to get rid of the minibus when the three entered, one firing a shot into the ceiling.

God, it's the IRA already, he thought.

'Would you like to lose your kneecaps?' the leader asked.

O'Connor never replied. His heart-rate had risen to bursting point; he felt his underpants wet, his anus damp.

'Who did you sell that boat to yesterday? What make was it? What is it called?' the leader demanded as the other two louts dragged O'Connor's wife screaming from the kitchen.

'Tie the tart up,' the leader ordered. 'Then shaft her.'

'No, no, don't do that. I told the Garda everything. How was I to know they had a trunk full of your cocaine?'

'Is that what he told you?' The leader laughed. 'It's more dangerous than a few hundred kilos of coke. Answer the bloody questions, or else she'll get the best shagging of her life.' He nodded to his men. One of them had already ripped her blouse and pulled her bra off. He was roughly fondling her breasts with one hand and groping between her struggling legs with the other.

'It was a ten metre Fairline, twin 200hp diesels, called the *Glengarriff*,' O'Connor screamed. 'There were five of them; an Australian and four shady-looking dagos. It had auxiliary fuel tanks and a hard-cased automatic lifeboat.'

'What time did they leave?'

'About three o'clock.'

'Thank you for being so helpful. Here's a souvenir of our visit.' And with that, he shot O'Connor in the knee. They turned and left, leaving his wife, tied-up, screaming.

Seconds later a phone call was received in North London. It was 1145 hours Greenwich Mean Time.

✳✳✳

During the previous night, the St Mawgan Nimrod Maritime Reconnaissance aircraft identified four possible vessels in the St Georges Approaches, west of the Isles of Scilly. Two had been eliminated when they had headed south-east for Brest; presumably French fishing boats. The two remaining motor launches, about 30 miles apart, were continuing to head towards Cape Finisterre when the RAF Kinloss Nimrods took over surveillance at 0830 hours. The aircraft remained five miles distant from their quarry, not wishing to alert the vessels' crews that they were under observation.

However, the two Nimrods had passed through the Prestwick Air Traffic Control Centre's radar 30 minutes after take-off. One of the Military ATC assistants on duty was 'Mac' McIver, a US Air Force Sergeant, one of several controllers on an exchange tour with the RAF. He watched the two identified aircraft on the scopes and began thinking, *Sunday? Two Nimrods heading south – supposedly on a training mission. That doesn't make sense.* He knew enough about Nimrods' modus operandi that they hunted in pairs. *But the RAF never trains on a Sunday!* He noted the time and their bearing. He would be off duty in half an hour and would report the incident to his US superiors.

Back in his room in the Sergeants' Mess, McIver removed his scrambler phone from his locker, and rang the duty officer at RAF Alconbury in Cambridgeshire. Although nominally called RAF Alconbury, the station is, in reality, a United States Air Force base. It is the home of USAF's U-2 spy planes that take-off daily from Incirlik in Turkey and fly overnight at 70,000 feet across eastern Europe; landing early in the morning beside the A1, three miles north of Huntingdon. The duty officer listened carefully, thanked his source, and entered the information into a computer that would share the data with computers as far away as Virginia, USA.

***

It was 1120 hours when Commander Tony Reid, the Royal Navy's duty officer in the MoD briefing room, asked the Chief of the Defence Staff, 'Now that we have sufficient information to positively ID the launch, when do you want to go in, sir?'

'I'm looking at the map, Tony. Just show me exactly where the *Glengarriff* is?'

'It's here,' he said, pointing to the large display-map, '160 miles north of Corunna; well outside Spanish waters.'

'What are the chances of the survivors being picked up there?' The man who had interrupted and questioned Tony Reid was the taller of the two strangers accompanying CDS. The commander had not been introduced to either but gathered they were high-powered; all three calling each other by their first names. His name appeared to be Charles.

'Excellent, I would say, sir. It's a busy sea route around Cape Ortegal and there will also be plenty of local fishing boats, mostly drifters, in the area.'

Charles nodded a silent thank you.

Sir David Craig ordered, 'OK. Tell Kinloss to go ahead.'

Seconds later the aircraft approached the two suspect vessels for a visual ID. Over flying at 500 feet, photographs were taken with powerful zoom lenses. The *Glengarriff* was easily identified by its yellow canister. The photos were transmitted back to Kinloss. The faces of two North Africans and a Caucasian looking up at Eddie Ledsom's Nimrod were instantly displayed on screens in both the Ops Centre and the MoD.

'That's Quayle,' announced Sir Charles to his two colleagues as he examined the pictures. Commander Reid nodded to the VDU operator, Sergeant Toll, to transmit the positive ID to RAF Kinloss.

Having taken their photographs, the Nimrods flew away from the vessels. As they retreated, confirmation appeared on their computer screens that the *Glengariff* was the target. The second Nimrod positioned itself exactly five miles to the west of the *Glengariff*, while Nimrod alpha took up a position five miles to the east. Both Nimrods were also exactly five miles ahead of where the *Glengarriff* would be in fifteen minutes time, assuming it didn't change course. The launch's profiles were entered in to the Sting Rays' micro-circuits; it was decided the approach speed of the torpedoes would be 40 knots. At a height of 300 feet, two torpedoes were released.

✦✦✦

On board the *Glengarriff* it was Anibal who asked the question, 'Who the hell are they? What are they doing?'

'It's the RAF. They've found us and are taking photos to confirm our identification,' replied Juan.

'What for?'

'I suspect they are planning to intercept us. As we speak there's probably a Royal Navy ship heading towards us from Gibraltar. There's no way anything could catch us from Plymouth; we're too far ahead.'

'What will we do?'

'There's little point in sailing south to meet trouble. I think our best chance may be to make for somewhere like San Sebastian and get inside Spanish territorial waters. They won't touch us there.'

'Why San Sebastian?'

'There may be a chance we can meet up with ETA, the Basque freedom fighters. They would help us escape. We'll change course at once to 130 degrees east.'

Anibal nodded. It made sense. What neither knew was that their best chance of survival lay in turning through 180 degrees and then, while heading due north, turn off the Volvo diesels.

As the *Glengarriff* began its turn east, the Tac Nav in Nimrod alpha, Tim Clarke, smiled. He watched as the course of his torpedo altered automatically. However, he knew that the torpedo from Nimrod beta would now hit the *Glengarriff* after his, unless he took action. A few depressions on his keypad, and his own torpedo slowed to make a simultaneous impact. He watched as his scope showed the two deadly missiles close-in on their prey. 'Impact in three minutes,' he announced as he read the data from his computer; his message was heard onboard the Nimrods, in the RAF Kinloss Ops centre and in the MoD.

The two Nimrod captains began to climb towards their cruising altitude; preparing for their journey home. They had been instructed not to approach the doomed vessel and to remain out of visual range. Nothing must be done to incriminate their participation in the sinking of the *Glengarriff*. The Tac Navs remained glued to their scopes. The minutes ticked by. 'One minute to impact.'

The scope registered the hit, and the *Glengarriff* disappeared from the screen. Seconds later an SOS message was being broadcast from the position of impact; the lifeboat had been ejected, the casket had opened automatically and the inflatable was operational. Tim Clarke immediately reported back to the Ops Centre, 'Mission completed successfully.'

'Let's go home,' announced Eddie Ledsom to the two crews. The Nimrods climbed steadily to 30,000 feet and headed north, 15 degrees east. It was 1140 hours GMT; 1240 hours European time.

***

The moment of impact on the *Glengarriff* was catastrophic. First, a horrendous thud, instantly followed by a shudder, as if the launch had hit a brick wall. Then, a deafening crack as the hull was split open and the ship retarded from 20 knots to a standstill in less than 20 seconds. Although still on deck with Anibal and Felipe, Juan could sense the sea rushing in to flood below decks. He knew they had collided with something big and could only imagine it must have been a submerged rock that wasn't on their charts. Instinctively, he jumped to the stern and pulled the quick-release lever on the straps that held the lifeboat. Instantly springs threw the yellow canister into the water, some ten yards from the launch. There was an enormous whoosh, as it opened automatically and the lifeboat self-inflated.

'Get off,' he yelled at Anibal and Felipe. 'Tell the others to abandon ship.' He could see the sea rushing up from the galley below. He knew at once Eduardo and Rodrigo would not get out. The realisation made his heart sink; they would be trapped below. With the deck awash with the foaming sea, he could do nothing for them. He jumped, saw the other two do likewise and turned to swim towards the inflatable.

'Help!' he heard from behind. Juan turned and saw both Anibal and Felipe thrashing in the water. Clearly, neither could swim. There had been no time to don lifejackets. He swam back, grabbed Felipe's arms and placed his hands on his own shoulders, 'Stay still,' he ordered. 'Lie quietly on your back, facing me.' He then swam breaststroke towards the lifeboat and pushed Felipe over the rubber side and into the dinghy. Seconds later he was with Anibal, the stronger of the two helpless men. In a similar fashion they returned to the lifeboat. Felipe, still gasping for breath, leant over the side and helped to pull Anibal to safety. All three sat on the rubber floor exhausted, catching their breath.

The *Glengarriff* had disappeared.

'We can never thank you enough,' said Anibal. 'You saved our lives. You are our brother. Allah will be forever grateful to you.'

Juan smiled and put one hand on each of their shoulders, nodding as if to say it's OK. *Phase one: getting their trust – completed,* he thought.

Many minutes passed in silence before Anibal asked, 'What the hell happened?'

Juan had been thinking the same thing. 'It can't have been submerged rocks,' he replied. 'There weren't any on our charts; look there's no evidence of there being anything there – no white horses, nothing.'

They resumed their silence as the enormity of losing Eduardo and Rodrigo dawned on them.

✶✶✶

In London, there was silence in the briefing room as it dawned on the top brass that a successful mission isn't always a satisfying one. Commander Reid felt distinctly awkward; it wasn't his place to say anything. The Chief of the Defence Staff's Personal Staff Officer hadn't said a word all morning. The equipment operator, the only other person in the room, was Sergeant Alec Toll. He remained rooted looking at the blank screens.

Minutes passed before the Service Chief asked the two intelligence chiefs, 'What happens next?' It was tantamount to saying *I've done my bit.*

Sir Peter looked at Charles, as if asking permission to answer the question, and then replied, 'We wait. I will move an operative from Madrid to our charge d'affaires office in Gijon, the regional capital. A rescue at sea will quickly become local news. He will gather all he can and find out where the Spanish take the crew who will, presumably, have no documents. Usual Spanish practice is not to release anyone until they have been identified and issued with new passports. They will probably be held in a detention centre for illegal immigrants.'

'That could be interesting as Quayle's passport says he is a New Zealander with the name of Quine. I am going to have to check we covered our tracks correctly when we issued him with his false ID,' said Sir Charles. He continued, 'However, I am confident that he knows how to keep in touch. Are your men in the embassies aware of his call sign and know what to do?'

'Yes. He will announce himself as Bradda Head and ask for his message to be passed to Dover Castle. He will relay it in Gaelic.'

'Good. Shall we have a spot of lunch in *The Royal Horseguards Hotel*?' asked Sir Charles.

David Craig smiled. He had a card up his sleeve but he wasn't about to show it; at least, not yet.

The three chiefs stood up, thanked Colonel Harrington, Commander Reid and Sergeant Toll, then left.

All right for some, thought Alec. *I've got to wash their coffee cups. The mean bastards didn't even leave me any chocolate biscuits.*

CHAPTER 16

Sunday 31st March 1991

The United States Air Force base in Zaragoza is located roughly halfway between Madrid and Barcelona. Primarily designated as a Master Diversion Airfield for space shuttles, the base had been winding down for several years and had become something of a sleepy hollow. Nevertheless, two E-3 Sentry aircraft, or AWACS, were always based there on detachment from their home base of Geilenkirchen in Germany. Their prime role was to patrol the western Mediterranean and Northern Africa. As he was about to sit down for his Sunday lunch at one o'clock Continental Time, the base commander, Colonel Harry Bamberger, received from his Duty Officer a 'flash top secret' scrambled signal from the CIA HQ in Langley, Virginia. He didn't doubt its authenticity, but was puzzled by its instruction.

An Airborne Warning and Control System aircraft was to fly immediately due west to the northern border of Portugal and turn north. It was to scour the coastal seas for a 30-foot Fairline motor launch, the *Glengarriff*, with a yellow casing covering its on-board lifeboat. It would be heading south at around 20 knots. The AWACS need fly no further than 100 miles north of Cape Ortegal. It was to remain on-station until the vessel was found, or the mission called off. The E-3 would be refuelled in-flight from aircraft based at the USAF Base Moron, near Seville. When found, the Sentry was to relay the *Glengarriff's* exact position on a frequency dedicated to communications between AWACS aircraft and nuclear submarines.

Bamberger could only imagine that the vessel was going to be taken out by a submarine using either a torpedo or, more likely, a SLBM: a submarine launched ballistic missile with a conventional warhead. However, he decided to check if a tanker aircraft from Moron had been allocated to the task and rang his buddy on the scrambled line – the base commander, Brigadier Mike Shriver.

'Yep, I've had that signal too,' he replied. 'When do you want the refill?'

'My duty crew can take-off within thirty minutes. They should be on-station by 1430 hours local; they should reach the northern limit of their patrol area an hour later. Plan for refuelling around 2030 hours.'

'Fine, if you want us sooner, give me a shout.'

***

Juan sat quietly pondering in the lifeboat. He was cold, wet, and exhausted. 'I think we struck a submarine,' he said quietly, articulating his thoughts. 'I can't see what else it could have been. I remember a fishing trawler being sunk in the Firth of Clyde last year in similar circumstances. Everyone said it had been dragged under when its nets were snarled-up by a nuclear submarine coming out of Faslane. The Royal Navy denied it, of course. I can only think our sub was either French or Spanish.'

Anibal and Felipe never heard him. Their thoughts were elsewhere – remembering their late friends.

Juan looked around the small inflatable. The radio beacon was working – there was a red neon light flashing on and off regularly. There was food and water. He wondered how long it would be before rescue arrived. His watch read 1245 hours local time; he closed his eyes.

He was awoken by the unmistakable *thud, thud* beat of a helicopter. His watch read 1400 hours. He had been asleep for over an hour. He looked up and saw a red and yellow chopper hovering above them at 100 feet. The down force of its rotors was smoothing the sea around them, but causing their dinghy to spin in a circular movement. A man wearing a one-piece waterproof Day-Glo suit was being lowered from the helicopter on a winch. He struggled into their tiny boat and over the roar of the engines from the helicopter, yelled in Spanish, 'Spanish Coastguard. Anyone injured?'

Juan replied, 'No, we're all fine.'

'I'll take you up one at a time.'

Ten minutes later, they were safely inside the helicopter. A flare was fired into their dinghy to sink it and they were flying back to the mainland.

The winch-man shouted, 'We are from Corunna but we are taking you to Gijon, our HQ.'

'Why?'

'There are facilities there to accommodate you while you are processed.'

And with that the three wet and tired friends pulled their blankets around them and supped their steaming coffee. Conversation above the noise was impossible.

∗∗∗

The crew strength of an E-3 can vary according to its mission, but the aircraft that had taken off from Zaragoza had ten members on-board. Six were *ears* – sergeant operators trained to listen to radio transmissions in a variety of languages. Half an hour out from their base, one of the operators was listening to frequencies used by the Spanish coastguards. Over the intercom he called to the Captain of the aircraft, 'Sir, a helicopter is reporting as having found three survivors from a motor launch that has sunk 130 miles north of Cape Ortegal.'

'So what, Number four?'

'The vessel was called the *Glengarriff*. Isn't that the name of the vessel we're looking for?'

'Tune me into that frequency at once, will you?' Captain Jim

McNaughton, having been half-asleep flying his AWACS on auto-pilot, suddenly sounded interested.

'It's in Spanish, sir.'

'Goddamnit, why can't these Dagos parley in English?'

'Two of the crew have drowned. Of the three rescued, one is Caucasian and two are Arabic.' Number four was enjoying the act of translation, knowing that his boss didn't understand a word of the local language.

'What else are they saying?'

'They are alerting Gijon to prepare for receiving them at their reception centre. Apart from the survivors being cold and wet, they have no injuries.'

'OK. Number one, transmit that info, scrambled, on the sub frequency we were given. Number two ditto to home, copy Langley and Moron. Tell them we're returning to base for the rest of our Sunday lunch.'

The computers in the CIA HQ in Langley received the information and automatically began digesting the data and cross-referencing it with other information received earlier. Sophisticated software on the IBM mainframes had been developed that could infer solutions to problems before a human could realise a problem existed. The computers knew the *Glengarriff* had left Kinsale at 1500 hours on Saturday, they knew the performance parameters of the Fairline launch, they knew the precise time when two Nimrods had passed through Prestwick's control centre and their bearing, they knew their capability to attack surface vessels. It was seconds later when the IBM machines were hypothesising the possible cause of the *Glengarriff's* demise and estimating within seconds the exact time of the sinking. They were even forecasting when the two RAF aircraft would pass through Prestwick ATC Centre on their return journey.

***

By 1415 hours GMT, Simon Rosenberg's mobile phone was ringing. The duty intelligence officer in the US Embassy in Grosvenor Square, London, was explaining that the RAF had sunk the *Glengarriff* in the Bay of Biscay where the depth of the sea was 20,000 feet. The bomb was no longer a threat, and two of the al-Qaeda terrorists had drowned.

Rosenberg thanked his caller, and hung up. However, he was not satisfied. He wanted revenge for Mannion's death and held Bradda Head, whoever he was, responsible. He knew better than the British or the Americans what a threat al-Qaeda was to world peace. Recent suicide bombings in Tel Aviv, orchestrated by them, had killed dozens of innocent civilians. Indoctrination of young Muslims to die for the cause was not new. Over 150,000 teenagers had died in the Iran-Iraq war on the promise of entering heaven. The trade of cheap arms from the IRA to al-Qaeda had to be stopped. He began investigating who his opposite number was in Madrid.

***

The three knights of the realm were having coffee, finishing their lunch at *The Royal Horseguards Hotel* when Sir David Craig's mobile rang discreetly.

'Excuse me a minute,' he said to his colleagues. He sat listening to his caller, occasionally murmuring a 'Yes' or a 'Good'. After almost five minutes, he hung up and smiled with satisfaction.

'Everything OK?' asked Sir Peter.

The CDS looked at Sir Charles. 'You'll be pleased to know that Quayle is safe. He and two of the Libyans have been rescued by a Spanish Coastguard helicopter and, as we speak, are on their way to a detention centre in Gijon. However, two Libyans were drowned.'

Sir Charles' face showed his astonishment. His eyes opened, his jaw dropped, he almost spilt his coffee. 'How do you know?' he spluttered.

'Like a game of chess, military operations have three phases. The St Mawgan Nimrod opened the game – it gave us the initiative; finding the quarry. The two MR2s from Kinloss played the middle game – attacking the enemy. However, there is always the endgame – the most difficult phase in a game of chess. Therefore, I sent a Nimrod R1, our electronic and intelligence gathering aircraft, from No 51 Squadron, to discreetly patrol the area.'

'The RAF's spy in the sky,' commented Sir Peter.

'Exactly,' agreed Sir David, 'and what you wouldn't have found out, if I hadn't sent it, is that the Americans were in on the act.'

'What?' Both the intelligence chiefs asked with one voice.

'The R1 picked up transmissions from a USAF AWACS based in Zaragoza that had been detailed to find the *Glengarriff* and report its position to a US Navy nuclear submarine. It looks as if the Yanks were planning to sink the *Glengarriff* as well. When the AWACS overheard the coastguards had rescued three survivors and the vessel was sunk, they called off their search.'

'But how the hell did the Americans get involved?' asked Sir Charles.

'I understand Langley was mentioned,' added Sir David.

'The CIA,' remarked Sir Peter. 'What I can't fathom out is how did they know the *Glengarriff* was the ship with the cargo?'

All three sat quietly contemplating the conundrum.

'Unless...' began Sir Peter then stopped.

The other two looked at him to continue his hypothesis,

'Unless...' he stopped again. 'You told me you thought Mossad had an agent on the Isle of Man who had been eavesdropping on telephone conversations?' He was looking to Sir Charles for a reply.

A nod was returned.

'Somehow Mossad found out how the device was being taken back to Libya, and persuaded the CIA to help them eliminate the threat.'

The others agreed. It made sense; Mossad and the CIA were now tracking Quayle.

'In which case,' began Sir Peter, 'I have a lot to do: either we tell Quayle and protect him somehow or I persuade Mossad that he's acting in their best interests.'

✴✴✴

At around this time, a phone rang in Rathmines, a middle class suburb of Dublin. The recipient simply answered, 'Derby.'

The caller replied, 'nil-two, Arsenal.'

It was a code used to confirm that the caller was a member of the inner clique of the Provisional IRA. By finishing the score of a match played within the previous week, John Gibney, at the receiver, knew that the caller was a fellow nodal point; he didn't have to know who he was. The various Provo brigades were to a greater, rather than lesser, extent independent. However, a communications net of nodal points tied them together. The nodes were the means by which one brigade could talk to another. The information path varied from day to day, week to week. The same pathway was never used twice. Conversation on the public network was always kept specific using coded acronyms; not an easy task.

'There's been a foreign LB *(Knee Capping)* in Kinsale.'

'Continue.'

'Two days ago, the TZA *(South Armagh Brigade)* bought BPT *(al-Qaeda's)* trawler in Carlingford.'

'The lot who bought the EA *(Derry Brigade)* parcel?'

'Yes.'

'TZA plan was to take the 5BPT south, dispose, and keep the N *(Money)* and the parcel.'

'So?'

'The 2TZA boys have disappeared; the 5BPT acquired a launch and left. Yesterday three thugs LB the ship's chandler.'

'So the BPT are away but someone wants to stop them?'

'Yes.'

'Ideas?'

'The CF *(British Government)?'*

'I'll report this upstairs; perhaps, FSZ *(ETA)* can keep an eye open for us in Spain.'

123

***

The Head of MI6 returned to his office. An excellent lunch, suitably fortified with a sherry, two bottles of Merlot shared between the three chiefs, and a brandy to finish was not the best preparation for what lay ahead. However, desperate times require desperate measures; contacting his opposite number in Mossad was something he had never done before. Establishing the lines of communication would have been difficult enough on a weekday, but having to do it on a Sunday without the help of his personal assistant might be impossible. He opened his safe and began looking through the piles of operation orders for all sorts of contingencies – all classified Top Secret.

Someday I must organise these things into some of sort order.

He fumbled through them, casting them to one side. Eventually, near the bottom, he found the file he wanted.

Why are these things always the last ones?

The red file was labelled: Contacts – Overseas Security Services. He began flicking through the file: CIA-USA, DGSE-France, GRU-Soviets, Stasi-E Germany, MAD-W Germany, SBMSW-Poland...

There's no bloody order in this file, I must get Rupert to go through it tomorrow. It needs pruning. Ah, here we are: Mossad-Israel.

Several phone calls later and after several 'Call you backs', Sir Peter found himself inviting Simon Rosenberg to come to his office 'first thing tomorrow morning – urgent.'

***

'Sit down, Simon,' gestured Sir Peter Stacey. 'I would like your undertaking that what we discuss this morning is not to go beyond our level. I could have involved the Foreign Secretary and your ambassador, but when you have heard what I have to say then I hope you will agree this is an operational matter, not a political one.'

Rosenberg nodded, intrigued at what might be coming next.

'We know you discovered a small nuclear device had been bought by al-Qaeda from the IRA and was being transported back to Libya. We know you informed the CIA, who persuaded their Navy to use a ballistic missile to sink the *Glengarriff*. You will also know that we used two Nimrods to sink the launch in international waters, and that three of the crew were rescued by the Spanish Coastguard. You probably know they are currently being held in a detention centre in Gijon awaiting processing.'

Sir Peter stopped to see what reaction, if any, Rosenberg had. He was met with a poker face that invited him to continue.

'You won't know that the Caucasian on the vessel is working for us.' He stopped again.

This time, Sir Peter was surprised when Simon nodded and asked, 'We're talking about Bradda Head?'

'Yes. What is important for you to understand is that he is trying to infiltrate al-Qaeda; it's in your interests as well as ours that he succeeds. You have my word that whatever he discovers relevant to Israel we will share with you.'

CHAPTER 17

Sunday 31st March 1991

The Gijon reception centre is the smallest and least busy of the four detention camps dotted around the Spanish coastline, used to house immigrants awaiting deportation or integration. Whereas those in Cadiz and Almeria, both near North Africa, are usually overflowing, Gijon's is often empty. Juan had his own room with a wash basin but everything else was communal. Anibal and Felipe's room, the same size as Juan's, had bunk beds. The lounge, library and games room were well equipped. However, the outdoor exercise yard, surrounded by a ten foot wall, hinted a prison rather than a hotel.

After a hot shower, they were given clean clothes, followed by a hot meal in an empty dining room. The site was eerily quiet; they appeared to be the only inmates. They were told nothing would happen until the following morning. On Tuesday, Juan would be 41. The thought made him more depressed than ever.

What a place to have a birthday!

They ate silently and slowly. Juan's two colleagues were still visibly shell-shocked by their ordeal. After a considerable time, however, Juan decided he had to broach the subject of ensuring they get their story straight about what happened on the *Glengarriff*. They discussed the matter at length. Four things were agreed. Firstly, Juan had met them by accident when they used to frequent *The Old Vic* between fishing trips off the Isle of Man. Secondly, he had revealed he was planning to travel overland back to New Zealand on a motorcycle through Africa and South America. Consequently, they had offered to take him to Ceuta. Thirdly, the *Dom Pedro* had broken down on their way home. As it could not be fixed, they were forced to sell her to buy the *Glengarriff*. Finally, if asked why they sank, they suspected an explosion in the engine room had killed their two friends and blown a hole in the hull.

'Surely, they will contact the Irish and Manx authorities to check our story?' asked Felipe.

'We must hope they don't,' replied Juan. 'Whatever happens we must stick to our story. Sooner or later they will have to contact the Libyan and New Zealand embassies in Madrid and give us access to our own diplomats. Remember, all we want to do is to go home.'

I just hope Sir Charles in on the ball, thought Juan, *and covers my tracks.*

Later, alone in his room, Juan thought over the day's events.

If we had hit the hull of a submarine, we would have risen out of the water; possibly we might have turned turtle. There would have been a terrible scraping noise, not a catastrophic bang. We would have seen its conning tower, surely? And wouldn't a sub have heard us approaching on their sonar and taken evasive action?

He sat on his bed, his knees bent under his chin. What had caused the *Glengarriff* to sink so quickly? Something at the back of his mind was telling him he knew the answer. He went over the time he had spent in the Army. His last tour had been an instructor at the Joint School of Intelligence at RAF Chicksands, near Bedford. He remembered seeing an RAF publicity film called *The Nimrod: The Mighty Hunter*.

Of course! The film showed the aircraft releasing anti-submarine torpedoes. What were they called? The Mark 46?

He looked up at the ceiling, pondering.

I'll bet the bastards have developed a torpedo that can skim under the waves to attack surface ships as well. But why weren't we blown sky high?

He rubbed his eyes; he was feeling exhausted and began undressing for bed.

Then the penny dropped.

They wanted us to escape but wanted the atomic bomb to sink in deep waters. I'll bet the torpedo that hit us wasn't fused and Sir Charles was behind it. He wants me to stick with the Libyans and try to infiltrate al-Qaeda.

The following morning the three breakfasted together. The centre had seven other in-mates: three Ecuadoreans and four Cubans – all seeking asylum in Spain. The Ecuadoreans told Felipe they had stowed away on a ship from Panama. The Cubans, by contrast, said nothing; appearing not to trust anyone except themselves. In a dining hall capable of seating 30, it struck Juan that the centre was something of a quiet backwater.

With luck, our interrogators will not be keen to disturb their lifestyle.

The initial questions held in Spanish were largely exploratory: gathering basic facts such as name, date of birth, nationality and address. 'I have no fixed abode as I am travelling in Europe for a year. I am returning to New Zealand.'

His reply seemed to satisfy his interrogator, a Captain in the Cuerpo Nacional de Policia – the National Police who deal with immigration. He explained that he would be contacting the New Zealand embassy in Madrid. They would send a representative to interview Juan and issue him with a new passport, after which he could be released to continue. He seemed more interested in what sort of motorbike Juan was thinking of using for his journey, rather than getting details of how he came to be on a motor launch with four Libyans.

He's too lazy to investigate further.

Juan was then left alone for two days. His birthday passed without anyone noticing. Anibal and Felipe, however, were interrogated at some length. The Spanish appeared to doubt their stories and were making exhaustive checks.

On Wednesday morning, one of the guards informed Juan that a representative from the New Zealand embassy had arrived. Juan was escorted to a room with soft furnishings where a smartly dressed, young man in his late-twenties was sitting in an easy chair behind a coffee table. He stood up to his full height: perhaps six feet three inches. Clean-shaven, with light brown curly hair, a smart grey pinstripe suit, collar and tie; he stretched out his hand.

'Roger Cadman, security, New Zealand embassy,' he declared.

Juan's guard closed the door, leaving them alone.

They exchanged greetings and sat down opposite each other. Cadman opened his brief case, took out some documents, and assured Juan, 'We'll get you out of here in no time, old boy. Just a few formalities to go through, you understand?'

Juan nodded but didn't reply. Something in his gut told him Cadman was not who he claimed.

Then his visitor surprised him. From the bottom of his attaché, he withdrew what appeared to be a small multimeter. He pointed it around the room, under the table and chairs, and at the window. 'Can't be too careful in this game,' he said smiling. After a minute of sweeping, he continued, 'The room is clean. Dover Castle told me to be careful. He sends you his regards and asked me to give you this.'

Cadman passed over a crisp New Zealand passport. Juan opened it; saw his photograph and details, and smiled. *That old so and so – Sir Charles, up to his usual tricks. To have a replacement this quickly, he must have planned it.*

'I was asked to check your operational name.'

'Bradda Head.'

'Excellent. The NZSIS, the New Zealand Security Intelligence Service, would normally handle this sort of thing but Sir Charles called in a favour. I hope you don't mind?' He continued without waiting for a reply, 'You probably realise I'm from the firm based in Madrid. I've been told to tell you that had your launch not been taken out by the simultaneous strikes of our torpedoes, then the Americans were planning to hit you from one of their submarines.'

'By a torpedo?'

'No, by a submarine launched ballistic missile. As far as we could tell there weren't any of their subs close enough to fire an underwater torpedo.'

'Then, we were lucky?'

'Yes. Apparently Mossad had found out about the *Glengarriff* and frightened the CIA sufficiently to persuade them that Billy Tote was destined for New York. I believe it was the PM's decision to stop you in your tracks. Sir Charles gambled on you escaping when he saw the photos, taken by one of the Nimrods, of you and two of the Libyans on deck. He knew you were a strong swimmer; it's on your CV.'

Juan sat quietly taking in the news and thinking about Eduardo and Rodrigo. After a while, Roger continued, 'I've also been asked to clear up something. What happened to the two Irish guys who drove you south in the minibus?'

Juan smiled as he remembered the effort he had made to strangle Martin. 'We learnt they were planning to shoot us so they could keep the money and the fishing boat – the *Dom Pedro*. We took them out first, and threw their bodies over a cliff. Why?'

'The Provisional IRA has a fairly sophisticated method of inter-brigade communications, but GCHQ intercepted something that suggests the IRA is trying to get the Basque terrorist organisation, ETA, to help them extract revenge. Apparently, one of the guys you killed was the younger brother of Warwick Nash – their top hit man.'

'So, Anibal, Felipe and I have a price on our heads?' Juan asked, as he remembered the ease with which Anibal had strangled Nash junior.

'Something like that.'

'But how do they know we are here?'

'Your rescue made the local TV: "Three men rescued from sinking Irish motor launch." You know the sort of thing.' After a brief pause, 'Sir Charles has told me that he will fully understand if you think things are getting too dangerous and want to call off the whole business.'

'We do seem to have come to a dead end. The Libyan Embassy staffs haven't been here to see Anibal and Felipe. I can't stay indefinitely waiting for them to turn up. And if I did, there's no way the Libyan Embassy is going to take me along for a ride.'

'True, but we may be able to use the ETA-IRA threat to our advantage.'

'How?'

'Warwick Nash, with an accomplice, is currently aboard the Brittany Ferry that docks in San Sebastian,' he paused to look at his watch, 'just about now. Also, about now a commander from the Anti-Terrorist Squad of the Metropolitan Police is due to arrive at Madrid Barajas airport. He will be travelling directly to a meeting with a brigadier in the National Police who deals with terrorism. Our man will suggest you and your two colleagues are evacuated for your own protection – to Madrid, or better still, further south; well away from the Basque threat. No doubt a trap will then be set by the Spanish government's counterterrorist unit, the GEO, to capture or kill the IRA men and any helpers they may have from ETA when they attack here.'

'So, we can expect to be moved soon?'

'Yes. Probably this afternoon. I will take back your passport and tell the immigration staff here that there is a small error on it and that New Zealand's formalities will be completed in a few days time. They, of course, have no idea what is about to happen and will be kept in the dark. A final point: did you salvage your credit cards when you sank, or do you need new ones?'

'I always keep my plastic and cash in this small wallet in my back hip pocket.' Juan took it out and showed it to Cadman.

'Excellent. If you let me note the numbers, I'll make sure any future transactions you make with them will be traced by us in London. We'll then know exactly where you are.'

They shook hands and pressed a bell for the guard to return.

Cadman left while Juan was escorted back to the lounge to find Anibal alone. 'Felipe is being interviewed by a representative from the Libyan embassy,' he said in Arabic.

'Your turn next, then?'

'No, I think not,' he replied.

'Oh?'

'I suspect they have discovered I'm not Libyan.'

'Then, what the hell are you?'

'Saudi.'

'Saudi?! Then why not tell them?'

'Because I'm wanted there.'

'For what?'

'It doesn't matter.'

The two men sunk into an uncomfortable silence; Juan eyeing up his companion: *Anibal hasn't shaved since we left the Isle of Man; his beard is beginning to mature; he's beginning to look Saudi whereas Felipe has remained clean shaven. The difference never occurred to me but now I think about it, their accents are quite different.* After several minutes, Juan asked, 'What are you going to do?'

'Somehow I've got to get to Ceuta.' He never expanded why, but instead asked, 'How did you get on?'

Juan thought quickly. How much should he tell Anibal about the threat from the IRA assassins?

'I don't want to upset you, but the guy you strangled in the minibus was the younger brother of the IRA's top hit man, Warwick Nash.'

'So?'

'The New Zealand embassy has been tipped off that he has sworn revenge and may come after us; with or without the help of ETA.'

Anibal shrugged his shoulders, indicating he didn't care. Soon afterwards, Felipe returned; it was time for lunch.

They had hardly begun when two guards came to their table and ordered them in Spanish, 'Hurry up! You three are being taken away by the National Police immediately.'

'Why?' asked a worried looking Anibal.

'I don't know. There is a van waiting outside. Go to your rooms, get your things and hurry up!'

CHAPTER 18

Wednesday 3rd April 1991

The three were bundled into the back of an unmarked van designed to carry prisoners, with a thick wire mesh screen separating them from the driver and his armed companion. On each side of the van, small dark glass windows allowed them to see out but prevented anyone seeing in. Wooden benches ran parallel to the sides of the vehicle; capable of seating six passengers. The rear door was closed and locked securely with what Juan guessed was a padlock.

Through the forward screen Juan could see a police car, with two policemen, driving ahead as they left the centre's compound. He looked at his watch; he wanted to calculate how far they were going by estimating their average speed. It was 1300 hours local. They trundled out of Gijon and after 20 minutes were in countryside. The sun was on their right: they were heading south-east.

As Cadman had predicted, thought Juan. *We're being moved for our own safety. I expect we're heading for Madrid. I wonder if the centre is to be reinforced with the Grupo Especial de Operaciones to meet the ETA attack.*

I guess it must be 250 miles to Madrid; if we average 50 mph – five hours minimum. It's going to be an uncomfortable journey.

At 1430 hours, Juan noticed road signs indicating they were by-passing Leon. They were maintaining a good average speed. He noticed other road users tended to pull over when they saw the escorting police car. However, what Juan couldn't see, as there were no rear windows in the van, was a dark grey Mercedes following at a discreet distance.

An hour later they stopped at a rest area. The three were allowed to get out singly, and stretch their legs. They were given a small bottle of water while the four accompanying policemen had a smoke and a cup of coffee. Other users of the pull-in tended to keep well away, no doubt thinking the three companions were dangerous criminals.

Two hours later, they bypassed Segovia and progress slowed as the road climbed up the Sierra de Guadarrama. They rounded a bend and Juan could see a road sign ahead indicating a diversion – *desviacion de la carretera* – landslide. The leading police car stopped, the driver got out, looked around, shrugged his shoulders, returned to his seat, and his companion appeared to call up someone on their radio. After a minute, the driver got out, approached their van and talked to their driver. After much discussion during which Juan heard the phrases, *poor radio reception* and *much interference*, he returned to the lead car and turned off into the narrow side road. Their van followed; their speed was now less than 20 mph. What none of them could see was the Mercedes stop, someone remove the diversion sign and put it in their boot.

To one side of the road was a wooded ravine; perhaps 30 feet deep with a small stream at the bottom. The procession was crawling when, around a right-hand bend, Juan saw the road was blocked by a fallen tree. Again the lead car stopped. Both policemen got out, went forward to look at the tree and then called for their colleagues in the van to come and help. They presumably thought four of them could push it out of the way into the ravine. As they began to move the trunk, four shots rang out in rapid succession. Juan, from his Army days, instantly recognised the noise of high powered rifles. The four policemen fell as one. He couldn't see they were shot through the head, but his gut told him they were dead.

Christ, it's Warwick Nash. The bastards must have followed us from Gijon.

It didn't occur to ask himself how they could have travelled from San Sebastian to Gijon and organised the ambush so quickly.

A few seconds later there was a deafening bang as the rear doors of the van were blown off their hinges. When the smoke had drifted away, Juan saw the two doors lying on the ground. Beyond, two men were pointing AK-47s at them. Slung over their shoulders, each had a snipers' rifle. Both were casually dressed in light-blue jeans, trainers and navy tee shirts. Both looked alike; they could have been twin brothers: five foot ten inches tall, athletically built, dark curly hair, brown eyes.

These guys might be ETA; they're not Irish.

One of the men demanded, in Spanish, 'Where is the money?'

'What money?' replied Juan.

'There is supposed to be 10,000,000 pesetas in this van.'

'Sorry, we are internees being taken to Madrid. You've stopped the wrong van.'

The two gunmen looked at each other, and swore profusely in Spanish. One violently kicked a door; the clang echoed around the hillside. Behind them, Juan could see a grey Mercedes with a driver inside. The two men, still swearing, turned, walked back to the car and got in. The car executed a five point turn in the narrow lane and sped away in a cloud of dust.

The three looked blankly at each other in amazement. The whole incident had taken less than five minutes. They never spoke as they jumped from the van and walked round to look at the murdered policemen.

'What do we do now?' asked Felipe.

Neither Anibal nor Juan replied for several moments; both deep in thought.

'Any ideas, Anibal?'

'Put the four bodies in the van and push it over the edge into the ravine. We take the car, their handguns and their ID cards. We get the hell out of here.'

'Agreed. With a little luck, no one will find them down there until tomorrow.'

It took 15 minutes to cover-up the crime scene. The van could not be seen from the road; it had passed through scrub bushes before nestling between two pine trees. They pushed the fallen tree over the edge; reducing the chances of someone stopping and, possibly, finding the van. Ten minutes later saw them back on the main road and driving the police car towards the outskirts of Madrid.

Anibal drove while Juan searched through the extensive maps in the glove compartment. 'There's a motorway from Madrid all the way to Malaga. It should take no longer than six hours. From Malaga we can get a ferry to Melilla.'

'No. We go to Algeciras!'

'It's further; maybe another hour.'

'There are only two boats a day to Melilla and it takes four hours. There's a fast-craft every two hours from Algeciras, it takes no time. Besides, we have a safe house in Ceuta; once there, we are safe.'

＊＊＊

The phone rang in Simon Rosenberg's office. It was Simon's opposite number in Madrid.

'We've done what you asked. They should be well away by now.'

'Excellent. I'll pass on the news. Keep in touch.'

Simon replaced the receiver; he waited a few seconds then picked it up. He dialled a number, waited for an answer, and asked, 'Sir Peter?'

＊＊＊

While negotiating the complex network of ring roads to the west of Madrid, the trio stopped, refuelled and bought provisions. If the attendant serving them was surprised to see a police car with occupants in civilian clothes, he said nothing. It was none of his business; you don't get involved with *policies vestidos de paisano* when you have a suspended sentence hanging over you for shoplifting.

As they sped south on the E-5, Juan began to wonder how long it would take before someone realised there had been a problem with their move from Gijon. Less than half an hour south of the capital, a voice came over the car's radio demanding, 'Inform us of your position.'

'They want to know where we are,' said Juan.

'Switch the bloody thing off,' replied Anibal, as he put his foot down on the pedal.

***

'They are not responding,' the sergeant said as he looked up at his boss, Inspector Rodrigo, in the police HQ, Madrid. 'We haven't heard from them in almost two hours. What do you want me to do?'

'Keep trying,' he retorted. 'Meanwhile, I'll get on to Colonel da Silva.'

Within 50 minutes, the crews of two Lynx helicopters of the Spanish Air Force were being briefed. Equipped with night vision goggles and infra-red search and rescue scopes, they were given the convoy's last known position and told to confine their search pattern to minor roads leading from the main Madrid road up to a distance of 20 kilometres. Colonel da Silva didn't hold out much hope of finding anything until first light – approximately 0400 hours. However, he knew that if he had postponed the search until sunrise then it might be too late.

Just before dawn the wreckage of the police van was spotted in the ravine. Owing to the nature of the terrain – dense forest and steep slopes – the helicopter could only hover while awaiting the arrival of ground forces. A further hour passed before da Silva was fully in the picture. His first thoughts were that there must be a link to the attack on the detention centre in Gijon and that ETA had to be responsible for springing the two Libyans and the New Zealander. But why? Despite the early hour, he knew what he had to do: ring General Felix Antolin, head of the GEO, the Special Operations Group based nearby in Guadalajara. The GEO, equivalent to Britain's SAS, is specifically focussed on dealing with terrorist attacks, usually organised by ETA. Colonel da Silva had heard about the shoot-out at Gijon the previous evening and the trap that had killed five ETA and two IRA terrorists. Something serious was going on over his head. He knew General Antolin personally. Antolin was used to his bedside phone ringing at unusual hours and patiently listened to Colonel da Silva before putting into practice a well-rehearsed contingency plan.

***

It was past 4 am when the three escapees arrived in Algeciras; the streets were deserted. They parked their car in a multi-storey; thinking it might not be seen if surrounded by other users later that day. They walked down to the docks; a glance at the ferry timetable revealed the first vessel departed at 0530 hours. They found an all-night café, sat down and discussed what to do next. Anibal took the lead.

'When we get to Ceuta, we can lie low for a while.'

'There's one thing that worries me,' said Juan.

'Yes?'

'Presumably we don't need passports to get to Ceuta as it's officially part of Spain?'

'Yes.'

'Then, how am I going to leave there and begin my journey home without a passport?'

'We'll get you to Libya and you can buy your Honda there. A passport will not be a problem.'

'How can you do that?'

'You'll see.'

Juan was surprised at how quick the journey was. They caught the first fast craft of the day – a twin-hulled Sea Cat – and in less than an hour they had disembarked. Many of their fellow passengers were soldiers. They seemed to know each other and Juan wondered if they commuted daily to the fort on Monte Hacho at the eastern end of the North African enclave.

Ceuta is a city on a peninsula, some six miles long with a mixed population of about 70,000. It is considered to be a part of the Spanish region of Andalusia. Within 15 minutes they had walked to the Berber quarter: whitewashed terraced houses with narrow deserted streets that can be found anywhere in North Africa.

Anibal knocked on a door.

After some moments of waiting, a voice asked in Arabic, 'Who is it?'

Juan could not decipher Anibal's reply. The door was unbolted noisily. A man stood before them dressed in a traditional white embroidered kaftan. For a few seconds, his dark brown eyes registered nothing; then a look of disbelief appeared on his bearded face. Finally, he beamed as he recognised Anibal. He opened his arms and hugged him warmly.

'Moab, it is you. We thought you were dead!'

***

It was 0600 hours by the time the emergency committee, under the chairmanship of General Antolin, sat down with the deputy minister of internal affairs, Antonio Rivas, and the head of the Civil Guard, General Mendes. Within minutes the Spanish borders, controlled by the Civil Guard, were put on *Red Alert*, the descriptions of the three former residents of the Gijon refugee centre were distributed and orders given for their detainment.

'Where do you think they are heading?' asked the Minister to General Mendes.

'My best guess would be Portugal, or Gibraltar. We will concentrate our efforts accordingly.'

'And if they have already left Spain?'

'We will know where and when within the hour.'

It was General Antolin who then spoke, 'I can have some of my men from the GEO follow them, and detain them.'

'More than that, General. You will have them eliminated. They have killed four of our own men.'

'Very good, sir. If that is your wish.'

'However, I have a problem. You are both assuming ETA is responsible for freeing them?'

Both generals nodded.

'Then why did ETA and the two IRA terrorists attack our detention centre in Gijon?'

'I'm not following you,' replied General Mendes.

'You told me you were tipped off about the attack at Gijon by a senior officer from the Special Branch of Scotland Yard.'

'Yes.'

'And he suggested you move the three detainees to the safety of Madrid before the attack?'

'Yes.'

'ETA wouldn't have known we were going to move them. Indeed, they didn't know the GEO had reinforced the centre in preparation for the attack.'

The mist of miscomprehension evaporated from in front of the two generals. A light of understanding began to glow.

'So what you are implying, sir,' said General Antolin slowly, 'is that the British are somehow behind the release of the New Zealander and the two Libyans.'

'Is he a New Zealander?'

'Someone from the New Zealand embassy saw him yesterday and assured Gijon's detention manager that Quine was genuine and would be issued with a new passport in two days time.'

'Did you have this official checked?'

General Mendes shuffled some papers in front of him. 'His name was Cadman. He carried the requisite papers.'

'I shall have my ministry check him out. If, as I suspect, Cadman is from the British embassy then they have a lot of explaining to do.' Without waiting, Minister Rivas had picked up the red scrambler phone in the centre of their table, and was dialling a number he knew well.

After a few seconds, he asked the recipient of the call, 'Give me section seven.' He didn't have to give his name. At the other end, the system was telling the receptionist who was on the line – his boss. The generals waited uncomfortably; the minister mumbling impatiently.

After a few minutes, Rivas sat upright, a grave look on his face. 'Cadman is a SIS officer in the British embassy. General Antolin, call London and insist on implementing Protocol 31. At once!'

CHAPTER 19

Thursday 4th April 1991

Standing at the door, 'Come in, come in,' he repeated; moving to one side as Juan and Felipe entered the dark hallway. There was a smell of coffee being prepared from the rear of the house. As his eyes grew accustomed to the lack of light, Juan could see the entrance had led them directly into the lounge. Beyond, an opening revealed the kitchen.

Juan stood awkwardly behind Anibal, or Moab, as the stranger had called him, while the tall, overweight, older man spoke rapidly. His dialect made it difficult for Juan to follow their conversation. Meanwhile, Felipe had disappeared into the kitchen; presumably he knew his way around.

'We thought you were killed at Gijon.'

'Why?'

'There was a battle there yesterday between the GEO and ETA. Many were killed. The police announced several inmates were casualties as well as a dozen members of ETA. We knew you were there.'

'Who told you?'

'The Libyan embassy in Madrid ran checks on you and Felipe. Our man in the Ministry of Home Affairs in Tripoli filled us in on what was going on.'

'I owe my life to Alan, here.' Anibal turned. 'Without him I would have drowned when our launch sank.'

'My name is Omar al Ouda. You must be the New Zealander of whom

I have heard so much. You don't know it, but by saving Moab, you have done our cause a great favour. Someday the whole world will know of him. We may have lost the bomb but we will think of other ways to dislodge the Zionists from Palestine.'

He turned back to Anibal. 'How long do you think we have before the Spanish realise you have escaped to Ceuta?'

'Not long. They will soon find the abandoned police car in Algeciras and put two and two together.'

'Then we must get you into Morocco as quickly as possible. Ceuta won't be safe when the GEO start crawling all over the place.'

As if on cue, Felipe entered with a tray of small pastries and cups of coffee. Omar beckoned them to sit on the cushions. He turned to Juan and explained that Ceuta was a Freeport; ships from all over the world were entering and leaving around the clock. The town was rife with smuggling. The Spanish authorities generally ignored what was going on as the consequent increase in trade suited their pockets. The border with Morocco was almost non-existent; border guards on both sides were underpaid and susceptible to bribery. 'Two 5,000 peseta notes are all you need – one to leave and one to enter. It's a month's wages to them. It will be the safest way to get you out. Sailing to Libya would be quicker, but we would have to pass close to Melilla and, by then, the Spanish will be stopping and searching anything suspicious. I suggest you and Moab travel together. Felipe can come with me; breaking the three of you up will be safer. We will meet in Tripoli.'

Moab nodded. He didn't ask how Omar would get to Libya.

Omar took a photograph of Juan, and within 30 minutes the two travellers had left Ceuta and were heading south on the dusty road to Tetouan in Morocco. Omar had been right: the border crossing was quick and easy – a casual look at a piece of paper purporting to be a visa with the mandatory 5,000 peseta note folded inside satisfied the guards. Juan and Moab, having changed into traditional Berber clothes, had loaded the back of their Toyota pick-up with empty pallets strewn with various damaged items of fruit and vegetables. They claimed they were

Moroccan farmers returning from selling their goods at market.

Anibal drove; Juan sat next to him looking at the maps. 'How are we going to get into Algeria?' he asked. 'These scruffy bits of paper won't work twice, surely?'

'Omar is arranging for us to have Libyan passports. We will pick them up at the border town of Oujda tomorrow morning. Tonight we will stop at Selouane, get a good night's sleep and cross into Algeria after picking up the passports. We should be able to get across Algeria in one day. Once in Tunisia, we can rest for a while before going to Tripoli. You've gathered by now that my name is not Anibal.'

Juan nodded, 'When you told me in the detention centre that you were a Saudi, I realised Anibal was a false name.'

'My name is Moab al Saidenn. Omar is one of several Saudi princes who support our cause to push the Zionists into the sea and so liberate Palestine. We are fed up seeing the Israelis expand their illegal settlements on the West Bank – financed by the Jewish-Yankee banks. When we negotiated the purchase of the atomic bomb from the IRA, I thought we could use it to hold the Israelis to ransom.'

'By doing what?'

'Initially threatening to use it in Tel Aviv unless they withdrew completely from Jerusalem.'

'And if they had refused?'

'Then Armageddon. The bomb was important to our cause. That is why I took part in the operation myself. As chief coordinator within our organisation, I normally use trusted operatives to carry out such tasks. It doesn't do any harm for them to see I can get my hands dirty from time to time.' He chuckled, that deep throaty laugh that came from the bottom of the earth and always sent a shiver down Juan's spine. 'However, losing it has been a body blow; but I have other ideas that will be just as spectacular. The IRA's Brighton bomb, six years ago, will look small fry.' Again, he laughed to himself causing Juan to shudder.

They drove on in silence. Moab didn't expand further on his future plans. Slowly Juan felt his eyelids becoming heavy; soon he was asleep.

From 0800 hours that morning, reports had been filtering into General Mendes' HQ. Firstly, Border Guards had remembered three people catching the first sailing of the day to Ceuta – two Arabs and a Caucasian. He cursed under his breath. He ordered the Algeciras police to search for the missing police car; the abandoned vehicle was found within minutes. However, an hour later, another report was worse. Two Berber farmers had passed into Morocco minutes before the border had been sealed. Instinctively, Mendes knew what this meant. He was too late to detain two men. He consoled himself that the house to house search, already under way, might find the third man.

Meanwhile, however, his colleague, General Antolin was preparing for greater things.

'Protocol 31' is an agreed European Union contingency plan for the meeting of heads of military and police intelligence officers. Rarely implemented, it is highly flexible but is legally enforceable within the constitution of the EU. Only in the most exceptional circumstances can deputies attend in lieu of heads. The number of attendees can vary from just two countries to all the member states. Large meetings are always held in Brussels but when the cause of the concern affects few states, a neutral site is chosen. As early as 1000 hours local time, 0900 GMT, Antolin's Personal Staff Officer had agreement with London that the Head of MI6 would meet the head of the GEO later that day. Such meetings are confined to as few staff as possible: two body guards and one bilingual secretary each – the *need to know* principle is enforced rigorously. France was the obvious venue for the meeting. A small but highly rated three-star hotel was booked: Auberge du Redier, Colomars – a quiet hilltop village five miles from Nice airport on the Cote d'Azur. For the Spanish general, Nice was a mere one-hour flight. For Sir Peter Stacey, it was nearer two. The meeting was to begin at 1700 hours.

The phone rang in Simon Rosenberg's office as he was having a mid-morning coffee. It was his opposite number in Madrid.

'Two of them, one the New Zealander, have just entered Morocco. Our sayanim in Ceuta watched the three of them arrive from Algeciras on the first ferry this morning and followed them to a house in the Berber district. They stayed there for less than an hour, and then two of them left in a pick-up truck dressed as Berber farmers. He believes that bastard al Ouda met them – he's one of al-Qaeda's chief Saudi financiers.'

'Who has gone with the New Zealander?'

'I don't know, but it's not al Ouda. He's still in Ceuta; or was a few minutes ago.'

'It might be worth putting a tail on him to see where he goes.'

'That won't be easy. There's no airport in Ceuta. He will have to catch the fast craft back to Algeciras; then fly to Libya.'

'OK. See what you can do. In the mean time I'll let our friends know their man appears to have successfully infiltrated al-Qaeda and is now in Morocco.'

***

Later that afternoon Simon received a second call from Madrid. 'You won't believe this, but al Ouda left Ceuta with one of the guys who had arrived there this morning. They were picked up by a chauffeur-driven limo, with *corps diplomatique* plates, at the port in Algeciras and driven to Gibraltar. Our man followed in a taxi but couldn't enter Gibraltar because he hadn't the necessary papers. However, he positioned himself so he could watch movements on the airfield, which is adjacent to the border. Ten minutes later, a Royal Saudi executive jet took off heading east.'

'So, al Ouda has Saudi diplomatic status?'

'Along with hundreds of other buggers. Al Ouda is a minor prince, 425th in line to the throne, but he has so much money he doesn't know what to do with it. He and his cousin al Zharwhiri are two of the prime sponsors backing al-Qaeda, but there are several others we don't know about.'

***

Juan awoke; he had been fast asleep. He felt terrible. His mouth tasted like a sewer, he felt filthy; he hadn't had a wash for over 24 hours. He blinked and looked around. Moab was driving and chewing something; how he managed to remain alert puzzled Juan.

'How do you stay awake?' he asked.

'Here, chew one of these,' he grinned, passing Juan a small pouch full of green leaves.

'What are they?'

'Coca leaves. They will keep you alert.'

Juan took one, albeit hesitatingly. He was about to taste a form of cocaine for the first time in his life.

The leaf tasted revolting; nothing like a mint leaf – bitter, more like a bay leaf. Minutes later, his weariness had slipped away. He began to notice the countryside through which they were travelling. The gentle hills on either side of the road reminded him of the A66 heading west from Penrith. There were differences, however. Instead of verdant fields with plump Herdwicks, there were dusty patches with scruffy, thin, sandy-brown coloured Barbary sheep that looked like goats. There was no sign of anyone tending them. The road surface of compacted coarse aggregate was covered in a dirty-yellow dust; the traffic was light. *They don't get 100 inches of rain here per year,* he thought.

They trundled along the so-called N2 – little better than a cow track in places, with intermittent straight stretches where everyone thought they were Stirling Moss. They reached the village of Selouane in the early evening. It was a one-eyed town, a crossroad with, at the four corners: a hotel, a bar, a shop and what appeared to be a mosque. Several stray emaciated dogs roamed around, hoping for a scrap to be thrown from someone. *Fortunately, the N2 bypasses this dump; at least it should be quiet.*

CHAPTER 20

Thursday 4th April 1991

Sir Peter and his team arrived at the auberge an hour late.

'I must apologise, Felix, but the air traffic control officers over central France called a lightning strike. We had to divert and fly over Switzerland and Italy.'

'That's the French for you,' joked the Head of the GEO as they shook hands, 'most unreliable!' The two secretaries attending the meeting were introduced and, as the four men settled around a square table in the hotel's conference room, the general added, 'I have taken the liberty of booking dinner for nine o'clock. That will give us two hours for the meeting and an hour to freshen up. Is that OK?'

Sir Peter nodded, knowing how the Spanish routinely ate much later than he would have chosen. He had discussed the unusual request for the Protocol-31 meeting earlier in the day with Sir Charles Gray. *Attack is the best form of defence,* they had agreed. With this in mind, Sir Peter kicked-off aggressively, 'Now, Felix, what's this all about?'

A fluent English speaker, Felix Antolin had attended the one-year Army staff course at Camberley before working in the London embassy for two years. He knew the form the meeting would take and was not going to be bullied by a possible future member of The House of Lords.

In a cynical voice, he replied, 'I think you know, Sir Peter.'

There was a moment of frozen silence. It was a test: who would break the ice? The two secretaries looked up from their notepads, biros at the ready.

'Yesterday, a commander from your Special Branch came to Madrid to warn our Civil Guards that an attack was being planned by the IRA and ETA to kill the two Libyans and the New Zealander who had been rescued by our Coast Guards.' He stopped, looking for a sign of confirmation from Sir Peter.

Sir Peter acknowledged affirmatively, but said nothing.

'Your man, not ours, suggested the three illegal immigrants, for that is what they were, theoretically, be moved south to Madrid for their own safety.'

Sir Peter nodded, knowing full well where this line of conversation was leading.

'The convoy moving them was diverted from their route, attacked, and four of our Civil Guards were killed. The three terrorists, for that is what we are now officially calling them, escaped.' He stopped deliberately, setting the trap.

'I wasn't aware of that,' offered Sir Peter apologetically.

General Antolin knew not to lose his temper. *Keep cool; you have him in the corner.*

'Don't play games with me, Peter. Only you and us knew of the plan to move them. We would hardly kill our own men and let the buggers escape; would we?'

'Someone must have followed them.'

'You'll be telling me next the New Zealand Secret Intelligence Service is responsible!'

Sir Peter shrugged his shoulders, but remained silent.

'We know that Cadman is one of your men, not from New Zealand House.' The General suddenly erupted. He banged the desk with his fist, 'Who killed my men? Was it you or someone acting on your behalf? It has to be one or the other.'

Both the secretaries and Sir Peter jumped when the table shook. Sir Peter swallowed hard and took a deep breath before replying. Not for nothing had he risen to the top of his profession. He knew not to be seen to be ruffled.

'I fear, old boy, the CIA and Mossad are responsible.'

'The CIA, Mossad?'

'Yes. The Americans sunk the *Glengarriff* as a result of a request from Mossad.' Sir Peter's secretary, his PSO, Rupert, didn't bat so much as an eyelid. He knew how murky the plot to keep Quine in touch with al-Qaeda was becoming. Setting dog against dog was a regular part of the *grand game* of subterfuge. It was vital that Sir Peter's lies would convince the Spanish general.

'I find that hard to stomach, Peter. How could they possibly have sunk the motor launch?'

'With a cruise missile fired from a nuclear submarine, the *Philadelphia*, 200 miles away in the Atlantic.'

'Impossible. A missile would have instantly destroyed the boat. There would have been no trace, no survivors.'

'Normally – true. However, in this case, not so. What Mossad had discovered was that the *Glengarriff* was carrying an atomic bomb – one of Gadaffi's prototypes that he had given to the IRA in the early eighties, but the IRA never used it.' He stopped to see his adversary's reaction.

The General remained poker-faced. He, too, could play the *grand game*. 'Go on,' he said quietly.

'The Provisional IRA is keen to be seen as enthusiastic as possible about the so-called Northern Ireland peace process. A strict condition will be that they disarm. Some of their brigades are selling their weapons before they get decommissioned and destroyed.'

'Selling to whom?'

'An Islamist fundamentalist group calling itself al-Qaeda. Their aim is to drive Israel into the sea by any means. Mossad learned that the atomic device was destined for Tel Aviv and asked the Americans to intervene. They used their latest cruise missile that can sink shipping without leaving a trace. A classical missile could have blown the *Glengarriff* to smithereens, but may have detonated the nuclear bomb.

Imagine the international outcry if there had been a nuclear explosion 100 miles from the Spanish coast. What the Americans used was a missile called *Porpoise*. When nearing its target, it dives under the water and hits the hull a few inches below the waterline.'

'Incredible.'

Rupert continued taking notes but knew his boss had pulled it off – again.

'So,' added Sir Peter after letting the message sink in, 'the three escapees are al-Qaeda terrorists and are somewhere in your jurisdiction.'

'I fear not,' the General replied sheepishly. He was now on the back foot. 'We know the New Zealander and one of the others, we think the one calling himself Anibal, are in Morocco. We don't know where the third one is.'

'Don't worry. They won't get far. Mossad won't give up until they have been found and killed.'

'Do you want me to put some of my GEO men on their tails?'

'I think we can leave that to the Israelis, don't you?'

General Antolin nodded. He hadn't forgotten about Cadman. He had already made his mind up to send an elite three-man squad after the criminals; after all, hadn't his minister ordered their elimination? He knew that if he pressed Sir Peter on who Cadman was, Sir Peter would have had a slick answer: *Cadman had been recalled to London for investigation pending rumours that he had been peddling secrets to the Israelis.*

Tomorrow, Friday 5th April, he, as Head of the GEO, would trigger Operation Catch-up.

✱✱✱

While General Antolin and Sir Peter had been meeting in their comfortable surroundings, Juan and Moab had booked into their hotel, if that is what it was. They had to share a bedroom. *At least there's two beds* thought Juan as they entered the hovel. A communal toilet, a

French-style hole in the floor, was at the end of the corridor. It stank; the flushing system didn't work. There was no bath or shower – just a chipped bowl with a pitcher full of cold water on top of a chest of drawers. Juan pulled back the sheet on his bed to reveal a damp, foul-smelling stain and several fleas hurrying to escape from their sudden intrusion.

I'm going to have to sleep on the floor. Then he noticed several cockroaches playing in a corner. *It's going to have to be that wooden chair. I must be mad to be doing this. Why didn't I pull out after meeting Molly?* He realised he hadn't thought about her for over a week. He felt guilty, even though she was still pulling his heart strings.

He ate one of the worst meals of his life in the back of the bar, opposite the hotel. Apart from the couscous, he had no idea what else it contained. He guessed it was a cheap cut of lamb; although this lamb had died of old age. The few herbs that had been added to the stew disguised neither the smell nor the taste. The only consolation was the local beer – a light-coloured brew that reminded him of 1664. He decided to drink copious quantities to help him sleep in the wooden chair.

Moab had said little since their arrival. He didn't seem to notice the unhygienic state of their bedroom and apparently enjoyed their meal. Juan decided to broach the subject of their journey.

'Tomorrow,' replied his colleague, 'we will leave early, get our passports at the border town of Oujda and hopefully traverse Algeria by nightfall. The roads in Algeria are much better. I apologise for the state of this hell-hole but when we get to Tunisia things will be much better. I have decided to leave you in Tunis and let you recuperate for a few days. I will arrange for Felipe to fetch you and accompany you to Tripoli. There, we will get you the best motorbike money can buy and you can start your overland journey home.'

Shite! That's not what was planned, thought Juan. 'I'm not in any hurry, you know,' he replied. 'I can stay for a while, if you want.' Perhaps Juan retorted too quickly for Moab gave him a stare that disturbed him. *Christ, I hope I haven't let the cat out of the bag.*

'I have much to do when I return to Tripoli. I have to inspect our madrassas in the Sudan and the Yemen.'

'You have so many schools? How do you get around? What training do your students get?'

Moab laughed; that awful, horrible, hollow laugh. A shudder passed through Juan's body. *For God's sake, Juan, stop asking too many questions.*

'Hitler supposedly said "give me a boy before he is seven and he will be mine for life." Our madrassas operate on that principle. Our aims are long-term. In ten years time the Americans will fear us. We will have an army of warriors prepared to die for our cause.'

Juan hadn't the heart to tell Moab that the *give me a child* expression was the principle behind the training of Jesuits. A shudder up his back told him someone was walking over his grave. He was feeling distinctly uncomfortable.

There was a consequent pause in their conversation while Juan realised he was looking at the cruellest face he had ever seen. Anibal, once a friend, had gone. He was now the fallen angel. Juan decided not to push Moab any further.

Tomorrow will be another day.

After his worst ever meal, came his worst ever night. Sitting on a wooden chair with his feet off the floor, resting on the edge of an open drawer was not conducive to sleep. Each time he nodded off, he moved and woke. His ankles hurt from the edge of the drawer. He pulled the drawer out, turned it upside down and used it as a footstool. It helped ease the pain but did not help the sleep. His back ached. His bladder worked overtime. He lost count of how many times his piss helped flush the shit from the loo.

On Friday morning, without any breakfast, they left at six o'clock. Moab knew where to go in Oujda – an insignificant house on the edge of town. He was greeted warmly but reverently by an older man, who clearly was in awe of Moab. His wife had prepared breakfast: honey, bread, fragrant herbs in couscous and black coffee. After the gastronomic disaster of the previous evening it was heaven and Juan made the most of the delightful meal. He smiled when he saw his name in the Libyan passport: Khalil el Majid – *the glorious friend*. The photograph, taken less than 24 hours previously, was a good likeness and he wondered how Omar had had it developed so quickly.

An hour later they were in Algeria where the roads improved considerably. They were able to cruise rapidly and, although it was over 600 miles to Tunisia, Moab seemed to think they would cross the border by late evening. They travelled all day, stopping only to refuel and drink strong coffee to reinforce the coca leaves.

***

While Juan was breakfasting in Oujda, General Antolin was doing likewise but on a Spanish Air Force executive jet over the western Mediterranean. He was planning Operation Catch-up and had ordered Major Tevez of the GEO to be in his Madrid office by 1000 hours.

General Antolin gave his orders personally to the Major. 'You can hand-pick your own men but they must be fluent Arabic speakers and totally loyal. It is vital that you can trust them to keep their mouths shut.'

It had struck Antonio Tevez that it was most unusual for the chain of command to be bypassed in this manner. Three-star generals don't normally call lowly majors into their office to give operational instructions. However, the General had emphasised the operation was to be carried out with utmost secrecy. 'The fewer who know about this, the better.'

The General explained that Mossad may already be chasing the same quarry and that the British were somehow involved. The General gave him three photographs of the trio, taken after they had arrived at Gijon.

'You must trust no one. If anything goes wrong the Spanish government will deny the operation's existence.'

'But how are we supposed to know where they have gone?'

'We think two of them are heading overland to Libya through

Morocco, Algeria and Tunisia. The third – that little squirt', he pointed to Felipe, 'is almost certainly in Libya already.'

'What if they have split up? Do I kill them singly?'

General Antolin stared at his junior officer through his steely, dark green eyes. He wished he could be undertaking the operation himself. Standing to attention in front of him was one of the best men he had. *Someday, my son, you could be sitting in this chair.* The General smiled, deciding to test him.

'Why do you ask?'

'Two reasons, sir. One – I assume there is a time limit on the operation. Two – if we kill one, then the other two may hear of it and take extra precautions.'

'Antonio, there is no time limit. From what I gleaned yesterday in Nice from the British, al-Qaeda is training youngsters to be terrorists in ten years time; they may well end up making ETA look like boy scouts. And, yes, you will have to risk killing them one at a time. The important two are the ones who entered Morocco yesterday morning.'

'So the New Zealander and this one called Anibal,' he pointed to the photos, 'have a day's start?'

'Yes.'

'Then I think the best plan is to fly to Tunisia and to start looking for them crossing the Tunisia – Libya border, don't you?'

'I couldn't agree more. I have already arranged for you and your team to fly to Tunis this afternoon.'

***

Whilst Major Tevez was putting his team together to fly to Tunis, Sir Peter, having breakfasted well at the auberge and caught the 1020 hours British Airways flight to Heathrow, arriving at 1130 – so making up an hour due to the time difference, was chairing a meeting at the National Liberal Club in Whitehall Place. He had invited Sir Charles Gray and General Sir Richard Vincent, Air Marshal Craig's successor, to attend.

'A late lunch at 1330 hours in the dining room overlooking the Thames followed by a review of Operation Third Leg. Is that OK?' he had asked his two colleagues when phoning them from Nice airport prior to take-off.

Arriving at the club, Sir Charles and Sir Richard were surprised to find a fourth attendee: Simon Rosenberg. 'I have invited Simon along,' Peter Stacey began after having introduced him to the others, 'because I feel this operation is of mutual benefit to our two organisations. However, let us eat first. I am famished; breakfast this morning in Nice seems a long time ago.'

They kept business to a minimum over their steak salads, followed by lemon meringue tart swilled down with two bottles of Sancerre. Coffee and petits fours, taken in a private room, preceded the serious matter of 'What to do with Quayle?'

It was Simon who took the lead. 'Since liberating them on Wednesday evening, we have kept tabs on Quayle's movements. He caught the first sailing to Ceuta on Thursday morning, spent about an hour in an al-Qaeda safe house and then, with the Arab calling himself Anibal, crossed the border into Morocco. From what Peter tells me, they are bound for Libya overland. They, therefore, have to pass through Tunisia, which as I am sure you know, security-wise, leaks like a sieve. Information is easily bought there. We are sending two of our best agents to Tunis to look out for them. They are supported by half-a-dozen local sayanims. As we speak, they must be well across Algeria. We will spot them, I am sure. The question is, what do you want us to do with Quayle?'

The three Englishmen looked at each other. Peter answered, 'Quayle is something of an amateur. He was chosen by Charles for his unique linguistic abilities: Gaelic, Russian, Arabic, French, Spanish and German as well as English.'

'Don't forget Japanese!' interrupted Charles.

Sir Peter nodded, accepting the correction, before continuing, 'He seems to be coping and I think we can assume he has been accepted by the two al-Qaeda operatives who survived the *Glengarriff's* sinking.

However, the real test will come when he reaches Libya. God knows what will happen then – the Libyans are terribly suspicious. He will be watched like a hawk. On top of that, there are the communications problems that only he will be able to solve. We haven't heard from him since he left Gijon. I am hoping he will, somehow, make contact when he reaches Tunis. Once he is inside Gadhafi's sphere, he may disappear for a very long time. I am not sure what we can do about it.'

'We may be able to help there,' suggested Simon. 'We have no embassies along the whole of the North African coast, but in Libya we have been sowing operatives for many years. As you are aware, Gadhafi has been training anti-Israeli terrorists ever since he came to power. It's possible that one of our men could make contact and act as an intermediary.'

Peter looked at Charles. He nodded. Simon, seeing agreement to his proposal, asked, 'Is Quayle's code name still Bradda Head?'

CHAPTER 21

Saturday 6th April 1991

After a long, saddle-sore day, Juan and Anibal drew wearily up to the Algerian – Tunisian border soon after midnight. The diet of coffee and coca leaves had done its job. They crossed into Tunisia and parked in a lay-by a quarter of a mile inside the border. They shut their eyes. Juan felt a load lift off his chest; somehow, he didn't know why, he felt safer.

When the pair woke, it was gone 6 am. They could see a roadside diner 100 yards away. They walked across the road, entered and sat down. What immediately struck Juan was the difference from their Moroccan hell-hole. The café was spotlessly clean; the proprietor friendly. Unfortunately, the menus on offer were strictly Arabic – no full English here. However, the coffee was strong, the bread fresh, and the honey aromatic.

Moab began, 'Omar has booked you into a five-star hotel in Tunis for three nights. I will drop you off. There will be an envelope waiting with enough money for you to buy whatever you wish: young girls, young boys, anything.'

He chuckled – that dirty deep snigger that without exception made Juan feel uncomfortable. 'The hotel bill has been paid. Felipe will arrive on Wednesday to take you to Libya. I am sorry to leave you like this but I have much to do. Once in Libya, Omar will ensure that all your wishes are taken care of. I am sure we will meet again someday. Take care, my brother, may Allah be with you at all times.'

It was a strange thing to say and Juan didn't know how to respond. He couldn't think how to reply. All he wanted was a long hot bath and a change of clothes.

They drove the rest of the morning on good surfaced roads, in silence. Juan was still recoiling from the idea that his colleague for the past two weeks could consider that he may have paedophilic homosexual tendencies and began to wonder about Moab's own sexual preferences.

By one o'clock, Juan was in the marbled foyer of the five-star Tunis Sheraton. Mingling with scantily dressed tourists, he felt distinctly uncomfortable. He looked and felt a scruffy wreck. He could smell himself – a bad sign. There was more than an element of distain on the receptionist's face when she asked, 'Can I help you?' in Arabic.

He replied in English, giving his new name: Khalil el Majid. Surprise registered on the attractive young lady's face. 'I'm sorry but from your booking I thought you would be Algerian.'

'Libyan,' he corrected her, as he handed over his new passport.

She handed him his keys, gave him an envelope from the safe behind her and remarked, 'Your things have already been taken to your room.'

Juan smiled but didn't ask what things? Instead, he opened the envelope and glanced inside. It was full of crisp American $10 bills; he guessed there were at least a hundred.

His en suite room had a king-size bed and all the facilities of a modern hotel. A balcony overlooked the swimming pool and faced south. He opened the wardrobe. Inside were two lightweight suits, and several pairs of lightweight slip-on shoes – his size. *How on earth did they know my size? The suits look as if they will fit too.*

The dresser contained shirts, formal and informal, underclothes, socks, even a swimming costume. He could not have chosen better himself. In the bathroom was a razor and the usual shaving accoutrements.

They haven't noticed I have a beard; however, in this heat, it would make sense to shave.

He ran a bath, using the hotel's shower gel to maximise the foam. It was a delight settling into ten inches of hot water below five inches of froth. After soaking for over half an hour, he noticed the grime of the past week floating on the surface. He got out and was ashamed to see the tide mark of dirt. He hadn't felt so clean since leaving Port St Mary, almost two weeks previously.

He shaved and, feeling like a new man, called for room service: a chicken baguette, yoghurt and a bottle of Sancerre.

When the attendant arrived, Juan asked, 'Where is the nearest barber?'

'There is an excellent Turkish barber just around the corner. Tell him Azi sent you from the Sheraton; he will give you special treatment.'

The barber's shop proved to be part of a Turkish bath complex. A haircut, the mandatory removal by flame of ear and nasal hairs, followed by a massage in the steam room by an 18-stone Turk, set up Juan for the rest of day: lounging by the hotel pool.

That evening he ventured into the dining room feeling a million dollars. He found a corner table and ordered a small lager for an aperitif. Eating alone is a miserable experience but as he looked around at his fellow diners, he noticed at an adjacent table an extremely attractive woman, in her late twenties or early thirties, eating with an older man. Her tight skirt emphasised her figure, shapely legs and fine ankles.

Lucky bugger. Probably loaded to have a bird like that in tow.

Juan was embarrassed when she noticed him looking at her. She gave him a beguiling, coy smile but continued talking to her companion. He could hear they were speaking German but wasn't close enough to understand their conversation. She was stunning but not typically Teutonic. With high cheek bones, she had dark brown eyes and jet black shoulder-length hair. Her skin hinted a tan.

Middle Eastern?

Perhaps 5ft 9 in tall, she was slim but with broad shoulders that suggested she kept fit. He was entranced with her long fingers, considered in the Middle East to be a classical sign of beauty, and noticed she wore no rings.

Juan was about to begin his dessert when the couple stood to leave their table. The old man needed a walking stick to lever himself up. As he rose to his full height, he stumbled and fell heavily to the floor. Instinctively Juan reacted. He threw his napkin down and went to help. He picked the old boy up and asked in German, 'Are you alright?'

'*Sie sprechen Deutsch?*' the raven haired beauty asked, showing surprise.

'Yes, a little.'

'Your accent is a Berliner's.'

'I worked there briefly.' Juan realised he was getting into hot water. How was he going to explain that his name was Libyan?

She thanked him and introduced herself. 'My name is Alida Cron and this is my father, Hans Noll. Will you join us in the lounge for coffee when you have finished your dessert?'

Noll and Cron – that can't be right, he thought.

'I'd be delighted.' He'd made his mind up. Despite the risk that she might find he was booked into the hotel under a false name, he continued, 'My name is Alan.'

'You are English?'

'No, I am from New Zealand. But you are either Danish or from Schleswig Holstein?'

She smiled, 'We're from Lubeck.'

'Ah, a naval town.'

'Yes, my father was in the Navy during the war.'

A few minutes later, Juan was sitting with them on the veranda. Conversation remained in German. Juan had some difficulty trying not to show he was proficient in the language or give away his reason for being in Tunis.

His story that he was travelling back to New Zealand overland intrigued them. Alida claimed she had never before been outside Europe, but Juan didn't believe her; he wasn't sure why. Her father recalled being a sailor on the Admiral Graf Spee; ending up in Argentina after the scuttling of the battleship in the River Plate in 1939. He saw out the war interned in Buenos Aires.

'So,' she asked after a short break in the conversation, 'Where are you going from here?'

'I am going to Tripoli where I will stay with some friends for a while. I will buy an off-road Honda then follow Ted Simon's route through East Africa to South Africa, across to South America, then the USA and finally go home.'

'So, you've read *Jupiter's Travels?*' She laughed as she said it.

Juan face expressed surprise, as she quickly added, 'It's the best travel book I've ever read.'

'It's one of only two books I've ever read twice. The other was *King Solomon's Mines* and together they are the reason I must travel through East Africa.'

'I don't know that one,' she replied, 'but Ted Simon's adventures were unbelievable. I envy you and would love to come along for the ride.'

'Well, if you want to!' he joked.

'I might take you up on that.'

Her father, perhaps thinking the pair were getting too familiar at their first meeting, coughed loudly. Looking at his watch, he mumbled, 'I think it's time to be going to bed. Will you excuse us?' He had emphasised the last word.

He struggled to his feet. Alida stood up, turned to Juan, her eyes rolling upwards. She smiled, 'Maybe we can meet tomorrow? We are thinking of going to see the ruins of Carthage. Perhaps you would like to come with us?'

'I would be delighted.'

When they had gone, he ordered a double scotch. Sitting under a starlit sky on the terrace he began fantasising about having Alida as a travelling companion. *Would two up on a motorbike be practical when travelling through Africa? What sort of a bike could do it? A large BMW, perhaps?*

A BMW, of course – that's it!

The idea of using a BMW had triggered his earlier thoughts and doubts about their names.

Of course! Noll and Cron were world sidecar champions on a BMW in the fifties when I was about six or seven. He remembered seeing them in the TT. *There's something bizarre here.*

Juan remained in the bar for about half an hour. His mind wandered everywhere; going over the events of the past days and weeks. He was still uncertain whether he had been accepted by Moab, despite saving him from drowning. *Did I put my foot in it by asking too many questions? I've got to persuade him that I can be of use teaching languages in one of his madrassas. Do the Germans know I am from the Isle of Man or is it pure coincidence?* He wondered if his imagination was getting the better of him.

Tired, he ascended the lift to his room, undressed, and climbed into bed still thinking about Alida. *Is her name really Cron? What makes me think she is Middle Eastern?* He knew he was going to have one of those terrible nights when sleep is shallow.

***

The phone rang in a permanently manned office of the Israeli embassy in Madrid.

'Agent Hans Uhlmann,' the voice announced, continuing in Spanish, 'Lubeck is the Queen of Hanse.'

There was a pause before a voice simply said, 'Continue.'

'Agent Cron has made contact with Bradda Head. How far do you want her to go?'

There was a further pause, longer than the first. Then a different voice said, 'Hans, it's me – Simon Rosenberg.'

'What are you doing in Madrid?'

'This business is getting top priority from Tel Aviv. I flew out here this afternoon from London. Those bastards in al-Qaeda were planning to detonate an atomic device in our back yard. Bradda Head is working for MI6 and we think he may have successfully infiltrated them. Tell

Cron to stick to him come hell or high water. It's our best chance of ever getting someone on the inside.'

'He's just told us that he's planning to travel overland through Africa on a motorbike.'

'That's a load of bollocks. It's a front he's using with al-Qaeda.'

***

When Juan woke on Sunday morning, it was already ten o'clock. Contrary to his expectations he had slept soundly; making up for the previous three nights when he had hardly slept at all. He'd dreamt that he was seven years old and sitting with his grandmother on a wall at *The Nursery* bend in Onchan, watching the sidecar TT. The noise of the bikes was deafening as they roared past his feet, barely a yard away. Suddenly, as the two leading bikes came towards the bend, the passenger on the first looked over his shoulder to see how far behind were the chasing pair. The consequence of not leaning out to balance the machine as it swept round the left-hander was that the combination's third wheel flipped upwards. It overturned, throwing the leading pair along the ground and finishing on the far side of the road. They were unhurt, picked themselves up and, cursing in German, removed their helmets. The two riders were Hans and Alida.

Having showered and shaved, *God it is good not to have all that fuzz on my face*, he was finishing dressing when there was a knock on his door.

He looked through the spyhole and saw Alida. He opened the door. She greeted him in German, 'Are you coming to Carthage? Papa is not feeling well and I don't want to go on my own. If you are coming, you'll have to miss breakfast as the coach is waiting.'

He looked at her. Any man would be proud to be seen in her company. Wearing a classic red sleeveless summer dress with matching white handbag and sandals, her thick white belt highlighted her stunning figure. Her jet black hair shone; he longed to comb it with his fingers. Momentarily he imagined himself pulling her towards him to kiss her luscious red mouth.

He managed to mutter a reply. 'I am sorry. I overslept. Will your father be OK on his own? Perhaps we can have a coffee when we get to Carthage.'

'Dad will be all right, but we must hurry if we're not to miss the bus.'

He grabbed his jacket and, as they descended in the lift to the foyer, she took his hand and smiled, 'We will have more freedom on our own.'

His instinct was to recoil and withdraw his hand. He didn't, but he wondered why she was encouraging him so soon. Along with the other holidaymakers, they boarded the coach.

***

As the trip to Carthage began, the main border between Tunisia and Libya at Ra's Ajdir on the North African coast had already been manned by Major Antonio Tevez and his two soldiers. Between the two countries, there is only one crossing open to general traffic. The control of travellers is strictly enforced. Visas are scrupulously examined. Even if correct, it can take up to 24 hours to cross the no man's land. Corruption is rife; precise paperwork is essential, but insufficient to guarantee passage. There are two other border crossings further south in the desert, but Tevez knew that using them would mean detours of hundreds of miles over roads little better than camel tracks: slow and dangerous as hijackings were common. He reasoned that anyone travelling overland to Tripoli from Tunis must use the coastal route. They positioned themselves on a hill, a quarter of a mile inside the Tunisian border. With their powerful Leica binoculars, they could see everything going on below. Night vision goggles supplemented their watch during hours of darkness. Using an eight-hour shift system, one of the GEO counter-terrorism specialists was always on the ground patrolling amongst the queuing vehicles – never less than one mile in length. Major Tevez was satisfied that if either Quine or Anibal tried to cross the border, then they would see them.

CHAPTER 22

Sunday 7th April 1991

The coach to Carthage, a short journey of 30 minutes, was largely full of German tourists. This surprised Juan as he hadn't envisaged Hans or his daughter as mass tourism types. Furthermore, he noticed that the others on the coach were elderly and in small groups, as if they knew each other. Coupled with the nagging suspicion that Alida was not her name, he wondered if she was German at all.

And yet, her German is perfect.

She was friendly and talked frenetically about the history of the Carthaginians and how Hannibal had crossed the Alps with elephants to attack Rome from the north. 'The beginning of tank warfare,' she postulated.

Juan knew that the Romans had the last laugh, raising Carthage to the ground some 15 years after Hannibal's victory.

Hopefully, the same thing will happen to al-Qaeda.

However, as they strolled around the ruins, listening to their guide, he was amused to find that peace between Rome and Carthage was not officially signed until 1985; the two cities had been officially at war for over 2,000 years. After an hour they broke away from the others and found a taverna with ample shade from the midday sun under olive trees.

Having ordered coffee, served with some tiny pastries, Juan decided to vent his doubts.

'If you will excuse my manners,' he said, deliberately speaking in English, 'are you really German?'

She frowned, narrowed her dark brown eyes, and stared fixedly into his. She said nothing for what seemed ages, and then replied in excellent English, 'What made you think I might not be?'

He ignored her question and probed further, 'You're not called Alida either, are you?'

She smiled, shaking her head to imply the negative.

'Then, who the hell are you?' He asked the question quietly, but authoritatively.

'I am surprised you haven't worked that out,' she replied, smiling broadly as if he was missing the joke. 'The clue is in our names.'

'Ah, yes. Noll and Cron were BMW world sidecar champions in the fifties. Indeed, I dreamt about them in the Isle of Man TT last night. They never won the TT, but it doesn't explain why you are here.'

Juan sensed where their conversation was leading but wanted to give away as little as possible. He knew only Sir Charles could have told them about his Manx connections.

He asked, 'What has Noll and Cron got to do with telling me who you are?'

She made no bones about hiding her cards any longer. 'Your operation is codenamed The Third Leg. Your operative name is Bradda Head and you work for Dover Castle. Right?'

She had him at advantage point. He knew it.

He said nothing and waited for her to continue. There was a long pause; then she asked, 'Who do you think rescued you from the Spanish police last Wednesday?'

'Tell me.'

'We did.'

'We?'

'Mossad. We have been keeping tabs on you ever since our sayanim blew himself up in the Isle of Man. My name is Lydia Lasker. Hans and I have been instructed to give you all possible assistance to help you infiltrate al-Qaeda. I am afraid to tell you that there is a price on your head. The Spanish GEO are at this moment trying to find you and your two al-Qaeda friends. Spain is not happy about losing four policemen last week.'

'But your lot did it.'

'Yes, but they think you plotted it.'

'I don't follow. Why should they?'

'The Director of MI6 met the Head of the GEO in France last Thursday. Your escape was the sole topic on their agenda.'

'You haven't answered my question.'

'Firstly, Sir Peter and our Head of Operations in London have agreed to share everything on this one. Your Head instinctively knew General Antolin was going to send some of his special service men after you. A Spanish team of three arrived on Friday evening at Tunis airport and were seen by one of our network. Secondly, one of our sayanims spotted you crossing the border into Tunisia. He works in the café where you had breakfast. The rest was easy.'

'You seem to know more of what is going on than me. So, what now?'

Half an hour had slipped by and the proprietor of the small restaurant was laying the tables around them for lunch. He asked, 'Will you be staying for lunch?' He clearly wanted to lay their table.

They looked at each other. 'Shall we?' asked Juan.

'That would be nice,' she replied, 'but we had better tell the coach driver we will not be returning with him.'

'Where are you staying?' asked the waiter.

'*The Sheraton*,' replied Juan.

'No problem. I will arrange a taxi for you afterwards.'

Juan left Lydia while he went to find the driver. He returned ten minutes later to find her sipping an aperitif, a cold lager waiting for him and a bowl of assorted olives on the table. 'I noticed you had a lager for an aperitif last night,' she said smiling.

'You don't miss much, do you?'

'I'm trained not to.'

'I know this sounds corny, but what is a nice girl like you doing in a murky business like this?'

She laughed. 'It's a long story. I was born in Iran. My father was a Jewish Iranian, Khalil Esfandi. He had married a Russian. I was fifteen years old when the Shah was deposed and my father realised that an Islamic State would not be safe for Jews. Even under the Shah, it was not exactly comfortable. We were treated as second-class citizens, but not persecuted.'

That makes her 27, he calculated.

'The danger was exacerbated with the pending invasion of Afghanistan. We moved to Neumunster in Northern Germany where there is a strong Jewish community and my father had contacts. In Iran everything was taught in Farsi at school. At home, my parents spoke a mix of Hebrew, Arabic and Russian. In Schleswig Holstein I learnt German quickly and went to university in Hamburg to read English where I was recruited by Mossad.'

'But you said your name was Lasker.'

'The name of my ex-husband; we divorced a year ago.'

'Do you live in Israel?'

'No. I really am German; however, Hans was originally American. His parents fled there in the thirties. It's what makes Mossad unique when compared to other security services. To be in the CIA you have to be American; to be in MI6 – British. Mossad agents can be any nationality, as long as they believe passionately about the right of Israel to exist.'

The remark made Juan think. Despite his time in the Intelligence Corps and working for BRIXMIS, this had never occurred to him. It explained the uncanny knack of Mossad turning up under every stone.

They ordered a light lunch: a pine nut risotto, a speciality of the house the patron assured them, followed by a tuna salad. *Similar to Salad Nicoise,* thought Juan. The local white wine was rather sweet but complemented the meal that was taken at a leisurely Mediterranean pace. It was past 3.30 pm when the taxi came to take them back to Tunis.

By then they had agreed there was little to be done until Wednesday, when Felipe was expected to arrive, except make contingency plans. In the meantime, they would keep their eyes skimmed for the GEO operatives. Juan agreed to make contact with the British embassy the following morning.

Together with Hans, they had dinner that evening to discuss the way ahead. Juan noticed Hans looked younger, and commented, 'I notice you no longer require your walking stick'.

'It's rather special,' Hans replied. 'The stick is actually a rifle loaded with six 9mm bullets. Holding it with one hand, I can hit a target at ten metres.'

'It must have quite a kickback?'

'It does,' he laughed, 'that's why I try and hold it with both hands.'

Conversation moved on. Hans' parents had fled Germany to America in 1936. He had moved to live in Israel with his wife, of German extraction, in the mid-sixties. He had fought in the six-day war of 1967.

'I think,' began Hans after a pause in the conversation, 'I should disappear into the background. I suggest you and Lydia are seen together as much as possible. Al-Qaeda knows you are here; fortunately, the GEO do not. My guess is that the GEO are waiting at the Tunisian border with Libya hoping to catch you and Moab passing through. Earlier today, when you were in Carthage, I anonymously tipped off the Tunisian authorities that a small group of terrorists are planning an international incident at the border with Libya. I am hoping the Tunisian police will act and remove the GEO threat. The danger, of course, is that al-Qaeda will realise there is a third party at work and be frightened off.'

'There isn't much we can do until Felipe turns up on Wednesday,' said Juan.

'If he turns up,' replied Hans.

They retired separately to their respective rooms. Juan lay in bed thinking of what the future might bring, half wishing for a knock on his door and for Lydia to enter, wearing a see-through nightie that would complement her figure. It never happened; *only in James Bond stories,* he thought, smiling to himself.

Instead he thought of Molly. It was two weeks since he had left her, but it seemed ages ago. *I wonder if George has transferred the car to her and explained what is going on. Is she coping with the boys? She'll be all right. She managed before I came into her life. At least she shouldn't have any financial problems.*

He felt tired. So much had happened in such a short time. Sleep was catching up on him.

Molly, my dear Molly... my Molly, my maiden...

***

While Major Tevez was patrolling the queue of vehicles slowly exiting Tunisia that Sunday evening, his two colleagues sat in their three-man tent eating their compo rations.

'We've been here twenty-four hours; there's no bloody sign of these two guys. I'd have thought they would have come through here by now. How long do you think we are going to be stuck on this hopeless task?'

'I've no idea. I'd have thought if they haven't turned up by tomorrow evening then Tevez will call off the whole thing and we can go home.'

They continued their meal; neither noticing how silent it had become.

Then, from somewhere nearby, a *crack,* followed by a mumbled curse.

Both knew instinctively from years of training and experience what the breaking of a twig from somewhere near the front of their tent meant. Someone had stepped into their shallow trap, covered with dry foliage.

In less than a blinking of an eye, both had grabbed their compact semi-automatics and were crawling on their backs, quietly shuffling out of the tent up two diagonally-opposed trenches at the rear.

The technique of creating escape tunnels from their wigwams by digging several two-foot deep passages, carefully camouflaged by covering stiff canvas with leaves, soil and grass, originated with the

Cheyenne Indians. The GEO had modified the system. Their trenches were only ten feet long. Each soldier had reached the end of their own tunnel in less than five seconds. Undertaking a well rehearsed procedure, they stood up, their coverings falling away, and opened fire in the direction of the tent's entrance. Three men dropped.

However, the Tunisian police were not fools. They had brought a dozen men and their captain had previously surrounded the tent with six snipers – his best shots. The two Spaniards never knew what hit them from behind; several bullets entering the nape of their necks and killing them instantly.

Down on the road, above the noise of the heavy diesels waiting in the queue to enter Libya, Major Tevez heard the commotion coming from the hillside above. He recognised the sounds of his own men's VP70s. He also heard the higher pitched noises made by the snipers' Russian Dragunov SVDs. He knew what it meant: he was on his own. No one around him had ears sufficiently tuned to recognise gun fire. He thought quickly. The police, or whoever had found his men, would be searching the tent and discover there was a third man. Two and two would put him in the valley at the border checkpoint. He had to move – and move quickly. He looked around.

A forty-tonner was coming towards him from Libya, having passed through the border checkpoint 200 yards away. He stepped in front of it, waving his semi-automatic pistol at the startled driver. He jumped onto the running board, and yelled in Arabic, 'Quick, the lorry in front is smuggling illegals into Tunisia. Follow him.' And without asking, he opened the door and jumped in beside the driver.

The terrified driver didn't ask questions. He put his right foot down as ordered; his eyes as large as organ stops.

Tevez thought quickly.

Who could have found them? The Tunisian police? But how would they have known? Someone must have tipped them off.

He thought back to his briefing with General Antolin. Something about Mossad being after the same quarry and the British being involved.

It doesn't make any sense; neither could have known we were here. Perhaps it was al-Qaeda?

He remembered, too, the general's warning, *'The Spanish Government will deny all knowledge of the operation.'*

He went over events, weighing probabilities against possibilities. *His targets passed into Morocco on false papers. To get into Algeria and Tunis they must have acquired forged passports – probably made in Libya by al-Qaeda. They may have realised they were being hunted by Mossad. They would have guessed the most likely place to be ambushed was the Tunisian – Libyan border. Then what would they have done?*

Of course! They would have transferred to a boat to take them from Tunis to Tripoli. How far is that? 500 kilometres? That would take some organisation; it would take time for al-Qaeda to find a vessel. They may still be in Tunis. But where? If I know the Libyans, with all their money, it will be in one of the five-star hotels. I'll look for the bastards there.

He thought about his old instructor at the GEO training school – a Warrant Officer, long passed retirement age, a veteran of the Spanish Civil War, but retained for his expertise in field craft. *'When you have to make a decision in a hurry without all the facts then use the formula: fgh=abc. Five good hunches = a bleeding certainty.'*

He looked at his driver; his hands were still shaking from the intrusion of the GEO specialist. Tevez smiled to himself. *There is something satisfying about having total control over a fellow human being.*

'Where are you going?' he asked the driver.

'You told me to follow the truck in front.'

'I asked where you are going.'

'I was going to the port in Tunis.'

'Excellent. Drop me off there and don't say a word about this to anyone. Understand?'

The driver nodded enthusiastically; glad to know that he was not going to be shot.

CHAPTER 23

Monday 8th April 1991

When Juan woke, it was past nine o'clock. He went down to breakfast and found Lydia sitting alone. He joined her, asking, 'Where is Hans?'

'He's already moved out to the hotel across the road. From now on he will be keeping a discrete watch from a distance.'

'What are our plans for today?'

'Up to you,' she smiled. Her reply was friendly; a suggestion in her tone that she would try anything once.

'How about going sailing?' he enthused. 'I have checked, and we can hire a dinghy from Sidi Bou Said, which is not far away. Have you ever sailed?'

'No.'

'You will enjoy it. We can have lunch on the beach and come back here later in the afternoon when it will be cooler to lie by the pool.'

'It will be a test to see if we can give Hans the slip,' she laughed.

***

The Tunisian police captain in charge of the partially successful operation at the border stood in front of his colonel.

'There is evidence that there were three of them. One has escaped. We set up road blocks and did a wide sweep of the area, but found nothing. The Libyans assured me no one escaped through their border, so he is still at large in Tunisia.'

The portly colonel nodded as he inhaled from his cheroot. 'Anything else?' he asked in a disinterested tone.

'They weren't terrorists.'

The colonel straightened up in his chair. 'Go on.'

'They had Heckler and Koch VP70Ms with stocks. As far as I am aware they were only issued to military units; mostly the Italians. They had compo rations; there were no personal identity markings on them of any sort; not even money. Furthermore, their sleeping bags, boots, and clothes were identical – standard issue. Their tent was of a quality suggesting they were undercover paramilitaries. They had powerful binoculars and night vision equipment. Their use of escape tunnels from their tent is the hallmark of a specialist team.'

The colonel nodded, 'But not proof.'

'No, but five hunches…'

'Yes, I know make a certainty. Any clues as to what country they may be from?'

'None, except they were neither Jews nor Muslims.'

'Really?'

'They were not circumcised. Therefore, your guess is as good as mine; probably southern European – Italian? Maybe Spanish or Greek.'

'It doesn't make any sense. What were they doing there? Our anonymous tip-off simply described them as terrorists. They must have either been waiting for someone or something to pass through the border.'

The captain nodded but said nothing.

The colonel sighed. 'Well, whatever it was they've missed their chance.'

'What will we do with the bodies?' asked the captain.

'Keep them in the mortuary for a week. If they are not claimed, then incinerate them.'

'What about the third man?'

'Is there much point in looking for a needle in a hay stack?'

'No, probably not.'

'I'll issue an amber alert to all stations, but without a description of him, I don't hold out much hope.'

***

Although the road from the border to the city of Tunis is well-surfaced by North African standards, the 500km journey took all night. The sun had been up several hours when Tevez's lorry trundled into the port area of downtown Tunis. The two men had not exchanged a single word during the entire journey.

'Where are you heading for now?' asked Tevez.

'Marsala, Sicily,' replied his driver.

'Then?'

'Naples.'

It occurred to the Major that an easy option would be to accompany the driver to Italy by smuggling himself in the rear of the 40-tonner. However, he had no documents and the Tunisian police would possibly be on the alert for a third man.

'I am going to watch you board the ship, so don't try anything silly. You'll do best to forget you've ever seen me. We have many contacts worldwide, especially in Sicily – our traditional home. Understand?'

There was a nervous 'Yes'. The driver was under no illusion that Tevez meant business and must be a member of the Cosa Nostra, the Sicilian Mafia.

During the hour waiting for the ship to sail, Tevez sat on the quayside analysing possibilities. He had sufficient money and a VISA card issued on a Swiss bank that gave him unlimited access to GEO funds. He was aware that his clothes were a give-away. As soon as the local shops opened he would buy a practical outfit. His weapon, concealed in his rucksack, was safe from prying eyes.

Two hours later, breakfasted and newly kitted, he found a B&B in a quiet cul-de-sac near the short-stay marina. Yachting marinas tend to operate like car parks: long-term and short-term. Patrolled by port officials, this one had a prominent douane post; other marinas for permanent moorings did not. *If a boat is going to pick them up and take them to Libya, then this is most likely the one they'd use.* He thought about visiting the local five star hotels for signs of the murdering fugitives but rejected the idea when a brochure from the information centre showed how many hotels there were.

With a commanding view of the marina, he was sitting on the quayside having a light lunch – a steak salad, a half bottle of Rioja, with a large bottle of San Pellegrino – when he saw a 100ft motor launch appear from around the furthest pier. Whilst it was tying up – Mediterranean style with stern to shore – he noticed the vessel flew the green flag of Saudi Arabia. The ship was named *Juheina Star*. He began musing on the wealth of Saudi princes. He gazed abstractedly while the douane went aboard, disappearing for a considerable time. Eventually, he reappeared clutching a small parcel; Tevez was prepared to guess it was a bribe.

Several minutes elapsed before four sailors disembarked. Dressed casually in jeans and tee shirts, they walked down the pier towards where Tevez was sitting. They were coming to the taverna for a drink. They sat down, several tables from himself. Now close enough for recognition, Major Tevez instantly knew one of them was the Libyan Felipe; his weasel-like face was unmistakable.

Eureka! He's here to fetch the other two bastards.

The four settled down, drinking copiously the local red. Antonio knew that to remain watching would attract attention. He finished his lunch and left, positioning himself discretely some 50 yards away where he could watch Felipe.

An hour had passed when, having finished their pasta lunch, Felipe rose and left the others who began drifting back to their ship. Tevez followed as Felipe headed towards the tourist hotels. He went straight to the *Sheraton*. The major followed – at a distance. In the foyer he could see Felipe asking for someone. The receptionist was shrugging her shoulders as if replying she didn't know. He was pressing her for something and she appeared to call for a senior member of staff. A smartly dressed young man arrived at the front desk, talked for some time to Felipe, and then went into the office behind. He came back and nodded.

Felipe smiled and sat down in the foyer, taking a position near the glass revolving doors from where he could see everyone coming and going. He was served a beer; presumably on the house.

Tevez remained outside, sitting down under a shade by the pool, but able to see Felipe through the large windows that formed the wall of the foyer. He bought a large bottle of a mineral water from the pool-side bar. He wanted steady hands for what he was planning.

Over an hour had elapsed when Tevez noticed a couple, hand in hand and apparently enjoying each other's company, enter the garden. They passed within a few feet of him and went into the hotel. Felipe stood up and began talking to the clean-shaven man. Their conversation appeared animated; there was much gesticulation and shoulder shrugging.

The couple eventually sat at Felipe's table. A waiter brought them three beers. Conversation appeared intense; there was clearly disagreement. Major Tevez reached into his rucksack. He withdrew a miniature telescope and looked carefully at the male Caucasian. *Can it be the New Zealander? He looks different from the photograph without a beard. It must be him, who else could it be? But who is the woman? Where is the tall Arab who called himself Anibal?*

He thought about moving closer to try and overhear their conversation but decided against it. *Be patient – the first rule of undercover work.* He would have to get nearer to his quarry later; there was no point in risking giving himself away.

After about half an hour of intense debate, the couple stood up and went to the lifts at the rear of the foyer. They reappeared 15 minutes later carrying small holdalls. Felipe joined them while they appeared to pay their bills at reception; then the three came out, heading towards Tevez.

The major turned away and left the hotel grounds. He knew the direction they would take. He quickened his pace to get well ahead of them. He found a shady side street and entered. In the step of a doorway he watched them pass. He re-emerged and was following them at about 30 yards.

His mind was racing. *Where to do it? Do I kill the female, or simply injure her? What setting do I use on the gun? Single shots or a small automatic burst?*

At 25 metres he knew he could kill three men with a three-round burst in less than one second. He'd practised on targets for many years.

A three-round burst at 15 metres will be kids' play.

As he followed them, one hand was in his rucksack carefully setting up the stocked pistol. *I'll wait until they're on the pier – there will be fewer people around.*

The couple had their arms loosely around each other, the Caucasian talking to Felipe most of the way. As they reached the pier, Tevez had quickened his pace and moved within range. He withdrew the automatic, glancing for a fraction of a second to check his rapid fire setting. He raised the firearm to his shoulder, took aim at Felipe and fired.

'Phut, phut, PHUT.'

Hundreds of seagulls, mostly dozing peacefully on the boats' superstructures, rose as one, their squawks deafening.

To the untrained ear, three shots were fired that Monday afternoon. Everyone in the vicinity, subsequently interviewed by the police, swore there were only three bangs.

Yet four bodies lay on the pier.

The douane was awoken from his afternoon nap by the noise. *Can I be dreaming?* Initially, he arose from his slumber slowly; nearly falling over. His left leg had been asleep too. He wiggled his toes to get the circulation going and went to the door of his office. What he saw filled him with horror. He ran towards the three bodies lying in a heap. One was still, the other two moaning. He summed up: one dead, two injured.

Then he noticed the fourth figure, 12 metres away. He ran to investigate. What he saw stopped him in his tracks: the man's face had been blown away; there was blood and gore everywhere. At his side lay a semi-automatic weapon. In a panic he ran back to his office, passing the other three. He never noticed five men coming from the nearby *Juheina Star*. Out of breath, he dialled the emergency number for the police. He knew they would arrive within three minutes – it was a procedure practised regularly. Over the phone he tried to explain there had been a shooting on his pier and two men were dead and two injured. He was regretting having finished the bottle of red wine with his lunch; it was taking him longer to explain what had happened. He was confused. At the other end of the phone, the police sergeant kept asking silly questions as if he didn't believe the douane's story.

When he finished, he re-emerged into the bright sunshine. The first three bodies were gone. *Was I dreaming? No, there is the poor bugger without a face.* He approached him again. *What the hell has happened to the other three?*

He looked around. He couldn't explain it. In his confused state of mind, he hadn't noticed the *Juheina Star* had slipped its moorings. Already it was disappearing around the end of the pier.

CHAPTER 24

Monday 8th April 1991

The *Juheina Star* began accelerating as soon as it rounded the pier. Its Italian captain, Romeo Felittini, in the ship's control centre on the top deck, had been given his instructions, 'Maximum speed, and fastest course for Tripoli.'

Although his ship was capable of 35 knots, he set the controls to accelerate gradually to 30 knots. They were some 400 miles from the Libyan capital – a shade over 12 hours. *I'm not going to shake to buggery my beloved, brand new baby just for an hour and a quarter, and certainly not for that little shit, Mousad.*

His boss was the motor yacht's owner, Prince Omar al Ouda. *I take orders from the Prince, not his bloody agent, Mousad Safahar.* The *Juheina Star* was less than a year old. Its lightweight, 120 ft-long hull, built from glass reinforced plastic, with its twin 3,500 HP MTU engines driving twin water-jets, meant that it could outrun anything the Tunisian Navy could muster.

On the executive deck below, Mousad Safahar stood with the crew's medical orderly, Azi al Wajh, in the premier suite. They had separated the unconscious Lydia, now lying on the suite's blood stained double bed, from the men who were next door in number-two suite. She had been shot in the back of her left shoulder. 'I suspect she has a shattered collar bone and the bullet, or a small fragment, may be lodged somewhere in or near her thyroid gland. Her pulse is high; a few centimetres to the right and the bullet would have killed her. She has lost a lot of blood, but I have patched her up; she is strong and should survive if we can get her to hospital. Her horrible facial cuts and bruises are where she fell heavily on the ground, breaking her nose and hitting her forehead. She will probably remain unconscious for several hours. She will not remember anything about the shooting.'

'The egg on her forehead; is that where she fell? Is that dangerous?'

'No. I would be more worried if it wasn't there.'

'When we get to Tripoli, will she be fit enough to return on a plane to Tunis?'

'Not straight away.'

'Have you checked her holdall?

'Yes. She carries a German passport in the name of Alida Cron. Her Visa card is issued by the Bank of Lubeck. Everything else is personal: perfume, a change of clothes, that sort of thing.'

'Good. Let's go next door.'

They moved into the corridor. Mousad called for an attendant to stand outside Lydia's bedroom.

'If she comes round, call me at once.'

'Yes, sir.'

They entered the bedroom.

Azi began, 'You can see Felipe is dead. The bullet entered the back of his head and he never stood a chance.'

'We will arrange a burial at sea shortly. I am more concerned about the Caucasian. This is the man who Moab calls his brother. I believe he saved our leader's life. He is the reason we went to Tunis. I understand Moab wants him for a special task.'

'It's going to be touch and go.'

'Why?'

'He was hit twice. The first bullet entered his chest and is still there. I am pretty sure it missed his spine, but not by much. However, I suspect it may have punctured his lung. He is on oxygen because of breathing difficulties. He really does need to see a specialist thoracic surgeon.

Again, I have stopped the bleeding but whether he will survive the journey to Tripoli is, at best, fifty-fifty. I have given him a mild tranquiliser to prevent him from moving and dislodging the bullet.'

'You said there was a second bullet.'

'Yes. Look at his left hand. He must have had it around the woman's left shoulder. The bullet that hit her had previously passed through his hand. I wouldn't be surprised if it has damaged the nerves leading to his fingers. He may partially lose the use of his hand.'

Mousad nodded gravely. 'We must pray to Allah that he will survive.'

'Shall I prepare Felipe's body for burial?'

'Yes. You will find all you require – weights, canvas bag and so on in the hold. I will inform Captain Felittini about the ceremony. I don't want it to slow us up. His life,' he looked at Juan, 'could depend on minutes.'

Safahar retired to the stateroom, went to the cocktail bar, and helped himself to a generous Glenmorangie with ice. He sat down.

What a cock-up. Who the hell shot Felipe, el Majid and the German woman? What was she doing coming anyway? Why were there four bodies on the quay? An assassin must have shot the assassin!

Mousad relived the episode. He had been in the yacht's control room on the top deck with Romeo when the incident occurred. They had witnessed it happening. He remembered el Majid coming down the quay talking to Felipe on his right-hand side with his left hand resting on the German woman's left shoulder. He remembered Romeo taking charge instinctively and giving the order to bring the three bodies on-board. He had started the diesel engines and immediately initiated the cast-off.

I only heard three shots. I never saw who shot the fourth man. Whoever did it must have fired at the same time.

He took a sip of his highland nectar. *Try and work this out logically,* he said to himself. *Who the hell would want to kill Felipe and el Majid? And why?*

He thought through their recent history, as told to him by Prince al Ouda.

The IRA had tried to kill them at Gijon. Could the assassin on the

184

quay have been an IRA hit man? Hardly. How could he have found them?
Could it have been the Spanish authorities or ETA?

None of it was making any sense.

And who shot the assassin? He must have been following them from
the Sheraton *to the quay. He must have been there to protect either el*
Majid or the woman, Alida. Who is she, anyway?

He began to theorise.

Let's assume the killer was IRA. Who could have known the IRA were
up to something? Only the British. Then the unknown gunman must be
MI6 and he was there to protect the female. She must be a British agent.

Alternatively, the Spanish GEO were after them because they were the
cause of the four Spanish policemen being killed when they escaped near
Madrid. And was Moab's escape pure chance or arranged by someone? If
so, who? ETA? No. The British? It must be.

Whichever way and whatever way he looked at it, he kept coming to
the same conclusion – *she is a British spy.*

He knew he would have to get rid of her. He thought about throwing
her overboard, but knew that Romeo, being a gallant Italian, would not
allow him. He decided to keep her isolated until Tripoli and send her back
under escort to Tunis. He picked up the ship's telephone and called Tripoli.

He explained his predicament.

'Get rid of her at once. It's too dangerous for her to see our yacht
here in Tripoli. Meanwhile, I'll arrange the very best private
hospitalisation for el Majid. We must keep him alive whatever happens.'

Mousad shuddered. He knew the voice on the end of the phone was
someone with whom you did not query orders.

He returned to the executive suite, dismissing the guard outside. 'I'll
sit with her for a while,' he said. The guard smiled inwardly. He had
looked in on her several times and taken more than a fancy to her slim,
trim body himself. He suspected Mousad might be having similar ideas.

Mousad closed the door, carefully locking it. He wasn't going to be
disturbed at any cost.

He picked up the pillow from the other side of the king-sized bed, admired her beauty, and thought, *what a waste.*

He placed the pillow over her face and held it down – firmly. He froze with the pressure he was applying. There was no resistance, just a few involuntary movements from the body's muscles that lasted less than a minute. Then nothing. He didn't let go. There could be no room for error. When he released his grip, he felt her pulse – there was nothing. He looked at the pillow, fluffing it up and replacing it would be futile – it was smeared with Alida's blood. He shrugged his shoulders. He unlocked the door and shouted up the corridor, 'Get me Wajh, at once.'

'I was sitting with her when she suddenly had convulsions then stopped breathing,' he said to Azi al Wajh.

'Probably a blood clot. It could have become dislodged from the shoulder area, travelled through the veins and entered the heart. She would have felt very little. Shall we bury her with Felipe?' He had noticed the stained pillow and guessed what had happened; he wasn't going to say anything. Mousad Safahar, suspected by the crew to be a hit man, was someone you didn't cross swords with.

'Yes. As Captain Felittini is the only Christian on-board, he will have to take her ceremony.'

Romeo had been brought up in downtown Naples. He hadn't attended church since the age of 13 after his confirmation. He struggled with what to say as Lydia's body rested on the plank, prior to it sliding over the side. He began, 'The Lord is my shepherd; I shall not want. He maketh me to lie down in green pastures…' but soon afterwards dried up. He momentarily felt ashamed that he could not recite any more of Psalm 23. As a boy of nine, he had learnt it word perfect.

Mousad read from the Koran before Felipe's body was released to the deep.

Within minutes the *Juheina Star* was back to 30 knots. Below deck Juan remained unconscious.

✳✳✳

186

'Just tell me those last details again, will you?'

Hans sighed. He knew the tape recorder was switched on. What he was about to report would be given close scrutiny by the hierarchy. He took his time, thinking through the afternoon's events carefully.

He began, 'I watched Lydia, Quine and the Arab, whom I took to be Felipe, leave the *Sheraton*. Lydia and Quine were carrying holdalls. They headed towards the quay. I hung well back. They were followed, at thirty yards, by someone with a rucksack. I had noticed him in the hotel grounds previously and wondered who he was. He left the hotel grounds ahead of them but ducked down a side street to let them pass. He was well trained in surveillance. I remained about forty yards behind him. As they began to enter the marina, he closed-up to within fifteen yards. I drew nearer too. I was perhaps thirty yards behind the unknown man. I could see Felipe was taking Lydia and Quine towards a Saudi registered yacht – the *Juheina Star*. I saw the killer remove a Heckler and Koch VP70 from his rucksack and raise it to his shoulder. I took my BUL-Cherokee from its holster and fired. I was praying I was not too late. He went down, but so too did Lydia, Quine and Felipe. A douane came running out from his office at the end of the pier. Four or five sailors came from the *Juheina Star*; the seagulls were making a deafening racket. I slinked back into the shadows from where I could not be seen.'

'Then what?'

'The douane inspected the damage and went back to his office, presumably to get help. The sailors whipped up the three bodies and had them on board in seconds. The yacht had cast-off by the time the douane returned to the scene. The assassin is dead.'

'So our agent, along with Quine, is on the *Juheina Star* bound for we know not where. Furthermore, we don't know if they are alive or dead.'

'Correct.'

'God, what a cock-up. We should be able to track the yacht, of course. Our friends will follow it by satellite. Wherever it is heading, we will have to make sure we have someone waiting. Is there anything else you want to add?'

187

'I have been back to the *Sheraton*. I have made sure both Lydia's room and Quine's are clean – absolutely no traces.'

'Excellent, then you'd better come home.'

✶✶✶

The Colonel removed his polished boots from his desk and sat up straight as his captain entered. He asked his subordinate, 'I gather from what you told me over the radio you have found our missing third man?'

'Yes, definitely. He carried the same semi-automatic as the two we shot at the border. His clothes were different, but this guy was the boss.'

'Why?'

'He carried money, and had a VISA card – on a Swiss bank.'

'Untraceable, then?'

'Yes.'

'What about the three he shot on the quay?'

'The douane swears they were hustled aboard a Saudi motor launch – the *Juheina Star* – which cast off immediately. By now it will be long gone and in international waters. We may never know who they were.'

'Have we no idea?'

'We are making extensive enquiries around the hotels, but so far no luck. What do we do with the third man?'

'The same as the others.'

✶✶✶

'I'm afraid we may have lost Quine, Sir Peter. And one of our best agents too, for that matter.'

'Why? What's happened?'

'You know they were waiting at *The Sheraton* for the Arab calling himself Felipe to turn up on Wednesday?'

'Yes.'

'Well, he turned up two days early. Our agent, Alida, and Quine

188

agreed to go with him and they walked to the marina to board a Saudi launch. On the quay, just a few yards from the boat, all three were shot by a professional hit man. We don't know the extent of their injuries as they were quickly hustled onto the yacht, which then left in a hurry. We suspect they're being taken to Tripoli where we have several sayanims. We will watch out for their arrival. Our second agent, Hans, watched the whole affair and managed to get a shot at the unknown assassin, killing him. However, he was a fraction too late to prevent our two being hit.'

'Who the hell was the assassin?'

'We don't know.'

'Well, if it wasn't us, and it can't have been the IRA or ETA, then it must have been the GEO. That bastard Felix Antolin offered to chase Quine, Felipe and Anibal to extract revenge. I thought I had managed to persuade him to leave it to you guys. Obviously, I was wrong. He won't be happy when he finds out he has lost one of his best men.'

'The problem is we don't know if Alida and Quine survived. I will let you know as soon as we find out anything. We calculate the *Juheina Star* will reach Tripoli around midday tomorrow.'

'We'll have to keep our fingers crossed that they're OK. Meanwhile, I'll brief Sir Charles.'

✸✸✸

The Head of MI5 listened to his colleague patiently.

'You know, Peter, this began as a simple operation to find out if there was any evidence of the IRA selling its weapons to al-Qaeda. That aim succeeded. The Navy have doubled the number of fishery protection vessels in the Irish Sea and there is no evidence of pair-trawling transfers or the use of Manx ports. Furthermore, the Irish Navy helped us catch a Liberian registered coaster last week off the Ring of Kerry heading for Libya. It was full of illegal arms, including 500 AK-47s and several tons of semtex. I am hoping that our vigilance has prevented the reversal of munitions and from now on the Provisional IRA will come clean with the decommissioning authorities led by General de Chastelain. For that, we have Quayle to thank. However, I now fear the operation has got out of hand. I doubt if we'll ever see Quayle again.'

'If Quayle has survived the assassination attempt, and al-Qaeda wants to keep him, he will be taken to a hospital in Tripoli. We will know then, for certain, that he is trusted by them.'

'True.'

'Mossad have two sayanims there. They will keep us in the picture.'

CHAPTER 25

Tuesday 9th April 1991

It was past midday when the *Juheina Star* entered Tripoli harbour. She had been given clearance to enter the quiet eastern dock usually reserved for the Libyan Navy, vessels with diplomatic immunity and those belonging to Gaddafi's clique. There would be no inspection by the Libyan authorities. A fully equipped ambulance was waiting. So too, posted on a five-storey apartment block, overlooking the harbour, was a sayanim with powerful binoculars.

He watched the paramedics go on-board. Ten minutes later they reappeared with a white unconscious male on a stretcher equipped with saline drips and oxygen. Shortly afterwards the ambulance sped away, blue lights flashing.

At the exit from the dockyard gate, an insignificant white Nissan followed. The driver suspected he knew where the ambulance's destination would be: the small private hospital used exclusively by Libya's inner circle. Situated off Al Fatah Street, it overlooked the sea near the Mitiga airport. He knew it well; passing it everyday to his job as a luggage handler at the airport.

The first sayanim kept his binoculars fixed on the *Juheina Star*. He remained there for three hours but no one else was evacuated. It was time to report.

***

'So, only one wounded body came off?'

'Yes.'

'Then the other two, including our own female agent, are either still on the ship or were buried at sea.'

'I can't see them still being on-board. Surely, they would have taken the corpses away.'

'Thank you for that. We'd be grateful if you can find out anything more about the state of the wounded man. His name is Quine but he may be registered as Khalil el Majid.'

'That won't be easy. There's no way we are going to be able to get into the al Maghribi hospital.'

'Then, we're going to have to think of something else.'

***

In 1991, the resumption of normal diplomatic relations between Britain and Libya was still eight years away. Following the Pan-Am bombing, relations had been severed; although a small charge d'affairs office remained. There were few staff: only four including the consul, plus two locally recruited low-grade administrative assistants. It was, therefore, something out of the ordinary when Brian Baxendale, the consul, received a ciphered request from Sir Peter Stacey.

Two days later, and after taking what he thought were tablets similar to aspirin, he complained to his wife of excruciating stomach pains. When he collapsed in his office, the authorities reacted according to his status and he was rushed to hospital with suspected appendicitis.

An inconclusive operation by the senior surgeon removed organs that were swollen and badly infected. Remaining in hospital for a further four days was recommended. It gave Baxendale sufficient time to befriend a medical orderly and discover that Quayle was next door, recovering from gunshot wounds. He was no longer on the critical list. It was thought he may be confined for a month before he would be strong enough to be released. Enquiries as to future plans for him were met with a blank stare.

A few days later, the diplomatic bag arrived in London partially answering MI6's director's questions.

The two Tripoli sayanims were told, via a chain of command that stretched from London to Tel Aviv via Rome, to watch the hospital round the clock, beginning in three weeks time.

***

'Where am I?'

'You are in a hospital in Tripoli,' replied the male nurse on duty.

'How did I get here? What happened?'

'I am not sure. You were shot twice and are lucky to be alive. You have been in a coma for the past three weeks. My instructions, now you are awake, are to ring reception.'

'Three weeks?'

'Yes, since you came here.'

He used the bedroom phone, and simply announced, 'Room 11 has come round.' There was a reply. The attendant nodded, saying, 'OK.'

'He will be here within the hour.'

'Who?'

'I don't know. Please try and remain as still as possible. One of the bullets punctured your right lung. It will take some time for the scars to heal. You are going to have to be patient.'

***

'My name is Mousad Safahar. I am Prince al Ouda's Private Secretary.'

Juan looked blank.

'You met the Prince in Ceuta.'

'Of course, I am sorry.'

193

'No, don't apologise. You have been through a lot during these past few weeks.'

'What am I doing here?'

'You may remember Felipe was to meet you at your hotel in Tunis and bring you to Tripoli?'

'Yes, but he turned up two days early.'

'Prince Ouda decided to use his yacht rather than drag you across the frontier by car. However, you had acquired an attractive female companion, I gather?'

'Yes, Alida.'

'She was German?'

'Yes.'

'We believe she was a British spy.'

'Rubbish!'

'Not so. We believe the IRA had somehow followed you to Tunis and were determined to assassinate you and Felipe for killing Nash in Ireland. However, the gunman who shot you on the quay was, himself, shot. We believe the so-called German female was keeping tabs on your movements. She had a colleague who, on seeing you about to be killed, opened fire in an attempt to save your lives. Unfortunately, he was a fraction of a second too late. Felipe and the girl died. We had to bury them at sea.'

'Alida is dead?'

'Yes, I am sorry.'

'It doesn't make any sense. Why would the British want to follow me?' And without waiting for a reply, Juan continued, 'I spent two wonderful days with Alida. She was holidaying in Tunis and she had agreed to travel with me on my motorbike as far as Cairo. If it had worked out, I was hoping to persuade her to come to Cape Town. When Felipe met her at the *Sheraton*, he was most reluctant to bring her along. However, I persuaded him it would be OK and Moab wouldn't mind. Furthermore, I speak good German and would swear she was German, not English.'

Mousad shrugged his shoulders. He was not convinced by Juan's protests. 'Talking of motorbikes,' he began, 'Prince Ouda has asked me to put two propositions to you.'

'Oh?'

'The first is that he is willing to buy you any bike you wish. He will arrange a genuine Saudi passport, with diplomatic status, that will get you across difficult borders such as between here and Egypt. If you wish to go home via Saudi and Pakistan then all will be arranged.'

'You said there was a second proposition.'

'He would like to meet you in Riyadh to discuss the details. I am not privy to the second option, except to say he is a most generous employer.'

'Employer?'

'Now you are stronger, we can arrange for you to fly to Saudi and meet him, if you wish? It can't do any harm.'

'No, I suppose not. At least I am heading in the right direction to get back to New Zealand.'

***

Two days later, the phone rang in the Rome office of the Israeli embassy; Mossad section.

'Tripoli is the city of three regions.'

There was a pause, before a voice asked, 'What happened there in 1804?'

'The USS Philadelphia was burned.'

'Report.'

'I was working at the airport this morning when a Royal Saudi HS125 executive jet arrived. It parked at the end of the runway and an ambulance drew up. I saw the New Zealander, Quine, go on-board. The aircraft took off at 1055 am.'

'Why have you left it until now to report? It's nearly 1800 hours.'

'I was not able to get away from work. I thought you would want to know.'

'Fine. Thank you.'

***

'So, we've no idea where the jet went?'

'No, I'm afraid not.'

'By now, if it went to Saudi, it will have landed. We must assume they want Quine for something; otherwise they would have eliminated him. Have you any sayanims in Saudi?'

'A few.'

'Then you must get them to keep their eyes peeled.'

'It has already been done.'

***

Having been met at the airport and transferred to a stretch limousine without going through customs, Juan found himself in a villa complete with a 30 metre oval-shaped swimming pool. In the large manicured gardens, sprinklers kept the grass green. Many varieties of conifers such as Korean firs, Lebanese cedars and Austrian pines provided shade and a heady aroma. The single-storey building was air-conditioned. He was shown to his room: a suite with a large sitting area and a veranda overlooking the pool and gardens. Nothing had been spared to make his visit as comfortable as possible. The fridge was complete with fresh fruit, various drinks, and his favourite snack – Danish pastries.

'If there is anything you desire, please ring the bell. It is my job to help you recover. My name is Fatima. I am your personal ayah.'

When she turned and was leaving the room, Juan noticed her colourful sari wrapped around her slim, petite figure. Until then he had been mesmerised by her large, dark eyes, smooth, swarthy skin and luscious, red lips. Standing no more than 5ft 4in, her long black hair, tied in a twisted ponytail, shone as if illuminated. He hadn't really heard what she had said. *What was her name?* he asked himself. He was

196

wondering if she was Indian rather than Pakistani when, in the doorway, she turned, smiled and added, 'Prince Ouda will meet you for dinner at 7.30 pm. If you wish to swim in the pool, please feel free to do so.' She turned and left; Juan was left admiring her beautiful, firm figure.

Juan decided not to swim. Instead, he settled on a sun-lounger in the shade on the veranda with a large orange juice and a Danish pastry. He soon nodded off.

CHAPTER 26

Wednesday 8th May 1991

'Shall I run you a bath or would you prefer a shower?'

He woke feeling groggy. He had been in a deep sleep. He rubbed his eyes. Standing in front of him was Fatima.

She handed him a large iced gin and tonic in a cut-glass beaker. 'It's a Tanqueray,' she said.

How did she know that's my favourite? I don't remember telling anyone.

He sat upright, thanking her.

'It is seven o'clock. Pre-dinner drinks will be on the veranda in thirty minutes.'

'I'll have a quick shower, thank you.'

She smiled and left. Juan was left noticing her dainty feet.

Half an hour later, refreshed and wearing a completely new outfit, laid out for him when in the shower, he ventured onto the veranda and headed in the direction of the conversations and laughter. Turning a corner at the end of the bungalow, he saw a group of three men in western lightweight suits, similar to his own. He recognised Prince al Ouda immediately. Behind them in a separate group, were three women in traditional Arab ankle-length dark dresses with long sleeves but not wearing head scarves.

'Ah, Alan. Allow me to introduce you to our dinner guests. This is Ali al Ghraizil, one of our Chiefs of Staff, and this is Mohammad Grilenci, a fellow backer of our organisation.'

Juan shook hands with each in turn before being introduced to the three wives. He noticed the women drank fruit juices; the men – G&Ts. Juan was not to speak with the wives again. Conversation before dinner was largely asking Juan to recount his experiences since leaving Ireland. Ali seemed to be the leader; his questions were more searching, more probing.

Is he trying to catch me out?

At the table, Ali asked, 'Why do you think we have brought you here?'

'I understood Prince Omar had a proposition to put to me.'

'We were wondering if you would undertake a task for us.'

'A task?'

'We need someone to teach English to some of our better students.'

'TEFL teachers are two-a-penny. Why me?' *I mustn't show too much enthusiasm.*

'Teaching English as a Foreign Language is one thing, but we need something else.'

'Oh?'

'We need someone with the motivation to get our students up to a good level of technical English. They need to know the difference between a resistor and a capacitor, implosion and explosion, how a detonator works, how to program a computer and so on.'

'My formal education in science stopped at "O" level.'

'Yes, but you have since acquired qualifications in marine engineering.'

'Well, sort of.'

'Don't be so modest. We will make it worthwhile.'

Juan said nothing; waiting for Ali to continue, but it was Prince Omar who offered, 'How about $20,000 per month paid into a numbered Swiss bank account. In addition you will receive free accommodation and so on.'

Juan said nothing for a while. He wanted to feign reluctance. 'Your students, what is their English like?'

'Virtually non-existent.'

'What age will they be?'

'Anything from sixteen to twenty-five.'

'Too late.'

'Sorry?'

'Too late. If you want youngsters capable of absorbing themselves into Western society, then you need to start teaching them English when they are five or six.'

'That could take time out from their studying the Koran.'

'Life is always a compromise.'

'You're saying we must begin teaching English as soon as we get them into our primary madrassas?'

'Yes, otherwise it will be hopeless. Give them to me as teenagers with a good command of English and within a year I will have them passing the Cambridge Overseas Examination Board's "O" level papers in science.'

'What do we do in the short term?'

'I will try my best. If they are bright and have a talent for picking up languages then, perhaps, in two years they may be reasonably conversant.'

'That's fine; our timescales are measured in decades.'

'I would need textbooks, audio-visual aids, a fully equipped laboratory with an assistant...'

'You can have whatever it takes.'

'I'm not sure; it's asking a lot to tie myself up for several years. I really would like to see Africa and South America before going home to New Zealand.'

'Look,' it was Mohammad, who interrupted, 'how much do you know about our cause?'

'Only what Moab told me.'

'Would you like to see life in the raw and why we feel the way we do?'

'What do you mean?'

'Let me take you to the West Bank and East Jerusalem. I'll show you how the Palestinians are being treated by the Yankee-backed Israelis.

You might come back feeling more sympathetic to our aim.'

'Which is?'

'To push the Zionists into the sea, or, at the very least, to their 1948 boundaries.'

***

Late the following afternoon, Juan found himself flying in a north-westerly direction with Mohammad as company. He guessed they were heading for Amman, but didn't ask. Juan was dressed in traditional Arab robes with a red and white keffiyeh. His beard had grown in the month since last shaving in Tunis; his skin had darkened. He could pass as a Saudi gentleman.

Mohammad had brought several maps, which he unfolded.

'Look at this map. It is of the West Bank of Jordan in 1971. Now look at the same map but dated 1991. What's the difference?'

'These red dots all over the place.'

'Exactly. Israeli settlements. 87 at the last count and growing at the rate of one a month. All illegal, of course.'

'I'd no idea there were so many.'

'No one in the West does. That's the bloody trouble. The Israelis get away with it because the UN is either too lazy or too impotent to do anything about it. As long as the US rules the roost and keeps the Saudis sweet by buying their oil, the Zionists are safe. With the fall of the Soviet Empire two years ago, Russian Jews are now pouring into Israel at the rate of 1,000 per week. Immigration is three times the annual population growth. They put them into Palestinian homesteads either on the West Bank or in East Jerusalem and boot out Arab families into squalid refugee camps. What I am going to do over the next few days is to show you the suffering we are undergoing. When we have landed in Amman, it is but an hour's drive to the border. We will enter the occupied territory through one of our safe passages when it is dark. We will stay near the Dead Sea until the early hours then cross the border on foot. One of our men will pick us up and drive us to Jerusalem in his Land Rover; be ready for a bumpy ride.'

Less than an hour after landing, Juan found himself in what he assumed was a safe house near the River Jordan. An elderly couple ran the house and seemed to know Mohammed well. They were used to him travelling through their home. While waiting to cross in the early hours, Juan had a chance to ask questions about al-Qaeda. He tried to be as subtle as possible. 'If I am going to work for the organisation, perhaps I should know something about it,' he began.

Mohammed was open with his replies; hiding nothing. Juan learned that there were ten madrassas in six different countries. Some countries he had expected: Afghanistan, Pakistan, Yemen and Libya; but two were a surprise: Syria and Somalia.

'None in Iraq, then?' he asked.

Mohammed laughed. 'No, poor old Saddam is bankrupt. He has lost Kuwait. He has no-fly zones imposed on him in the north and south. He has UN weapons inspectors crawling all over the place. I'm afraid Saddam is shafted. He was initially sympathetic to our cause and was friendly with Moab; after all, Iraq is still officially at war with Israel. But they fell out and now he doesn't want to know.'

'Where will I be teaching?'

'We are setting up what you might call an academy with selected pupils who show exceptional promise. We want them educated to a standard acceptable in the West that will allow them to go to American or British universities, then after graduating become sleepers.'

'Sleepers?'

'Yes. In the West they will gain skills useful to us. They may become pilots, doctors, scientists, computer programmers and so on. When the time is right they will use their skills to our advantage. You are the first link in a chain that may take ten or twenty years to come to fruition. I believe the plan is to build the academy in Syria near the Turkish border, but I am not sure. We operate like a multinational company and set-up local franchises. Whereas Honda produce motorbikes and then train technicians, salesmen and help create dealerships, we do the same except our product is the eventual capitulation of Israel. Our franchises, such as, say, the Yemen Group, will be tactically independent but operate within our strategic framework.'

'Where does your hardware come from?'

'The Irish source has recently dried up. However, with the Soviet empire collapsing, most of what we want comes from Russia through Turkmenistan and Afghanistan.'

'Not Libya, then?'

'No. Gaddafi is friendly but is trying to play it both ways. He wants to sell his oil for the best price, which means keeping the West sweet.'

He paused, and then added, 'We'd better get some shut-eye. We have a long night ahead of us.'

They left the safe house at 0200 hours. They walked, mostly in silence, for two hours. Juan estimated they had travelled about five miles, largely through scrub and lightly wooded terrain with some rock scrambling, before eventually rendezvousing with a battered Land Rover. Mohammed introduced Abu, their driver. 'Our journey will be uncomfortable as we have to travel over some rough ground. The Israelis patrol the main roads and stop anything suspicious. Palestinian registered vehicles with blue licence plates, like this one, are not allowed to travel on the main highways.'

During their passage, Mohammed explained that Abu's parents used to own a farm with 80 acres of olive trees; their main source of income.

'It was on a hillside and one day Israeli bulldozers arrived, ploughed-up the olive trees, some hundreds of years old, and burned them. They were dispossessed of their home and livelihood at a stroke. No compensation or explanation was given. Today, it is the site of a settlement called Maale Adumim with over 15,000 Jews living there, and growing all the time. Within ten years, it will be a city. You will see when we arrive there how the Israelis build wide roads to gain fast, easy access to the townships. The roads are barred to vehicles that have not got

Israeli permits. The police will shoot our tyres, laugh, and leave us abandoned if we try to travel on them. The dispossessed Palestinians live in a shanty town at the base of the hill. You will be appalled by the squalid conditions. Needless to say, Abu is one of our strongest supporters. We will rest with his parents for a while, and get some breakfast before we show you what is going on in East Jerusalem.'

Juan was shocked by what he saw when they arrived. It reminded him of the shanty townships he had seen on TV in South Africa: no proper sanitation, electricity cables lying on the ground, broken windows covered by sheets of polythene, communal water taps. The warmth of friendship offered to him, however, was genuine. Abu's mother proffered warm, newly baked bread with honey, and tea. They stayed until mid-morning when Mohammed announced it was time to go to watch a demonstration.

'Where?' asked Juan.

'There is a meeting to object to the building of 2,000 Israeli homes in the Har Homa district near Bethlehem. We will go there. I want you to see how Israeli justice is one-sided. There is to be a peaceful march to the central square in front of the town hall.'

***

Even though several miles from the gathering point of the march, they encountered road blocks and indiscriminate searches being carried out by Israeli troops.

'They are afraid of car bombs and are searching for anyone with arms,' explained Abu as they were stopped. 'We must walk the rest of the way.'

It seemed that most of the protesters were youths; all male. Juan noted most were dressed like youths anywhere in the West: jeans, tee shirts and trainers. In their traditional dress, he thought Mohammed and himself looked distinctly out of place. Nevertheless, the march went peacefully as it meandered through the narrow streets of old Bethlehem.

Eventually, they arrived in a small, open square. A row of police in riot gear, with shields and batons, stood three-deep preventing access to the town hall. Several protesters went forward to hand in what appeared to be a petition, but were pushed away. Shouting broke out; a few youths began picking up stones and throwing them. People were being pushed forward and the inevitable clashes began. Several groups of policemen broke ranks and, acting in a well-rehearsed manner, formed snatch squads. The unfortunates, who were caught, were beaten brutally. The effect was to inflame the crowd. Within minutes it was total chaos. Then several shots rang out. Juan, from his position at the rear of the action, noticed for the first time snipers on the roofs surrounding the square. There was screaming and terror as the protesters turned and tried to run away.

Mohammed grabbed Juan, nodded as if to say come with me and, together with Abu, they took shelter in a recessed doorway on the edge of the square. The protesters were running past five or six deep; the police giving chase. At least a dozen went by, hell-bent on catching the stragglers; no doubt to mete out punishment. The door behind them opened and an old woman beckoned the trio, 'Come inside.'

'Follow me.' She led them upstairs to a bedroom window overlooking the square. Already the square was empty except for three dead youths being dragged away by the militia. She turned to look at Mohammed, as if sensing she knew he was their leader, shrugged her shoulders, made the motion of spitting on the floor and said bitterly, 'They must be stopped.'

Clearly moved, Mohammed had difficulty in replying, 'They will be someday.'

'I won't live to see it, but make sure you do.'

CHAPTER 27

Friday 10th May 1991

They stayed with the old widow for several hours. She was glad of their company and insisted on giving them a late lunch – a lamb stew with black bread. When they left, she had tears in her eyes, 'Don't forget your promise, Mohammed.'

'I won't, someday there will be a Palestinian state with access to the sea.'

The streets were quiet; *had there ever been a riot?* They found their Land Rover and headed north into East Jerusalem. As they drove around, Mohammed pointed out numerous Jewish settlements expropriated from Arabs. 'In 1966, before the war, there were fewer than 1,500 Jews in East Jerusalem. Today they number over 150,000 – one hundred times as many. Forty per cent of East Jerusalem's population is now Jewish. They grab the title to the land and ignore the planning regulations that they strictly impose on us. They destroy our mosques. Their goal is the annexation of East Jerusalem and to unite it into a complete city – the capital of Israel.'

They carried on for some while, Juan noticing the obvious differences between new Israeli neighbourhoods and older Palestinian ones where paths were seas of mud and gravel, houses often little better than wooden shanty towns.

'Over there you see Pisgat Zeev,' said Mohammed pointing. 'It is one of the biggest Jewish communities; currently it has a population of

29,000. And over there on that hillside, Ramot has 16,000. When I was a boy they didn't exist.'

The rate of expansion jolted Juan. *That's the size of Douglas; built in less than 25 years. I'd no idea this was going on. I can see why they hate the Americans for all the backing they give Israel.*

'Mohammed, I've seen enough. I'm ready to go back.'

'We'll wait at Abu's parents' house until dark, and then retrace last night's journey.'

While they were waiting to leave, Juan spoke quietly to Mohammed, 'I've been thinking about the demonstration in Bethlehem.'

'Yes, what about it?'

'Do the Israeli police always give chase when the demonstrators flee?'

'Yes. They enjoy giving them a beating; often shooting them in the back.'

'If one of us had been dressed identically to them, they would not have noticed us joining them as they ran past the doorway?'

'No, I suppose not.'

'If we had strapped a bomb to ourselves, then we could have worked into their centre and blown them up; killing maybe a dozen of the bastards at one stroke.'

'Welcome to al-Qaeda!'

'Another thing, have you ever wondered where Israel gets its oil from?'

'We suspect much of it is from either Angola or Venezuela. There was a period when it came from Iran.'

'Iran? Surely not.'

'It was while the Iran contra affair was going on. Israel was supplying Khomeini with spares for his American Phantom aircraft. Iran had bought them when the Shah was in power. In exchange they were getting Iranian oil. But that has now stopped. Why do you ask?'

'You know I have a master mariner's ticket?'

'Yes.'

'If we could hijack a tanker bound for their oil terminal at Ashdod, south of Tel Aviv, and fill the bow with explosives, then we could set it to ram the port. It would destroy their facilities for months.'

'It would have to be planned carefully. I am not sure we have the skills to sail a tanker.'

'I will be able to help you and, no, I don't intend to blow myself up.'

'I'll put the idea to Moab when we get back to Riyadh.'

***

Not fully recovered from being shot in Tunis, Juan was surprised how long it took him to recover from his trip to Jerusalem and the West Bank. Several weeks went by with only Fatima, a well-stocked library, a fully equipped gymnasium, the swimming pool and Sky television for company. Mohammed had disappeared, as well as Prince Ouda. As the third week began he asked Fatima, who had kept their relationship restrained despite his attempts to be less formal, about leaving the compound and exploring the surrounding countryside.

'My instructions are strictly to accompany you at all times. I will have to get the chauffeur to drive the limousine.'

Juan had not realised Prince Ouda had so many staff. Fatima explained that she was one of twenty full-time employees. The cooks, gardeners and house servants were accommodated in staff quarters adjacent to the bungalow, but beyond a high wall.

'Riyadh is a city with a population of over two million people. Where do you want to go? If you read the guide book this evening, then we will be able to plan your trip. Perhaps you may wish to visit the Al Masmak Castle and go to the top of the TV tower?'

'I would like to buy you kabsa for lunch somewhere.'

She smiled briefly. 'I am sorry, but Prince Ouda has explicitly said I must not fraternise with you. I do not wish to be sacked. The walls have ears. I understand he will return tomorrow evening and has arranged for several important people to come and meet you. Wherever we go tomorrow, we must be back in plenty of time.'

It hadn't occurred to Juan that his apartment might be bugged. The thought, however, made him wonder how she knew there may be listening devices. He pondered about the conundrum for some time but drew no conclusions. He wondered, too, about Fatima. She had a rounded face; more Indian than Pakistani, he thought. Pakistani women, whom he had met, had more chiselled features and yet he knew her name meant *the daughter of Mohammad.* He puzzled no further and planned his day out.

Juan decided to visit the Al Masmak Castle in the morning followed by lunch at the top of the TV tower. Fatima accompanied Juan around the castle. As they listened to the guide, he noticed how her dress was much more conservative than usual: a black ankle-length dress with a white head covering – the hijab, instead of the multi-coloured saris she wore indoors. Coupled to her throwaway remarks the previous evening about the house being wired and her sober dress today, he began cogitating. A feeling in his waters was telling him something was not as it seemed.

When they arrived at the tower, Juan again asked her to accompany him. She shook her head, 'I am not fond of heights,' she replied. 'Please go on your own. The chauffeur and I will wait for you.'

There was only one entrance; presumably this was why she was happy to let him go unaccompanied.

'I could be as long as an hour,' he warned.

'That's all right,' she replied. 'We will wait for you.'

It would be the first time since the Isle of Man that he had been alone and unsupervised. One hundred and seventy metres high, the view from the observation deck was spectacular. He chose to lunch in the restaurant and ordered a fish kabsa. As he ate, he continued to think about Fatima's odd behaviour. He smiled to himself, as he paid by VISA, knowing that within hours the trace on the card would alert London to his location and, perhaps more importantly, assure MI6 that he was alive. *That's it – she wanted me to be alone!*

Within an hour of Juan returning to Prince Ouda's palatial residence, MI6 officers on the Middle East desk at Vauxhall Cross had picked up the VISA transaction in Riyadh. The phone rang in Sir Peter's office. 'Phil Jay here, sir, Middle East desk.'

'Yes, what is it Phil?'

'I thought you'd want to know that Bradda Head used his VISA card to buy lunch in the restaurant at the top of the TV tower in Riyadh earlier this afternoon. Looking at the amount, I'd say he was alone.'

'Thanks, Phil, leave it with me.'

He put the receiver down for a few seconds, and then dialled his opposite number. 'Charles, it's Peter.' He repeated what he had been told.

There was a brief silence before the Head of MI5 replied, 'Quayle has obviously been accepted by al-Qaeda but I am worried he may not be up to the job. How long do you think we should leave him out in the cold before we bring him back? What is he getting up to? Our problem is communications. It's all very well Mossad keeping an eye on him, but they haven't seen him for weeks. I'm worried, Peter, that he may disappear and not be seen again. At some time we've got to get him back and tell us what he knows.'

'OK. Let's think this through. Only we know he is in Riyadh. We know he is residing at one of Prince Ouda's several residences; he has at least three. I have three operatives in Riyadh and will transfer two more this afternoon from Amman. By tomorrow morning they'll be able to watch the houses round the clock. If Quayle so much as farts, we'll know about it.'

'That's fine until they move him.'

'If they fly him to another country, then as long as we know what aircraft he is on, our satellites can follow. Don't worry. We won't lose him again.'

That evening, as Juan dressed for dinner, he wondered who the important people would be. Prince Ouda greeted him as he entered the ante-room. He recognised his number-one wife. Also present was Ali al Ghraizil, but the big surprise was to see Moab.

'Moab,' said Juan, 'it's good to see you. Are you keeping well?'

'Yes, my friend, but more importantly are you fully recovered?'

'Thanks to your friend's kindness, yes. I am fighting fit.'

'I have been hearing about your ideas from Omar and Mohammed. It is good that you have agreed to join us. We have sourced a secure estate from where you will be able to teach our best students English, Japanese and Russian.'

'Japanese and Russian? I didn't agree to that.'

'Ah, but you told me that you could speak Japanese and we have to buy equipment from them. They are cunning little bastards who will rook us if we're not on our guard.'

'Why? What do you do want from them?'

'They are the world's leaders in electronics. We need sophisticated and specialised tools for our work, especially in the field of communication switches and relays. We will require remote electronic detonators that can be triggered by radio signals, computers that can handle our growing need for worldwide communications without the Yankees knowing. That sort of bespoke equipment is not off-the-shelf. Our negotiators will have to speak Japanese fluently.'

'And Russian? Don't forget I have only agreed to stay for two years. I can't do everything.'

'Now that the IRA is being watched by the British, we are sourcing arms from the former Soviets. We need fluent Russian speakers too. You will get us started. Our exceptional pupils will become our future teachers. You will be our teachers' teacher.'

'And when am I supposed to start all this?'

'Tonight.'

'You're joking.'

'No, my friend. As soon as we have finished dinner, you and Ali are leaving for our new college in Naxcivan.'

'Naxcivan in the Caucasus?'

'Yes. It's an enclave of Azerbaijan between Turkey, Armenia and Iran. It's perfect for our needs – out of the way, a good climate; no one will bother you. We have sourced a 1,000 hectare estate with suitable buildings that will make a perfect boarding school. We have already installed a small domestic staff. Your job is to set the whole thing up: select academic staff and acquire the equipment you need. In effect, you will be the university chancellor.' He laughed at what he thought was a joke. 'Prince Ouda's PPS has agreed to be the bursar. You will fly there tonight. It is only three hours away.'

'When can I expect the first students to arrive?'

'We have selected them already. We thought about two months for you to get things up and running should be enough.'

'The school might not be very efficient in that timescale.'

They all laughed politely. 'Don't worry, my friend. I am not expecting instant results. Remember, this is a ten or twenty year project. Rome, they tell me, wasn't built in a day.' There were further polite laughs.

For some reason the others fear this man. What is there about him that makes him so special?

By ten o'clock local, 7 pm Greenwich Mean Time, Juan and Ali were leaving Riyadh for their two and a half hour flight to Naxcivan City. Accompanying them was Mousad Safahar, who, when greeting Juan, enthused at becoming the bursar. There was little conversation; it was time to get their heads down. On arrival, Juan noted the airport buildings were modern and the roads well surfaced. The clock in the terminal showed the same time as his watch; they were in the same time zone as Riyadh.

Probably about a 1,000 miles further north.

'We have about a seventy mile journey to our estate, near the second largest town, Ordubad. However, as we go further into the countryside, the roads become narrow and twisty. It will take about three hours to get there.'

Juan shut his eyes and was soon asleep in the back of the warm Mercedes.

✱✱✱

After the women had retired, Moab and the Royal Prince sat relaxing together with a bottle of Glenmorangie.

'Ossie.'

'Yes?'

'Do you really trust him?' asked Ouda.

'No, of course not. How can you ever trust an infidel? However, he is useful to us. I can't believe it was three months ago when he casually dropped into the conversation that he could speak Arabic, Russian and Japanese. I saw his potential, but knew then that he was a plant. I realised he was no Kiwi travelling around Europe; it didn't add up. Consequently, I deliberately didn't quiz him too closely how he could speak so many languages. It was a clever ruse; he's CIA, MI6 or an Israeli agent. We will let him get the madrassa started, but make sure he cannot communicate to his masters where we are. In a year's time when it is fully operational, we will have our own trusted teachers in place and then Mousad can get rid of him.'

CHAPTER 28

Wednesday 29th May 1991

The sun was rising by the time Ali, Mousad and Juan reached the site of the new madrassa, two miles east of Ordubad. Juan instantly recognised, from his experience in the Army, that their estate was a former Russian military encampment. He stopped and stared.

Ali saw his reaction and explained, 'It's the site of a former Soviet Army fort from the days when Naxcivan was one of the Soviet Socialist Republics. It has been closed for two years since the Russians left, but is ideal for our purposes. Everything works: the water and sewers are sound; we can generate our own electricity. It's well situated on high ground and there's plenty of space to expand. It was probably sited here because we are only a mile from the Iranian border across the Aras River, over there.' He pointed south. 'The fort could accommodate up to 500 troops.'

'But we're not going to be that big.'

'True. However, the soldiers' ten-man huts are being converted to four-man units to give each student his own room; other ex-dormitories will become classrooms. The former officers' mess will accommodate the academic staff while the old NCOs' mess will house the domestics. Eventually we envisage there will be one hundred students here, with twenty academics and, perhaps, a further twenty domestics. It will bring in a fair income for the locally employed servants and suppliers.'

'But we must be close to Nagorno-Karabakh? I thought there was a war going on there.'

'There has been a struggle going on for three years, but it's all over, bar the shouting. Nagorno is being annexed by Armenia with Azeri's consent in exchange for Armenia agreeing Naxcivan its independence. We will be quite safe here as the Muslim states, Turkey and Iran, are acting as guarantors to Naxcivan's freedom. The Armenians won't do anything as Gorbachov brokered the deal at a treaty in Moscow.'

Despite Ali's assurances, Juan felt uncomfortable. He knew some of the history of the Caucases from his Russian language training at Beaconsfield. He remembered how Lenin had tried to set up a Transcaucasian Soviet Republic in 1918 that lasted five minutes before wars broke out between Georgia, Armenia and Azerbaijan, the latter supported by Turkey. By 1922 Stalin and the Bolsheviks had absorbed all three countries into the Soviet empire. He suspected Gorbachov's promise to enforce boundaries that had been disputed for centuries could be meaningless.

The largest of the buildings was the original mansion of a once rich estate. They were met by the domestic manager who appeared to know Mousad and welcomed him warmly. Juan was taken to his en suite rooms before the three met in the dining room for breakfast. There were already several local servants in attendance.

Later, Juan spent the morning wandering around the patch. The site's boundaries were triangular, covering about two square miles. The ground sloped gently south towards the Aras River. Beyond the camp's boundary there were vineyards and in the distance he could see what appeared to be fields of cotton. He was surprised such crops could grow in the Caucases.

In two days time it will be June, perhaps I can expect a hot summer.

The original barrack-block huts were spaced with shrubs between them, ensuring privacy. There was a football pitch, a running track and a gymnasium at the north end of the camp. He had to agree with Ali, the site was ideal for a madrassa. However, the parlous political squabblings between the surrounding countries worried him. So too did the lack of communication facilities with the outside world. Apart from the phone in Mousad's office, there was nothing. He was well and truly on his own.

He began his job in the time-honoured way: drawing up a list of requirements and apportioning priorities. After a week of brainstorming, the list had 77 tasks. He costed them with Mousad, altered some priorities and set to work.

Six weeks had passed when his first monthly statement arrived from his Swiss bank account, via a forwarding address in Riyadh. It triggered an idea. Since arriving at the madrassa, he had given the problem of communications considerable thought. One day, when Mousad appeared to be busy, he approached him. 'Look, Mousad, I'd like to transfer a small sum of money to my widowed mother's account so that I can boost her pension. I was thinking of $500 per month.'

'Fine.'

Juan was surprised. He had expected some opposition. *He has other things on his mind.*

Mousad gestured to the fax machine. Juan wrote out the instructions direct to Switzerland: Beginning on 1 Aug 91, **$500** monthly to be sent to – **Isle of Man Bank, Athol Street, Douglas. Sort Code: 55-91-00. Name: Alan Quine. A/C No: 10799436. Authority: 2211630310404477.** Mousad neither checked the instruction nor noticed the slight smile on Juan's face as he left the office.

Mousad proved to be a competent bursar; he had the knack of getting equipment quickly. By late July, the first students began arriving. Juan had given considerable thought to how he would teach English from scratch. He need not have worried. The initial ten students, with ages varying between 15 and 20, had different nationalities: three Afghans, three Pakistanis, two Yemenis, an Omani and, rather surprisingly thought Juan, a Chechen. All ten had a good smattering of English, albeit with different accents.

He found the medium of film helpful. The class would initially watch a film, then when they saw it the second time, Juan would stop the projector every few minutes to discuss what had not been understood. After three weeks he insisted English had to be spoken at all times. He wanted their accents to improve and used suitable recordings to highlight the BBC dialect. A system of fines was agreed if students broke the *English-only* rule, such as having to clear the dishes from the table after meals. Each pupil built their own dictionary of difficult words and colloquial phrases. Progress was rapid.

By early October, he began science lessons. Mousad had provided two well equipped laboratories, each with their own lab assistant – one for physics and one for chemistry. The technicians were both Jordanian and spoke good English. He was able to rope them in to assist with lessons. The enthusiasm from his charges created an atmosphere with students competing to outshine each other.

***

Meetings between the Heads of the British Security Services take place regularly each month, except in August – the month for holidays. Hosting the gathering rotates. On Wednesday 4th September, it was the Foreign Office's turn and Sir Peter Stacey was chairman. Sir Charles represented the Home Office, Sir Richard Vincent represented the Ministry of Defence. Sir Peter Imbert – the Commissioner of the Metropolitan Police – represented Special Branch.

Whilst going round the table under 'Any Other Business', the Chief of the Defence Staff asked, 'By the way, whatever happened to that fellow the RAF sunk in the Bay of Biscay?'

Peter Stacey looked at his colleague from MI5 before replying, 'To be quite frank, we're not sure where he is. We know he was in Riyadh on 29th of May. He was recovering from being shot in Tunis.'

'Is he OK?'

'Yes, we think so. Al-Qaeda took him to a hospital in Tripoli where he underwent an operation. They then flew him to Riyadh for R and R. We mounted a twenty-four hour watch on where we thought he was staying but never saw him. We called it off after two months. I'm afraid he could be anywhere. We are certain he has al-Qaeda's confidence and is probably at one of their madrassas where they could be using his linguistic skills.'

'How many madrassas have they got?'

'Again, we are unsure. We suspect five or six: Iraq, Afghanistan, Pakistan, Yemen and maybe Somalia. It's that sort of info that we were hoping Quayle would come up with.'

'But he's no use if he can't communicate.'

'Quite. However, we do know he is alive. For two months now, small sums of money have been transferred into his Isle of Man bank account from Switzerland.'

'Can't you trace from where the money came?'

'I'm afraid not. We can't even find out which Swiss Bank is used as the Swiss centralise money transfers through a holding company to guarantee anonymity. I believe Quayle set up a Standing Order to let us know he is safe. Now we have simply to wait.'

***

Unconsciously, Juan was modelling the madrassa on St Bees. He insisted the students should partake in sport and persuaded Ali, who was effectively the school's governor and sponsor and regularly visited them, to employ a physical education specialist. He insisted lunch was communal in the large messing hall. He believed the success of the madrassa would depend on everyone knowing what everyone else did: contentment was the key.

The two Imams, who had arrived with the first students, were flexible with prayers, despite being radical Islamists. However, studying the Koran took three hours daily. They mixed well with the other staff and Juan was surprised how relaxed they were in his presence; frequently joking about him being a bloody infidel. He was left in no doubt, however, that they were the powerhouse behind the madrassa's *raison d'etre*: to brainwash the pupils into risking all for the future of Islam.

The first English teacher to join the staff in October, Nasser Khouri, had spent time in the Royal Jordanian Air Force as an aircraft technician. He had been trained by the RAF: firstly learning technical English at the RAF School of Education at RAF Upwood in Cambridgeshire and then undertaking an eighteen month long course at RAF Cosford, near Wolverhampton. Juan saw him taking over the reins in the future. By December progress was so rapid, thanks to Nasser's help, that Juan entered all ten students for the June 1992 Cambridge Overseas GCSE papers in Chemistry and Physics. He told Ali that the first students would be ready to leave in July.

'Excellent. We will begin preparing the necessary paperwork for their entry into Britain and the United States.'

'What plans have you for them?'

'Some will train to be pilots in the US where it is quicker and cheaper than anywhere else. It also raises fewer questions; especially in Florida where every youngster wants to fly. In Britain, the medical professions are more highly considered and some will become doctors; others, perhaps, train drivers or master mariners like yourself. One or two may come back here and teach the future students.' He added that four exceptional students had been selected to learn Japanese and would be arriving in April, along with a further 26 for Russian and the rest – English.

'We will be almost full up.'

'Yes, the grand plan is beginning to be played out.'

'I am going to be heavily reliant on Nasser to teach the English students as Japanese and Russian will become my full time job.'

'As you asked, Mousad has begun the process of acquiring two suitable language laboratories and thinks he has found a Japanese technician and a Russian speaker to help you. Moab is delighted with the overall progress you have made.'

CHAPTER 29

Monday 4th May 1992

The monthly meeting of the security chiefs on Monday 4th May 1992 was held in the Main Building of the Ministry of Defence – seventh floor. Field Marshal Sir Richard Vincent, CDS, chaired and began by declaring that Item One on the agenda would move to Item Two.

'You may not know, gentlemen,' he began, 'but this morning at 0500 hours local time, that's about six hours ago, Armenia invaded Naxcivan. It is, of course, a consequence of the breakup of the Soviet Union. Although you will remember that last August's Coup against Gorbachev failed miserably, many of the hardliners escaped prosecution, frequently returning to their ethnic states to continue creating trouble. One of the most dangerous areas is Nagorno-Karabakh where the Christian population, mostly Armenian by background, was ruled from Muslim Azerbaijan. The invasion of the Muslim populated Naxcivan by the Armenians is a desperate attempt to get Nagorno recognised, once and for all, as part of Armenia. Your reaction may well be, "So what?" However, the situation is explosive. Already the Turkish Prime Minister, Suleyman Demirel, has announced that he considers the shelling of Naxcivan towns as a breach of the 1921 Treaty of Kars. He has made it clear that if the Armenians don't withdraw then he will declare war against them. Typically, Russia has, within the last hour, come into the dispute by declaring that an invasion of Armenia by Turkish forces, a part of NATO don't forget, could trigger a Third World War. I have just been passed a signal from Washington, that the American forces based at Incirlik have been put on Red Alert.'

It was the Metropolitan Police Commissioner who asked, 'What is this Treaty of Kars?'

'In effect it was an agreement that the sovereignty of Naxcivan would be guaranteed jointly by Turkey and Russia. The problem is the old thorny one of religion. Turkey is Muslim, Naxcivan is Muslim, Russia is Christian, and Armenia is fiercely Christian. I over simplify, perhaps, but that's the nub of it.'

As he spoke, his Aide de Camp knocked, entered and gave CDS a further signal. He read it to himself and then issued a deep sigh. 'And just to confirm what I have been saying, gentlemen, American satellites are reporting seeing Iranian troops moving towards the southern Naxcivan border town of Ordubad.'

'More bloody Muslims!' exclaimed the policeman.

It was Sir Charles who asked the Service Chief, 'Have we many servicemen in Incirlik?'

'About 100 RAF personnel. There is a squadron of Tornadoes there helping patrol the No-fly Zone over Iraq. They're supported by technicians, intelligence analysts and a few administrators. They are all under the command of the US-NATO Base Commander.'

'How long have the Turks given the Armenians to withdraw?' asked Peter Stacey.

'Demirel hasn't said, but I can't see the Turkish Army being ready to invade Armenia in anything less than three weeks,' replied the general.

'In that case,' replied Stacey, 'the next few weeks could be interesting.'

'The situation is made more complicated by the fact that the Armenians are trained by the Russians. There are hundreds of Russian so-called advisers in Armenia and each of their divisions has at least one Russian liaison officer.'

***

When in May 1992, Armenia declared war on Naxcivan, their excuse was that Naxcivan had been shelling Armenian villages in the former Nagorno-Karabakh from the hilltops for some time and they had lost patience. Their initial advances had been minimal; capturing Naxcivan's exclave of Karki, a tiny village with a few farms through which Armenia's main north-south highway passes.

On Thursday 21st May, alarmed at the reaction of Iran to send troops to their northern border with Naxcivan, but fortified by Russian moral support, the Armenians decided to make a belligerent gesture by advancing along the southern border of Naxcivan from Agarak in the former Nagorno-Karabakh. A squadron of 200 troops in armoured personnel carriers met no opposition and advanced some 12 miles in under two hours. The Naxcivan road ran parallel to the Aras River on the north side and in places was clearly visible from the parallel Iranian road to the south. The forces could wave to each other. The Armenians then received an order to stop and take up a position five miles east of Ordubad.

'There's an old Russian base a further mile or so from here. I remember it when I was a subaltern,' remarked Captain Anatoly Smyslov, the Russian liaison officer to his Armenian Major, Tigran Akopian.

'OK. Let's stop there.'

Who was the most surprised that morning will never be known. Was it the Armenian troops, with their Russian adviser, at finding the former camp being used as some sort of international school, or was it Juan with his staff and students being surrounded at 11am by a squadron of armed troops who herded them into the large mess hall? It soon became obvious that language was a problem: no one in the madrassa spoke Armenian while none of the troops spoke Arabic. After several attempts to find a common tongue, Juan asked if anyone spoke Russian.

Captain Smyslov introduced himself. 'You speak Russian?' he asked.

'Yes, but it is a long time since I used it. What are you doing here?'

'Don't you know? Armenia has invaded Naxcivan.'

'No, we are cut off from the outside world. We are an international school.'

'I am sorry, but our orders are to stay here until we are told to advance or withdraw.'

'Then, can I ask we conduct ourselves in a civilised manner?'

'Of course.'

Juan and Anatoly announced to their own sides the agreed stalemate in Arabic and Armenian respectively.

The solitary telephone line to Ordubad was cut.

That afternoon the Armenians began digging in and organising their guard rota. Everyone was to remain in the main hall sitting on the floor, there were to be no prayers, no talking, and toilet facilities were supervised. The domestic servants were allowed to manage water and food. Juan and Anatoly remained in each other's company in a small office next to the hall where they were easily accessible; they were the only way of communicating between the two groups.

Captain Smyslov was of average height, but slim build. Fair haired with bottomless pale blue eyes, he commanded attention and respect. Although junior in rank to the Armenian major, Juan felt he was in charge. There was something about him – Juan couldn't put his finger on it. *Arrogance? No, the wrong word. An air of self-esteem? Better. He comes from an important Russian family, perhaps?*

'What are you doing here?' asked the Russian. 'You are obviously not a Muslim like the rest.'

'It's a long story. Can we talk confidentially?'

'Of course.'

'Why has your advance into Naxcivan been stopped?'

'I suspect a ceasefire is being negotiated as we speak.'

'What will happen then?'

'I expect we will withdraw back to Armenia with a guarantee that Nagorno-Karabakh will be finally accepted as being part of Armenia by Azerbaijan, Turkey and the other Islamic States.'

'Can I suggest that when you withdraw you take some hostages to ensure your safety?'

'Why?'

'It will be a cover for me to leave.'

'You are being held here against your will?'

'Yes. I could be a useful source of information to your intelligence people.'

'What nationality are you, then?'

'I am a New Zealander.'

'Then I will repeat my first question. What are you doing here in the middle of nowhere, so far away from home?'

'I wish I could tell you. You're going to have to trust me. If you can get me to your Senior Intelligence Officer in Yerevan, I promise he will appreciate your foresight in rescuing me.'

'Why should I trust you?'

'I'll give you two reasons. Firstly, have you ever heard of BRIXMIS?'

'Yes, of course, but I never served in East Germany. How do you know of it?'

'How do you think I can speak such grammatically correct Russian?'

'I did think your Russian was rather formal!'

They both laughed at the observation that Juan's Russian was rather old-fashioned and lacking modern colloquialisms.

'Then isn't it obvious how I know about BRIXMIS, or do I have to spell it out?'

'You were in British military intelligence!' exclaimed the captain.

Juan merely nodded, before adding, 'The second thing is this. One of those students your men are holding in the main hall is a Chechen.'

'Which one?'

'I'll leave you to find out. It will be more convincing if you singly interrogate them. Ask Mousad, the bursar, for their passports. You will find they're false. Mine is also a forgery.'

'I am prepared to help, but you must answer my question. What are you doing here? Indeed, what is an international college doing here?'

'The school is a front for training Islamic fundamentalists.'

'God, if I tell Major Akopian he will massacre the lot of you before

224

we leave. You know what the Armenians are like, they hate Muslims and any excuse…' His voice tailed away.

'You mustn't let that happen. Less than a mile away, across the river, is the Iranian Army. They will be watching us as we speak. As soon as you withdraw, a platoon will be sent across to see what has happened. If they find something like that, they will cut you off before you get back to Nagorno-Karabakh. Indeed you may already be cut off.'

'No, we left twenty-man patrols every two miles. They are in constant touch with us. So far everything is quiet. But, I agree with you. It will be sensible if we take half a dozen hostages with us to guarantee our safety from the Iranians.'

The following day, a Friday, the tension mounted. For the Muslims it was their holy day and not being allowed the freedom to go to prayer was creating an explosive situation. It was alleviated when Captain Smyslov confided with Juan that a declaration of peace and an agreement was to be signed that evening between the President of Armenia, Levon Ter-Petrossian and Heydar Aliyev, the leader of Naxcivan. The deal was being co-signed by Gorbachev and Suleyman Demirel.

'Major Akopian has been instructed to withdraw at once. We will be leaving within the hour. However, he wants six hostages. We will take five students, plus yourself.'

Juan sought out Mousad. 'Look they are returning to Nagorno-Karabakh and will be gone within the hour. However, they are taking half a dozen hostages to ensure they are not attacked by the Iranians en route. They wanted either you or me to go. I have volunteered. They will release us when they are safely over the border. Perhaps you can arrange for transport to come and pick us up?'

An hour later, Juan was bundled with the students into the rear of a five-tonner, including, he noticed, the Chechen. As the choking dust from the road entered through the canvas covers, Juan watched their madrassa disappear over the tailboard of their truck. Progress was steady, the convoy growing as the dispersed Armenian troops were picked up. Juan assured the five students that once at the border, they would be released and he had arranged with Mousad for transport to come for the return journey of some dozen, or so, miles.

It took nearly two hours to reach the deserted border post. They drove through the barriers and stopped. They were ordered out and Captain Smyslov appeared from his leading Lada 4x4 jeep. 'You are to come with me,' he ordered. 'The others will remain here under guard. Major Akopian wants to ensure we are not followed.'

It struck Juan as a strange thing to do, but he didn't query the order. They drove away, leaving the Armenians and students behind.

'I have been in touch by radio with our HQ in Yerevan. As soon as I said you had been in BRIXMIS, they demanded to see you as soon as possible. They are sending a helicopter to pick us up. When we get to Agarak, we can have a light lunch before it arrives.'

'Are you accompanying me to Yerevan?'

'Yes.'

Agarak was little better than a border village. The lunch in the police barracks broke up the two hour wait. A journey that would have taken eight or nine hours by road was reduced to a one-hour flight. They arrived at Erebuni Airport, on the southern edge of Yerevan, at almost exactly 1700 hours.

A staff car was waiting to take the two officers to a military complex at the edge of the airfield. The airfield had been built by the Russians in WW2 and Juan could see a pair of Mig-23 aircraft of the Armenian Air Force in front of a hangar. The style of the military complex, surrounded by a two-metre high fence, reminded Juan of many of the RAF stations, usually built in the late 1930s, that he had visited whilst in the Army.

They entered the officers' club and Juan was introduced to a tall, well-built, fifty-something, uniformed officer.

'This is Alan Quine, about whom I told you,' said Captain Smyslov.

The Colonel offered his hand and shook Juan's warmly. 'Colonel Vasily Veresov, Soviet Security Service, formerly KGB. We have the same traditions as you Brits on a Friday evening – Happy Hour.'

He slapped Juan on the back and practically knocked him over as he led him, still gripping his shoulder like a vice, to the bar. There was no asking what he would like to drink. A full glass of vodka was pushed into his hand. Veresov raised his own, 'To glasnost and Anglo-Russian cooperation,' he boomed, and downed his drink in one.

Juan repeated the toast; obliging his host but struggling with his drink. The bar was full of officers – all drinking vodka. By the third drink, Juan was beginning to realise he could not keep up with Colonel Veresov and dearly hoped they would soon adjourn to the dining room. It was Captain Smyslov who stepped in to save the day.

'Colonel, Alan has not had a substantial meal today. Perhaps, he may be allowed to freshen up and have dinner. Then I am sure he will rejoin you in the bar.'

'An excellent idea, Smyslov. Take Major Quayle to his room. I will join you both for dinner when you come down.'

It wasn't until Juan was ascending the stairs with Anatoly that the significance of what had been said sunk in. Three treble vodkas had slowed his instincts: *How the hell did Veresov know my real name?*

CHAPTER 30

Friday 22nd May 1992

Mousad had not bothered to send the madrassa's minibus to fetch the six hostages. *It won't do them any harm to walk.* Instead he concentrated his efforts that Friday afternoon getting the telephone working. He needed to make contact with Riyadh and inform them of developments. It was almost 1800 hours by the time the engineer from Ordubad had fixed the line. Mousad contacted Ali al Ghraizil at Prince Ouda's residence soon afterwards.

'We heard about the Armenian invasion and hoped it wouldn't affect you,' Ali said.

'The Armenians, with a Russian officer, were here for twenty-four hours. When they left this morning they took six hostages: el Majid and five students. They said they would be released when they reached the Nagorno-Karabakh border, twenty kilometres away. They will be walking back now and should arrive here in the next hour or two.'

'Fine. When they return contact me again. In the mean time, I will alert Moab and the Prince to let them know what's going on.'

It fell dark soon after nine o'clock, but no one had returned. Mousad felt uncomfortable but consoled himself that the students and el Majid had either decided to stop for the night or else they hadn't been released immediately. *In the morning I will send the minibus to look for them,* were his last thoughts before retiring for the night.

Juan remembered little of Friday evening. He went to bed, head spinning and woke up with a thirst in the middle of the night. He quenched it, reinvigorating the alcohol, and fell into a deep slumber.

He dreamt he watched five men being marched into the shallows of a river as he hid behind nearby rocks. Ten troops armed with sub-machine guns lazily stood in a group smoking until their officer shouted for them to fall into line. 'Aim, fire.' The five men fell as one into the shallows of the river; their bodies floating as the water turned red.

He woke; sweating all over. The room was hot. He was thirsty – again. He opened the window and a cool breeze entered. He drank more water to help his dehydrated body. With the alcohol reignited, he fell onto the bed. Soon he was asleep; this time peacefully.

It was almost nine o'clock when he woke. He shaved, showered, dressed and wandered downstairs to the dining room. Captain Smyslov was waiting for him. They ate together while Smyslov explained that, despite it being Saturday, Colonel Veresov wished to interview him at ten o'clock.

'How did he know my name was Quayle?' asked Juan.

'I didn't know he did,' replied Anatoly.

'But that's what the Colonel called me last night.'

'Then you'd better ask him. I merely signalled Yerevan HQ that I had met someone claiming to have been in BRIXMIS and gave them your description. I mentioned you spoke Russian and Arabic. They insisted I bring you here and sent the helicopter.'

Juan's question was soon answered when they arrived in the Colonel's large, dark, wood-panelled, sombre office. The three men sat in comfortable chairs around a small coffee table.

'Smyslov's description of a forty year old dark-haired officer claiming to have been in BRIXMIS who spoke Russian and Arabic allowed our computer in Moscow to identify you in seconds. I have here a fax of your file, Major Quayle. It makes interesting reading. I see Brigadier Lutikov set you up with a seventeen year old German girl. The affair seems to have ruined your career. I am sorry about that.'

'In some ways he did me a favour. She was nearer twenty-two, by the way. I was never very happy in uniform and have always been something of a black sheep. I completed my sixteen-year commission in the Army and became a teacher of modern languages. Why did Lutikov want to set me up, in particular?'

'Lutikov is one of the old school. I am surprised he and his cohorts survived last August's *coup d'état*. However, he was always a slippery bugger. Someday he will come a cropper. He probably saw you as a rising star and a potential long-term threat. He knew of your penchant for the ladies, saw it as a weakness, and, being something of a pervert himself, decided to trap you.'

Juan smiled, 'And I fell for it. I admit I was rather wayward ten years ago. You mentioned an August coup. What coup? I never heard of it.'

The Colonel frowned. 'Are you saying you never knew we had a two-day revolution in Moscow last August?'

'No. In Naxcivan we were cut off from the World's news.'

'Smyslov can fill you in on the details but last year a group of old time communists tried to take over control of Russia, believing that Gorbachev was giving away too much power to the republics. The coup collapsed and the gang of eight who had elected themselves to run the country were tried and either executed, imprisoned, or committed suicide.' He shrugged his shoulders as if to indicate he couldn't care less. 'I have often wondered if Lutikov was involved.'

He paused before continuing, 'However, to get back to you. Smyslov tells me you have information that might be of interest to us. First of all I would like to know how a former British Army Officer comes to be in a terrorist training camp in the middle of nowhere.'

Juan saw little point in concealing the *raison d'etre* of his mission that began with the visit of Sir Charles to St Bees almost two years previously. He avoided details such as the attack by the Nimrods, and the cooperation between Mossad and MI6. However, he admitted Billy Tote was a crude atomic bomb acquired by al-Qaeda from the IRA, but was now at the bottom of the Atlantic as a result of the *Glengarriff* sinking. *'An explosion in the engine room.'* He described their rescue, their escape thanks to the bandits making a mistake, their travels across North Africa and the mysterious shooting in Tunis. *'Probably the GEO.'*

It was one o'clock by the time Juan had brought the officers up to date. Apart from coffee and biscuits being served, there had been few interruptions. Captain Smyslov was the unofficial secretary and took notes.

They adjourned for lunch and, during the meal, preceded by several vodkas in the bar adjacent to the dining room, Colonel Veresov admitted, rather surprisingly, that he knew nothing of al-Qaeda. 'Perhaps someone higher up knows something and considers their threat is purely against the West. However, if they are now training Chechens, Moscow will be interested. I have been ordered to send you to Moscow on the evening plane with Captain Smyslov. I will fax ahead my report. You will meet Brigadier Beliavsky, one of Lutikov's men. His staff will give you a fuller interrogation. I am sure that if you cooperate, everything will work out all right.'

Juan wasn't convinced.

Nevertheless, he was reassured to some extent when Veresov added, 'It is in both our interests that we pull together on this one. The threat from suicide bombers in Moscow's Metro could be as great as it would be in London's underground.'

The Colonel had made a valid point, and Juan felt Veresov was taking the threat from fundamental Islamists seriously. Here was one senior Russian officer who was open to believing there may be an enemy within both their midsts. It was strange and worrying, however, that he had never heard of al-Qaeda.

★★★

Meanwhile in Naxcivan, after breakfast, Mousad asked Nasser to accompany him to the border. An hour later, they were staring at an empty guard post. The barrier across the road had been left upright. The area was deserted, the barren rocky landscape eerily silent, except for a flock of buzzards picking and squabbling at what appeared to be the flesh of some sheep on a small rocky beach in the bend of the river, 50 metres away.

They approached the birds, Nasser firing shots with his revolver to frighten them away. The sight that awaited them made them stop in their tracks; both were physically sick. Partially eaten bodies, covered in congealed blood, lay in a heap; their flesh hacked off their backs by the claws and beaks of the buzzards. There were swarms of flies. In the small inlet, the water was red. It didn't need a criminal pathologist to see that the men had been shot by automatic gun fire. Some bodies were riddled with as many as half a dozen holes.

'Who could have done this?' asked Nasser.

'The bloody Armenians,' replied Mousad.

As he walked slowly towards the stinking corpses, a flash of light suddenly hit Mousad in the eyes. Someone was looking at them from the southern side of the River Aras. Their binoculars had caught the sun and reflected it onto Mousad's face. 'We're being watched,' he said.

Nasser looked over the river, but could see no one.

'I am going across to see if they know anything about this.'

Mousad found a stick, tied his white handkerchief to it, and waved. Then, fully dressed, he walked into the river. It was shallow enough for him to cross; at no point was it higher than his waist. As he reached the other bank, Nasser, who had remained behind, saw two armed soldiers emerge from behind some scrub. Mousad met them, shook hands, and then fell into a parlay with much gesticulation and pointing. After five minutes, Mousad returned.

'Have you counted the bodies?' he asked as he approached Nasser from the shallows.

'No, I was too shocked to even think about it.'

They counted; there were five.

'As I thought,' said Mousad. 'El Majid is missing. The Iranians watched the whole thing. El Majid was driven away by the Russian liaison officer as soon as they crossed into Nagorno. The Armenians remained here at the border until 1800 hours when the armistice was simultaneously signed in Moscow, Ankara and Tehran. Then they lined up our boys in the shallows and shot them.'

'The bastards!'

'You stay here to keep the buzzards away. I'll go back as quickly as possible and return with some volunteers, sheets, and the madrassa's truck. We will take the bodies back as quickly as possible and get the Imams to bury them.'

By mid-afternoon, the bodies were being buried according to Muslim traditions in the grounds of the former Russian Army camp. Mousad made contact with Riyadh to explain what he had found at the border. It was Prince Ouda who listened carefully, seething with anger.

'I have still not been able to contact Moab; he is at one of our remotest madrassas in Afghanistan. However, I will act on his behalf. He told me he suspected el Majid could not be trusted and was a spy. Now I believe he is right. He was planning for you to eliminate him when he had completed setting up the school. He knows too much. I want you to go to Agarak and sniff around. See if you can find out where the Russians have taken him. Whatever happens, at whatever cost, we must get rid of him.'

'I will leave immediately. What do you want me to do when I find where he is?'

'Report back. I will keep trying to get hold of Moab. He is due in Peshawar early next week.'

That evening, Mousad found a small, shabby hotel in Agarak, ate dinner, drank some local beer and went to bed. It had been a hell of a day.

✳✳✳

The Saturday evening's flight to Moscow in the Air Force's Tupolov Tu-

154 had been uneventful. Juan was surprised to see pretty hostesses in military uniform; he had expected the crew to be male. The food they served, however, was not as attractive.

Worse than school dinners.

Captain Smyslov explained that they would be landing at Chkalovsky Airport, some 20 miles north-east of Moscow.

'It is used as a Transport Command airfield but its claim to fame is it is the home of cosmonaut research and training. You will stay at the base this weekend and, with luck, tomorrow I may be able to find someone to show you around the Yuri Gagarin museum in Star City. I have been ordered to return to Yerevan on Monday. I don't know what will happen to you after that.'

It was dark when they landed after their three-hour flight. A car met them at the terminal and took them to their quarters.

'Would you like a drink before retiring?' asked the captain.

Juan nodded and they entered an empty bar where the duty airman sat passively waiting for customers. The whole mess seemed to be deserted. 'We are probably the only ones in the mess this weekend,' remarked Anatoly. 'Being so near to Moscow, most of the officers who live here during the week will have buggered off for some night life.'

The same as in British messes, thought Juan.

***

Sunday morning was, to Mousad's surprise, market day in Agarak. The traders were a mix: half Azerbaijani Muslims and half Armenian Christians; they mingled amiably and, like tradesfolk the world over, there was plenty of good- humoured banter. He soon discovered that a Russian military helicopter had landed on Friday afternoon in the grounds of the border police, kept its engines running for ten minutes, and then taken off in a north-westerly direction. He could only assume that el Majid had been taken to Yerevan. He looked at the map. The journey ahead of him would be at least eight or nine hours over the mountains in his Nissan truck. As there wasn't a bus until Monday, he decided to leave at once. He bought some bread, fruit and bottled water.

After seven tortuous hours, he reached Garni, a small town some two hours from Yerevan. Exhausted, he stopped for the night. In the distance he could see Mount Ararat: of considerable importance in both Christian and Muslim folklore. Despite recent fine weather, it was still covered in snow.

***

A late breakfast on Sunday morning was taken in an empty dining room. At eleven o'clock, a retired military officer arrived to show Juan and Anatoly the cosmonaut centre. A whole town had been created to house the trainee spacemen and their dependents. Star City had its own shops, schools, kindergartens, cinemas, sports halls, soccer pitches and running tracks. The scale of the facilities was staggering. It took many hours to walk around the museum that included a planetarium, an underwater training module used to simulate weightlessness and a gigantic centrifuge to create "G" forces.

The weather had been pleasantly warm and dry, and time had passed rapidly. Juan felt his friendship with the captain strengthening. After their tour, and over a late lunch taken in the space centre canteen, Anatoly began to express his fears for Juan's future. 'Although Colonel Veresov was up-beat, I am concerned about your safety,' he said.

'Why?'

'My instructions are to treat you as someone under arrest. You do realise they could see you as a spy: a British Army Officer caught in the Soviet Union wearing civilian clothes.'

'But I am no longer in the Army.'

'Maybe not, but you were in BRIXMIS and must know the score. Whatever happens over the next few days, don't trust your interrogators. Not all the senior officers in the Army, or the politicians, believe in glasnost. The coup of last August failed but it was a close-run thing. The chief players have disappeared but there remains a lot of sympathy for their cause.'

'Do you really think I am in danger?'

'My honest answer is: I don't know. I know little of the reorganised KGB, now renamed the FSB. They operate from the old KGB HQ in Lubyanka Square in downtown Moscow. I suspect little has changed – I don't know. I shouldn't talk to you like this. Tomorrow I have to hand you over to one of their agents. He may be all bonhomie, but remain on guard at all times.'

That Sunday evening they dined together in the mess. There were a few officers with their wives in the bar, but they tended to keep to themselves. After dinner, Juan and Anatoly sat quietly in a corner, playing some chess – very one-sided chess. 'My uncle taught me the game,' Anatoly had remarked at one point. 'He was briefly world champion.' Consequently, Juan was unable to give the captain much of a game, and they agreed to retire early.

As they were putting the pieces back into the box, Anatoly said, 'You are going to be on your own in Lubyanka. Is there anything I can do?'

Juan looked into his pale blue eyes. *He is genuinely concerned for my safety.*

'There is something.'

'What?'

'Make an anonymous phone call to the British Embassy.'

'And say what?'

'Simply say: "Bradda Head is in the Lubyanka." Then put the phone down.'

CHAPTER 31

Monday 25th May 1992

Mousad arrived in Yerevan before noon. *What now?* he thought.

He was surprised by the city's size: a population of well over a million people. He drove towards the centre and found a five-star hotel, the *Hotel Ararat.*

What the hell? I may as well have comfort. Ouda will pick up the bill!

His Pidgin English was as bad as the receptionist's but they managed to make each other understood. She looked at his Saudi passport, shrugged as if to ask *what are you doing here?* and handed it back. He found the chambermaid, a Muslim, still working on his floor – the fourth – and made discreet enquiries. She spoke some Arabic – it helped. She told him that the Russian military complex was situated on the edge of Erebuni airfield, some six or seven kilometres south of the city centre.

He drove out of town, passing many Soviet-era apartment blocks; mostly dull-grey and dilapidated. Nearing the base, he saw two women, wearing the hijab, walking in the same direction; it gave him a ray of hope as they appeared to be going to work. *I'll bet they work at the military complex as cleaners.*

He parked about a quarter of a mile away from the main entrance. Some bare-footed children were playing football in the wide road. They looked curiously at him getting out of the truck, but ignored him. *A good sign, I am insignificant.*

The two women he had seen earlier were approaching him. He

decided to take a chance and asked in Arabic, 'Do you work at the base?'

They stopped. Their faces registered surprise at a stranger in western clothes asking them a question in Arabic.

'Yes,' one replied. 'Why?'

'Do you mind me asking what you do?'

'I work in the officers' club, cleaning. Why?'

'Would you like to help the cause of Allah?'

'Go on.' The youngest seemed intrigued. The elder never spoke; age brings caution of the unknown.

'Did a stranger, either American or English, arrive here on Friday and is he still on the base?'

'Someone stayed in the officers' club on Friday night. I cleaned his room on Saturday. He only slept there one night. I never saw him.'

'Did he leave anything that might indicate who he was?'

'No, except he left the room immaculate; unlike the Russians who think nothing of puking all over the place after they've been on the vodka.'

'Could he have been flown out of Erebuni?'

'There's a daily evening flight to Moscow.'

'Thank you, ladies. I would appreciate it if you said nothing to anyone.' And with that he handed them a US $10 note each; still the international currency, even for a Saudi. They didn't know it but, in accepting their treasure, the two women had put themselves in considerable danger.

So our friend has flown the nest and is now in Moscow. Moab is not going to like this one little bit.

The two Muslim cleaners, Aida and Leila, chattered excitedly as they resumed their walk to work. Neither had ever seen a US $10 note before, yet alone owned one. They showed their passes at the guard room and carried on chatting. They met up with their colleagues at the gathering point in the civilian administration centre for the distribution of the day's late shift duties. The Armenian manager of the civilian workers always doled out jobs to ensure the Azerbaijani Muslims got the worst tasks. That day the two cleaners were allocated the officers' club kitchen. It meant they would be washing dishes and clearing tables until 9 pm, under the supervision of the Russian warrant officer who ran the officers' mess.

They arrived at the rear of the club, and were met by the Russian WO, known to all the civilians as *The Bear*. A giant weighing 17 stone, 6ft 3in tall, he was respected among the civilians for treating everyone fairly. He wanted them to '*finish doing the bedrooms first*' and then report back to the kitchen. By 6 pm, an hour before dinner was to be served, they found themselves laying the tables. As they placed the cutlery carefully on the tables and arranged the napkins, the pair continued to whisper excitedly about their new found wealth.

'What are you going to do with the money?' one asked.

'I am spending it on myself; my lazy husband isn't going to get his hands on it, that's for sure!'

'A new bra and some stockings, I thought.'

'That's a good idea. That way he'll never notice.'

They giggled at the thought that neither of their husbands would notice their new bras.

Unknown, however, the Armenian corporal head waiter was overhearing them.

'What have you two slags got to laugh about?' he demanded.

They stopped in their tracks; their faces paled.

He was a known bully, rumoured to have forced himself on one of the younger girls. His eyes were too close together, his lips thin, his skin pale; all the civilian workers hated him. He advanced and grabbed Leila by the arm, twisting it to the point where she thought it was going to break. 'What have you got? I won't ask you twice.'

'Nothing. Let me go.' As she tried to wrest away, there was a crack as her arm broke. She yelled in agony and fell to the floor, her eyes welling up. She screamed loudly.

The mess manager, in the adjacent kitchen, ran through the swing door. 'What is all the commotion about?'

'These two have been up to no good,' replied the corporal, as he pulled himself up to his full height, but was still dwarfed by The Bear.

'He's broken Leila's arm,' shouted Aida.

'They're hiding something,' explained the corporal, 'I know it. They've been thieving from one of the officer's rooms.'

The WO looked at Aida. 'Have you?'

'No, we were given some money,' she blurted; more concerned about her friend writhing on the floor in agony than hiding the facts.

'Corporal, I am going to take these two to see the medical officer at once. Rest assured I will get to the bottom of this and if I think you were bullying them then I will have you on a charge. You will be doing night duties for six months. Understand? Now get the tables ready for the officers' dinner; they will be coming through those doors in ten minutes and everything had better be shipshape.'

The Armenian corporal stood to attention. He knew better than to cross swords with the Russian WO. It was just about the worst thing he could do.

Although the medical centre was closed, the duty medical orderly was called out. An X-ray confirmed the break.

The WO was fuming. 'I'll have that little shite, so I will,' he said.

Leila's arm was cast in plaster.

'Don't worry; I will make sure you are put on light duties for the duration. Now tell me what happened.'

The two cleaners told their version to The Bear. He listened intently and realised he would have to get them to repeat their story to the security officer.

Major Alexi Troitski listened and understood that he, too, would have to elevate their tale to higher authority. He knew of the British officer arriving with Captain Smyslov on Friday and being sent to Moscow.

Things may be getting out of hand.

Finally, the two Muslim women found themselves repeating the afternoon happenings, for the third time, to Colonel Veresov. He asked some probing questions.

'Describe him.'

'An Arab, swarthy skin, 5ft 10in, well-built, strong-looking, shaved beard, hooked nose,' said Aida.

'Yes,' added Leila, 'with podgy hands.'

'Podgy hands?'

'Yes. He's never worked manually. His nails were manicured.'

Both the Colonel and the Major smiled at each other.

'What was he wearing?'

'A western-style, beige-coloured suit, matching shirt and collar. Brown shoes,' replied Aida.

'They looked as if they had been polished recently,' added Leila.

Amazing what these two can remember thought Colonel Veresov.

'What car was he driving?'

'It was a white Nissan truck with a registration plate I have never seen before.'

'And he gave you ten dollars each?'

'Yes.'

'And why were you so sure the man who stayed here on Friday night was either English or American?'

Aida hesitated, she had to be careful. 'Because he left his room so tidy.'

Ah, British Army Officers; scrupulous in their habits, thought the colonel.

He turned to his major. 'Get the Arab's description out to all border posts. He is to be stopped. Then get as many troops as you can muster and find what hotel he is staying in. With a bit of luck he might still be in Yerevan. Start at the centre and then work outwards to the east. My hunch is that he came from the Nagorno-Karabakh area.' He looked at his watch. 'It is already 8.30 pm. I will go and get some dinner. Report to me immediately when you have news.'

Veresov was in the bar two hours later joking with some of his staff when Major Troitski entered. 'We have him, or at least we know where he was staying – the *Ararat Hotel*. When he checked in this morning, he had given an address near Ordubad. He returned to the hotel around three o'clock this afternoon, made a phone call to Saudi Arabia, paid in cash and left.'

'Do you know whom he rang?'

'Yes, I had the call traced to a Prince Ouda, apparently a lowly member of the Saudi royal family.'

'Then we must assume he has decided to get back to Naxcivan. Make sure the Armenian police are manning the border at Agarak. If he doesn't stop when ordered, then they are to shoot to kill. Have him brought back here – alive, if possible.'

'Yes, sir.'

★★★

When Mousad decided to return to Naxcivan it was mid-afternoon. He filled the Nissan with diesel and the two spare 5 litre cans that were always carried in the back. He calculated that, with luck, he could be in Agarak before midnight. He checked out of his hotel after making a phone call from his room to Prince Ouda. Moab, he discovered, had still not been contacted and, therefore, was unaware of the events of the previous few days.

'We must inform Moab immediately,' said Prince Ouda. 'I will send Ali al Ghraizil to Peshawar at once. He can be there in a few hours. If el Majid is in Moscow then we are going to have a hell of a job finding him. I think the best thing is for you to return as quickly as possible to Naxcivan and await instructions. Moab has many contacts. I don't know if he has anyone in Moscow. He may have a Chechen there who could sniff el Majid out.'

The journey over the mountains proved more difficult in the dark than the previous day. The tight bends had to be negotiated carefully and it was past midnight when he reached the Nagorno border town. With everywhere closed, and although desperately tired, Mousad decided to press on.

Nearing the border, he was surprised to see the Armenian post lit. The road barrier was down and he could see armed police. One hundred metres beyond, across the no man's land, the Naxcivan post was also manned. He stopped about 50 metres short of the barrier and hesitated, wondering whether to turn around and take his chances by foot over the mountains to the north or try crossing the River Aras to the south and into Iran. He put the Nissan into reverse and began to make a three-point turn when there was a hard metallic tapping sound on his window. He looked up. He was staring into the barrel of an automatic weapon. The guard motioned with it for Mousad to get out. For a fraction of a second, he thought he should put his foot down and go for it. However, common sense and fear made him stop. He wound down the window.

'Yes?' he asked.

'Get out.'

He opened the door. There were two of them with Kalashnikovs.

'Turn round. Put your hands on the roof, feet apart.'

He felt shackles being put on his ankles.

One hundred and fifty metres away, a Naxcivan guard was watching through his binoculars. He made a note of the incident in his diary. It was exactly 0113 hours on Tuesday 26 May 1992.

CHAPTER 32

Monday 25th May 1992

On the same day that Mousad had been in Yerevan, Captain Smyslov shook hands with Juan in the foyer of the officers' club after breakfast. Juan's guard for the journey to the Lubyanka had arrived wearing a bespoke Armani light blue suit, a white shirt and a red tie – very dapper. He had expected someone stocky in a black leather knee-length coat with a Fedora hat, as worn by most of the Russian operatives in the 1980's BRIXMIS. *Things must be looking up in the new Russia.*

'I shall remember what you said,' remarked Smyslov as they departed.

The car, a large saloon of indeterminate Soviet make, made slow progress through the Moscow rush hour. His guard sat with Juan in the rear whilst the driver and his passenger, an armed soldier, sat in the front. Few words were exchanged; the atmosphere eerily cold. Over an hour passed before they drew up at the front of a yellow brick building. With the smartly suited but monosyllabic escort, Juan entered the front door into a gigantic neo-baroque foyer. From the ceiling, at least three storeys high, hung a multitude of large chandeliers. He was reminded of the Royal Liver Building in Liverpool, but this was on a grander scale. He was unaware that the Lubyanka was also originally built for an insurance company.

They were checked in at the reception desk, after which the unnamed bodyguard ushered Juan to the bank of lifts, 'This way, please, Major.'

They ascended to the seventh floor and went down a long corridor.

They stopped at Room 723. Underneath the number on the door was the name: Brigadier Beliavsky. Juan's keeper knocked. They entered an outer office. A plain-looking, broad shouldered, shapeless woman, in her late twenties, wearing a brown uniform in the rank of a captain, stood up from behind her desk.

'Major Quayle for Brigadier General Beliavsky,' announced his escort.

She nodded, but did not reply. She went to a door behind, to the right of her desk. It gave Juan an opportunity to see her shape: upside-down legs, exaggerated by flat heeled shoes, a broad beam and no waist. Her short cropped hair hadn't seen a stylist in years, if ever. *Not chosen for her looks. Perhaps she is the sister of Tamara Press?*

She entered and disappeared briefly. When she came out, he saw a round face with vacant, hard eyes. She said nothing but indicated with a toss of her head for him to enter. Juan looked at his guard who nodded, *you go first.*

He went through and heard the door being closed behind him. He was alone with a small, uniformed officer, no more than 5ft 4in, but square-shaped like his assistant. *I wonder if they are siblings.*

'Ah, Major Quayle. I am Brigadier Beliavsky and have read Colonel Veresov's report – most interesting.' There was no greeting, no warm introduction, no offer of a coffee, not even a chair. It was like being ushered into the headmaster's study prior to being caned for a minor misdemeanour. He wondered if he was expected to stand throughout his interrogation.

The Brigadier came straight to the point.

'What is a major in the Intelligence Corps of the British Army doing in a Soviet State, out of uniform?'

Juan knew immediately where this line of question was leading. However, his training from so long ago had not been forgotten. He didn't answer immediately, but looked around for a chair.

'May I?' he asked, as he carried the chair towards the Brigadier's desk.

The bemedalled uniform nodded – begrudgingly.

'I am no longer in the British Army,' Juan said quietly, sitting down

245

slowly, as if suffering from piles. *Take your time. Make him wait for your answers.* He made a show of getting comfortable before continuing, 'I retired four years ago.'

'Ah! Retired but not resigned.'

'What's the difference?'

'You are on the Reserve for another two years, are you not?'

'Technically, yes.' He feigned a yawn. 'Pardon me; I didn't sleep too well last night.' He shifted in his chair. 'As you know, you are only recalled to serve under exceptional circumstances when the Government has declared a State of Emergency.'

'But you are serving in an active role on behalf of your Government's security service. To be technical, your words not mine, you are a spy and I could have you put in front of a military tribunal. Technically, you could be shot.'

Juan smiled, uncrossing his legs to get more comfortable. He said nothing for a while, as he considered his position.

'I have the right to see a member of the British Embassy.'

'From your time in BRIXMIS, you know that is rubbish. Spies have no rights.'

Juan knew the little creep was correct. *What the hell is he doing? I wonder if he's calling my bluff.*

'You will see from the report in front of you that I volunteered to be a hostage, along with some others, to help the Armenians and Captain Smyslov retreat from Naxcivan safely. I would hardly have done that if I was spying on the Soviet State.'

'Yes, but why were you there in the first place? Volunteering to be a hostage could have been a clever ploy. This cock and bull story of an Islamic Fundamentalist Army being set up doesn't hold any water with me. What are they called?'

'Al-Qaeda. In ten years time everyone will have heard of them.'

'Who are they?'

'As far as I have been able to find out, they are sponsored by a group of dissident Saudi princes and businessmen. I have met only two: one calls himself Ali al Ghraizil and the other is Prince Omar al Ouda. However, the top man seems to be Moab al Saidenn.'

'Spell them, please.'

Juan spelt the names as best he could. The Brigadier wrote the names out slowly, repeating the letters singularly.

When he had finished, Juan continued, 'Their prime aim seems to be the liberation of Palestine by driving the Israelis into the sea.'

'Amen to that!'

'Yes, but their greater aim is the total Islamification, if there is such a word, of the whole world.'

'Impossible. They must be a bunch of idiots.'

'Agreed, but dangerous idiots. You must never underestimate your enemies; remember what happened to your troops in Afghanistan. Ten thousand dead?' As soon as he had said it, Juan bit his lip. He knew he had put his foot in it. He had just made an enemy of Brigadier Beliavsky.

'We were underfunded and then Gorbachev came along with his bloody glasnost.'

'Well, al-Qaeda is certainly not without money. As far as I have been able to determine they have at least six military training establishments called madrassas. They have chosen their sites to be as isolated as possible. The young men chosen are wrapped in a close-knit family where their *esprit de corps* matures. It is the only family they know; they have a pride in their achievements. There are madrassas in Afghanistan, Pakistan, Yemen, Somalia and the one I was in – Naxcivan. They use their Imams to convince the trainees their cause is worth dying for. They are in it for the long term. An army is being prepared to commit suicide in some incredible ways.'

'Such as?'

'One idea is to capture a tanker full of oil or liquid gas, plant bombs on board and sail it into a refinery such as Southampton or Rotterdam.'

'Not a problem for us. Our refineries are in Siberia.'

'OK. How about hijacking several aeroplanes simultaneously and flying them, fully laden with fuel, into one of your refineries such as the one in Omsk?'

'We would shoot them from the sky as soon as we knew the planes had been hijacked.'

'Suppose four or five bombers blew themselves up on different trains whilst travelling on the Moscow Metro in the rush hour?'

For the first time, Beliavsky looked grave. He peered over his desk at Juan, his eyes narrowing. 'Is that one of their plans?'

'I don't know but what I do know is they are radicals with a ten-year plan. By 2002 all the world's advanced countries are going to be at war with al-Qaeda.'

'But they're a bunch of loners. How can they terrorise us?'

'You've hit on the right word and the wrong word. Firstly, terror: they are endowed with hatred for what they see as a decadent world; even their own Saudi government is not safe. The key to terror is hatred. Deep in their background these recruits have experienced something that makes them hate you and me. It could be a mother who gave them no love, or a father who was a brute. The Imams cultivate their psyche to a fanatical hatred of all non-Muslim societies. Secondly, the wrong word: loner. Moab and his lieutenants are out there now, recruiting. They are finding talented young men who are not inadequate loners or drifters. I have seen their best. The madrassa in Naxcivan is a college where languages are being taught: English, Russian and Japanese. They study sciences such as physics, chemistry and computing. When they leave they plan to infiltrate Britain, America, Russia and Japan. There, they will study further to become doctors, lawyers, pilots, sea captains, policemen, computer programmers and so on. When they are qualified, we can look out. The doctor who releases virulent cholera into a city, the veterinary who deliberately introduces anthrax into farms, the pilot who crashes a plane into a skyscraper, the computer hacker who closes down a banking system; these men, who are beginning their training now, see the whole thing as a big adventure in the name of Islam. They thrill at the thought of being long-term sleepers, knowing that some day they will make history.'

'I think we should take a break. I have ordered some sandwiches for lunch.' He pressed the intercom on his desk and asked for them to be brought in.

The Tamara Press lookalike appeared with a tray.

'I hope mint tea is to your liking,' he said.

Is he warming to me? 'I was worried I might have to drink more vodka.'

Beliavsky laughed; even his ADC's frown broke into a half smile.

'This afternoon I want to begin to go through your story, from when you were recruited by MI5 to the present, blow by blow. It will probably take until the end of tomorrow. Tonight you will be accommodated in a secure suite on the top floor. The rooms are quite comfortable. Malenkov was held there in 1955 before being ousted and replaced by Bulganin who was Khrushchev's puppet, of course.'

'Of course.'

'So, you are joining good company.' He roared at his little joke. 'While we are eating you can be thinking how to answer my first question: What makes you so special that you were recruited from a small school in Cumbria?'

***

Captain Smyslov's flight to Yerevan was not leaving until 1500 hours. He decided to make an unannounced visit to see his widowed mother in her apartment on the west side of Moscow. They enjoyed catching up on family news and, like all mothers worldwide, she insisted she prepared him his favourite dish for lunch – a dumpling stew. He hadn't the heart to tell her that his tastes had changed since leaving home 15 years previously. When she was preparing the dish, he asked, 'Mum, there is something I want you to do for me.'

'What?'

'Make a phone call from a public box in the centre of town.'

'Why should I go into Moscow to make a phone call?'

'I don't want the call to be traced and the ten boxes on the south side of Red Square are always busy. No one will notice you making a call from there. I will give you the money for the Metro and the call. I will also give you enough to buy a new coat from GUM.'

'There's no need for that.'

'Consider it a birthday present for next month. I won't be home for another three months.'

'What do you want me to do?'

'Ring this number and simply say what is written on this paper. Then put the phone down at once. Make sure you wear gloves. By the time you are doing that, I will have taken off for Yerevan.'

***

The afternoon's questions proceeded slowly.

God, at this rate, I'll be here all week.

Every answer was written down or notes added to the report in front of him, presumably the one faxed from Colonel Veresov. By the time the brigadier-general seemed ready to stop, the office clock showed 1830 hours and yet they hadn't got to the sinking of the *Glengariff*.

He's flagging. What a pity he will be fresh in the morning for the trickier parts of the saga.

'I would like to stop here,' he said wearily. 'Your guard, Inspector Georgiov, will accompany you to your quarters. Dinner will be served in your room. I will see you in the morning.' He pressed his intercom. Tamara's sister appeared and nodded for Juan to exit. To his surprise, his guard was the same dour escort from the morning.

***

By the time Mrs Smyslov had said her farewells to her favourite son, tidied her kitchen, walked to the local metro station and found herself in the centre of town, it was almost five o'clock. Office workers were already pouring out of the government offices dotted around the square

250

and heading home. She did what Anatoly had asked. She phoned the number, meaningless to her and heard in Russian a female greeting, 'Hello'. She didn't wait. *'Bradda Golova v Lubyanka,'* she shouted and slammed the phone down. She hated phones – so impersonal – and didn't have one of her own; she couldn't afford one. She was looking forward to getting a warm coat in the GUM department store, a short walk across the square.

✳✳✳

All calls to British embassies are recorded. However, they are often recorded elsewhere, when made from insecure lines. The message heard in the FSB suggested an elderly person had made the call. It was too short to be traced by the duty officer. And anyway, he was about to put his coat on to go home. He scribbled a note for action by the night staff. *They do bugger all,* he thought.

✳✳✳

In the embassy, the mention of the word Lubyanka rang an alarm bell with the receptionist. The message was passed upstairs immediately to the security officer, John Hartston. He looked at the note and then listened to the recording. It made no sense but he remembered something about a code name. He retrieved the archive orders book. After much flipping backwards through the entries, sure enough, there it was:

Order No 18/91, dated 31 Mar 91. Top Secret

All messages in Gaelic using call sign 'Bradda Head'
for 'Dover Castle' to be transmitted FLASH to Hd MI6
IMMEDIATELY.
Add time of receipt.

Well, he thought, *there's no mention of Dover Castle and it's not in Gaelic, but I'll send it anyway.* He looked at his watch: 1710 hours Moscow – 1410 hours London. *They've plenty of time this afternoon if they want to come back to me.*

By 1430 hours GMT the news was on Sir Peter's desk. His first reaction was to think it was some sort of a joke. By 1500 hours the Moscow embassy had confirmed the message was genuine. He called Sir Charles.

'What the hell is Quayle doing in Moscow?' the head of MI5 asked his colleague.

'I've no idea, but we must pursue this even if we end up with egg on our faces. I am going to see the Foreign Secretary in fifteen minutes. I will ask Douglas Hurd to call in the Russian Ambassador immediately to investigate and give us an explanation by tomorrow morning.'

'I can't see how it can be anything other than genuine. My guess is that somehow the Russians have captured him in the Yemen, perhaps, or Somalia? Quayle must have somehow charmed someone to make a phone call to our embassy.'

'By now the Russians will know that we know. That could complicate matters. If there are any developments this afternoon I'll let you know.'

✳✳✳

Ali al Ghraizil had arrived at Peshawar late that Monday evening. He discovered that Moab had still not arrived and was now overdue. He went from one safe house to another in the districts of Sher Ali Town, Faqeer Kalay, and Pajagi Village; no one had seen him, no one seemed surprised. 'Don't worry,' said one. 'He's coming from Kabul, he'll turn up tomorrow.'

Ali went to bed; there was little he could do but wait.

CHAPTER 33

Tuesday 26th May 1992

Ali al Ghraizil was surprised when he awoke to find Moab waiting for him at breakfast. He had arrived in the middle of the night. 'Much safer to travel in the early hours,' he said. 'What's the panic all about?'

Ali related the story of the massacre, the flight of el Majid to Moscow, the efforts of Mousad to track him down in Yerevan, and how Mousad, after phoning Prince Ouda, had been told to return to Naxcivan.

Moab listened intently. Ali sensed the anger in Moab as his black pupils grew, his nostrils enlarged, the veins on his neck flared. His blood was boiling. The rumour that Moab possessed the power of hypnosis, Ali could now believe. He'd read of Rasputin having supernatural powers over the Russian royal family. The similarity explained why he was undisputed leader of al-Qaeda, even among men from higher social standing. 'Prince Ouda didn't know what to do. He thought you might have a contact in Moscow who could find out where they are keeping el Majid.'

'Oh, I know where he will be. I must ensure Lutikov eliminates him before they hand him back to the British. It's time he did something for himself.'

It was 0800 hours Pakistan time, 0700 Moscow time, Tuesday 26th May.

***

Juan ate well that Monday evening – some sort of beef goulash. The bottle of Lubyanka's house red, *probably Hungarian or Bulgarian,* enhanced the experience.

The night was spent dreaming of the Cuban missile crisis, *had Khrushchev slept here?* Breakfast was brought in at 0830 hours. Half an hour later, he was accompanied back to room 723 by the mute Inspector Georgiov. In the outer office there were signs of a panic.

Juan heard Tamara speak for the first time. 'The Brigadier has been called away to see Lieutenant General Lutikov. He may not come back until this afternoon. You will have to return to your room and wait there.'

Something's up.

Back in his suite, there was little to do other than watch Russian day-time TV. The choice of programmes lay between game shows that were worse than those in Britain or dubbed Australian soaps. He switched from one channel to another indiscriminately, but soon gave up.

He inspected his room. He could see there was a magic eye camera in the ceiling rose and possibly another behind the wall-mounted mirror in his bathroom.

I might be out of practice, but I'm wiser than I was in Berlin.

Amongst a small pile of books on a shelf, he found an old book of the 1953 Zurich Candidates Chess Tournament – won by Anatoly's uncle. In a cupboard the previous evening, he had spotted a wooden chess set. He settled down for what could be a long wait. While playing through some of Vasily Smyslov's games from the tournament, he wondered if his nephew had made that phone call. *It could explain the flap.*

***

As Chairman of the Military Intelligence Committee, Lieutenant General Mikhail Lutikov's office was in the Kremlin – the heart of government. Brigadier Beliavsky had served under Lutikov when he had been supreme commander of Soviet Forces in Afghanistan and greatly admired the man whom he considered to have the finest tactical brain in the Russian army.

Lutikov's Personal Staff Officer, Colonel Victor Suetin, ushered him into the inner office of his old regiment commander.

'Sit down, Boris,'

'Thank you, sir.'

'Last evening our ambassador to the Court of St James was called to see the British Foreign Secretary. The British know we are holding Major Quayle. Any ideas how?'

'None at all.'

'Pick your best man. Get him to do some delving. Begin by seeing if the British Embassy received any unusual visitors yesterday or had any phone calls. If some lazy bugger has missed something, then I'll have his guts for garters.'

'I'll get on to it right away.'

'How's it going with Quayle, by the way?'

'He's definitely working for MI6, and was chosen because of his unique ability with languages. Apparently, he can speak Irish Gaelic as well as Arabic. MI5 thought al-Qaeda was getting its arms from the IRA.'

Lutikov chuckled, 'And, of course, we know that is not the full story.'

'Exactly. However, he infiltrated al-Qaeda successfully, but I don't think he knows about us. He doesn't know who their leader is either.'

General Lutikov paused, thinking of a time long passed. Then warned, 'I remember Quayle in BRIXMIS: gifted but flawed. His weaknesses were wine and women. I accept, however, he may have changed in ten years. Whatever you do, don't underestimate him.'

'Shall I get one of our girls to take his dinner to him this evening?'

'Yes. Make sure she is slim, fair haired and looks younger than her years. Let's see if he makes the same mistake as last time. Unfortunately, however, there may be a spanner in the works.'

'Oh?'

'Yesterday afternoon, Colonel Veresov, our senior liaison officer with the Armenians, discovered a member of al-Qaeda spying near our base at Erebuni. He was, apparently, making enquiries about our friend Quayle. By the time Veresov found out, the Arab had left Yerevan. However, he was caught trying to cross the border into Naxcivan in the early hours of this morning. His name is Mousad Safahar, a private secretary to Prince Ouda.'

'Never heard of him.'

'There's no reason why you should, except I know he's used by al-Qaeda as an occasional hit man. He can be a ruthless little shite. The problem is I've no idea whether Safahar knows about our connection.'

'What are we going to do?'

'American sponsorship of Hamas buggered us in Afghanistan. Now it's our turn. We'll use al-Qaeda to hit the Yanks. Colonel Veresov is a Gorbachev man, so I've ordered him to send Safahar here immediately without interrogation. When he arrives, you know what to do?'

'Siberia or an accident?'

'Both. Quayle must go too. Unfortunately, that may be trickier now that it is up at ministerial level. Are you absolutely certain he knows nothing about our links to al-Qaeda? Don't tell me what you think I want to hear, Boris. Our future and the resurgence of the Soviet State depend on it.'

'He knows their recruits are gifted young men, he thinks they are funded entirely from Saudi, he believes their arms are now coming from dissident states such as Turkmenistan, he only has vague ideas where the madrassas are, he knows strategic terror plans such as mass hijackings, he hasn't a clue we are backing al-Qaeda.'

'I'm seeing our Foreign Secretary, Andrei Kozyrev, in an hour's time at eleven o'clock. He wants to draft a formal reply for our ambassador in London to give to the British Secretary of State, Hurd. I am inclined to hang on to Quayle, if we can, for a few days. If he's as ignorant as you say he is, we could use him as a bargaining counter to get one of our own men back.'

'Who?'

'I was thinking of Steerforth – the V-bomber pilot who infiltrated the RAF in the seventies and gave us the details of their atomic targets. He was caught at RAF Waddington, pushing his luck. He's been in Wakefield prison for almost ten years; it's time we brought him home.'

✱✱✱

General Lutikov's PSO, Colonel Victor Suetin, was used to receiving strange phone calls from his boss' wife and having to cover for his absences. However, that morning after the General had left to see the Foreign Secretary, the message was one of the oddest.

'Will you tell Mikhail that I have just received an urgent phone call from his tailor? He wants him to go for a fitting of his new suit this afternoon at three o'clock. If he doesn't turn up, then the suit will not be ready on time. I didn't know he was having a new suit made. He never tells me anything.'

'I will tell him the minute he comes back from his appointment with the minister, Mrs Lutikov.'

I didn't even know the old man had a bespoke tailor.

It was past 1330 hours when the General returned to his office. Colonel Suetin thought he looked exhausted, but gave him his wife's message.

'Are you sure the call was urgent, Victor?'

'Yes, sir. That's what your wife said.'

Lutikov looked at his watch. 'I'll change into civvies and get some lunch on the way. If anyone calls, make the usual excuses, will you? I should be back around 1630 hours.'

Colonel Suetin was used to making excuses; Lutikov was something of a ladies' man and the Colonel knew at least two of the general's mistresses. Normally their frissons were taken after light lunches in the swankier hotels. He wondered if this was a new ploy to meet a new girlfriend.

General Lutikov knew what to do. He made several unnecessary changes on the Metro to ensure he wasn't followed; then, satisfied, he headed for Frunzen Place, a station near Trubetski Park. He sat by the bandstand and waited. At precisely 1500 hours a young man in jeans and trainers approached. 'Do you want a game of chess?' he asked.

'I only play for a bottle of claret.'

'So, it's to be a French Defence.'

'What is the message?'

'The leader is concerned about the capture of Safahar and el Majid. They know too much. He wants you to eliminate both of them.'

'Tell him Safahar will disappear in Siberia. El Majid, or Quayle, is not so easy.'

'Quail?' The stranger was confused. *What has a game bird to do with this?*

'At the moment, everything is under control, but Quayle is an Intelligence Officer in the British Army. His detention in the Lubyanka is up at ministerial level. He may be repatriated to Britain and I can't stop it. Tell your leader that he may have to wash this particular dirty linen himself.'

***

Dimitrievich Pankin had been ambassador to the United Kingdom for almost a year, but this was the first occasion on which he had been called urgently to explain what the Foreign Office had called 'the illegal imprisonment of a British citizen'. After the usual pleasantries, Ambassador Pankin read a prepared statement.

'My Government wishes to point out that Major Juan Quayle, of the British Army Intelligence Corps, has been detained while undertaking suspect activities in a former State of the Soviet Union. As such, he could be found guilty by a military tribunal of espionage and dealt with according to Russian Law. However, in the spirit of glasnost my Government is prepared to consider an exchange of prisoners under a pro rata agreement.'

He stopped and looked up from his paper. Douglas Hurd was sitting before him behind the largest oak desk he had ever seen.

'Ambassador Pankin,' he said slowly, 'that is poppycock. We both know that Quayle was discharged from the Army almost four years ago. He is a civilian attempting to uncover information about an international terrorist organisation that is a threat to both our governments; indeed to all civilised governments. However, we are prepared to meet your government's terms. For whom do you wish to exchange Quayle?'

'Alexander Steerforth'

'The RAF pilot who gave you our V-bomber secrets?'

'Yes.'

'We agree. We would like to make the exchange as soon as possible. When can you arrange the deal?'

The sudden acceptance of his government's terms surprised the ambassador. He had been briefed that the UK Government might hesitate, arguing that Quayle was innocent until proven guilty, whereas Steerforth was a known traitor who had been found guilty in an open court. Stumbling to give a sensible reply, he suggested what seemed to be a reasonable timescale.

'How about the day after tomorrow?'

'Fine. Shall we agree Vienna, as usual?'

This suggestion, too, surprised the ambassador. The exchange was his first. He had not realised that in the 1950s, during the height of the Cold War, such exchanges of agents had been common place. Vienna, then under joint Allied rule, was always used and a well established procedure had been created. Douglas Hurd, however, was a keen political historian and knew the ropes.

The ambassador left the Foreign Office feeling somewhat deflated. He knew he had agreed to something that might create ripples in Moscow.

✳✳✳

By the time Lieutenant General Lutikov had returned to his office, Minister Kozyrev had reluctantly agreed to the timing of the exchange

259

as proposed by his London ambassador. The Minister had been pleased when he found Lutikov absent from his office *on urgent business* and had to speak with Colonel Suetin. It saved him having an unpleasant row with one of the Army's senior men. He informed the general's personal staff officer that he had already arranged for one of his secretariat to collect Quayle from his room in the Lubyanka.

When he learned of the deals that had occurred in his absence, Lutikov was furious. Colonel Suetin had never seen the old man so ill-tempered.

Perhaps his new girlfriend didn't come up to standards.

After shutting himself in his inner office for ages, he came out and suggested his staff leave early. It was only 1730 hours, normal departure could be as late as 1900 hours; the old boy was usually something of a workaholic after having an extended lunch break.

That definitely confirms it; she either didn't turn up or she greatly disappointed him.

With the office empty, Lutikov took a file out from his drawer. He opened it to the first page – a summary of its contents:

Confidential

Major Juan Quayle RAIC (retd)

D o B:	2 Apr 1950
P o B:	Isle of Man
Educ:	Durham Univ, Leeds Univ
Career brief:	...

He looked no further before photocopying the page, folded it into an envelope, wrote a Moscow address on it, found a stamp in the typist's drawer and put it in his inside pocket for posting on his way home. He sighed, it had just dawned on him that it was his wife's birthday. Cursing, he returned to his office, and phoned her favourite restaurant. Fortunately, there was a table. *The first bit of luck today,* he thought.

He turned to leave. The phone rang. He thought about not answering it; *I'd better get home quickly or there'll be trouble.* He picked it up. 'Yes?' he snapped.

'It's Beliavsky here, Sir. You wanted me to find out if anyone had approached the British Embassy.'

'Well?'

'Someone rang them yesterday evening around five o'clock and simply said "*Bradda Golova v Lubyanka.*"'

'Why was this not passed up the line?'

'The night shift had not come on duty and the day shift had left half an hour early.'

'That's no excuse.'

'I agree. The problem is that we have no reference in our files as to what Bradda Golova is. The night duty officer, after investigating our files thought it was a crank call.'

'And who or what the hell is Bradda Golova?'

'I have done some searching. It is a promontory on the Isle of Man.'

'Bloody Hell, Quayle!'

'Sorry?'

'Quayle was born in the Isle of Man. Someone was telling them that Quayle was in the Lubyanka. I want you to begin an investigation. There can't be that many people who knew we had Quayle.'

'Where shall I start?'

'Begin at the beginning. That's Veresov and come forward from there.'

★★★

The junior secretary from the Foreign Ministry and Juan travelled by staff car to Moscow's international airport at Domodedovo. There, he was introduced to a young man calling himself Grigory Panchenko. 'I am a second secretary in the Viennese embassy and am returning to Austria this evening after two weeks leave. We are booked on the 1830 hours flight and should arrive at Schwechat Airport, Vienna, at 2130 hours. I have been instructed to tell you that you are being exchanged for another prisoner the day after tomorrow. You will be confined to our embassy until the exchange.'

When the plane's wheels left the runway, a huge weight was lifted off Juan's shoulders. He felt safe; he was on his way home.

CHAPTER 34

Tuesday 26th May 1992

Douglas Hurd rang his Director of MI6. 'They have agreed the exchange as you hoped. It will take place the day after tomorrow in Vienna. I'll leave you, Peter, to take care of the details. I never checked with Ambassador Pankin, but I assume the Russians are aware of the usual protocol.'

'Thank you, Minister. I'll let Sir Charles know at once. We are both looking forward to getting Quayle back.'

'I shall be interested in what he has to tell us.'

'Never fear, minister, I will keep you informed of all developments.'

What is the usual protocol he's talking about?

MI6's Head of the Eastern Europe desk was Grade 3 Donald Pownall, fluent in Russian, Hungarian and German. He couldn't answer Sir Peter's query about the usual protocol.

Over an hour later, he rang his boss back. 'Apparently, the exchanges always used to take place at 1000 hours in the café Salm-Brau in the Belvedere Gardens. It is a short distance from both Vienna embassies. The usual procedure was then to give our man lunch in the embassy and bring him home courtesy of the RAF that afternoon.'

'The RAF no longer flies regularly to Vienna. Book him on the first BA flight. I'd like you to accompany Steerforth and do the exchange. When you get back, I'll meet you at Heathrow.'

The flight from Moscow took three hours, but the time zone difference between the two cities meant that when Juan and his escort arrived it was only 1930 hours local. The Russian Embassy in Reisnertstrasse is situated in the centre of Vienna and, having been shown to his room, Juan was surprised to find himself being taken out to a nearby restaurant for dinner.

'What's to stop me making a break for it?' he asked his companion, Gregory.

'You wouldn't get far,' smiled his dinner partner. 'See those two over there?'

Juan turned around. He saw two dark-suited, stocky individuals with what his father would have described as *seven-o'-clock shadows*. They stared back intently.

'They are members of the FSB. I suspect they were formerly KGB. We will try to make the next thirty-six hours as pleasant as possible, but please realise that until you are released, you are under house arrest. Tomorrow I will attempt to show you some of the city, but be aware those two bruisers will never be far away.'

***

Alexander Steerforth had languished in Wakefield gaol for nigh on ten years. He had been kept segregated from other prisoners for his own safety. Traitors were a different breed – even from murderers and rapists. Having aged nearer 20 years than ten, he had resigned himself to dying in prison as he couldn't envisage seeing his 35 year sentence ever coming to an end. It was a shock rather than a surprise when, on Wednesday morning, he was taken to see the governor.

'You are being sent back to Russia as part of an exchange. Put your personal belongings together and be ready to move in an hour.'

Ninety minutes later, he found himself handcuffed to a warder, who was dressed in civvies. Sitting in the back of a limousine speeding south of Doncaster on the A1, he hadn't seen beyond the prison walls for so long that everything appeared new. It was unreal. He was amazed to see fields of yellow rape and blue linseed. It wasn't until south of Newark that he began wondering where he was being taken. He ventured to ask his escort, 'Where are we going?'

'You'll find out soon enough,' was the gruff reply.

He decided the rest of the journey would have to pass in silence.

When they eventually hit the M25, they turned west and Steerforth guessed they were heading for Heathrow. There, they met Donald Pownall, dressed immaculately in a dark suit, light blue shirt, with an MCC tie. A tall, slim-waisted man in his forties, his presence exuded importance. The warder called him 'Sir'. Unfortunately, Alexander realised the warder was accompanying them on the plane. His handcuffs were to remain locked.

'We're flying to Vienna this evening. Tomorrow you will be exchanged for one of our agents,' announced the dapper civil servant whose body language told him there would be no more dialogue.

Steerforth thought, *Tomorrow, I'll be free!* At a stroke, he felt ten years younger.

***

Soon after 0930 hours on Thursday 28th, Juan, his escort Gregory, and the two badly-shaved bodyguards left the Russian Embassy and began walking south. They crossed a main road and Juan found himself in a lovely green park. The University's Botanical Gardens were to his left, but they turned right towards a café. Sitting outside in the sunshine, he could see four people. Two smartly dressed men, whom he took to be from the British Embassy, and an older grey-haired man, rather haggard, handcuffed to a thick stocky individual who looked inappropriately dressed in sports jacket, jeans and a pair of trainers. They all stood up as they approached. The elder of the two pinstriped men came forward and asked, 'Mr Panchenko?'

'Mr Pownall?'

They shook hands acknowledging each others assumption to be correct.

Pownall turned to the ill-dressed heavy and nodded. The older man's handcuffs were unlocked and Pownall nodded for him to come forward.

Gregory turned to Juan and formally said, 'Farewell Major Quayle and good luck.'

The two exchangees passed each other without a word or a smile.

'I'm Donald Pownall, MI6 Eastern European desk. Welcome home, Major Quayle.' He was smiling and held out his hand. He was introduced to the other two: Philip Carr, Vienna Embassy and Lee Bates, Wakefield Prison.

'Would you like a coffee before we return to the embassy?' asked Donald. 'We are catching the 1430 hours flight to Heathrow after an early lunch.'

***

Sir Peter Stacey was waiting to greet Juan in the VIP lounge. It was 1600 hours local. 'Welcome home, Juan. It's been a long time, almost two years since you met my colleague, Sir Charles, at St Bees.'

'It was a lifetime ago, Sir Peter. Much has happened.'

The four men sat down to tea, sandwiches, and cakes. Bates looked distinctly uncomfortable and said nothing. Sir Peter got straight down to business. 'Juan, I have booked an RAF 32 Sqn HS125 aircraft to take us to RAF Chivenor in North Devon; take-off 1730 hours from RAF Northolt. We will be at our training centre, Woodside, in time for dinner.' Looking at Bates, as if to say – *you shouldn't be here* – he added, 'We can discuss your future on the way down.'

When Sir Peter and Juan climbed into a waiting chauffeured RAF car to take them to Northolt, Donald Pownall and Lee Bates left for the Piccadilly Line to take them into central London.

'Now that we're alone, I can outline our plans. I expect you would

266

like to have some time on your own; do your own thing. However, I'm afraid that first of all, we would like you to write a report on all that has happened since you were birched in the Isle of Man: list the people you have met, summarise your opinions of them, put together any ideas you may have formed, that sort of thing.'

'How long have I got? So much has happened and I haven't kept a diary.'

'We realise that and there is no hurry. Sir Charles will join us towards the end of next week. Together with several of our staffs from the appropriate departments, we would then like to spend several days going through your report and analysing it with you. I think you'll be at Woodside for three or four weeks. We also have a proposition for you to chew over.'

'What?'

'We, and by we, I mean the Foreign Office, would like to offer you the position of an ambassadorship.'

'You're joking?'

'No, I am serious. Douglas Hurd and I have discussed it. Your linguistic abilities must not be wasted.'

'I thought you had to be a career civil servant to rise to an ambassadorship.'

'No, not at all. The appointments are frequently made for political reasons.'

'I can't see myself entertaining foreign dignitaries to tea and cakes in somewhere like Paraguay.'

'There's no hurry to make a decision. Mull it over during the coming months. First of all, there is much work to be done.'

***

The flight in the RAF 125 took less than an hour. Thirty minutes after landing at Chivenor, they had arrived at Woodside. Juan found a small wardrobe laid out in his room.

'The things in your room are really only for tonight. First thing tomorrow you can go into Barnstaple and get whatever you need. After almost two years away, your allowances have built up considerably. I will return to London in the morning, but will return with Sir Charles in about ten days time.'

Juan had a restless night – he couldn't get to sleep as he began drafting his report on the previous two years; trying to remember names and events. He spent Friday wandering around Barnstaple buying clothes and personal effects. He found a suitable pub for lunch and enjoyed eating fresh fish swilled down with real ale. It was heaven to be home in Britain and feel safe.

Although a Saturday, he settled down in the college's library with pen and paper to plan his report. He had been told that a senior secretary from London would be arriving on Monday. She would collect his written work each day, type it double-spaced, correct it as necessary and offer suggestions. She had full security clearance for such work. When the pair had agreed content, copies would be securely faxed to London for Sir Peter and Sir Charles to begin preparing their analysis. Time passed rapidly that weekend and on Sunday afternoon he took the opportunity to play golf at Westward Ho! with one of the staff whom he had met 18 months previously.

On Monday afternoon, he met the senior secretary, Barbara. She was of a similar age to him, perhaps a few years older, in her mid-forties. She was joyful, pleasant and vivacious. She had a full figure that was well preserved. Her red henna hair was immaculate, her make up not overdone. Her nail polish matched her hair and lipstick. She had several rings on the fourth finger of her left hand. They looked expensive. She was dressed in a matching jacket and skirt – knee length. Nice ankles above high-heeled shoes, she was every inch a neat and tidy secretary. Her typing was good too, she could read his handwriting. A friendship began to develop rapidly; Juan had felt within minutes of meeting her that they were kindred spirits. She joked about his misuse of the apostrophe and a tendency to split his infinitives. It triggered further conversation about his schooling and education. He began to suspect she knew his true identity and had read his personal file; although she never admitted it. He asked questions about her background. She was openly honest: she was divorced and had a small house in Barnstaple as well as a flat in Holland Park, London.

On Wednesday, their third day together, he took the plunge. 'Would you be offended if I asked you to come out to dinner with me one evening,' he asked.

'No. I would not be offended,' she smiled.

'When?'

'Why not tomorrow night?'

'That's fine, but I don't have a car.'

'I'll pick you up at 7.30 and take you to a nice restaurant near Bideford.'

***

It turned out that Barbara was older than Juan had thought: early-fifties.

She doesn't look it.

She had married when barely 18, and had three children by the age of 22. They were now grown-up and had fled the nest. Her divorce had been traumatic; her *ex*, as she referred to him, turned out to be a philanderer and spendthrift. At the height of her depression, when after 20 years of misery and the children adults, she had packed her bags and left for London. There she had become a personal secretary to a senior civil servant, but not before trying to murder her husband.

'Murder?!' exclaimed Juan, as she regaled the story.

The claret had begun to take effect. She laughed. 'I had read somewhere that if you gently warmed dog meat, then let it cool, it became deadly poisonous.'

'So, what did you do?'

She giggled, 'I made him a casserole with dog meat.'

'What happened?'

'Nothing. He said it was the best casserole he'd ever had.'

They roared together. *God, being with this woman is fun, but I'm not sure I'd want to marry her.*

He vowed to take her out again as soon as possible.

The following week he would hire a car; he had plans to see more of Barbara.

CHAPTER 35

Thursday 11th June 1992

On the following Thursday, a week later, Juan arrived at Barbara's terraced, two-up, two-down house in the older part of Barnstaple in his hire car. She had clearly spent money on the property. The front door entered into a modern, newly fitted kitchen-diner. Beyond was an immaculate lounge, full of knick-knacks with memorabilia that looked faintly Turkish or middle-eastern. The colours exuded warmth, friendship and, somehow, joyousness. There was a faint fragrance of incense. She had a sparkle in her eyes as she greeted him with a gin and tonic. Her backyard was designer built: potted plants, a raised bed, a clematis climbing along one wall and a water feature. The house was a reflection of herself.

They sat in the lounge with some nibbles before leaving for her choice of restaurant. 'I hope you like Indian,' she remarked.

'Great. The food at the college is good, but tends to be bland. I'm looking forward to it already.'

Over dinner they discussed progress on his report; after nine days they were about halfway finished. That day they had covered Juan's narrow escape from assassination on the quay at Tunis.

'Reading your account on the aftermath at Tunis, there was something that didn't ring true,' she said.

'Really? What?'

'You describe being shot through your left hand that was around Lydia's shoulder.'

'So?'

'Can you show me exactly where your hand was?' She stood up and moved nearer to him.

'I had my hand here,' he said, standing beside her and putting his left hand on the corner of Barbara's left shoulder.

'Are you sure it wasn't here, near the carotid artery.' She put his hand closer to her neck, 'or here.' She moved his hand under her armpit. He could feel the firmness and warmth of her left breast. Instinctively, he squeezed her gently. She smiled, but didn't resist. Others in the restaurant were watching. He withdrew his hand, embarrassed at his forwardness.

'No, it was resting on her bone here. Is it called the scapula?'

'Then there is no way she could have died from her wound.'

'Why?'

'When travelling through your hand, the bullet would have slowed down. It would then have lodged in the scapula. There is no way it could have killed her.'

'She may have fallen heavily on the ground.'

'Yes. That might have caused a nasty graze; even broken her nose. But it wouldn't have been fatal. She was murdered on the boat.'

'Why murder Lydia?'

'They clearly didn't want her to accompany you to Riyadh.'

'Why?'

'Because they realised she was a member of Mossad.'

'Do you think they thought that I was aware of that?'

'Probably, yes. I suspect they used you after that and intended at some stage to kill you too.'

'And there I was, all the time, thinking I was indispensable,' he smiled.

'The graveyards are full…'

'Yes, I know, of indispensable men! Who said that? George Washington?'

'No, much more recent than that – an American basketball coach called John Wooden, although some say it was General de Gaulle.'

'Ah, Wooden. He famously said, "*It's not who starts the game that counts, but who finishes it.*" Or something…'

'Anyway, I think Sir Peter's team will want to ask you a lot more about that boat trip.'

There's more to Barbara than meets the eye. She gives the impression of being something of a dizzy woman; I think she is deliberately misleading me.

He tucked into his prawn Madras. After a few minutes of silence enjoying his hot curry, he remarked, 'You know, Barbara, this is the one thing – a good curry – I have missed more than anything else since being away.'

'Really? How sad!' She chuckled – a beguiling come hither grin that spelled: *I thought it would have been something else.*

He took her home, but didn't receive an invitation to come in for coffee. He found it strange after her manner in the restaurant. Somewhat disappointed, he returned to Woodside.

The following morning when Barbara came into his small office to take away his work, Juan asked the most commonly asked question on a Friday: 'What are you doing this weekend?'

'Waiting for you to ask me where we are going.' She laughed. He wasn't sure whether she was joking.

'Are you serious?'

'Of course. There are more spicy things in life than a Madras curry.'

'But I've no idea where we could go.'

'Leave that to me. With a bit of luck we'll get a room in *The Rising Sun* at Lynmouth. You won't get a curry there; rather a steak to give you strength.'

∗∗∗

While Barbara and Juan were discussing their weekend trip to Lynmouth, thousands of miles away in NW Pakistan, a coded message was being received from Moscow. Moab read it with disbelief. Alan

Quine, alias Khalil el Majid, was Juan Quayle – a British Army officer. He had been planted by the British Security Services to infiltrate al-Qaeda. His first reaction was anger; he was furious with himself for being duped. *How could I have been so stupid? I suspected all along something was not right about him – he was too good to be true. All those languages – so useful to us. Blast him; Ouda did warn me. I should have let him die in Tripoli. That birching – just to gain my confidence. Then he saved my life – at the risk of his own. Or was it? He never explained the sinking of the* Glengarriff. *I'll bet the whole charade was contrived by the bloody Brits, including the escape from Spain. I'll get the bastard for this; he will die in agony.*

He began analysing what Quayle knew of his organisation. He would have to close the madrassa in Naxcivan. *Move it to Azerbaijan, perhaps? He knows Prince Ouda supports our cause. Who else has he met? He has seen me but doesn't know my real name. I must sit down and think this through carefully. There must not be any future cock-ups like this.*

***

The drive from Woodside to *The Rising Sun* took 40 minutes. They booked in to a double room with a king-size bed. Barbara, totally relaxed and unabashed, unpacked and began to undress. Juan, awkward and uncomfortable, didn't know where to look.

'Before or after?' she asked.

'Pardon?'

'Do we shower first or afterwards?'

'I'm not sure.'

She stood close to him in her transparent underwear; the bright sparkle in her hypnotic eyes. 'Kiss me,' she said.

He put his arms around her and did what he was told. It was the warmest, deepest kiss he had ever experienced. His face was pressed against hers. He didn't want it to finish. *By God, she knows how to kiss.* She had skilfully undone his belt and had begun pulling down his trousers. He cooperated, slipping his shoes off as his trousers fell to the floor. His inhibitions had started to vanish. He felt her firm body while she unbuttoned his shirt. They were both breathing heavily as they laid backwards onto the bed.

'I've always had a strong libido,' she gasped as she pushed him onto his back. 'I will come quickly this way,' she said as she mounted him. Soon she was out of control. Seemingly temporarily satisfied, she slid under him; her body wriggling furiously as he pushed deeper. The hang-ups he had minutes previously disappeared; he wanted it to last all night. The eruption was volcanic, but he heard nothing. Only silence as his heart rate steadied. His exhausted body clung to her, never wanting to let her go; his mind blank with the release of the pent-up testosterone. They lay together recovering for many minutes. Eventually he began to hear the sound of the waves in the harbour outside their partially open window. It gently broke the tranquillity.

They bathed together sharing the half bottle of champagne they had found in the minibar. During dinner, Barbara raised the subject of his report.

'You mentioned that you had an Indian ayah in Riyadh.'

'Yes – Fatima.'

'Was she a Muslim or a Hindu?'

'I'm pretty sure she was a Muslim. She wore the hijab when we went outside the compound. Why?'

'Two reasons. Firstly, Fatima can be a Hindu name as well as a Muslim one. Secondly, she left you alone to go up the TV tower. She must have known you would use your credit card to pay for lunch and the transaction would be intercepted. I think she left you alone deliberately.' She paused, and then declared, 'I'll bet she is a member of the Indian NSG.'

'The Indian National Security Guard?'

'Yes – India's counter-terrorism unit. It is a tri-service paramilitary force; often called the Black Cats.'

'Ah, Sunderland Football Club!'

'Sorry?'

'It's OK, just my little joke. Sunderland are called the Black Cats.'

She smiled politely; neither understanding the joke nor its relevance.

'What you're saying is that the Indian Government may already have an agent inside al-Qaeda.'

'It's a possibility. Sir Peter may ask you more about it next week.'

If you are just a secretary, Barbara, then you know a lot about espionage. I suspect you are a plant of Sir Peter's. But why?

'When will the team of questioners arrive?'

'They are due down on Friday and will begin questioning you immediately after lunch. So, you'd better make the most of this weekend.' She giggled. Her eyes sparkled brighter than ever. He could feel his libido strengthening his muscle again. He wondered, however, whether his could keep up with her.

The weekend went by quickly; much of the time spent in their bedroom. Juan was surprised at his stamina; Barbara had the knack of bringing the best out of him.

After Sunday lunch they trundled back to Barnstaple. 'Would you like to stay the night?' she asked. Her main bedroom was tastefully decorated with matching colours: cream curtains, carpet and bedcover. Barbara prepared a light evening supper, downed with a Sancerre. They went to bed early; Juan falling asleep, totally exhausted. He was not to wake until it was time to return to Woodside the following morning.

CHAPTER 36

Monday 15th June 1992

Juan and Barbara, in attempting to finish the report for Thursday, worked long hours that week. Barbara was not work-shy. She corrected his errors and made useful suggestions for improvement. Her ideas were always relevant. His suspicion that she was something more than a gifted secretary was confirmed when she showed special interest about his time spent at the madrassa.

She seemed intrigued about Naxcivan. She asked searching questions about the school's role, its location and position relative to Nagorno and the River Aras. She wanted to know what had been left behind by the Russian Army, an estimate of the number of troops that the site could have supported and whether there was any evidence of there having ever been a detention centre. Where did the students come from? Their ages? Their previous education? What nationality were the Imams? What were their names?

Deep down, Juan developed a gut feeling that Barbara knew more than she was letting-on about the history of Naxcivan, and its importance vis-à-vis Armenia and Azerbaijan.

The Russian military generated more questions. What impressions had they made on him? Were they pro-Yeltsin?

'I'm asking these questions now because it's the sort of information the committee are going to ask,' she said on one occasion.

They finished on Thursday afternoon and he spent that night at

Barbara's. He had become confident when in her presence; no longer worrying that he might put a foot wrong. He enjoyed her company and looked forward to spending more time with her in the future. He thought his feelings were reciprocated. The excitement she generated had made him forget Molly. He was besotted; he could not hide his fervour. He had never met another woman like her: the first to love sex for its own sake. It was intoxicating. Barbara was something altogether different from anyone else. She was bewitching, but bewildering at the same time. Together in bed was so intense that he thought *no one else could possibly have had this experience before.*

That Thursday night he articulated his thoughts when they were lying together. 'I would like to spend the rest of my life with you,' he whispered.

She pulled away, a puzzled frown on her face. Her look said: *you fool.*

'There's no way I shall ever live with a man again. I'm not going to start cleaning up after them, washing and ironing their shirts and stained underpants, and forever having to put the toilet seat down. When you leave Woodside next week, forget me. Tomorrow Sir Peter and his team arrive. Concentrate your efforts on them, not me. I will always remember you as one of the best lovers I've ever had. But that's all – another lover. Find yourself a good woman who can give you children and long-term happiness.'

He was speechless. Dumbfounded, he could only look at her; disbelief registering on his face. He felt his body was collapsing inward as it dawned on him that he may have been used as a tool; literally nothing else. He turned over and thought *I must have been mad to think of giving up Molly.*

✳✳✳

By lunchtime on Friday the team had assembled. Sir Peter, as chairman, introduced the Head of his Middle East desk – Phil Jay, the Head of MI5's Irish desk – Sean Doran, and to his surprise – Barbara Renton.

'I think you've met Barbara, our man in Georgia and the Caucasus,' he smiled knowingly.

You bastard. She's been a plant all along. My instinct about her was right. No wonder she asked so many questions about Naxcivan. I wonder if she knew Fatima was an Indian NSG operative.

'Hardly a man, Sir Peter,' remarked Juan.

'No, quite!' He looked sheepish; Barbara blushed. The joke had misfired.

'We've read your report and have many questions we want to ask. As we go along, we will make our own notes. It will take several days; probably into the middle of next week. You appreciate the importance of getting everything right. I can't exaggerate this enough, but your sterling efforts may yet save the lives of millions of people.'

Using their copies of the transcript, they were largely happy to keep questions in chronological order of events.

'I'd like to begin with your first contact with the man who called himself Anibal Esmando. What were your impressions of him?' asked Sir Peter.

'Initially, he told me he was the mate on the *Dom Pedro*. The captain was a nasty piece of work called Carlos Marcial.'

'Yes, he was convicted of money laundering and given twelve years imprisonment, along with the Irish skipper, Tom Murphy. They now reside in Douglas gaol. Please continue.'

'I began to realise when we escaped to Ireland that he was in fact the real leader. Subsequent events proved me right.'

'You said in your report that he told you his real name when you reached Ceuta.'

'Yes, he said he was Moab al Saidenn.'

'Note anything unusual?'

'No. What?'

'His two names are anagrams.'

'I hadn't noticed, but then I was never much good at crosswords.'

'We believe he is the supreme leader of al-Qaeda. His real name is a third anagram: Osama bin Laden. He is the son of a wealthy Saudi businessman and is totally disillusioned with western society. Capturing him in future will be one of the West's top priorities. There is evidence to suggest he is currently in the Sudan.'

'That wouldn't surprise me; he is highly peripatetic. He has a madrassa there.'

'You don't mention that in your report.'

'Don't I? I must have forgotten, but I think he told me sometime on the journey across Algeria.'

'What makes him such a powerful leader?'

'He has hypnotic eyes and even Prince Ouda seemed to be in awe of him. He also understands the significance of the exponential.'

'The exponential?'

'Al-Qaeda, we believe, was formed four years ago. Yes?'

'Yes.'

'Suppose they began with ten supporters and each year they manage to double their numbers.'

'So?'

'Then today they will have eighty hardliners in their organisation, but in ten years, it will have grown to over 80,000. Imagine that number of fanatics happy to blow themselves up for Allah and the potential damage they could cause.'

'Mmm, I can't see them ever growing to that size without us getting wind of it.'

Juan shrugged his shoulders. He knew his four listeners were thinking linearly. 'Perhaps not, but even if they only doubled their numbers every two years, then by 2006 they would have over 10,000 ready to die for their cause. Western Governments are going to have to increase their level of surveillance on potential suicide bombers, that's for sure.'

'Somewhere in your report, you list the sort of threats they could pose.'

'Yes – page 23 or thereabouts.'

Sir Peter and the others fumbled through the papers in front of them.

'You envisage they could hijack an airliner and fly it, full of passengers, into a building such as the Pentagon or the Empire State Building. How would they train their terrorists to fly a modern aeroplane?'

'Simple. Young men are currently being trained to acquire western scientific qualifications. They will emigrate to Britain and America. They will attend university prior to getting themselves on flying courses. Already al-Qaeda is planning how to bypass airport security systems.'

'But pilot training is expensive.'

'Money is not a problem when you're backed by Saudi princes.'

'Such as Prince Ouda. You met him initially in Ceuta. Then you stayed at his residence, or should I say one of his residences, in Riyadh. What did you make of him?'

'I think he is one of many backers of al-Qaeda. He and Ali al Ghraizil are the only two sources of finance I met.'

'You know Ouda has Saudi diplomatic status?'

'Yes. It must be a good camouflage for al-Qaeda.'

'Barbara tells me he gave you a servant to look after you.'

'Yes, an ayah called Fatima.'

'Do you think she could be an Indian NSG operative?'

'When Barbara mentioned it, I thought about it and yes, I think it is possible.'

'Why?'

'When she allowed me to go up the TV tower on my own, she must have known I would use my VISA card. I think she deliberately gave me the chance to touch base.'

After a pause, Barbara asked, 'I'd like to concentrate on the Russians you met. The first was Captain Smyslov; your opinion?'

'Without his help, I would not be here. Firstly, he persuaded Major Akopian to take myself and five hostages back to Armenia to protect their withdrawal...'

'Can I interrupt there? Are you saying it was your idea that the Armenians took hostages?' asked Sir Peter.

'Yes.'

'What happened when you reached the border between Naxcivan and Nagorno-Karabakh?' pressed the Director of MI6.

'I joined Smyslov in his jeep and we went to Agarak. We waited for the helicopter to take us to Yerevan.'

'The other five remained at the border with the Armenians?'

'Yes.'

'Did you notice anything on the journey from the madrassa to the border crossing?'

'You mean did I see if we were being watched?'

Sir Peter nodded.

'Three years in Baghdad and a further three in BRIXMIS, usually inside East Germany, gives you a sixth sense when you are being observed. Although my senses are not as honed as they once were, I felt the Iranians were watching us from the south bank of the River Aras.'

'Did you know the Armenians massacred the five hostages?'

'No, I didn't. Why didn't the Iranians intervene?'

'Possibly because the al-Qaeda five were Wahhabi Sunnis – extremists who believe Shias are not true Muslims. And, of course, the Iranians are Shia.'

Barbara looked at her boss as if to ask *can I continue?*

She asked, 'So Smyslov saved your life?'

'Yes, I guess he did. After Yerevan, he accompanied me to Moscow and entertained me that weekend. I formed the opinion that he is pro-glasnost.'

'What of Colonel Veresov?'

'Also inclined towards modernism. He gave me the impression he didn't like Lutikov. He had never heard of al-Qaeda, which struck me as strange bearing in mind his position in Armenia. Although he knew my real name, his ignorance made me doubt the efficiency of the internal comms within the Russian military.' Juan paused, and then added, 'Later, I wondered if there was a deliberate block on publicising al-Qaeda activities.'

She nodded, as if signifying agreement, continuing, 'Beliavsky?'

'Ah, a different kettle of fish. Definitely old school. If he'd had his way, then I would have been shot at dawn. He knew I still had two years left to serve on the Retired List and saw me as a spy. I don't think he was happy that I was trying to infiltrate al-Qaeda. He seemed overly keen to know what I had discovered about them; particularly their source of weapons. I played up the IRA connection. My knee-jerk reaction is that there is a conspiracy somewhere.'

'What do you mean?' It was Sir Peter interrupting again.

'Well, it was on the morning of day two. Beliavsky was called away to see Lutikov. I formed the impression the shit had hit the fan; presumably because Smyslov somehow had got the message through to our embassy that I was in the Lubyanka...'

'It was Smyslov who rang us?'

'Yes. I was desperate and told him to tell you that Bradda Head was in Moscow. I had to keep my fingers crossed he would help. At that stage, I believed I would disappear in Siberia. Suddenly it all changed, I was on my way to Vienna. Do you know why I think Lutikov and Beliavsky were so concerned about my release?'

'No, go on.'

'Because they are in league with al-Qaeda.'

'Surely not!' exclaimed Sir Peter.

'Lutikov was in overall charge of the Soviet troops in Afghanistan when Gorbachev brought them home. He knew better than anyone how much support the Americans were giving the Mujahideen. He wants al-Qaeda to do the same thing to the Americans. I believe he strongly resents the decline of the Soviets as a World Super Power. I'll bet my bottom dollar there is a secret clique within the Russian Army, led by Lutikov, giving al-Qaeda support.'

Barbara was nodding, as if agreeing. 'Unfortunately, we have no proof,' she added.

'However, I think the Russians should be warned at the highest level that there may be a third party fermenting trouble.'

'I'll bring that up with Douglas next week,' agreed Sir Peter. 'He will have to make the decision as to whether to go further.'

Phil Jay asked whether Juan had any more thoughts about Lydia's disappearance.

'The captain of the *Juheina Star* was an Italian. I never met him. The man in charge seemed to be Mousad Safahar. I worked with him subsequently at the Naxcivan madrassa where he was the bursar. He was some sort of personal secretary to Prince Ouda. I never liked Safahar – I don't know why. If, as Barbara pointed out to me, Lydia's injury could not have killed her then I can only assume Safahar had her murdered. I was told she and Felipe were buried at sea. My guess is that Safahar must have rumbled that she was an agent, but that begs the question: Who shot us and why?'

'I thought you knew. You were shot by the sole remaining GEO operative who was, himself, killed by Hans – the Mossad agent.'

'But how did the GEO find us?'

'He was lucky. He must have seen Felipe coming off the *Juheina Star* and followed him. He then followed the three of you to the quay. Hans kept watch, but was fractionally too late in preventing the Spaniard shooting.'

Barbara took over. 'I would like to move on to your recuperation period in Riyadh.'

And so the questioning continued for the rest of the day. Minor points were slowly cleared up. Juan thought at times that trivia had become the master of the game.

At 6 pm Sir Peter called a halt. 'Tomorrow I would like to begin speculating on al-Qaeda's organisational wiring diagram and their likely targets.

CHAPTER 37

Saturday 20th June 1992

After some discussion, they agreed Osama bin Laden was the undisputed leader of al-Qaeda. He had a small cabinet, perhaps five or six, each with a specific role. Prince Ouda was probably his chancellor and chief money raiser; Ali al Ghraizil, his Chief of Staff, was possibly head of procurement – both personnel and arms. 'He had a lot of involvement with setting up the Naxcivan madrassa,' said Juan. 'I never met any others at that level.

'It's ironical,' said Sir Peter, 'but they have organised themselves like the American Government.'

The others looked at him to continue.

'They have allowed each country's groups considerable independence. Rather like the American states, such as Nevada and Kansas, the al-Qaeda organisation in the Sudan, Yemen, and so on, do what they like within the hierarchy's rules. Money and supplies come largely from the centre. Long-term strategy and training is centralised whereas tactical decisions and recruiting can be made locally. The bomb attacks in Israel last week would have little to do with bin Laden and were probably organised by a Palestinian group. The planning of the so-called spectaculars will be central, as they will take years to set up. Causing maximum confusion by making simultaneous attacks on geographically adjacent targets is a central strategy of their terror campaign, but will be left to individual groups to plan and execute. As for communications, I imagine they use nodal points like the IRA. Unassuming, insignificant houses receive mail, suitably encoded, and act as post boxes. Unless we are certain of the nodal point, little can be done. Telephone calls are also nodal and encoded; but in a much simpler manner. They are kept short and to the point. We use GCHQ as much as possible to snoop, but it's rather hit or miss.'

'If we are to crush them we must target their weakest point,' asserted Barbara.

Juan's estimation of her in MI6 was rising by the day despite her using him as a toyboy. He could see her replacing Sir Peter in the future.

They looked at her to continue.

'We must stop their recruitment and destroy their madrassas.'

'Preventing recruiting is surely a matter of education,' said Phil. 'We must find out where they target their efforts and try to ensure their propaganda falls on deaf ears.'

'That won't be easy. At the madrassa in Naxcivan, of the twenty or so students I met, there were at least eight nationalities. The only common thread was that they were all Muslims.'

'Then governments are going to have to be warned of the threat and clamp down on radical mullahs,' said Sir Peter.

'Again, easier said than done,' replied Barbara. 'Take Pakistan, for example. The government is fiercely Islamic; its existence is historically due to the fact that had it remained part of India in 1947, they would have been swamped by the 80% Hindu majority. I suspect, too, that those recruited in Pakistan come from the northern border regions near Afghanistan where Juan thinks their primary madrassas are.'

'Primary madrassas?' queried Sean.

Barbara looked at Juan to answer.

'Like we have primary and secondary schools, so do al-Qaeda. They are giving their students a degree of education that is superior to that given by governments. Al-Qaeda's recruiting and training, coupled to their long-term aims is going to make them a force to be reckoned with. It will take the combined resources of the west to deal with them.'

'Moving onto likely targets. You conjecture quite a few ideas. Do you wish to amplify?' asked Sir Peter.

'Their aim will usually be to kill as many people as possible, preferably Americans, in the most spectacular way. Attacks will be multiple and simultaneous. We mentioned airline hijacking yesterday. I can envisage two or three aircraft being hijacked simultaneously and converging on a crowded city such as London or New York. Imagine the havoc of three packed airliners crashing into Canary Wharf, a packed football ground, such as White Hart Lane, or the Houses of Parliament.'

There was silence before Sean asked, 'Why White Hart Lane?'

Barbara answered immediately, 'They're the Jewish team.'

Juan continued, 'An even greater threat to London could come from hijacking an oil tanker or a gas tanker.'

Sir Peter's eyes narrowed. Juan realised he hadn't explained what he meant. 'I intended to say a ship carrying oil or, worse still, natural gas. They could capture it, like pirates, outside Rotterdam and load it with explosives. They sail it up the Thames, ramming it into the Thames Barrier just before a spring tide.'

'The City would be flooded to a depth of 10 ft. Electricity cuts, computer basements ruined. Billions wiped off the Stock Exchange in minutes,' added Barbara.

'Exactly. I keep coming back to the same conclusion. Your Service, and that of MI5 and Special Branch, are going to have to get ready for a terrifying future. Fail to prepare will prepare to fail.'

***

Peshawar in the North West frontier of Pakistan is a remote town. Rule of law is a mix of Sharia law and knowing the right person, whether he is the local head of police, or the current tribal chief with the most militia. It is, therefore, a haven for unscrupulous organisations such as al-Qaeda. Osama bin Laden had made the town his HQ four years previously when he had fallen out of favour with Saddam Hussein.

He had received the single sheet photocopy of the summary of a Russian FSB file, marked *Confidential,* and had read it many times. On each occasion his fury had increased. He knew it was providing him with most of the information to have his revenge. He called one of his more intelligent analysts to attend a meeting to discuss the brief report on Quayle.

'I want you to do some research on the Isle of Man.'

'What exactly do you want?'

'Specifically, I want you to go there and find out as much as you can about this individual. You have his date of birth, his place of birth, where he went to school, and the names of his parents. I see his mother was Egyptian – that explains how he spoke fluent Arabic. Find out if he still lives there, where, what he does, his habits and if he has a family. If he doesn't live on the island, then it will be more difficult. However, he taught at a school in Cumbria for a while. Go there. Someone must know where he is. Trace him down. Take as long as is necessary. Keep in touch in the usual way. Report to me every month. This task may seem trivial, but it has top priority.'

'May I ask what is so special about him?'

'I want him to die the most horrible death known to man – to be burnt alive!'

✦✦✦

By the afternoon of the fourth day, the analysis of Juan's report was finishing. Juan was exhausted, but so too were the committee members. The conclusion of the amended report was headed *Actions to be Taken.* It agreed that the Foreign Secretary would be briefed by Sir Peter. The recommendations included:

The Foreign Secretary seeks a face-to-face meeting with his opposite Russian number to alert him that General Lutikov may be fermenting trouble by supporting al-Qaeda.

The Foreign and Home Secretaries seek extra funding in cabinet to begin recruiting additional MI5 and MI6 agents, preferably with Asian backgrounds. Their training courses commence as soon as possible as a matter of urgency.

An edited version of the report be produced for Mossad and the CIA by Sir Peter.

Sir Peter to contact his opposite number in the Indian NSG to ascertain whether Fatima was an agent and, if so, whether the NSG would be prepared to share future intelligence.

The Foreign Secretary to discuss privately with the Prime Minister the possibility of raising concerns with the Pakistani Prime Minister, Nawaz Sharif, of the potential dangers of al-Qaeda and the belief that recruiting and training is predominantly taking place in the North West of his country.

Sir Peter to consider the possible means of finding Osama bin Laden using current resources and taking action to arrest him.

***

That evening the five had dinner together in a bistro chosen by Barbara. 'Have you given any further thoughts to the proposition I put to you when you returned from Russia?' Sir Peter asked Juan.

'To be honest, sir, no I haven't. I've been too busy putting the report together. I really would like to take a break for a few months and recuperate. Was there a time limit for me to give a reply?'

'No, you can take as long as you want. Barbara tells me she has been impressed by your performance and thinks I should encourage you to join our ship.'

His phrase *your performance* caused Juan a wry smile. In a jocular fashion that would be lost on Sir Peter, he replied, 'I must say Barbara's performance impressed me too.'

Barbara coughed, smiled and, somehow, scowled at the same time. She had got the point.

'What are your immediate plans, then?' asked Peter.

'I was thinking of returning to the Isle of Man for a while and see how things pan out. I might take up Barbara's suggestion to settle down.'

***

The following day, Sir Peter sat alone in his office at Vauxhall Cross, pulled out a memo pad and began to write to his opposite number, Robert Gates:

TOP SECRET
Memorandum

SUBJECT:	AL-QAEDA THREAT	
From:	Director MI6	**Date:** 23 Jun 92
To:	CIA Director, Langley	**Ref:** VB/CIA/AQ92/1

Dear Robert,

1. You are aware we successfully infiltrated an agent into the terrorist organisation calling itself al-Qaeda. Our operative recently returned to us after 18 months in the field and has been questioned at length about his report. I enclose a summary at Annex A. However, I would draw your attention to the type of threats al-Qaeda pose to our societies. In particular, their aims are long-term. Potential suicide martyrs are being educated to infiltrate the West and become airline pilots, computer hackers, doctors, etc. Therefore, in the future we can expect aircraft and ships to be hijacked simultaneously and be used as human bombs, targeting The Empire State Building, The White House, New York harbour, and so on. In the short term, however, we believe car bombs will become more sophisticated and attacks more ambitious. Underground car parks are particularly vulnerable where the foundations could be disturbed in an attempt to collapse a whole building. Your World Trade Centre could be a good example. I cannot stress enough the importance of this memo. Could we meet to discuss more fully Major Quayle's report ASAP...?

290

Sir Peter's PA took the finished handwritten document and typed the message into the cryptographic coding machine. A hard copy of the text, to be kept on file, appeared...

ONRC EDCE SECI NALK HDIL WLSA MNSA RMHA WGKG RLEA...

Compressed into a package the size of a micro-dot, it took less than a second to traverse the Atlantic and appeared on a de-coding computer in Virginia looking like...

YOUA REAW AREW ESUC CESS FULL YINF ILTR ATED ANAG ...

An experienced de-coding operator was, within minutes, presenting the Director of the CIA, Robert M Gates, with the message...

YOU/ARE/AWARE/WE/SUCCESSFULLY/INFILTRATED/AN/AGEN T...

CHAPTER 38

Thursday 25th June 1992

A few days later, Juan arrived at Douglas. He drove to Port Erin and booked into the *Falcon's Nest Hotel*. It was only four o'clock. Excited, he unpacked and then drove the three miles to Port St Mary to knock on Molly's door. His heart was thumping like a teenager on his first date. A middle-aged man, perhaps not much older than himself but looking more like 60, answered.

'Yes?' he asked, in a grumpy manner.

Juan was surprised and confused. It took less than a second for him to think, *My God, has she married this old buffer?*

'Is Molly, I mean Mrs Kelly, in?'

'She doesn't live here anymore.'

He had never been hit in the chest by a rubber bullet but he imagined it felt like the blow that had just stunned him.

'She's moved away?'

'Yes.'

'Do you know where to?'

'No. All her mail is redirected by the Post Office. I never met her. The house was already empty when I bought it last October.'

'Ten months ago?'

The man nodded.

'I am sorry to have bothered you.' He turned and slowly went down the front steps – shell shocked.

Why has she moved? Where could she have gone? I know, I'll walk down to her sister-in-law's house and ask Pam.

In Lime Street, there was no reply. He couldn't be sure, but he felt there was someone inside. *Am I being paranoiac?* He walked to the quay, hoping to find Mark's boat. Nothing, all the fishing fleet were at sea. Disconsolate, he walked back to his car.

What do I do now? I know, I'll ring George Costain.

He had long ago lost George's phone number. He returned to Port Erin and checked in the hotel's telephone directory – nothing. *George must be ex-directory.*

He knew he would have to go to Douglas in the morning and ask for George at the Police HQ.

He booked a table for dinner – eight o'clock – and decided to drive to Fleshwick Bay for pure nostalgia. The farm house blown to pieces by the so-called German WW2 bomb was still a wreck. The fragile pier, used by the IRA, had disappeared; presumably in a gale.

I can't believe it was only 15 months ago; so much has happened.

The following day, before nine o'clock, he was talking to the same portly desk sergeant that he had met when asking to see the Chief Constable about phone tapping. To his surprise, the sergeant remembered him.

'Mr Quine isn't it, sir?' he asked. 'You caused quite a stir when you were birched. PC Corlett wouldn't let on what it was all about. Most of us thought it was some sort of conspiracy.'

'That would be one way of describing it, sergeant. Would you contact DC Costain and tell him that I would like to see him?'

'He's Detective Sergeant Costain now, sir. He was promoted soon after your affair died down.'

A few minutes later, they were greeting each other like long lost brothers. 'I never thought I'd see you again,' exclaimed George.

'Well I have been torpedoed, shot and imprisoned in the Lubyanka. And that's just for starters.'

'I'd love to hear all about it, but I'm in the middle of an investigation into child abuse at the moment. I could grab an hour at lunchtime, if you like. Could we meet? I want to know what happened after your punch-up with Corlett.'

'It's going to take longer than an hour, George. But, yes, lunch would be fine.'

'Shall we say *The Liverpool Arms* at 1230?'

'Fine. There's one thing I'd like you to do for me, however.'

'What's that?'

'Do you remember Molly Kelly?'

'Yes, of course. I transferred the ownership of your car to her, as you asked. Why?'

'She's moved. She no longer lives in Cronk Road. Can you find out where she has moved to?'

'Sure, it shouldn't be difficult. I'll bring you her new address at lunchtime.' He looked at his watch. 'I must go. See you later.'

Juan filled in time by wandering through Strand Street and then walked up Crellin's Hill to the Manx Museum. He'd visited it many times as a child, but was surprised to see so many improvements. From the rather drab and dull experience he remembered, it was now lighter, brighter, and better designed to grab your interest. He found himself staring at a large three-dimensional model of the Island. He could see the farm where he grew up outside Bride. The farm's lease was due for renewal in six months. He wondered whether to renew it for another ten years or run the farm himself. It would be a hard life, but a satisfying one.

But a farmer needs a wife.

When he arrived at the pub, locally known as *The Halfway House*, George was already waiting.

'The interviews went quicker than I thought. Child abuse cases are the worst of all; I would prefer a good murder anytime.'

'Do you get many?'

'There have only been two since I've been on the Force, and one of those involved abuse as well.' He paused, and then continued, 'I've found

294

Molly's address. She now lives in Ramsey.' He handed Juan a piece of paper: *50 Hespra Terrace, Ramsey.* 'If I remember rightly, it's on Lezayre Road, near the Grammar School.'

'Yes, I know it. Don't forget I went to Ramsey Grammar School.'

'Of course.'

'What I can't understand is why she moved. It's about as far away from Port St Mary as you can get.'

George shrugged his shoulders, before asking, 'What are you drinking?'

An hour and a half, and two pints later, George having been totally absorbed as he listened to Juan's tale, asked, 'What are your future plans? Anything now is going to be awfully dull.'

'It's time to settle down, George. I think I'll take over the farm at Ballajorra. Rather than try to run it like my dad, I'll go in for one or two rare breeds, Llamas and Loghtan sheep, perhaps.'

'And does Molly feature in these plans?' he asked smiling.

'Wait and see, George. Wait and see. Fancy being a best man?'

They shook hands, vowing to meet up again shortly.

Juan drove north; 20 minutes later he was knocking on the door of No 50. The house was not dissimilar to that of Cronk Road: pre-war terraced, with a dormer third storey.

The door opened. Molly stood in front of him, looking dishevelled. In her arms was a crying child. 'What?' she asked, annoyed at having been disturbed.

'Molly, it's me, Juan.'

She blinked, and then screwed her eyes. She peered unbelievingly. Her frown disappeared; her frown became a ray of sunshine as her face lit up. 'Is it really you?' Her eyes welled-up as she moved awkwardly towards him, not knowing what to do with the baby. He opened his arms wide and gently caressed them both without wishing to harm the child. He kissed her forehead. She smelt of baby milk, but it was wonderful. He didn't care that her hair was a mess, or her pinny stained, or that there were no stockings on her legs and her slippers were worn. He moved his mouth down, licking her nose and kissed her lips. She had her eyes closed as she tried to respond as best she could with the babe in her arms. It was Molly, his Molly.

'Come in,' she begged and stood to one side.

She led him into the front room. She put the baby into its cot. She had clearly been in the middle of giving it a feed.

'Who is this, then?' Juan asked, bending over the child and touching its cheek with the back of his hand. He turned to look at Molly.

She registered surprise on her tear-stained face.

'Don't you know?'

'No.'

'She's your daughter, Sophie.'

Without stopping to think, 'You're joking,' he exclaimed.

'Well, it's no bugger else's.'

CHAPTER 39

Friday 26th June 1992

'Molly, that's marvellous.'

'It hasn't been for me.'

'Why?'

'Having a bastard in Port St Mary to a stranger, who just happened to be your lodger for a few weeks? And him guilty of assaulting the police? Then he was birched! What do you think the gossips made of that? Losing my job was the least of it. I was sent to Coventry, people turned their backs on me in the street. The boys were bullied at school. I was even nicknamed The Baker.'

'The Baker?'

'I had a bun in the oven, didn't I?'

'Molly, I'm so sorry. I had no idea.'

She sat down and wept profusely. 'It's not your fault. You told me to believe in you and I did.'

She paused for what seemed a considerable time, then added, 'Honestly.'

She looked up at him. She was in shock and shaking. Her eyes – wet, red, and full of suffering.

He knelt down in front of her. 'I have thought about you every day.' He lied convincingly. She believed him; she wanted to believe him. He held her hands and looked into her tear-stained face. That beautiful face, that unique face, which he knew he would never tire of looking at.

'I had to leave Port St Mary. Get as far away as possible. I put the house on the market, moved out the next day and rented this place. It sold about three months after I left.'

'And when was Sophie born?'

'On Christmas Day, six months ago. Pam took a while to get over the fact that she was related to someone seen locally as a scrubber, but looked after the boys for a week. No one knows me here; it's Ramsey's main advantage.'

'Where are Peter and Mikey?'

'At school. I must go and pick them up in five minutes. Mikey goes four afternoons a week. He starts full time in September.'

'I will come with you. You can tell the other mums that your husband has come home.'

'Is that a proposal?' she asked, still looking unhappy.

'Yes. Will you?' He was still kneeling in front of her holding her hands. Mysteriously, Sophie had been quiet in her cot throughout their conversation.

'Will I what?' She had started to smile.

'I'll take that as a yes!'

He pulled her up and gave her the longest, warmest, tightest kiss he could.

Three weeks later, on the 17th July 1992, they were married at the local registry office. George was best man and his girlfriend was the second witness.

Juan gave notice that he would not renew the lease on the farm. Molly was excited at the thought of living on a farm again. The boys began to make a list of the animals they wanted to keep.

They lived at Hespra Terrace where they celebrated their first Christmas and Sophie's first birthday. It had been an idyllic six months.

On New Year's Eve, the BBC News at Ten announced simultaneous bomb attacks had taken place at two hotels in Aden, the *Movenpick* and the *Golden Mohur*. Both were used by the US Army to billet troops whilst on furlough from peacekeeping duties in Somalia. Luckily, only two were killed – a tourist and a hotel worker.

Simultaneous bombings, the hallmark of an al-Qaeda attack thought Juan as he listened. *Bin Laden won't stop there; more attacks will occur.* He didn't know it, but the US would withdraw from using Yemen as a base for operations in Somalia a few weeks later.

On Monday January 4th, they moved to Ballajorra. A week later, Peter and Mikey started at the little primary school in Bride village that Juan had attended almost 40 years previously.

Juan managed to acquire five llamas, a flock of 40 Hebridean black sheep and half a dozen goats; Peter's favourites. He had given the goats names and, when called, they would come to him for feeding and milking. The farm was never going to make a fortune, but Juan's plan was to make it a happy, largely self-supporting unit. He built a piggery, and Molly's hens were laying sufficiently to keep the family in eggs. Two beehives were bought. Negotiations began to obtain a small herd of Belted Galloway cattle.

Once a week they would go to Ramsey for shopping. With the boys at school, they would take Sophie and usually had lunch in a bistro near the quay. The more exotic restaurants – Chinese and Italian – necessitated a trip to Douglas. Getting a babysitter was not a problem. The local vicar's 15 year old daughter was reliable. They would go, typically, every six weeks. It was a good life; a simple life. They were happy in each other's company. They often noticed in restaurants how frequently other couples never talked. Their own conversation never dried up.

Their tranquil, idyllic lifestyle blossomed. Their only contact with the outside world was watching the news on TV in the evening, before going to bed. They didn't receive any daily papers. On their weekly trip to Ramsey, they would buy a copy of the local weekly, *The Isle of Man Examiner;* their only newspaper.

International events were occurring, however, that troubled Juan. On 26th February a bomb exploded in the underground car park of the World Trade Centre in New York, killing six and injuring 1,000. He felt it had the hallmarks of al-Qaeda; confirmed when a week later Mohammed Salameh was arrested.

∗∗∗

TOP SECRET
Memorandum

SUBJECT:	AL-QAEDA THREAT	
From:	Director MI6	**Date:** 28 Feb 93
To:	Director CIA	**Ref:** VB/CIA/AQ93/1

Dear James,

1. Firstly, let me congratulate you on your recent appointment. I hope we have many years of successful cooperation ahead of us.

2. Secondly, my commiserations on the recent outrage at the World Trade Centre. You have come to your chair at a most difficult time.

3. However, may I draw your attention to a memo my predecessor sent Robert Gates last year. In it he warned of the threat posed by al-Qaeda and specifically mentioned tower blocks with underground car parks being vulnerable.

4. He invited your organisation to join a small group with vested interests in sharing information on the growing threat of al-Qaeda. The Israelis, the French, the Germans, the Indians and ourselves meet informally biannually and would welcome your attendance at our next meeting in Tel Aviv on 10 Mar 93.

Yours etc,

    Barbara

∗∗∗

On March 12th simultaneous bombs killed over 250 people, mostly Hindus, in Bombay. Juan remembered Fatima and wondered if she had been an Indian NSG agent.

Was the Hindu government worried about the extreme Islamists too?

In early October, 19 US soldiers were killed and 70 injured fighting in Mogadishu, Somalia. Juan's gut told him there was a link between the so-called rebels and al-Qaeda.

About the same time, trouble broke out in Russia. Boris Yeltsin, the Russian President, dissolved parliament but had to resort to violence to keep control. He shelled the Russian White House, killing several hundred. Juan remembered Lutikov and Beliavsky and imagined their having a hand in the revolt. Perhaps they had already been removed from power. There were occasional reports on the news that trouble was brewing in Chechnya. His mind went back to the students at Naxcivan; he hadn't thought about the madrassa for ages.

In March 1994, six months after the killing of 19 soldiers in Mogadishu, the TV news announced that the Americans were withdrawing all their forces from Somalia. A week later, on al Aljazeera TV, a statement, reputedly made by bin Laden, claimed the US were no longer "leaders of the New World Order, they were cowards and afraid to confront him."

God, I'm lucky to be out of it. Life here with Molly and the kids is all I want.

The same week a new restaurant opened in Douglas – *The Taj Mahal*. A big splash in *The Examiner* described it as 'an upmarket Indian.'

'We must give it a try when we are next in Douglas,' said Juan.

'I've never eaten Indian food,' replied Molly.

'I see the proprietor is actually from Pakistan, most so-called Indian restaurants are not Indian at all; mostly they're Bangladeshi.'

A few weeks went by; it was approaching Juan's forty-third birthday.

'I'd like to take you somewhere for your birthday,' said Molly. 'How about trying that new Indian?'

On Saturday evening, the 2nd April, Molly and Juan put Sophie to bed at seven o'clock and allowed the boys to stay up for another hour with Jilly, the vicar's daughter. Their table was booked for 8 pm.

Greeted at the door by a bearded proprietor wearing a Kashmiri jacket and turban, the restaurant and food was a cut above the usual curry houses found in Britain.

They drove home in the dark, over the mountain road towards Ramsey – in the reverse direction of the famous TT course. It was a beautiful night, a half-moon and the stars shone brightly. They pulled into a lay-by above Sulby reservoir to admire the moon's reflection on the lake. He put his arm around her shoulder and smiled at her. Her flaxen hair reflected the light. She smiled back but said nothing, her eyes shone with expectation. He kissed her. With both breathing heavily, his hand fumbled to undo her bra. Soon he was kissing her firm breasts, his hand sliding up her thigh.

'Let's get in the back,' he suggested.

With Molly on top of him, the excitement of making love outdoors had them gasping as they quickly climaxed together in a sudden, sharp frenzy.

They collapsed into each others arms, each holding firmly to their partner until they began to feel the nip in the night air.

'We'd better get back for Jilly,' Molly said. 'Her mother will be wondering where we've got to.'

'That's the first time we've ever done it in a car,' remarked Juan as he started the engine.

'Then we'd better have Indian food more often.'

***

At The Taj Mahal, a handwritten note was copied three times. They were put into three envelopes and addressed to three different addresses in Bradford, Birmingham and East London. From there, they would be duplicated and sent to various addresses in the Middle East. One could be guaranteed to arrive at its ultimate destination in Peshawar.

The gist of the letter was simple: *Found Major Quayle. He lives in the North of the Island and has a wife. What next?*

A month later, a reply was received at The Taj Mahal: *Find out if he has a family. What he does for a living. There is to be nothing left when he is destroyed – nothing. We need to know everything about him.*

***

It took over six months for a report to be finalised and returned to Peshawar. The two operatives, trained in Afghanistan, had perfected their scouting skills. Even Juan had never noticed he and his family had been under considerable observation for almost half a year.

He has a sixty acre farm – Ballajorra. It is bounded on one side by the sea. The farmhouse is 400 metres from the main road. Access is by a single, rough track – not tarmacked. He has about forty sheep – a rare breed, ten unusually marked cattle, five llamas and some goats. They keep chickens and have several pigs. There is no dog but several Manx cats.

There are three children; the two boys attend the village primary school. The daughter is about two and a half. His wife is approximately seven or eight months pregnant and helps run the farm. They rise at 0700 hours and usually retire around 2230. They regularly attend the village church on Sunday morning. He is a member of the Ramsey golf club and plays regularly on Thursday afternoons with the same friends. The only time we have seen them leave the farm en famille was on July 5th – Tynwald Fair Day, a Manx bank holiday. After attending the fair, they went for a picnic on a beach in Port Erin. They appear to be a very happy family.

***

On the last day of November, Heather Indira Quayle was born; so named as she had been conceived in the back of a car on the heather-covered slopes of Snaefell after an Indian meal. Sophie, about to become three, had her nose put out as her brothers now transferred their attention to the new member of the Quayle family.

***

In the middle of January 1995, a reply was received at The Taj Mahal: *A specialist will arrive in May. His name will be Mwt al-Swd. You will do as he says – to the letter.*

The two Pakistanis had no idea what the meaning of his name was; neither understood Arabic. Had they known, they might have worried what the future would be for the Quayle family.

CHAPTER 40

Thursday 29th June 1995

During the winter months, The Isle of Man Steam Packet Company run a twice-daily service between Heysham and Douglas. As the summer months approach, their level of service increases to accommodate the holiday traffic. Services from Belfast, Dublin and Liverpool are introduced.

The ship from Dublin arrived on Thursday 29th June 1995 at precisely 1300 hours. Stepping onto Victoria Pier, Douglas from the *Lady of Mann* was a chisel-cheekboned, tall, slim Afghan with several suitcases. Dressed in a smart charcoal-grey suit, he looked to be a salesman carrying samples. Indeed, had he been asked to open his cases, they would have revealed samples of Kleeneze brushes and kitchen utensils, including many containers, apparently plastic, but in reality glass covered with plastic, labelled with products for cleaning ovens, work surfaces and tiled floors.

A taxi took him to the Villa Marina, situated in the central part of the two mile promenade; he didn't want the driver to know exactly where he was heading. A 50 yard walk up Broadway placed him in front of The Taj Mahal. He entered. It was half-full of workers enjoying the lunchtime special for £4.99. He sat down without asking for a waiter to show him to a table. A swarthy, bearded attendant, perhaps in his early thirties, wearing a bottle green shalwar qameez, approached and gave him the menu. 'Our special today,' he said, 'is chicken korma, followed by mango and ice-cream.'

'Fine, I'll have it with a pint of Kingfisher. Tell Gopal that Mwt al-Swd has arrived.'

'I am Gopal, sir,' replied the surprised waiter. 'We were expecting you to arrive last month.'

'Naturally, my movements must be kept secret. I have had to come here via a circuitous journey through France and Southern Ireland. It has taken longer than I thought. The fewer people who meet me *en route*, the better.'

'Of course, of course. I didn't mean to imply any criticism. We have a room ready for you above the restaurant, if you wish to stay here.'

'That will be fine. When can we get down to business?'

'The lunchtime trade will be over in half an hour. We close from two o'clock until seven this evening.'

'Excellent.'

'I'll get Ajit to come and introduce himself. He's in the kitchen.'

The stranger ate his curry but opted for a black coffee instead of the dessert. He was shown to his room on the second floor by Gopal. He unpacked his personal belongings and looked around. There was a wash basin that had been there since the former Victorian boarding house had been built. It was cracked and stained. The wallpaper, pale blue flowers of indeterminate species on a white background, was in places hanging off the wall – *winter damp,* he thought. The carpet on the floor was badly worn.

Thank Allah this exercise won't take too long.

He would have to use a communal bathroom at the end of the corridor. It was as unappealing as his bedroom.

He returned to the empty dining room.

'Is everything all right, sir,' asked Gopal.

'It'll do,' he growled

'We have copied the Ordnance Survey map of the farm for you,' enthused Ajit, 'and sketched further details on this drawing.'

'How remote is this place?'

'It's about a mile from the small village of Bride. The road that passes the bottom of the farm lane is very quiet. The track to the farm is less than half a mile. Hedges mark the boundaries of the fields. It is easy to hide and not be seen. I could take you this afternoon if you want. We have a small Ford car,' replied Ajit. He struck the stranger as the smarter of the two.

Having changed into suitable clothes for country tramping, half an hour later al-Swd and Ajit were descending down the mountain road into Ramsey. In his haversack, the Afghan carried powerful binoculars, the maps provided by Ajit and several marker pens.

'Where have you been parking the car when you have been reconnoitring the farm?' asked al-Mwt.

'We have varied. The nearest place is at the side of the church in front of the village café, but it's too obvious. We generally leave it miles away and walk across the fields. Another option is to leave it in Ramsey and catch the bus, but they are infrequent.'

'So wherever we park, we're in for a short hike?'

'Yes.'

In the event, they drove through Bride and took the road towards the Point of Ayre lighthouse. They parked beyond the cottages at Cranstal and walked south along the shore.

'This is a safe approach,' said Ajit.

'Who collects the children from school?'

'Usually the wife. It's near that time now.'

'So, we must be careful.'

They found a spot to observe the farm from the rear. The field with the llamas was adjacent to that with the black Hebridean sheep. Beyond were the Belted Galloways. The goats seemed to be allowed to wander wherever they wished. The two men saw Molly return from the school-run, and go inside with the children. There was no sign of Juan.

'Where do you think Quayle is?'

Ajit shrugged his shoulders before realising it was Thursday. 'I know, he'll be playing golf in Ramsey,' he remarked.

'What time does he normally get back?'

Again Ajit shrugged.

'We'll better wait and find out then,' said al-Swd in a tetchy way that conveyed annoyance.

By half-past five, Ajit was beginning to get agitated. He kept looking at his watch.

'What's the matter?'

'I am thinking of Gopal. He will be wondering where we are. The restaurant will be opening again in an hour and a half.'

'Bugger the restaurant,' spat al-Swd. 'Details such as this are far more important than your bloody restaurant. Fancy not knowing the times of comings and goings, did they teach you nothing at Miranshah?'

He knows we attended the madrassa at Miranshah!

Miranshah is a small town on the north-west frontier of Pakistan, equally populated by displaced Afghans and local Pakistani Waziris. In a hidden valley to the west lies one of al-Qaeda's military training areas.

'I'm sorry, sir. I never thought it would be significant.'

'Everything is significant; the time they put the children to bed is significant, the time they normally go to bed themselves is significant; even the number of pigs is significant.'

Ajit felt a cold shiver run up his spine and tried to rescue the situation.

'They have two pigs and usually go to bed around half past ten.'

'Yes, I read your report. Now belt up and wait here. I am going for a closer look.' And having rebuked Ajit, Mwt crawled away. Within a few seconds he had disappeared – as if he had never been there.

It was almost a quarter to seven when Ajit saw Juan return from golf. He was getting nervous. The Afghan had been gone over an hour and he had no idea where he was. He looked at his watch. *What will Gopal be thinking?*

Suddenly a hand grasped his shoulder from behind. He jumped out of his skin. He turned around. It was Mwt smiling at him.

'Still worried about the time? I have finished here for now. I will come back tomorrow night on my own. Let's go.'

They crept away.

Ajit took the fastest road towards Douglas – the TT course past Snaefell mountain. He eventually plucked up the courage to ask the stranger, who hadn't said a word, what he had found out.

'The house has no alarm system, the lock on the French window into the dining room is easily picked, the boys share a bedroom, the little girl has her own, the baby's cot is in the main bedroom, which has its own shower room.'

'You've been inside?' asked a disbelieving Ajit.

'Of course.'

'But the wife and the kids were inside too.'

'Yes, so what?'

He paused, looking at the view of Douglas as they turned a corner leading to a long descending straight with a pub at the bottom. He continued, 'The house has an Aga oil burning stove that supplies the central heating as well as acting as a cooker. I think I've seen enough to formulate a plan. All we need now is to get them out of the house for a few hours.'

'Well last year they all went to Tynwald Fair for the day.'

'When is that?'

'Next Wednesday – the 5th July.'

'Is it a bank holiday?'

'Yes.'

'Then, I want you to close the restaurant that day for lunches. I have jobs for you and Gopal.'

It was almost eight o'clock when they arrived back in Douglas.

CHAPTER 41

Friday 30th June 1995

On Friday morning, the Afghan never came down for breakfast. Ajit and Gopal instinctively knew not to disturb him. They were in awe of his presence and authority. They knew their place in the organisation – troopers ready to die if necessary. But al-Swd was something different. He gave orders, others obeyed them. He finally appeared at midday, asking where he could get some basic electronic equipment. He wanted, he told them, to make an eavesdropping microphone that he could plant in Quayle's house to listen to conversations.

'We must be certain that they will be away next Wednesday to give me plenty of time to implement our plan.'

Although he had called it their plan, neither Ajit nor Gopal had a clue what was planned. They weren't going to ask. They would do what they were told when the time came. They just hoped it wouldn't entail pressing the self-destruct button. They had come to like their quiet life on the island.

'I've seen an anorak's shop like the one you want in Back Strand Street,' replied Ajit.

'I'll go on my own,' he replied when Ajit volunteered to show him where it was. 'I don't want you guys more involved than necessary.'

The shop turned out to be a wonderland of parts for almost anything: washing machines, valve radios, computers, calculators, even black and white TVs. The owner, Geoff Callow, was most helpful – suggesting chips and processors that would work better than others. 'Simultaneous timing devices triggered by mercury can be awkward to handle,' he said. 'These radio controlled solid state relays are more reliable. The problem with mercury switches is that the smallest thing can start them off. I've known a mouse trigger them.' Al-Swd thanked him, paid cash and, armed with a soldering iron, left. He then disappeared for the rest of the afternoon into his room.

On Saturday 1st July he took the Ford and was gone all day. Ajit suspected he had returned to Ballajorra and was planting the bugs. The Quayles were probably doing their weekly shop in Ramsey. He didn't reappear until Monday lunchtime. They didn't ask where he had spent the two nights, but they noticed an agricultural odour from his clothes; they suspected he had spent them in a barn.

'It looks as if we are on for Wednesday,' he said. 'They are planning to go to the fair and then picnic at Port Erin, like last year. The two boys have bullied their parents. It's what they wanted. They are planning to leave at ten o'clock to go to the fair at St Johns, so we must leave here by 8.30 am at the latest. I want you to wear distinctive coloured shirts that day. They will help you to be seen at the fair and be remembered by witnesses. If necessary, ask a policeman the time, make sure you get a good score at the shooting booth, anything like that. When this is all over and I am gone, the police may come snooping. It is vital that you both have alibis on Wednesday. Also, clean up my room. Make sure there is nothing left that can be linked to me staying here this week.'

On Tuesday, the Afghan spent most of the day in his room. He appeared for some lunch in the kitchen and went for a walk. The restaurateurs never asked where.

On the morning of the fair, they drove through the centre of Bride village and parked the car among the sand dunes beyond Cranstal. Mwt then explained what he wanted them to do.

'You are to return to the farm road and wait near the entrance. When the Quayles leave in half an hour or so, you are to follow them at a discreet distance. You know where they are heading, so it shouldn't be too difficult. Take turns to watch them carefully at the fair. When you are certain they are heading to the south of the Island for their picnic, you are to return here and pick me up. That should be around half past one. If at any time you think they have changed their plans and are coming home early then you must get ahead of them. Drive past the farm entrance and blow the car's horn for all its worth. I will then know to get out quick. I'll then meet you here thirty minutes later. Understood?'

They both nodded. It seemed simple enough.

Al-Swd took his packed rucksack and headed towards the shore. He arrived at his observation point in time to watch Mrs Quayle load the back of their Volvo estate with the essentials for a day out: a hamper, wind-breaks, inflated rubber rings, canvas chairs, a child's push-chair and the other necessary paraphernalia needed to keep young children content. He watched the two boys enthusiastically jump in the back seat. Sophie was less keen to sit between her brothers. With the baby on her mother's knee and Quayle driving, it was 10.20 am when the packed car moved down the farm lane.

He waited, enjoying the warm sunshine where he lay among the sand dunes. *I'll give them half an hour in case they return.*

At 1100 hours he moved towards the house. Picking the lock on the French windows, he gained entry and started work on the Aga in the kitchen. He opened the burner door and lifted off the inner cover to reveal the safety valve phial. He took off the phial protector. He had noted the automatic timer was set for the hot water and central heating to start at 1800 hours. The central heating thermostat in the hall was set for 15 degrees, therefore unlikely to come on during the warm summer weather. He removed the oil control valve and inserted a timing device linked to the detonator embedded in the Semtex that he had brought halfway across the world. He connected the miniature transmitter to the timer. He put the control back, replaced the inner cover and the burner door. The most intricate and awkward of his jobs had taken 50 minutes. It was already midday.

Next, four incendiary devices, with their detonators and receiver relays, were placed strategically. They would fire simultaneously when the explosion occurred in the Aga. The first he placed under, but inside the padding, of the lounge settee. The second was hidden in the cupboard under the stairs inside a cardboard box used to contain furniture polishes and dusters. The third he positioned inside the 1,000 gallon oil tank near the rear door. Finally, on the landing at the top of the stairs was a padded armchair. He turned it upside down, cut a hole in the canvas, pushed the device inside and taped up the hole.

He then went around all the upstairs windows; they had been conveniently closed before the family had left home. Each was carefully opened and several drops of superglue applied to the frames. Within minutes they would be impossible to open. Before moving outside, he double checked he had left no clues to his presence.

He looked at his watch. It was one o'clock. He returned to the dunes. Using a folding spade, he dug a four-foot hole in the soft sand. He buried everything; finally throwing the spade into the hole and kicking back the sand. He smoothed the site over; no one would ever find his tools. He walked the mile to Cranstal. A few minutes later, his colleagues arrived.

'Any problems?' he asked.

'None,' replied Gopal. 'They left the fair after about an hour. We followed them as far as Foxdale and then we turned around. We went back to the fair for half an hour. Ajit won that teddy bear on the hoop-la stall. I met one of our regular customers and chatted to him for a while.'

'Excellent. You can take me back to Douglas. I have a boat to catch.'

'You're leaving so soon?' asked Ajit.

'Yes, my work is done. I will catch the 3.30 pm boat to Liverpool.'

'Then what?'

'You don't need to know. Nothing will happen until late tonight. If the police come nosing around tomorrow you have never heard of me. There is no evidence. You know nothing.'

The two men nodded their heads up and down rapidly; a worried look on their faces.

***

Four hours after leaving Douglas, the Afghan was walking from the Pier Head, up Lord Street towards Lime Street Station. He was in no hurry. His train for Euston didn't leave until 2040 hours. There would be plenty of time to make a phone call and have something to eat. His train would arrive in London a few minutes before midnight. An al-Qaeda sleeper would meet him there, put him up for the night, and take him to catch the 0735 hours train to Dover; in plenty of time to catch the 1000 hours boat to Calais. From there, someone would drive him to Charles de Gaulle Airport to catch an afternoon flight to Riyadh.

As his train sped through Rugby station, he looked at his watch. It was 2248 hours. He smiled. *It should all be over by now.*

***

The afternoon had been warm and sunny. The children had played in the sea making sandcastles with moats; shouting excitedly as they dug channels to allow the sea to surround their forts. Juan had been buried alive; only his head left above the sand. This had excited the boys but Sophie had been worried her daddy might never recover. Molly had even managed forty winks. The nearby ice cream shop had been visited twice.

When Molly suggested they should be packing up, it was approaching six o'clock and the beach was almost empty.

'I think we should go via the Port Jack Chippy in Onchan and finish the day off properly,' replied Juan. The boys pricked up their ears at the idea of prolonging their day out; especially having a fish and chip supper.

It was past nine o'clock when the family arrived back at Bride. By the time they had bathed the children and got them to bed, an hour had passed.

Juan and Molly came downstairs. Exhausted, they flopped onto the settee and put the TV on to watch the news. The news had almost finished. It was 1030 pm, their usual time to go to bed. Partially recovered from their exertions, Juan felt he needed a nightcap.

'It's been a wonderful day. Would you like a drink before we go upstairs?' he asked.

'Yes, that would be nice.'

'What would you like?'

'I rather fancy a glass of red,' she replied, smiling mischievously.

Juan had seen that look before. He knew what Molly was thinking.

'In that case,' he replied, 'I'd better go down into the cellar and get a special bottle?'

'Yes, and while you're doing that I'll slip upstairs and check they're all asleep.' They rose together, and Juan couldn't resist slapping Molly on the back of her tight jeans.

You've got a lovely ass, he thought.

She giggled and wiggled as she went towards the stairs. She was imagining what might happen after they had consumed a glass or two.

He went into the kitchen, passing the Aga. In the utility room, he lifted the heavy trapdoor, switched on the cellar light, and began to descend the concrete stairs. He had taken five steps down when there was an enormous bang behind him. The force of the blast threw him forward and he caught his head on the floor of the basement. There were stars, then nothing.

CHAPTER 42

Wednesday 5th July 1995

Juan lay on the cellar floor, unconscious; he didn't know for how long. The light had gone out. His head hurt like hell. He could feel a bump on his forehead as big as a golf ball. He felt blood trickling down his face. Reacting intuitively, he fumbled up the steps and put his shoulder to the closed trapdoor. Nothing; it was jammed tight. It wouldn't budge, not even a fraction. He couldn't get out.

Something solid has fallen on top of the trapdoor.

He fretted and began worrying what had happened in the house.

Are the children safe? Is Molly OK? She is sensible and will do the right thing. Perhaps what is preventing me from getting out is too heavy for her to shift. She will go to the village for help, or ring the police. Stay calm.

The silence triggered more unease. *Surely, if everything is all right upstairs then he would hear Molly calling to him? Or else, hear the children crying? Why did the light go out? Surely, the oil-fired Aga couldn't have exploded?*

There was nothing; the eerie quiet was only disturbed by what he imagined was the cracking of burning wood. *Something is burning.* He could smell it. *At least there is no smoke down here. What could have caused an explosion? The Aga was only serviced a month ago.*

He waited.

And waited.

And waited.

He estimated an hour had passed since he had come round when he heard the sound of the fire brigade arriving from Ramsey.

And about bloody time too. I'll soon be out of here.

He could only imagine what was going on outside. There were sirens – *the ambulance, or the police?* He thought he heard water being hosed on the floor above. He shouted, but no one replied.

***

Above him a well-practised routine was in operation. The Ramsey fire service, mostly manned by volunteers, had been called out when a passing motorist had seen the farmhouse on fire. He had approached the inferno but could see no sign of life. He had driven into the village and dialled 999 from the phone box. He had returned to the farm gate to ensure the firemen came to the right place – unnecessary as the flames could be seen miles away. In Ramsey, the sound of the fire station's siren, to call out volunteers, could be heard all over the town. It automatically triggered the local police as well as the ambulance from the local cottage hospital to attend.

After two hours of hard work, the flames were largely quenched. The house was a smouldering shell; the first floor having collapsed completely. Only parts of the outer walls stood. The firemen began rooting among the scorched embers using high powered torches. The fire chief at the scene was Sub-Officer Bill Chapman. He shouted to PC Bob Corrin, 'You'd better come and look here.'

The sight that greeted the young police constable was not pretty. His stomach churned, but he kept control. However, he impulsively turned away.

'Five bodies huddled together: I would say one adult, three children and a baby,' remarked the fireman. 'I think you'd better get your inspector out here pronto.'

'Why?'

'Until proper investigations have been carried out by our investigator from Douglas I can't be sure, but I suspect this fire is the result of a deliberate act.'

The inspector of the northern division, based at Ramsey, was newly promoted Inspector George Costain. He knew Ballajorra belonged to his old buddy Juan Quayle. He had listened to his PC's phone call and, despite it being three o'clock in the morning, even before the PC could finish, he had shouted, 'Don't touch anything, I'm on my way.'

The drive from Ramsey took less than 15 minutes.

'Only one adult?' Inspector Costain asked the Sub-Officer.

'Yes, almost certainly female, judging from her size.'

'Then where the hell is Juan?'

'Juan?'

'He's the owner of the farm. Those are the remains of his wife, Molly, and their four children.'

'We've searched the rest of the house. There's no one.'

'These old Manx farmhouses have cellars. Have you looked there?'

'We haven't seen a cellar.'

'There will be a trap door. It could be covered by falling debris.'

'I'll get my men to search.'

'I suggest you start in the kitchen area.'

***

Ten minutes later, the catastrophe had been brought home to Juan: total devastation. His family and home destroyed by the inferno.

'I'd gone to the cellar to get a bottle of wine to finish a perfect day,' he sobbed to his Best Man. 'I can't believe it. We only had the Aga serviced a few weeks ago.'

George looked at Bill Chapman – *Do I tell him?*

The Sub-Officer shrugged his shoulders.

'I don't want to upset you, Juan, but there is a possibility the fire had nothing to do with the Aga.'

Juan's eyes widened and he stood upright. He stared disbelievingly at George. 'Are you telling me this was arson?'

Bill answered, somewhat apologetically, 'I can't be certain, but so much devastation suggests an initial explosion that triggered further incendiary devices.'

'But that would take planning and expertise,' remarked George.

'Well, I've never seen a house go up so quickly in my twenty-five years of being in the Fire Service, and I was at Summerland. It wasn't like this.'

Summerland, the Island's biggest ever fire, had killed 51 holidaymakers 22 years previously. The cause, attributed to some boys smoking, remains disputed.

George looked at Juan. The white of his eyes were red, but not from crying; this was sheer anger. Rage was bursting inside, causing the veins on his neck to rut. He had grown several inches taller.

'George, you'd better get the Chief Constable immediately. Is it still Colonel Madoc? We know the possible background to this.'

'It's four o'clock in the morning.'

'Sod the time; this is either the IRA or al-Qaeda.'

***

Colonel Madoc had been reluctant to come out from Douglas to a farm fire, but when George had mentioned Major Quayle, and a possible IRA connection, he had called his driver immediately. He duly appeared an hour later.

Juan was holding up remarkably well. George marvelled at his calmness and apparent self-control. *Surely any minute now, it will sink in what has happened and he will collapse.* However, he was keeping his emotions under control. *Tragedies affect people in different ways,* thought George. *He's so stoical; it's as if he didn't care. If I didn't know, I could be thinking he planned this himself.*

'Colonel,' greeted Juan. 'I think you'd better contact Sir Charles Gray at once.'

319

The Chief Constable stopped dead in his tracks and stared in utter amazement at Juan. Here was a man whose family had been murdered – burnt to death – and he was giving orders as if nothing had happened.

George looked at his chief and rolled his eyes as if to say: *I can't believe it either.*

Not noticing their reaction, Juan continued, 'It is over four years since we last met and you will remember I was sent here by MI5 to investigate the Provisional IRA arms sales. Either they or al-Qaeda have done this, the bastards.'

Suddenly, he sank to his knees in front of the Chief and was crying like a child. Sobbing and muttering incomprehensively, his hands covering his face, the change had been instant. Colonel Madoc placed his hands on the shoulders of the snivelling wreck kneeling in front of him. He had seen the sudden effects of shock before when he had been a captain in the Royal Welsh Fusiliers during the Korean War.

'It's OK,' he whispered. 'We'll find out who did this; we'll get the bastards.' They remained motionless for many minutes, before Juan slowly pulled himself together, rose and began drying his tears with his handkerchief.

'I'll call Sir Charles first thing in the morning,' began the Chief.

'No, that'll be too late. By then the press will have got hold of the story.'

'What has the press got to do with this?'

'If we're to take advantage of this mess, then this is what we have to do...'

***

An hour later, Sir Charles was listening to the Manx Chief Constable regale the tragedy from the Ramsey police station.

'What you are proposing makes sense,' he replied, 'but it will be up to the new Head of MI6 to implement the plan and execute it. I'll ring Barbara Renton at once. She's their new Head, and I'll suggest she flies to the island first thing.'

'There's a flight from Heathrow at 1040 hours,' suggested the Colonel. I'll meet her at Ronaldsway.'

'Fine. If there's a problem, I'll get straight back.'

By 1300 hours, Barbara Renton, Henry Madoc, Juan Quayle, George Costain and the Head of the Isle of Man's Fire Service, Finlay White, were discussing the problems of implementing Juan's plan in Douglas police HQ, fortified by a buffet lunch.

'How many know the truth?' asked Barbara.

Inspector Costain answered, 'Apart from us, the five fire crew who attended the fire, the two ambulance men, the local PC and the Colonel's driver.'

'No one else?'

'No. Juan came back to Douglas with Colonel Madoc and will stay at his house. I warned Bill Chapman and his crew that they were to say nothing to anyone about what happened. I laid it on thick; I think they are sensible and can be trusted to keep their mouths shut.'

George looked at Finlay White, who nodded agreement. Finlay then added, 'On occasions like this it is usual practice for me to issue a statement for the local press. I have prepared this draft.' He handed everyone a copy.

They read the bulletin in silence. After several minutes, Barbara said, 'It looks OK to me, but I suspect this tragedy will make the national papers as well. They may send reporters over to the island for the funeral. Have you thought about that, Juan?'

'No, not really. Could it be kept private?'

'We've never done anything like this before,' interrupted the Chief Constable. 'It is going to have to be handled carefully to prevent rumours circulating. The funeral director is going to have to be put in the picture, as is the coroner and the hospital pathologist.'

'We're dealing with ruthless thugs,' said the Head of MI6. 'The World Trade Centre bombing two years ago killed six and injured over one thousand. The figures could easily have been the other way around. The bombing in Oklahoma three months ago, that killed over one hundred and fifty, shows how sadistic al-Qaeda can be.'

'But wasn't that conducted by two Americans?' interrupted the Chief Constable.

'There is evidence emerging that one of them had contacts with fundamental Islamists. I am inclined to think this is their work also, and not that of the IRA. The Northern Ireland Peace Process is proceeding well. At last, all parties concerned are pulling their weight, including Sinn Fein. What that means, however, is that al-Qaeda may have a cell on the island; possibly fronting an Indian restaurant?'

The Chief Constable looked to his Inspector for help. After a pause, he replied, 'We have only two or three such restaurants.'

'Unfortunately, that's all it takes. I suggest you get your Special Branch to make contact with Scotland Yard and do some checking. It may, of course, be too late; the cuckoo will probably have flown the nest.'

Colonel Madoc nodded, but didn't reply.

Barbara continued, 'I think this plan could work as long as everything goes all right at this end. I would like you to take personal control Chief Constable. You are going to have to get the Coroner to agree to an indefinite postponement pending the Fire Brigade's inquiry. Then there's the pathologist. What are we going to tell him? Will he co-operate?'

'The head pathologist at Noble's Hospital is Dr Tony Carlton. I know him well through the Bridge Club. He's an ex-RAF doctor and would have signed the Official Secrets Act. I am sure he will help us out.'

'Good. I can handle the national press; I'll slap "D" notices on them if necessary. Juan, do you intend to come back to the Island to attend your family's funeral incognito, or what?'

'I think Molly would want this plan to work. I am sure she would forgive me not being present. And, anyway, there would always be a risk of someone recognising me. That would blow the whole thing sky-high.'

'In that case Mr White, I suggest you release your press statement with these additions…'

A day later, on Friday 7th July 1995, the front page of the *Isle of Man Examiner* read:

FARM HOUSE TRAGEDY: FAMILY OF SIX DEAD

By Mike Cringle

Head Reporter

A gigantic fire two nights ago swept through the northern farm of Ballajorra, near Bride. The owner, Juan Quayle (45), his wife, Molly (37), and their four children Peter (7), Mikey (5), Sophie (3) and Heather (6 months) were found dead, huddled together, by firemen from the Ramsey brigade after the fire had been extinguished. It is believed they were overcome by smoke inhalation and burnt alive.

The Island's Head Fire Officer, Finlay White, in a statement said that it appeared the oil boiler may have exploded showering the downstairs with burning oil. The family, who were upstairs at the time, stood no chance of escaping. Investigations are not yet complete, but foul play is not suspected. For further details and a photograph, see page seven (Northern News).

The following day, a similar article appeared on page five of *The London Times* by the newspaper's Isle of Man correspondent, Mike Cringle.

CHAPTER 43

Monday 10th July 1995

TOP SECRET

MEMORANDUM

SUBJECT: AL-QAEDA THREAT

From: Director MI6   **Date:** 10 Jul 95

To: Director CIA, Langley   **Ref:** VB/CIA/AQ95/1

Dear John,

1. Firstly allow me to congratulate you on your recent appointment. I hope we can successfully work together for a safer future. It is on this theme that I write.

2. My predecessor, Peter Stacey, wrote to Robert Gates 3 years ago about the perceived threat from an emerging Islamist terrorist organisation called al-Qaeda. Our intelligence at that time was based on an agent who had infiltrated al-Qaeda for approximately 18 months, during which time he had worked in their madrassa in Naxcivan. I invited your predecessor, James Woolsey, to join an international forum that meets regularly to share information on 28 Feb 93.

3. The Indian NSG, the French DGSE, the German BND, Mossad and ourselves meet biannually. The NSG has established agents within al-Qaeda as well as inside Pakistan's ISI. They are providing an invaluable insight into what is going on. The French are monitoring immigrants from North Africa, particularly Algerians; the Germans closely

watch for extremists within their Turkish population; we know hardliners come back from Pakistan and stir up hatred within towns such as Bradford, Luton and Rochdale. The overall picture is one of a deteriorating situation where further outrages are going to be committed; not if, but when.

4. Last week, for example, the agent mentioned in para 2 above was murdered along with his wife and 4 children by a sophisticated arson attack that had all the hallmarks of al-Qaeda.

5. I write on behalf of our forum to invite you to our next meeting to be held in Paris on 28 Aug 95.

Yours etc
    Barbara

Helen, Barbara's PA, took the handwritten memo, and began typing. The hard copy appeared…

ROEI CERT AFAU MACA MWHE FEKA AEON SSNH TSO4 TACE…

And seconds later in Virginia…

MYPR EDEC ESSO RPET ERST ACEY WROT ETOY OURP REDE ECES…

✱✱✱

After the meeting on Thursday afternoon, Juan had spent the rest of that week and the following week arranging his affairs with George: the funeral arrangements, the death certificates, the correspondence with insurance companies, the selling of the farm – even his car, and the legal aspects of the will. Monies due to him would be transferred to a numbered Swiss bank account. He left the island as a foot passenger on the afternoon boat of Saturday 15th July to Liverpool, with only a small overnight bag. Barbara had flown back to London immediately after the meeting on the evening plane and agreed to meet Juan at Exeter on Sunday 16th. Juan would then lie low at Woodside whilst a new identity would be found for him. Juan Quayle, Alan Quine, and Khalil el Majid would no longer exist.

As the ship left the Island he went up on the open deck. He looked at Douglas Bay slowly receding in the distance. He knew he would never see it again. He was leaving behind a part of him; no, he thought – all of him. Molly, the kids, the farm on which he grew up and his Manx roots were gone forever. He looked down at the waves below, perhaps five yards beneath him. They were mesmerising as they sloshed against the steel hull. The green, white and dark blue merged into each other as they sped past. It occurred to him to jump; what was there to lose? He had lost everything.

He remembered the last time he had been in the sea. *I should have let Anibal drown – the bastard. If only I had known what I know now.*

He continued staring at the sea rushing past. He knew he wouldn't stand a chance. He would be sucked under the ship as it raced along at 20 knots, get minced in the twin propellers and become fish food in a matter of seconds. A chill went up his spine.

No, it's not what Molly would have wanted. I have a duty to you and I promise you, Molly, I'm going to get even.

He caught the 2330 hours train from Lime Street to Euston, arriving at 0510 hours. He wandered down Tottenham Court Road, found somewhere for a greasy spoon breakfast and decided to walk to Paddington. He hardly slept a wink on the train, mulling over the loss of the only people he had ever truly loved. He knew he would never forget the wonderful times he had with the children. Molly would, forever, be the only girl in his life; whether he would ever feel the warmth of a woman's body again he was unsure, but it would make no difference. He believed that the only one he would remember would be her.

It was a strange sensation walking up a deserted Oxford Street, the shops not yet open for Sunday trading. He felt empty. Like a blown egg shell, the slightest knock and he knew he could crack and crumble. He felt totally numb. He walked instinctively in a trance, not noticing his surroundings; engrossed in his own world. Deep inside him, the seed of hatred was fuelling revenge. The acorn's roots were spreading malevolence through his veins.

If I have to walk to the ends of the Earth, I will find and kill bin Laden.

He arrived at Paddington in plenty of time to catch the 0905 hours train to Penzance; first stop – Swindon, second – Exeter, arriving 1112 hours.

Barbara was waiting for him. Wearing a figure-hugging black suit, ochre-coloured blouse with matching shoes, she looked and smelt a million dollars as she hugged him warmly. 'Are you all right?' she asked. From the look on her face, he felt she was genuinely concerned for his welfare.

'I'll be fine as long as I'm kept busy,' he replied.

He had expected her to be in a chauffeur-driven vehicle, but she drove herself in her unremarkable, silver-grey Ford Mondeo. She headed into the countryside without explaining where she was taking him. 'I thought we might have lunch in a quiet spot and discuss your plans further,' she said.

Juan nodded, but didn't reply. He could feel his eyes closing; sleep had been in short supply for some weeks.

He awoke when the car stopped outside a thatched hotel – *The Royal Oak Inn*. The village, he later discovered, was called Winsford. 'What a beautiful place,' he remarked casually.

'Yes,' she replied. 'My ex and I spent our honeymoon here and I've always had a soft spot for it ever since.'

'It didn't put you off then?'

'No, he was quite good in bed; it wasn't until later that he became a philanderer and a drunk. Perhaps I drove him that way,' she joked.

Her laughter was infectious – it always had been. For the first time since his tragedy, he found himself smiling weakly. Barbara was chalk and cheese to Molly. However, he had always been fascinated by her. In her presence he somehow felt light-headed. She was *joie de vivre* personified.

If anyone can lift my spirits, it's you, Barbara.

They lunched in a corner of the saloon – alone, except for a couple of old boys who sat at the bar, sipping the local ale. They cast furtive glances at Barbara; looking at her shapely legs and wishing wishful thoughts.

'I have been putting some flesh on the bones of your plan,' she began after they had ordered. 'Are you up to discussing it?'

'Yes, but first of all, what happened to all those recommendations we made to the Foreign Secretary about the danger of al-Qaeda? I would like to know; we didn't get a chance to discuss anything in the Isle of Man.'

'There were several successes. First of all, we were right about Fatima. She did work under cover for the Indian NSG and, as far as I know, still does. I now have a good relationship with my opposite Indian number, Lieutenant General Gobal Rao. At his suggestion we formed an interested group that meets every six months to discuss al-Qaeda developments and share intelligence. The Israelis, along with the French and the Germans – the main countries with Islamic immigrant fundamentalists – attend. We suspect there are rogue elements in the Pakistani ISI who actively support al-Qaeda and help them to source arms as well as give them information.' She paused for a moment.

'What about the Russians? Are they on the al-Qaeda committee?'

'No, they're not. But do you remember Boris Yeltsin having a problem in September of '93?'

'Vaguely. I didn't follow international events that much.'

'Well briefly, Russia's President, Yeltsin had a bust-up with his parliament. There was a constitutional crisis caused by his privatisation reforms that were too liberal for the old communist school. The parliament booted Yeltsin out, impeaching him. There was a stand-off that lasted for ten days and ended when he ordered the Army to shell the Supreme Soviet Building. The Army split into two factions: some pro-parliament, others pro-Yeltsin. About 180 or more were killed. Yeltsin regained control and imposed rule by decree. The hard line communists were rounded up, including guess who?'

'Lutikov.'

'A hole-in-one. Along with the others, he disappeared. They're probably shovelling salt in Siberia. What else do you want to know?'

'Did we warn the Americans of the danger?'

'Yes. Peter Stacey tried to arrange an international conference with other directors of intelligence. He sent Robert Gates a memorandum warning him of impending long term and short term attacks. He predicted the World Trade Centre car bomb of two years ago. Did you hear about it?'

'It killed six but it could have been hundreds.'

'Exactly. The Americans' reaction was one of arrogance – it won't happen in our back yard. Someday they'll come to regret not heeding our warnings. After the World Trade Centre attack, however, I wrote another memorandum to the CIA. By then, Robert Gates had left under a cloud. He was associated with the original Iran-Contra affair. His successor was James Woolsey but he pooh-poohed my suggestion that he join our al-Qaeda group. I wrote a second memo pleading he reconsider, and warned him of pending attacks on western embassies worldwide. I made the point that our member countries were building road blocks in front of our embassies to prevent car bomb suicide attacks. But I never received a reply.'

'So, the memoranda fell on deaf ears?'

'I'm afraid so. Someday they'll wakeup to the fact that they're not invincible. By then, I have a horrible feeling it will be too late. Now, getting back to your future, there are some weaknesses in the plan we must sort out. Firstly, can you speak Urdu?'

'No, and I suspect I might have to learn Pashto as well.'

'You've been thinking about this, then?'

'Yes. What are the other problems you foresee?'

'Secondly, your *raison d'etre* for being there.'

'Not so easy.'

'My thoughts are you should become a freelance journalist, or better still, a Middle East correspondent for *The Daily Telegraph*.'

'Why?'

'You could write some anti-Israeli, anti-American articles from the Lebanon. The view as seen by Hezbollah – that sort of thing. Then with a reputation of being pro-Palestinian, you might get invited to visit al-Qaeda's leaders in Afghanistan.'

'Why *The Telegraph*?'

'It's about the only British paper with gravitas that doesn't have Jewish ownership.'

'OK. What else?'

'How to get close enough to bin Laden to guarantee a hit. He will not have to recognise you and the weapon used will have to get past his minders. Anything with metal will be spotted a mile away. All this preparation is going to take time.'

'In my experience, Barbara, the quickest way of learning a language is to be thrown in at the deep end. I need to live with a family that speaks Urdu and Pashto.'

'For how long?'

'Based on picking up previous languages, I should be proficient in six months.'

'Fine, I'll get on to that. Getting you on the staff of *The Telegraph* should be straight forward. It may take several years, or longer, to build up a reputation for being a radical pro-Palestinian. The weapon, however, could be tricky. I am currently thinking along the lines of something chemical or biological; they can easily be disguised in a spray of some sort.'

'And my appearance?'

'We've plenty of expertise there. We can have you looking like Cary Grant, if you want.' She laughed at her own joke.

Juan laughed as well; she had lifted his spirits in a few minutes. *Why does the sun always shine when you're around?* he asked himself.

She continued, 'This morning I had a call from Colonel Madoc. It looks as if the bomb that blew up the farm was located inside your Aga. The fire brigade's arson specialist believes it was linked by radio signals to incendiary devices in your lounge, under the stairs, at the top of the stairs, and inside the oil tank.'

'My God.'

'It proves beyond any doubt who did it.'

After lunch, Juan and Barbara continued their journey west. 'I am pretty well tied up for the rest of this week,' she said at one point. 'I will not be able to get down to my cottage next weekend. If you feel you want to get away from Woodside, I can let you have the spare key. It's up for sale, by the way. I've found a dream house in the South of France that I am doing up for my eventual retirement.'

'You're not retiring yet, surely?'

'No, but when I saw this place at a bargain price, I knew I had to have it. It'll probably take five or six years to get it the way I want. The French workmen are not the quickest.'

'Where is it?'

'A little village called Belveze in the Aude.'

'Ah, near Carcassonne?'

'Yes, not far.'

'It's a kind offer, but I'll live-in at Woodside. Funnily enough, I've been thinking of investing some of the money from the sale of the farm in an apartment in the South of France.'

'Oh, anywhere in mind?'

'I was thinking of Antibes or Juan les Pins.'

'Yes, it's lovely down there, perhaps I can help you to find a nice flat?'

'Why not? A few days on the Cote d'Azur would make a pleasant break.'

'Will you be OK at Woodside?'

'I expect one or two of the students will want a game of golf at

Westward-Ho! If not, I can always go for some long walks.'

She turned and looked at him quizzically. 'You won't do anything stupid, will you?' she asked.

'Would it matter if I did?'

She took her left hand off the steering wheel and placed it firmly on his knee and squeezed. 'Yes, you know it would. Between us we'll find a way of getting your own back and stop al-Qaeda in its tracks.'

He noted her use of the royal *we*. Somehow it reassured him. The best espionage brain in the country was on his side. Perhaps, after all, he would get over his tragedy and survive.

***

A cutting from *The Times* had arrived by fax in Peshawar. The recipient read it and smiled. *It's taken almost three years to get you off my back.*

CHAPTER 44

Monday 17th July 1995

It only took a week for Juan to be given a new persona. The documentation arrived: a national insurance number, an NHS number, a driving licence and a bank account: Lloyds, Davies Road, West Bridgford, with debit and credit cards. The rigmarole that he had gone through to become Alan Quine five years previously had been relatively simple. To become John Pearson, however, was more complicated. Whereas previously he took on the identity of a fellow Manxman, with similar origins, and no one likely to closely investigate him, John Pearson was altogether a different matter.

When he received his CV, he knew he had to study it carefully. Born in West Bridgford, Nottingham, on 29th March 1950 – *a few days older than me* – the only son of a policeman, he was educated at Lady Bay Primary School from where he won a scholarship to Nottingham High School. There, Pearson had been an all-rounder, never excelling in anything other than having a gift for languages. After a family holiday to Egypt and visiting the Pyramids, the boy had decided he wanted to study Arabic at university. With three reasonable 'A' levels, he found himself undertaking an Arabic degree at Exeter University from 1969 to 1973. The degree included a year in Cairo.

Pearson then joined the civil service as an interpreter in the Foreign Office; initially in London and then four years in Cairo – a city he came to know and love. On promotion to a senior grade, he had returned to work in England. However, bored with routine work, he had taken time out to travel through South America, improving his Spanish and learning some Portuguese. After three years, he arrived in the United States to discover his linguistic ability was a commercially valuable asset. He worked for Chase-Manhattan Bank dealing with their Saudi customers' investment portfolios.

A chance meeting with the Foreign News Editor of *The Daily Telegraph* at a cocktail party led to him being offered a job as correspondent for the newspaper in Beirut.

At 45, he was still a bachelor.

His mentor at Woodside was a six foot three inch tall Liverpudlian, Bill Bradley. He met Juan on the evening of Sunday 23rd July in the bar to explain the following week's programme.

'Tomorrow morning, you will see our plastic surgeon for a medical. If you are to meet bin Laden then we must ensure he doesn't recognise you; at least not immediately,' he added, laughing.

'I always had a beard and long hair when I was with him. I thought shaving and getting a number-two haircut would suffice.'

'It will help, but there are other things we can do.'

'Such as?'

'Wear glasses, use coloured contact lenses, put on weight, remove or add distinguishing features, that sort of thing.'

The following day, he lay on a couch for the specialist, Dr David Skelly. 'These two scars: the one on your hand and the other in the right of your back, are they bullet wounds?'

'Yes.'

'They are healing up nicely, but I think we should eradicate them completely.'

'How?'

'I will give you a cream to use twice daily. Apply an infra-red heat lamp for fifteen minutes afterwards. The scars will have disappeared completely in three months. Now, what weight are you?'

'About thirteen stone.'

'Nearer fourteen I would say. When bin Laden knew you, were you this weight?'

'About the same.'

'Then I think you should go on a diet, rather than put on another two stone. I want you down to eleven stone. Plenty of sit-ups will get rid of that pouch. What height are you?'

'Five foot, ten and a half inches.'

'OK. I am going to get special shoes made that will give you an extra 1/2 in. I want you to hold yourself more erect from now on. With an effort and some stretching exercises that I want you to do at the same time as the sit-ups, you should make an extra inch. I think we should give you a tattoo, say on your forearm.'

'Why?'

'They are an excellent distracter. People notice them and ignore other features. Any ideas for one?'

'No.'

The doc looked at Juan's notes. I see you are taking the place of someone from Nottingham.'

'Yes.'

'Then, how about Nottingham Forest's badge – a tree with the word *Forest* underneath?'

'Fine, if we must.' Juan was neither a Forest supporter nor keen on tattoos.

'We also need facial distracters.'

'Such as?'

'We will break your nose and set it slightly crooked. Coupled with contact lenses to change the shade of your eyes and some artificial eye bags, you will be a new man!'

'I assume the plastic surgery is done under anaesthetic?'

'Yes, of course. You won't feel a thing.'

'When will you do all this?'

'Oh, no hurry. Perhaps when you are nearer to completing your training. Meanwhile, I am prescribing a drug that will make your somewhat swarthy skin go pale.'

'You're joking?'

'No. There is an American pop star who has tried to become white using it and it caused side effects. Don't worry. The doses you will be taking will be harmless. Your own mother won't recognise you when we're finished.'

Now I think about it, there was little mention of Pearson's parents in the CV.

Having listened intently to Dr Skelly, Bill intervened, 'As you can see, John, there is a lot to learn. There is even more to forget. They say a leopard can't change its spots, but I'm afraid you are going to have to learn. We will begin tomorrow by visiting Nottingham. Over the next ten weeks we will travel to Exeter, Cairo, Rio de Janeiro and Washington DC. You have not only to become John Pearson, but you must forget everything about who you really are. It is not easy, believe me.'

'But what about the paper trail – the records?' asked Juan.

'Don't worry about them. Our specialists have an easier job amending school records and so on than you have of remembering them. You've already received new social security numbers, driving licence and bank details?'

'Yes.'

'There you are then. Anyone checking them will find they are genuine.'

At Nottingham he saw where he was born, his first school, where he played soccer and cricket. He visited Forest's Ground and Trent Bridge where his father had taken him as a lad. He listened to records of the local Nottingham dialect and began mimicking their accent. They went to Skegness – an occasional weekend treat with his parents. He got to know the cinemas in the city, where the trolleybuses used to take him when he went to High School; where he learnt to swim and places in the nearby countryside where he would cycle with pals. A month went past rapidly; he slowly began to feel like he was John Pearson. He was no longer reacting to being called Juan and was ignoring remarks made in languages such as Russian and Gaelic that Pearson never understood.

'The secret is not to compare your new identity with your own. When you were eighteen and about to go to Exeter, how did you get there?'

'I imagine I caught the train via Birmingham and Bristol.'

'No. You DID catch the train. You mustn't fall for that trap.'

At Exeter, they called on the professor of the Arab Studies Department, Professor Eric Adamson.

Having been introduced, Bill remarked, 'I am leaving you with the professor for the rest of the day. He will talk to you in Arabic and describe the courses here. He will tell you what books you must read.' He laughed and turned to the academic, 'Won't you prof?'

'Yes. Our course is heavily based on classical Arab texts that you probably have never read. I'm afraid you should read at least some of them if you are to convince any future interrogator that you really studied here.'

Juan nodded apprehensively. He was fluent in Arabic, but knew his limitations when it came to reading. A few days later, they left Exeter; Juan armed with half a dozen texts: 'Essential reading,' according to Professor Adamson.

They returned to Woodside. 'A few days rest to let it sink in,' remarked Bill. 'Next week we are off to Cairo. We will need to scout out where you used to live and work. There won't be any time for sightseeing, I'm afraid.'

It was then back to base before leaving for South America on Sunday 3rd September. 'How's your Portuguese?' asked his companion.

'Not great. Why?'

'Good. We don't think Pearson knew that much, either. He didn't stay long in Brazil.'

It was the first time that there had been a hint that John Pearson had been anyone other than imaginary.

'You mean there really was a John Pearson?'

'Yes, of course.'

'What happened to him?'

Bill smiled. 'He died of septicaemia from a snake bite in Bolivia.'

'I didn't know there were snakes in Bolivia.'

'Maybe not in La Paz, but the northern part of the country is mostly jungle. Many of the rivers are tributaries of the Amazon.'

'So, how much of his CV is real?'

'He was born in Nottingham, did go to the schools we have visited and did a degree at Exeter. He travelled through South America for three years. Most of the rest is fabricated; but don't worry, no one will ever find out.'

They spent three weeks travelling through Brazil, Argentina, Chile and Bolivia before heading to the United States.

'So Pearson never went to the States, if he died in Bolivia?'

'No, not as far as we know. The ten years you worked for Chase-Manhattan in Washington has been engineered by our friends in the CIA.'

'Does the CIA know about our plan to infiltrate al-Qaeda and assassinate bin Laden?'

'God, no! We tell them as little as possible. The need to know principle, and all that.'

Juan and Bill had been away six weeks when they returned to Woodside on 13th October.

'There is no formal review of your progress, John. However, there are still some weaknesses that need to be improved. Your Nottingham accent is still too variable. From tonight you are to play these tapes when you go to bed. They are on a loop so will play all night. We have also acquired a copy of *Saturday Night and Sunday Morning* and I want you to watch it until our speech therapist is happy with your performance. OK?'

338

Juan nodded.

'Otherwise, I think you have done pretty well. How do you feel about your ability to take over the role of Pearson?'

'It's the little personal things that worry me. Who was his first girlfriend? When did he lose his virginity? Who was his best pal at school? Indeed, what happened to his parents?'

'Ah, that's one of the reasons we chose Pearson. They were killed in a car accident in 1975 just up the road from where they lived; at a place called Radcliffe on Trent. The A52 is particularly dangerous thereabouts. You have no close relatives as both your parents were single children. As for girlfriends and pals, you can make them up for yourself. Believe me, no one will ever get down to that detail if al-Qaeda check up on you.'

On Saturday evening, Barbara appeared in the bar as Juan was about to go in for dinner.

'I'm down for the weekend. I gather you're picking up your new ID very well. I've come to hear your thick Nottingham accent,' she joked.

'I'm afraid I'm not up to Albert Finney standards, but I'm working at it.'

'Why don't we go for a curry in town, then you can show me how hard you are working at becoming Albert Finney?'

The innuendo in her suggestion didn't go amiss. The 1960 film had Arthur Seaton, the anti-hero, sleeping with an older woman, Brenda, played by Rachel Roberts; ironically similar to Barbara in looks. Shirley Anne Field who played Doreen, Seaton's girlfriend, could have been Molly, except for the colour of her hair.

Although still mourning his family's death, three months ago, and having occasional flashbacks, the offer was too tempting. Having already consumed two large glasses of Tavel Rose, he thought *what the heck?*

'OK,' he replied.

'You'd better pop upstairs and fetch your tooth brush.'

Forgive me, Molly. I know where this is going to end. Barbara used me, now it's my turn.

The Saturday night sexual revel was followed by the Sunday morning recrimination. *John Pearson's first fling,* he thought bizarrely. However, it was Barbara's conscience that surprised him. She was full of remorse. As they lay in bed, loathed to get up, she asked innocent questions about Molly and the children. Her attempt to excuse her behaviour made him feel worse. His monosyllabic replies hinted that the subject was taboo and they lay there for ages, saying nothing. He knew he had broken his own moral code. Barbara could sense the guilt running amok within him.

After what seemed an interminable time, she knew she had to break the silence.

'I know this sounds cruel, but if you are going to extract your revenge on bin Laden then it's what Bill Bradley told you, "It's harder to forget the past than it is to learn the future." You told me that Molly would want you to go through with this plan. In order to do it, you have to believe you are John Pearson. I've hinted to you in the past that I'm not totally happy with the plan. It's too risky in my opinion, but if it works, then I'll be here for you. You know that.'

'Three years ago, I wanted to move in with you and you turned me down. I would have married you. Are you saying you now regret it?'

'I might be.' She smiled beguilingly, leaning towards him and kissing him like no one else ever could. His body out of control, he felt himself getting excited. He pushed her backwards...

Later, they drove out of Barnstaple for a lunch in a little country pub, *The Hunters Inn,* at Newton Tracey. Afterwards, they drove to nearby Appledore and went for a walk on the sands. Holding hands, he was happy to be with her; her with him. She was responding in a way that suggested she would be his mate if that was what he wanted. They talked through the problems facing the plan and went over his schedule for the next few months.

'After the next three weeks studying journalism, I have arranged for you to visit Porton Down.'

'To discuss weapons?'

'Yes. It's not going to be easy. Anything with metal, even deodorant

340

sprays will be confiscated. We have a ballpoint pen made of plastic that can shoot a chemical that melts the skin in seconds and kills within a minute. However, his guards, who will be present, will kill you as soon as you try to use it.'

'You know that doesn't worry me.'

'Yes, but it worries me. I want you to come home safely.'

She's softening with age.

'The two aims might be incompatible.'

The thought silenced Barbara.

I think she really does want me to come back in one piece.

They continued walking along the beach for some distance before she said, 'When are you seeing our cosmetic surgeon again? Is he recommending facial surgery?'

'He wants to break my nose.'

She stopped. 'What? That seems excessive.'

'Yes, he thinks I need a good distracter to convince bin Laden that he has never seen me before. I always had a beard when I was with him, and longish hair. I thought being clean shaven and having cropped hair would be sufficient.'

'Dr Skelly is probably right, but it might be less painful if he gives you a scar on your cheek, or something like that. I'm not sure I fancy the idea of a broken nose.'

'He wants me to lose several stones. I've lost sixteen pounds already. He's designing special shoes to make me an inch taller. I am taking a pill daily that makes my skin go pale.'

'I like you the way you are.'

I think she means it.

'Ironically, so do I.'

'It's getting cold. Shall we go back? Do you fancy me cooking this evening? I've some nice fillet steaks in the freezer. They would go down well with a Chateauneuf-du-Pape. Incidentally, when you're in London working at *The Daily Telegraph*, would you like to stay at my flat?'

CHAPTER 45

Monday 16th October 1995

Juan, now thinking of himself as Pearson, found the week's journalism course at Woodside a waste of time. His tutor, an overseas correspondent with *The Daily Telegraph*, covered subjects such as research techniques into the background of a subject, interview techniques – both face-to-face and by telephone, spotting an interviewer's hidden agenda, news and précis writing, meeting deadlines and understanding your audience. He had undertaken writing courses and interview techniques whilst in the Army. The work experience at *The Daily Telegraph* would, he thought, prove to be more relevant.

In the evenings, he used the time to study his CV further and consider where he was going with Barbara. She was fantastic company. She was fun. There was never a dull moment. Even when she was talking about her friends and relatives, about whom he hadn't a clue, he would listen and laugh at her jokes. His plan, however, had been to get even for killing Molly and the kids. He had thought that if he never returned it wouldn't matter. Now he found himself changing his tune. Maybe there was a future with Barbara. She was almost ten years older than him. What would happen to their relationship when the attraction of the bedroom had worn off? Perhaps it never would. Surely he hadn't the stamina to go on satisfying her libido? And yet it was wonderful to find someone with whom he was 100% compatible between the sheets.

During his fortnight in London, the work at *The Daily Telegraph's*

Foreign Desk was challenging and tiring. The work in Barbara's bed was equally challenging and tiring; her repertoire seemingly unending.

One evening Barbara brought up the subject of Juan speaking Urdu. 'I have discussed your need to learn Urdu and Pashto,' she said. 'I am receiving advice that it is unnecessary.'

'Really? Why?'

'It's too obvious. A journalist fluent in Arabic and just happens to be able to speak the languages of NW Pakistan and Afghanistan. How likely is that?'

'I see what you mean.'

'We are proposing you live with a Pakistani family for a month that has been given security clearance. You should pick up sufficient Urdu to allow you to get around in Pakistan.'

'Like schoolboy French?'

'Yes, that sort of thing. If anyone quizzes where you learnt your smattering of Urdu, you tell them you had a Pakistani friend in the cricket team at Nottingham High School. You can always joke that you fancied his elder sister.' She laughed.

At the end of a fortnight staying with Barbara, an exhausted Juan returned to Woodside. That weekend Yitzhak Rabin, Israel's Prime Minister, was assassinated after attending a mass meeting in Tel Aviv to support the Oslo Peace Initiative. Initial news reports speculated that the assassin, Yigal Amir, may have been an al-Qaeda operative. Watching the events unfold on TV, Juan thought a single murder was not in al-Qaeda's style. *They would have used a suicide bomber to blow up dozens of others as well.*

Subsequently, Juan was proved right. Amir turned out to be an extreme orthodox Jew opposed to the Oslo Accord.

Bill picked him up after breakfast on Monday morning and they drove to Porton Down, arriving in time for a mid-morning coffee. Greeted by the head of Biological and Chemical research, Dr Mike Cochrane, they were shown around the campus before lunch. In his office afterwards, the plan for Juan to become a journalist in Beirut was outlined. It was explained that it could take a considerable time for his reputation – that he was anti-Israeli and pro-Palestinian – to be established. Any weapons that he might take to the Lebanon would have to lie dormant for several years. If he was invited to interview bin Laden, it would probably be in either Pakistan or Afghanistan. The weapons would have to be portable, small and easily concealed.

Dr Cochrane listened intently, occasionally nodding and asking a question to amplify points. 'Am I right in thinking this could be a suicide mission?' he asked.

'Yes, if necessary,' replied Juan quickly before Bill could put any dampers on his reply.

'If you hadn't told me about the possible long delay of targeting bin Laden, then I would have suggested using Sarin. We could inoculate you, so that you would survive, but he wouldn't. However, it degrades rapidly. After two or three weeks' storage it's useless. Is there a possibility of poisoning his food?'

'I shouldn't think so. I can't imagine him inviting me to lunch.'

'As a reporter you will have a legitimate need for a ballpoint pen. We have several designs that are multifunctional. One even shoots a bamboo needle coated with a curare derivative that we have developed. The poison is called *turbocurare* as it paralyses instantly, the heart stops and it kills in seconds. The problem is that if he is accompanied by guards, they will see you taking aim.'

'They may even have inspected the pen beforehand.'

'I see from this file that you have seen the plastic surgeon about facial changes.'

'Yes.'

'He is having shoes specially made to increase your height by half an inch?'

'Yes.'

'Therein is our best bet.'

'I don't follow.'

'Do you know of trainers called Nike-Air?'

'No.'

'They use compressed air between the inner cushion and the sole to provide support to the foot. The air is under pressure, similar to that in a car tyre.'

Juan was wondering where Mike's logic was leading.

'There's only one biological agent that I know that could survive indefinitely if pumped into the gap of a shoe – anthrax spores.'

'Go on,' Juan encouraged.

'Anthrax can infect humans in three ways: absorption through a cut or graze, ingestion by eating infected meat, or inhalation. The most deadly method is, rather surprisingly, the latter – inhalation. A human breathing in sufficient anthrax spores will, within twenty-four hours, have the symptoms of a common cold or mild influenza: a runny nose, a cough, a sore throat, that sort of thing. If they do nothing, thinking they have caught a chill, then a day later they will have difficulty in breathing as the lungs begin to flood with excess fluids. By then it is too late to save them; they will be dead the next day. The lethality depends, as you would expect, on the number of spores inhaled.'

'What you are suggesting then, doctor,' said Bill, who had been quiet up to this point, 'is that Juan gets close to bin Laden and somehow releases the spores hidden in his shoes?'

'In essence, yes.'

'But that means Juan would also die from anthrax.'

'Not necessarily. The Americans have produced a vaccine, *Biothrax*. It would give protection. Unfortunately, it needs a booster every year, or so, to retain total immunity.'

'I am sure that could be arranged,' said Bill, eagerly nodding his approval of the plan.

'My advice would be, after successfully releasing the spores, you give yourself a high dose of penicillin as soon as possible to make sure you are safe. We would use the most deadly strain of the eighty-nine different forms of anthrax, Vollum 1-B. It was developed here at Porton after the experiment on Gruinard Island in 1942. The most difficult thing might be the design of the shoe. That will be a job for our dirty tricks department.'

The outline of a plan of attack decided, Juan and Bill returned to Woodside the same evening.

'Your training is nearly over,' said Bill as they drove down the A303. 'Tomorrow you are off to Blackburn to live with a family from Pakistan. How do you feel about that?'

'It could be interesting as I understand the plan is they will not speak any English after the first week. I hope the housewife cooks good curries.'

The family turned out to be nothing like what Juan expected. They lived in a detached house in a village called Mellor with a large rear garden that looked over the Ribble valley. The head of the Khan family, Ali, was a chief inspector in the Lancashire Police, based in Preston. His wife, Amana, was a midwife and their two children attended the near-by Queen Elizabeth Grammar School. Seven months pregnant, Amana was on maternity leave. She would be his fulltime teacher. Living with the Khans – clearly a happy family – reminded him of Molly and the kids. The Black Dog would then bite him and depression set in. However, there was no time for moping. The Khans kept him busy. At weekends they went for walks in the Forest of Bowland, or the Lake District. For their last weekend, they travelled to Blackpool Pleasure Beach. At the end, Juan was conversing competently and could understand much of the Urdu TV and radio broadcasts.

The next week was spent in a private clinic in Bath. There, he underwent an operation to alter his nose, create a scar on his forehead and was tattooed on his left forearm.

He returned to Porton Down on Monday 4th December. Mike Cochrane was enthusiastic when showing them the prototype shoe. 'At a glance it looks like any other shoe with a thick modern composite sole,' he declared. 'However, if you press here, on the inside of the arch, you can feel a switch.'

He handed Juan the shoe.

Juan nodded and handed the shoe to Bill who also nodded.

'The switch triggers a nylon needle to puncture the wall of the sole on the opposite side, releasing the spores that are under pressure in the heel's cavity.'

'Won't there be a loud hissing sound that would be noticed?' asked Bill.

'No. Experiments at different pressures have shown that ten psi is sufficient. The shoe's cavity is sufficiently large to contain 20,000 anthrax spores. If you release them from both shoes, then the concentration in the air will be sufficient to kill everyone in a large room.' He paused, as if expecting applause.

'Yourself excluded, of course,' he added as an afterthought. 'I suggest you use it like this.'

He crossed his legs, putting his right ankle on top of his left knee. With his left hand he pressed the switch. 'You can see it looks a perfectly normal procedure. Later on, you do it with the other foot. The spores are colourless and odourless. No one in the room will know that they will be dead within forty-eight hours.'

'I'll have to do it differently than that,' remarked Juan.

'Why?' asked the scientist.

'Showing an Arab the sole of your shoe is about the worst thing you can do.'

'Then perhaps you can bend down and pretend to tie up your shoelaces.'

'OK. I'll think of something and play it by ear.'

Later that week, Barbara and Juan flew to Nice. They found a luxury, top floor apartment near the bottom of Rue Albert 1st in Antibes. Purchased from the sale of Juan's farm, they registered the flat jointly.

'Someday, when I return from killing bin Laden, this will become my bolt-hole from all the world's insanity,' declared Juan.

CHAPTER 46

Tuesday 2nd January 1996

Juan joined the staff of *The Daily Telegraph* after spending Christmas with Barbara at her flat in Holland Park. They had used what little time was left together wisely: going over and over Juan's CV. They spent a few days at a hotel in the centre of Nottingham and explored the city. They went to one of Forest's soccer matches, visited *The Trip to Jerusalem Inn*, walked around Wollaton Park and the adjacent university grounds to try and get the feel of his adopted city.

The two weeks with the Middle East news editor, who would be his contact when he sent reports from the Lebanon, went rapidly. The desk was headed by an old pro, Charles Carter. 'The first thing, when you get there, is to get yourself a pimp,' he remarked when they met on the first day.

'A pimp?'

'A scout, a fixer, a gopher – whatever you want to call him. Someone who knows everyone and knows his way around. He can make the difference between you getting, or not getting, a scoop.'

'How do I get one?'

'Don't worry; once it is known you are our Lebanese correspondent, they will come looking for you. When I was our Egyptian correspondent in Cairo in the early 70's, I had an excellent minder called Azi. He knew when things were going to happen long before anyone else. As a result, I was the first reporter on the spot in the Sinai when Egypt began the

Yom Kippur war. My report was twenty-four hours ahead of everyone else. He was also a good photographer; my reputation was made.'

'Who pays the gopher?'

'You do. Your salary will incur a bonus for such expenses. We have opened an account for you with the Royal Jordanian Bank in Beirut. They have branches all over the Middle East. Jordan is seen as something of a neutral country so you should have little trouble withdrawing funds wherever you are. Your monthly salary and expenses will be paid into it. If your *Man Friday* is any good, give him the equivalent of a third of your wage; exceptionally slightly more. You'll find local government officials expect bribes for any assistance they may give you. A good pimp can get round that by knowing a relative who knows someone who owes them a favour. Remember, corruption is a way of life out there.'

Time was spent learning how to précis reports, how to use fax machines, the best time to meet deadlines, a simple code to guarantee it was his report and not someone trying to impersonate him. He met an official from the Foreign Office who gave him a presentation on how to avoid being held hostage in the Lebanon: 'Perhaps write a sympathetic article on Hezbollah early on.' There were Visas to collect and immunisations to be had.

The Daily Telegraph had arranged accommodation in a small apartment in a safe area of Beirut, at the rear of the St Nicholas Greek Orthodox Cathedral. There was an office in town equipped with the necessary communications facilities.

★★★

'Simon Rosenberg to see you Mrs Renton,' announced the Director's PA.

'Thank you, Jill. Show him in, please.' Barbara stood up and moved around to the front of her desk.

She extended her arm and shook hands. 'Simon, it's good of you to come over and see me like this.'

'Hello, Barbara. What can I do for you?'

'First of all, let me congratulate you on your promotion to Head of Mossad Europe.'

Simon looked surprised. 'You're not supposed to know that,' he laughed.

'Of course not, the best kept secrets and all that.' She grinned, ushered him to sit down in an easy chair and asked, 'How do you like your coffee?'

She sat opposite; a small coffee table separated them. He noticed she was wearing a smart, loose fitting two-piece navy blue suit, edged with red. Her knee length skirt revealed shapely legs.

Not bad for a woman in her mid-fifties, thought Simon.

Jill entered with a tray containing china cups, a coffee pot, a milk jug and some biscuits.

'Allow me to start at the beginning. I know we see each other at our six-monthly al-Qaeda group meetings, but humour me for a few minutes. You will remember my predecessor, Peter Stacey, contacted you nearly five years ago to help us monitor an agent who had managed to infiltrate al-Qaeda.'

'Yes – Bradda Head. I remember him well. After he returned to the UK, Sir Peter gave us as much detail as he could. We lost a good agent in Tunis before your man disappeared for almost two years in the Balkans. The Russians captured him, as I recollect, during the Nagorno-Karabakh war. Some of his intelligence was used to scour out one or two hardliners in the Russian hierarchy. He discovered Indian Intelligence had also infiltrated al-Qaeda, and thanks to him our group has been so successful. He retired to the Isle of Man, I believe. Why, what's the problem?'

'You know he and his family were killed last year when their farmhouse was burnt to the ground.'

'It was a tragic end to a brave man.'

'It wasn't quite true.'

'Meaning?'

'Meaning, Quayle survived.'

Simon sat up straight from his relaxed posture. Barbara took the break to pour coffee thinking *if he doesn't know...*

'Quayle was trapped in the cellar when the fire was started by a clever series of linked incendiary devices that had all the hallmarks of an al-Qaeda attack.'

'I didn't know that.'

'We never told anyone that he survived – deliberately. If you didn't know, with your network of sayanims, then al-Qaeda doesn't know either. Quayle swore revenge and we have begun a long-term plan to assassinate bin Laden that might take several years. We have given him a new identity and completely changed his appearance. His own mother wouldn't recognise him, nor will bin Laden. However, his main problem will be getting close enough to carry out the attack.'

'And you want us to help?'

'He leaves next week for Beirut where he will become *The Daily Telegraph's* Middle East correspondent. He will establish himself in the Lebanon by writing pro-Palestinian, anti-Israeli articles. Hopefully he will get to meet Hezbollah and other radical politicians. A sufficiently sympathetic Palestinian profile will, we hope, get him an interview with bin Laden.'

'An admirable plan, but why tell me?'

'We need your help to establish his bona fides.'

'How?'

'You can arrange two things. Firstly, he will need a local scout. A gopher if you like, who will help Quayle make contacts, sniff out good stories and make sure he is in the right place at the right time; preferably when trouble is likely to break out. I was wondering if you have someone undercover in the Lebanon who could be diverted to become his fixer.'

'I know we have many agents in the Lebanon; some have even infiltrated the Lebanese Government. What sort of qualities would this man need to have?'

'I see him being able to smuggle Pearson, that's his new name by the way, into Israel to report on so-called Israeli aggression towards Palestinians, to act as his cameraman, to make introductions, to keep an eye on him and make reports to you. He must, above all, be flexible and occasionally do things that, in the short-term, are against Israel, but will eventually be beneficial.'

'You said two things.'

'Yes. I think, at some point, your soldiers should shoot him, not fatally, but make it serious enough for him to get plenty of Palestinian sympathy.'

'That's a hell of a plan you've got, Barbara. Does Quayle know you want him shot?'

'No, of course not. It must look real.'

'I'm glad I don't work for you!' He laughed.

Barbara wasn't sure how to take the joke.

'What sort of timescales are we talking about?'

'You haven't long to find the right man. As I said, he leaves for Beirut next week. The timescale for this plan is anything between two and five years. Surviving a spurious Israeli assassination will be crucial if he is to achieve notoriety.'

'How will Quayle kill bin Laden?'

'All I can tell you is that he will only need to be in the same room with him for half an hour.'

'So it's a CB weapon?'

'Yes. And one other thing.'

'Go on.'

'I have agreed I cannot communicate with Pearson while he is in Beirut. It would be too risky.'

'So you want our man to keep you up to date with any developments?'

'Yes, but through you.'

'Am I to tell him the true intention of the operation – that Pearson plans to assassinate bin Laden with a CB weapon?'

'NO! Definitely not. Again that would be too risky. He must think his role is purely to support Pearson as a gofer. Their's not to reason why, their's but to do and die.'

352

John Pearson flew from Heathrow on Monday 22nd with Gulf Air. He was met by his predecessor, Jack Bolton, who would stay with him for a fortnight before coming home to retire. As Jack so eloquently put it as they drove north through the war-scarred city, 'I've had enough of Arabs. When you get to know them better, you will see why the Israelis always wallop them in a war.' Juan had to fight hard not to give away his true background and tell him that he had once worked for several years in Iraq. He remembered Bill Bradley's warning – it is harder to forget the past than it is to learn the future.

It is one thing answering questions when your guard is up, it's another thing altogether when in the field.

'Why can't they win?' asked Juan, feigning innocence.

'They can't organise themselves,' he replied. 'They have no concept of teamwork outside their own family. The Syrians and the Iraqis were on the same side in the Yom Kippur War, but hated each other. Then there is this Sunni – Shia thing. They're worse than Catholics and Protestants. No, I'm going home to retire to Somerset. East Coker will be Shangri La after this place.'

'Have you a fixer? I've been told they are essential out here to get things done.'

'True, but my old hack is past his sell-by date – like me, I suppose. But the word is already out; you'll be swamped by eager youngsters wanting to make a name for themselves.'

'How will I select the best one?'

'Interview half a dozen and then give them a task: *get me a scoop.* See who comes up with the best opportunity for a story. Find out if he can handle a camera. How many languages can he handle? If he's any good, offer him a quarter of your salary.'

'Charlie Carter said a third.'

'Yes, but they expect you to barter. Never offer what you can afford immediately – not for anything.'

'What languages should he have? I can speak Arabic.'

'Yes, I know. But can you speak Hebrew?'

'No.'

'If your gofer can, so much the better. It means he probably knows someone, perhaps a relative, on the West Bank and can smuggle you into Israel. That's where the real stories are these days.'

Juan was impressed by his new flat: a one bedroom apartment on the fourth floor of a seven-floor tower block. Jack helped him move in and later took him around the local area showing him the shops and eating places. 'This is a good neighbourhood, you will be safe.' They ate at a nearby Thai restaurant that evening.

The next morning Jack picked him up and drove to the office. He discovered he had a secretary who worked three mornings a week. Emily Sharif was originally from North London but had met her Lebanese husband when he had been a student at Imperial College. She had lived in Beirut for 20 years. Juan would be her third *Telegraph* correspondent.

'Emily looks after the office, keeps the paperwork in check and knows the city like the back of her hand,' said Jack. 'I expect she has your agenda for the rest of the week sorted already.'

He looked at her for agreement.

'You have five applicants for an assistant,' she replied. 'I have arranged for them to have one-hour interviews with you, starting tomorrow morning.'

***

Of the five interviewed, three were chancers. Jack recommended the other two be given a week to come up with proof of their claims that they could handle photographic equipment, including a TV camera, had important contacts within the Lebanese authorities and find a potential scoop. Emily took notes of the interviews and coordinated the day impeccably.

A week later, Kazim Madani arrived for the second interview. A 28 year old, he looked like thousands of other Lebanese young men – tall, slim, almost gangly, dressed in jeans, soiled tee shirt and trainers. *Do they never wash their tee shirts? Perhaps they throw them away and get a new one from time to time.* However, he was full of enthusiasm and clearly wanted the job. He offered Juan an interview with a senior officer of Hamas – a friend of a distant cousin. He also claimed to be able to give Juan exclusive details of how the Israelis assassinated Yahya Ayyash, the master bomb maker known as The Engineer.

Juan looked at Jack, giving him a puzzled frown.

'It could be a good start. Everyone knows the Israelis killed Ayyash, but how they did it remains a mystery,' replied Jack.

'When was he killed?'

'About three weeks ago. It was a big blow to the Palestinian cause. This could be quite a scoop.'

Juan returned his gaze to Kazim who enthusiastically continued with details of how his aunt, with whom he had grown up, lived on the West Bank and he regularly travelled to see her illegally.

'I can get you into Israel whenever you want. My Hebrew is very good,' he enthused. 'There is to be a demonstration in a few weeks in Jerusalem against the proposals for extending the apartheid wall the Israelis are building. I could take you there too, if you want.'

I suppose I can forgive him for not washing his shirts!

Juan looked at Jack, who looked at Emily.

'The other candidate has not arrived,' she whispered.

Juan stood up, held out his hand, and asked, 'When can you start?'

The non-arrival of the other candidate was never explained.

CHAPTER 47

Friday 2nd February 1996

Kazim had arranged a meeting with the member of the Hamas inner council in Jordan. Two days after appointing Kazim, Juan found himself flying to Amman with his new gopher.

'Who is this leader you are taking me to see?'

'His name is Hassan al-Shapi, one of the senior Hamas officials in the Gaza Strip. Hamas use Jordan as their base for training operatives and getting supplies from Iran. We will be travelling overland to the south of the country; it will take most of the day.'

They hired a 4x4 at the airport, booked into *The Palace Hotel*, and left early the following morning. By late afternoon they reached Ma'an, a small town despite being the capital of the region. Their *Hotel Nabataea* was a comfortable family run establishment.

'Al-Shapi is to join us for dinner,' explained Kazim, 'if he turns up.'

'You don't sound too hopeful.'

'Don't forget, my contact is in Lebanon. Communications can often go wrong out here. It's not like being in London.'

Nevertheless, Hassan arrived promptly at seven o'clock. Juan was surprised that he came alone. The story he told of Ayyash's assassination could have been pure science fiction. Juan took copious notes, at times in disbelief at the sophistication of the Israeli attack.

'If Israel can do this to Ayyash, what chance have you got of ever defeating the Jews and pushing them into the sea?' Juan asked.

'We believe our cause is just. Allah will guide us. The more atrocities the Israelis commit in Gaza and the West Bank, the more volunteers we get. They come to help from African Islamic countries like Somalia and the Sudan, as well as from all over the Middle East. The war has barely begun. Suicide bombers are currently single and kill a few hundred at a time. However, the day will come when dozens of our heroes will simultaneously attack and kill thousands of infidels at once. It may be years away, but mark my words, it will happen. America will sit up and take notice.' Then, changing the subject, he asked, 'When will your article appear in *The Daily Telegraph*?'

'Hopefully, the day after tomorrow.'

Seemingly satisfied, he left. It was exactly nine o'clock.

On Tuesday 6th February 1996, a report in the foreign pages of *The Telegraph* read:

SOPHISTICATED ISRAELI TECHNOLOGY KILLS PALESTINIAN ENGINEER

By John Pearson, our Lebanon correspondent

On Friday 5th January, one of Palestine's chief bomb makers, Yahya Ayyash (29), was assassinated by the Israeli Shin Bet – Israel's Security Agency – the department that answers directly to the Prime Minister. For the past month, speculation has been rife as to how the murder was achieved. Yahya was, after all, one of the most wanted men in Palestine and had become a master of disguise to fool the Israelis and so avoid capture.

As a result of an exclusive interview with a leading Palestinian official, I can now reveal how sophisticated the Israeli operation was.

Three days after the killing, Yassir Arafat accused Israel of the assassination, saying, 'We demand that the other side be committed to peace and not kill our people in the lands of Gaza.'

There has been no denial from the Israeli Government that they had carried out the attack.

Apparently, a Hamas traitor, who I shall call Hameed, was in the pay of the Shin

Bet. He had been given Israeli identity documents for himself and his family with a guarantee of protection. Hameed was persuaded to give his cousin a mobile phone as a present. Ayyash and the unnamed cousin were lifelong friends and Ayyash frequently stayed with the cousin when in Gaza. The Israelis knew that Ayyash regularly used the cousin's phones believing them to be secure. He thought that if he used his own mobile the calls would be monitored.

Shin Bet told Hameed that the phone was bugged and all they wanted to do was monitor his conversations. However, the phone also contained 15 grams of RDX explosive. At 8 am on Friday 5th January, Ayyash's father rang him on the cousin's phone. Overhead, an Israeli warplane picked up the conversation and, having confirmed it was Ayyash, transmitted a signal to an Israeli command centre. Shin Bet then remotely detonated the bomb, blowing off Ayyash's head.

The degree of sophistication of the attack must be a worry to the pro-Palestinian groups such as al-Qaeda, Hamas and the al-Qassam brigades. A 40-day period of mourning will shortly come to an end and then, I believe, we may expect retaliatory attacks. Israel, once again, through its thoughtless actions has stuck its head in the hornets' nest.

Kazim's next success was to arrange a visit to the West Bank where a protest was to be held about proposals to extend the segregation wall. The wall had begun two years previously when Yitzhak Rabin, the Israeli Prime Minister, approved a mile-long concrete security barrier at a communal settlement called Bat Hefer. Rabin had set up a commission to make recommendations for the wall's expansion. A 465 mile-long wall, four times longer than the Berlin wall, and up to 30 feet high in places, was proposed. Plans showed that Palestinian homesteads would be razed, and journeys that currently took ten minutes could, in future, take three hours as a result of necessary detours and checkpoints. Israelis were calling it 'The Fence for Life', while the Palestinians, seeing families being split who only lived 100 yards from each other, were calling it 'The Apartheid Wall'. The formal announcement of the Shahal Commission was to be made in Jerusalem. Juan attended, along with dozens of other journalists. The peaceful march to the town hall by, perhaps, 10,000 placard carrying protestors was heavily policed by troops in riot gear. There was the usual fracas of barging, pushing and cudgel wielding that characterises such peaceful demonstrations. Strategically positioned barriers prevented the march getting near the town hall. As attempts were made to remove the barriers, the police opened up with tear gas, rubber bullets and water cannon. Snatch squads with shields and truncheons would charge into the crowd and grab individuals at random, dragging them away whilst coshing them indiscriminately.

The ructions lasted for over an hour before the disillusioned crowd drifted away. The next day, back in Beirut, Juan filed his report on 'the brutality of Israeli police in breaking up the legitimate protest by Palestinians about to be deprived of their homes and livelihood'. His report predicted that the building of the barrier would, within five years, directly affect 250,000 Palestinians who would lose their homes, and reduce their access to water, hospitals, schools, work and religious facilities. His and similar reports in other broadsheets fell on the deaf ears of western politicians.

Typically, each month, Kazim would find Juan an exclusive interview with someone. Often they were officials of the Lebanese government; occasionally, a leader of a rebel brigade of which there were many. Poor organisation and a lack of coordination were rife. *If only they could pool their resources then Israel would not be in such a strong position,* was the conclusion Juan came to on each occasion he met yet another brigade commander.

The Daily Telegraph Thursday 6th August 1998
HAMAS LEADER CALLS FOR HOLY WAR
By John Pearson, our Lebanon correspondent

I recently had an exclusive interview with Mohammad al Zakbarwi, the leader of the militant South Lebanon Brigade of Hamas. He claimed it was time for Muslims around the world to unite and liberate their countries from American inspired Zionist influence. 'Sons of Islam must unite to establish the rule of Allah on Earth,' he said.

'There is only victory or martyrdom.'

This pronouncement could be a change of policy as, until now, military action by Hamas has been confined to Israel and the Palestinian territories. Their battle has been against Zionist occupation of their land.

Al Zakbarwi claimed that he believed Palestinian leaders were abandoning their cause. 'The Muslims need a king, like Saladin, to conquer Israel and make it disappear from the map.' I hadn't the heart to tell him that Saladin was not nearly as ruthless as the popularly held belief: he spared his captors and held them to ransom. However, if the ransom was not redeemed they were sold as slaves. Saladin was quite an entrepreneur; an accusation usually slung at the Jews.

Al Zakbarwi went on to praise the suicide bombers, mentioning that the West can expect to see an escalation of such attacks over the next 18 months. Female bombers will be used in future, he said. He praised the al-Qaeda organisation as holding true to the Jihad – the holy war – and thought that its leader, Osama bin Laden, would 'rank up there with Saladin'.

I asked him about Yasser Arafat. 'His time has passed,' he said. 'He has grown lazy and fat whilst his people continue to suffer from increasingly deteriorating living conditions. We must prepare for a lengthy fight. Only when Israel withdraws from the West Bank and East Jerusalem, evacuates its settlers and frees its prisoners will we be prepared to consider an armistice,' he added.

My final question was to ask what he thought Hamas' priorities should be. 'Palestinians, men, women and children must be ready for the conflict. They need to be trained militarily to assist our warriors in our struggle against the Zionist enemy.'

∗∗∗

TOP SECRET
Memorandum

SUBJECT: Al-Qaeda Threat

From:	Director MI6	**Date:**	6 Aug 98
To:	Director CIA, Langley	**Ref:**	VB/CIA/AQ98/1

Dear George,

I am attaching a copy of an interview in today's *Telegraph* with Mohammad al Zakbarwi and would draw your attention to para 2, re 'a change in policy'. As you know, we have regular meetings with the Israelis, the French, the Germans and the Indian NSG to monitor developments and share intelligence about the threat posed by al-Qaeda. In the past, we have sent memoranda to all three of your predecessors asking your department to join our working group. I would ask you to reconsider your position and join us, as at our last meeting Indian intelligence was suggesting that attacks against foreign embassies were imminent within the next year.

Yours etc,

Barbara

***

A day later, on 7th August, bombs exploded simultaneously at the US embassies in Dar es Salaam and Nairobi, killing hundreds. Juan knew it was the work of bin Laden, and his interview with al Zakbarwi had been a test. Although he'd been in Beirut for two and a half years, there had been no contact with anyone from al-Qaeda. He hoped the time was approaching when tentative contacts would be made to interview the key player. However, as more months passed, he began to despair and his reports of suicide bombings, no matter how horrific, became routine and therefore, boring. Neither Europe nor America was interested in yet another Israeli settlement being created illegally. The world's press barons seemed to be indifferent.

A further six months had passed when one day Kazim urged Juan to accompany him to Israel to witness the destruction of a small village that was to become a new settlement. They travelled through the night over rough terrain and, at one time, crawled through a tunnel. They arrived the following morning at a shanty village, consisting of six houses and outbuildings situated in the middle of 20 acres of olive trees on a south-facing slope. A small stream ran through the estate. It transpired an extended family lived in the houses: grandparents, their five married sons, with wives and their children. They had lived on their farm for many generations. Today it was to be razed to the ground to make way for a settlement of orthodox Jews. In Juan's eyes, the adults looked old. He explained their apparent age by their living conditions: no running hot water, external wiring that must have made the electricity supply erratic and a common sewage system to an overflowing cesspit. The 40-year old Palestinian men and their spouses looked more like 70.

On the top of the hill, overlooking the site, two bulldozers had assembled.

'The Israelis will do nothing until the troops arrive,' explained Kazim, 'then we can expect fireworks.'

To Juan's surprise, they were the only members of the press present. 'How did you know something was going to happen here?' asked Juan.

Kazim said nothing but stroked his nose with his index finger and smiled.

✷✷✷

The Daily Telegraph Monday 15th February 1999

MASSACRE AT PALESTINIAN FARMSTEAD
TWO SHOT BY ISRAELI SOLDIERS

By John Pearson, our Lebanon Correspondent

On Friday last, the 12th February, I found myself at a small farmstead, called Bil'sallin, in the middle of the occupied West Bank. The farm of some 24 acres, mostly consisting of olive trees, but with a few fields for a flock of sheep and some goats, has been the home of the al-Aluris for over 100 years. It sustains the family of Jamal al-Aluri and his five sons with their families.

At 0900 hours precisely, two bulldozers descended the slope towards the farm buildings, crushing the olive trees in front of them. The father and his sons stood their ground in front of their homes. Behind them, their wives and children shouted insults and waved placards declaring Israelis to be the direct descendants of Satan. Behind the bulldozers, silhouetted on the top of the hill, as if in the Ingmar Bergman film, *The Seventh Seal,* stood a dozen Israeli soldiers watching and waving their rifles. They laughed to see the trees being ripped from the ground and I was reminded of Bergman since so many of his films were of insanity and death. What I was witnessing was madness; I wasn't to know the Grim Reaper was around the corner. The relentless advance of the JCBs seemed to be taking place in slow motion and I wondered what would happen when they neared the first building in their way – a ramshackle barn.

What happened was unbelievable. As the barn was smashed to the ground, two of the brothers ran towards the JCBs, waving their bare hands and screaming for the diggers to stop. The bulldozers halted and for a moment there was an impasse; shades of Tiananmen Square. Not for long, however. Two shots rang out, and both the men fell to the ground. Instinctively, I ran forward, waving my white handkerchief and yelling for the troops to stop firing. I reached the fallen farmers in seconds. One was moaning in agony, a bullet hole in his shoulder. The other lay still – quite dead. As I bent down to help the injured man to his feet, hoping to retreat, a third shot rang out. I felt a stab of excruciating pain in my thigh. I had been shot. By this time all hell had broken loose. The women and children were running forward and screaming into the line of fire. The other men had arrived and were pulling me away, along with their brothers, towards the farm houses. The bulldozers remained stationary; their drivers didn't know what to do.

My photographer, Kazim, was busy recording the scene. I was to learn later that the civilian drivers refused to go any further. They turned their machines around and retreated. The shattered al-Aluri family is now minus a bread-winner; the Israeli soldiers think they have got away with murder. However, as a British citizen, I have been able to persuade our diplomats to pursue prosecution through the Israeli courts. Whether this will achieve anything, or not, will remain to be seen. I have my doubts, despite our photographic evidence.

The question Western Governments must ask themselves is, when are they going to take action to stop Israel's gung-ho treatment of the Palestinians? Uncle Sam can no longer continue to turn a blind eye. For heavens sake, Mr President, act now before the sleeping tiger of the Arab World wakes up!

∗∗∗

The Daily Telegraph Monday 7th June 1999

ISRAEL DESTROYING LEBANESE TOWN A PRECURSOR TO WITHDRAWAL?

By John Pearson, our Lebanon Correspondent

The small town of Khiam in South Lebanon overlooks Israel's northern border, a geographical accident that has brought it devastation for the second time in 21 years.

On Friday 4th June a methodical, systematic destruction began. House by house, district by district, everything was razed. Even the ground was levelled. The town's 30,000 residents have mostly fled north to escape the battering from the Israeli Army and Air Force. Air raids have included the use of incendiary bombs as well as high explosives. Tanks and bulldozers are completing the work done by artillery shells.

The Israelis appear to be determined to wipe Khiam from the map. Already the town is unrecognisable as the streets are a pile of rubble from the shattered houses and burnt out vehicles. Schools, mosques, municipal offices, the police station, even the football pitch have all gone.

I have been unable to confirm the rumour that the UN Observation Post was blown up, killing two of the UN troops.

Why?

It is widely believed here in Beirut that a general election is soon to be called in Israel and that Prime Minister Netanyahu is trying to gather support from right wing members in the Knesset who see him as being too soft with the Palestinians, especially after the signing of the Wye River agreement last year.

Opinion polls are suggesting the centre left party led by Ehud Barak will win. It is hoped, perhaps unrealistically, in the Lebanon that the Israeli socialist party will withdraw from the occupied territory when they get into power, providing certain security guarantees are given by the Lebanese government.

✱✱✱

The Daily Telegraph Thursday 25th May 2000
ISRAEL BEGINS WITHDRAWAL FROM S LEBANON
By John Pearson, our Lebanon Correspondent

Ten months after becoming Israel's Prime Minister, Ehud Barak has kept his promise to withdraw troops from southern Lebanon. Yesterday, the first Israeli tanks began to pull back across the border and are being replaced by a UN peacekeeping force known as UNIFIL. The process will occur in stages and will depend on the strength of the UN troops and the perceived ability of the Lebanese Army to take effective control of the area.

I observed about 80 Lebanese military trucks and jeeps carrying soldiers and equipment heading south through central Beirut yesterday afternoon. When the process is complete, it will be the first time Lebanese troops will have been so close to the Israel border in almost 30 years.

The Barak plan calls for the UN team to increase to 15,000 and be joined by an equal number of Lebanese troops. However, the feeling I am getting from members of the Government here is that if the fundamentalists, such as Hezbollah, begin stirring trouble, then the Israelis will return with even more force. "The problem is that the guerrillas will not give up their arms," said a Lebanese spokesman. He could have added that the Army will not confront the freedom fighters and drive them from their entrenched positions in towns such as Tyre. Ambivalence and indecisiveness are the masters.

✱✱✱

The Daily Telegraph Tuesday 1st May 2001
TORTURE AND DETENTION IN ISRAELI PRISON
By John Pearson, our Lebanon Correspondent

On a recent secret visit to northern Israel, I was fortunate to meet a 27 year old Palestinian journalist, Rihab Ibrahem. Her story is one that will move the hearts of all free-thinking people.

It was a sunny, balmy day in early March 2000. She was finishing a late lunch with her family in Nazareth when a car pulled up in the driveway of her father's house. Two men got out, one a Palestinian and the other, she suspected, an Israeli. They asked her to accompany them to answer a few questions. She asked, 'Why?'

The Palestinian introduced himself as Abu Hasheem, a member of the discredited Palestinian militia, the PLA, known to be in the pay of the Israelis. He explained that if she refused then she would be arrested by his colleague, a member of the Israeli Shin Bet and taken to the notorious El Main detention centre.

A bewildered Rihab climbed into the car and soon realised that they were headed towards the prison. Although she had never met him before, she was to learn that Hasheem was the Shin Bet's liaison officer for Nazareth. At the detention centre she was one of 1,500 people held under the most primitive of conditions.

That afternoon she was quizzed for six hours while being made to stand the whole time. 'Most of the questions I couldn't answer as I had neither the information to give them nor did I understand what they were wanting,' she said. 'I formed the impression that Hasheem held a grudge against my father who is an educated man and a leader in the community. This was his way of getting revenge.' She was to discover later that many prisoners at the centre were also held purely because of personal grudges.

Every day for the next 20 days, two women guards fetched Rihab from her cell and took her for interrogation. A bag would be placed on her head and, handcuffed, she would be dragged to a room where for eight hours she had to stand while being asked questions. 'The first three days were OK, I was not beaten. But then it got worse. I was made to kneel and hold a chair above my head. If I dropped it, they threw cold water over me and I received an electric shock.'

Subsequently she was kicked in the face and they broke her nose. She began to develop an allergy over her body. She received no medical attention. Despite her appalling treatment, she says she was lucky as the women were not subjected to the same degree of torture as the men. Confined in a solitary cell, she would cry herself to sleep.

'Ironically, it seemed worse when they stopped coming to get me for interrogation and punishment. For six weeks no one came at all. My measly ration of one meal a day was slipped through the door and the bucket for my slops was removed at the same time. I fell to an all time low and would have committed suicide if I had had the means,' she told me.

Then one day, she was put in a cell with three other girls. One, Najwa, a mother of four young children, also had her husband and brother detained at the same time. However, they were able to give each other some comfort and try to keep a positive outlook. They knew that Ehud Barak had promised to release political prisoners who had not been put on trial.

Then on May 24th, they heard cries of 'Allah Akbar' resounding in the courtyard of the detainment centre. 'It was a cry I shall always remember,' she said with tears in her eyes. 'We thought it was the Shin Bet killing some of the male detainees, but then a man opened our door with a crowbar and we were free. We went out into the bright sunlight. No one was crying, no one was laughing. Everyone was too stunned. The whole place had been deserted by the guards.'

For Rihab, and thousands like her, the freedom is heavenly, but the scars run deep. 'Until Israel realises it cannot destroy a nation and it must begin to talk with us, then the fear that has been created will shape our lives,' she said.

Rihab Ibrahem spent three months in El Main. No one knows why.

Three months after penning the moving account of Rihab's incarceration, Kazim came into the office clearly excited. 'Boss,' he said, 'do you remember interviewing Hassan al-Shapi?'

'The guy we met in Gaza?'

'Yes, it's over five years ago.'

'What about him?'

'He made contact with me yesterday and asked whether you would like to interview bin Laden.'

'You're joking? What did you tell him?'

'I said "Yes".'

'And?'

'We are to go to Peshawar in Pakistan and ask for Hammed Mir.'

***

A few days later, Barbara received a call from Simon Rosenberg. 'They're off to Pakistan next Wednesday – the 29th August.'

'God, it's taken five years. Let's hope it works.'

CHAPTER 48

Wednesday 29th August 2001

After making all the necessary preparations to travel, such as arranging to withdraw cash from any of the branches of the Allied Bank of Pakistan, Kazim and Juan flew into Karachi on a PIA flight direct from Beirut, arriving late afternoon. They booked into the airport's *Hilton Hotel* and had previously organised a 4x4 from Avis. Their plan was to travel to Peshawar the following day. However, after almost ten hours driving they were shattered; 600 miles of hot and dusty roads had taken their toll. They pulled off from their route and stopped the night at the *Hotel Continental* in the centre of Multan in the Punjab.

★★★

TOP SECRET

Memorandum

From: Director MI6   **Date:** 30 Aug 01
To: Director CIA, Langley   **Ref:** VB/CIA/AQ01/1

Al-Qaeda Threats

Dear George,

1. In my last memorandum to you on this subject, dated 6 Aug 98, I asked you to

consider joining our international working group on al-Qaeda threats. Somewhat ironically, the following day al-Qaeda attacked two of your African embassies. I don't wish to rub salt into the wound, but it's possible it may be about to happen again. Early next week I have a meeting with my Foreign Secretary, Jack Straw, when I will be tendering my application to take early retirement at the end of September. Notwithstanding your department's reluctance to share information with us, I am taking it upon myself to let you know what we have on al-Qaeda and bin Laden before I leave MI6. Please take this letter in the spirit in which it is intended.

2. As long ago as 23 Jun 92, a memo from my predecessor, Peter Stacey, to Robert Gates warned that al-Qaeda's aims were long-term. An operative of ours, a Major from the Army Intelligence Corps, had spent 18 months under cover with al-Qaeda and provided us with invaluable information when he returned. My predecessor's memo warned that aircraft hijackings would be coordinated and the planes used as flying bombs to target buildings such as The White House.

3. In 8 years things have moved on apace. The AIC Major was targeted by an al-Qaeda assassin in Jul 95. His family – a wife and 4 children – were murdered, but the Major survived. However, only a few in my department and Mossad know this. He was officially buried with his family. With his appearance dramatically changed to avoid recognition, for the past 5 years he has been undercover as *The Daily Telegraph's* correspondent in the Lebanon, aided by a Mossad agent acting as his gofer. By writing anti-Israeli articles, he has gained the trust of various terrorist organisations.

4. This culminated last week when he was invited to interview bin Laden somewhere in northern Pakistan. The operation was originally set up, not to interview bin Laden, but to get close enough to assassinate him. I fully expect the operation to be a success, but whether our operative will ever return from NW Pakistan is doubtful. He always knew it could be a one-way trip, but revenge for the massacre of his family was overriding.

5. I won't go into details of the plan, but our agent will be using anthrax spores as a biological weapon. A check by your staff will, I am sure, reveal an outbreak of anthrax

within the next week or two somewhere near the Afghanistan border. The strain being used is Vollum 1-B, developed at Porton Down; it is the most dangerous in our arsenal.

6. I understand your Government is planning the invasion of Afghanistan imminently with the aims of destroying the Taliban, al-Qaeda and bringing Osama bin Laden to justice. In view of the above, the latter aim may be redundant. However, knowledge of the anthrax strain we are using may help in your planning.

7. Our committee's best source of data has been, for some time, the Indian NSG. They have been picking up vibrations from their agents in Pakistan that something big is afoot. I am only speculating, but I wonder if our agent receiving an invitation to meet bin Laden has been co-ordinated by al-Qaeda to coincide with a spectacular attack. Bin Laden is hoping an article in a newspaper such as *The Daily Telegraph* will maximise publicity. I, therefore, urge you to be *en garde*. I shall be writing to our international committee members in due course about my retirement but am taking the liberty to invite you to the next meeting to be held in London on 1 Nov 01, which will chaired by my successor. Perhaps, by then, and with luck, our man will return safely having achieved a successful outcome to the operation.

8. Finally, George, may I wish you the very best for the future.

Yours etc
    Barbara

✳✳✳

It was another hard day on Friday, as the 400 plus miles took a further nine hours. Fortunately, Juan and Kazim's hotel, the *Al-Mansoor*, was comfortable, air conditioned, the staff friendly and the bath water hot. Situated near the railway station, it was a few minutes' walk to the office of The Salt Valley Star.

The following day, Saturday 1st September, Juan and Kazim went to the newspaper's office and asked to see Hammed Mir. 'He's not here,' the receptionist replied.

'But we're from *The Daily Telegraph* of London and have come a long way to see him.'

She shrugged her shoulders, as if to gesture that she couldn't care less.

'I insist I speak to your Editor.' Juan was pleased with his command of Urdu. *Must let her know who is boss,* he thought.

It surprised the young girl. She stared for a moment trying to read from Juan's face whether there would be a fuss upstairs if she turned away what could be an important stranger. She swung around and shouted through to the back office, 'Raz, go and get Ibrahim. Tell him there's someone here who claims he's from some paper in London.'

Juan decided to let the sarcasm ride. He looked at Kazim and rolled his eyes upwards, saying in Arabic, *'You can't get the staff anymore.'*

The office junior had already resumed her place behind her VDU, presumably to continue to play her game of patience.

A few minutes later, Ibrahim appeared. Tall, slim, with chiselled features and a dark olive complexion, he wore jeans and, yet another, grubby a tee-shirt. 'Can I help you?' he asked politely.

'We've come to see Hammed Mir. I gather he's not here.'

Ibrahim looked furtively around to ensure no one overheard his reply, 'Have you come from Beirut?'

'Yes.'

'Then, please, follow me.' He took them up some stairs to the first floor. 'Can I make you a drink of tea, perhaps?' He was somewhat obsequious and had obviously been expecting them.

'That would be nice,' replied Juan as they were invited to sit down.

'I'm afraid Hammed is away in the Tora Bora at the moment. He's been called away to convince your interviewee that you are genuine, and a sympathetic article published in *The Daily Telegraph* would add great weight to his cause. He has to be careful, you understand?'

'How long will he be away?'

'I am expecting him back in the next day or two. Travel up-country is very unpredictable. He left here as soon as you confirmed that you would travel. Have you been to Pakistan before?'

'No. We are not impressed by your roads.'

Ibrahim laughed in a jovial manner, apparently thinking Juan's remark was a joke. It wasn't. 'You would have done better to come from Karachi by train. We have two expresses a day that only take ten hours; that is when they run!' It was his turn to make the joke about transport in Pakistan. He continued, 'Where are you staying?'

'The *Al-Mansoor*.'

'A most excellent establishment. The manager is a distant cousin of mine. I will ensure you are looked after admirably. I will give you one of my juniors to guide you around our beautiful city, if you like. As soon as Mir has returned I will contact you.'

'That would be very kind.'

And so for the rest of that day and the next, Raz showed the visitors around the city. It proved to be an eye opener to Juan. He'd expected Peshawar to be some backward frontier hovel teeming with poverty. Instead he was shown the beautiful architecture of the City District including the Islamia College and the Sunheri Mosque. At the city museum he learnt that Alexander the Great's successors influenced the layout of the town. Later, it subsequently became a centre of Buddhism, and the monks built a temple with a 400 ft tower in 120BC. Called a stupa, it existed until 634AD. They saw its foundations and Juan marvelled at its size. Everywhere there was evidence of both Persian and British influence. The two days passed quickly.

On Monday, Hammed arrived and met them at their hotel. 'Osama has agreed to an interview with certain conditions,' he said.

Not wishing to show his delight that, at last, his plan was within sight of its climax, Juan asked with a scowl, 'What conditions?'

'You will travel with me and a minder he has appointed in a blacked-out vehicle so that you do not know where we are taking you.'

'OK.'

'All you can take with you are the clothes you are wearing and a small bag of toiletries.'

'What about Kazim's camera?'

'We will inspect it first and it can only be used when you are given permission.'

'Fine.'

'You will conduct your interview in the presence of his bodyguards. The notes you take are to be written up immediately afterwards to become the article to be published. He will then give it approval. I am to bring it back here and fax it to London.'

'Still OK.' Juan had begun to wonder if Mir was al-Qaeda's official spokesman, handling dealings with the international press and, probably, Al-Jazeera TV.

'In that case we leave tomorrow after breakfast. We will pick you up from your hotel at nine o'clock.'

'How long will the journey take?'

'All of three days. I gather you told Ibrahim you were not impressed with our highways. You haven't seen anything yet.' He chuckled at his own joke.

The following day a four-seater truck arrived, loaded with tents, food and water. The minder carried an AK-47 and made no effort to hide it. Karim and Juan sat in the rear; the windows were blacked out. Juan guessed they were, in general, heading in a northerly direction. The roads gradually worsened to being little better than cow tracks.

Although difficult to assess, Juan's excellent sense of direction was telling him they were zigzagging to confuse him from knowing where exactly they were heading. *Three days travelling like this,* he thought, *could have us in Afghanistan, perhaps in the Hindu Kush.*

CHAPTER 49

Wednesday 5th September 2001

'Mrs Renton has arrived, Mr Straw.'

'Show her in, Judy. Oh, and Judy...'

'Yes, Jack?'

'Can you make us some coffee?'

'Of course.'

The Foreign Secretary's PA went back to her outer office where the Head of MI6 was waiting. 'You can go in now, Mrs Renton.'

'Barbara! I was surprised when I received your letter. Is it something I have done?'

'Of course not, sir. I have been thinking of taking early retirement for some time. The imminent Afghan invasion has raised the stakes in my battle with The Treasury to get money for more staff with Arabic qualifications. You can only hit your head against a brick wall so often. It's not only the New Labour administration that is reluctant to spend money on intelligence; the previous government was no better. The threat from al-Qaeda has been around for ten years and I have become tired of working in the dark with too few staff.'

'Barbara, please take a seat. Let me assure you I have to battle with The Treasury over everything – even paperclips; it was the same when I was in The Home Office. All I can say is that the PM has pledged President Bush our fullest support in Afghanistan. I'm not happy about it either. I worry it could become another Vietnam. However, it may work to our advantage. Gordon Brown will have no option but to find extra funds for our department, as well as the MoD. The cabinet will back me and agree to increased recruitment. Providing, of course, the graduates come from a mixed background and are not exclusively Oxbridge!'

The latter comment was made with a grin; a sly dig at MI6 and, possibly, Barbara's Oxford education.

'That idea is, if I may say so Minister, fallacious. Less than half my staff are from Oxford or Cambridge; we even have Leeds graduates.'

'Touché, Barbara! Touché!'

'However, if there is to be an expansion of our service, then I feel this is the right time to be going. A new broom and all that...'

'So, I can't persuade you to stay?'

'No, I have a small property in the Languedoc where I intend to spend my retirement.'

'Whereabouts?'

'In a village called Belveze, near Limoux.'

'It must be near Carcassonne?'

'Yes, not far.'

'A lovely part of the world. I don't want you to go, Barbara, but I wish you every happiness for the future.'

'Thank you, minister.'

'Please, call me Jack. There are two subjects, however, I must discuss with you. The first is, who do I recommend to the PM as your successor?'

'Historically, the Head has always been someone with Soviet experience. I was, as you know, a specialist on the Caucasus States – Georgia, Armenia, Chechnya, Turkey and Azerbaijan – a mixed bag. However, I think you should appoint the next head to be our current Head of the Middle East desk, Phil Jay.'

'Fine, I will recommend him. The second thing may take longer. I would like you to fill me in on all you know about al-Qaeda. I have always read the minutes of your meetings with the international committee, but why haven't the Americans joined? Aren't they taking al-Qaeda seriously?'

'No, but they should do. My predecessor, Peter Stacey, sent a warning memo to the CIA nine years ago; June 1992 to be precise, when Robert Gates was their head. At that time, we had managed to get an agent called Quayle inside al-Qaeda the previous year. He worked undercover in one of their madrassas before returning to us. The trouble with the Americans is they won't listen. The Atlantic and the Pacific isolate them and they feel impregnable. I clearly remember Quayle debriefing Peter Stacey and warning us that al-Qaeda was planning to train suicide pilots to hijack aircraft and smash them into the Empire State Building. I have a feeling he may soon be proved right.'

'What happened to Quayle?'

'He went to the Isle of Man, married and had a family. Three years later his farmhouse was attacked by an al-Qaeda arsonist. All his family were burnt to death. He was lucky to escape and he returned to work for us.'

'Was the assassin ever caught?'

'No. He was a professional hit man. Quayle returned to us vowing to eliminate bin Laden, al-Qaeda's leader. We gave Quayle a new identity and changed his appearance so no one would recognise him. For the past five years he has worked in the Lebanon as *The Daily Telegraph's* Foreign Correspondent, writing predominantly anti-Israeli articles. We hoped his pro-Palestinian stance would merit him being invited to interview bin Laden so that he could gain revenge.'

'What happened?'

'He's in Pakistan now. It took five years to gain the trust of the terrorists. All foreign correspondents in the Middle East have a local man on the ground – a gofer. Pearson's success – that was his operational name – was largely due to my arranging with Mossad for his minder to be one of their agents posing as a Lebanese. Pearson, however, never knew his helper was a Mossad agent keeping tabs on him. Pearson has successfully interviewed leaders of Hamas, Fatah and Hezbollah. All the contacts were made by an undercover Mossad operative. Ironical isn't it?'

'Can we trust Mossad?'

'Yes, Israel has more to fear from al-Qaeda than us. His gofer was tipped off a week or two ago that if they made their way to Peshawar, then someone on the staff of the *Salt Valley Sun* – the local newspaper – would guide them into the hornets' nest to meet bin Laden.'

'So we can only wait to see if the operation will be a success?'

'Yes.'

'How does Quayle hope to assassinate bin Laden?'

'Our best scientists at Porton Down came up with a scheme to release anthrax spores into the room during the interview.'

'Wouldn't that kill Quayle too?'

'Yes, but we have taken some precautions. He has been inoculated and will be carrying antibiotics in his wash bag.'

'Would that be sufficient to keep him alive?'

Barbara shrugged her shoulders and nodded. She hoped it would, but secretly had her doubts.

'How long does anthrax take to kill?'

'Without immunisation – two or three days. On the first day, those exposed to the spores would show the symptoms of a cold: a runny nose, a cough. On the second, their lungs would be full of discharging fluids. By then it would be too late to save them. Antibiotics have to be given within the first twenty-four hours, or else…'

'So, you think Pearson will kill bin Laden but could die himself?'

'Yes, I fear so.'

'What other information about al-Qaeda did Quayle bring back in 1992?'

'He was initially recruited by MI5 to ascertain whether there was a link between al-Qaeda and the IRA. The Provisionals were selling as much of their stock as they could prior to their arms being decommissioned by General Chastelain as part of the peace process.'

'I didn't know that. Was there a link?'

'Yes. He found out how the arms were being transferred at sea and intercepted the infamous Gadhafi atomic bomb.'

'I didn't know there had been a Libyan atomic weapon.'

'Gadhafi had sold the IRA a cheap nuclear device back in the mid-80s. The IRA ran scared, thank God, and never used it. Al-Qaeda was prepared to buy it and paid a million US dollars for it. It was transferred from an Irish fishing boat to a so-called Spanish boat in the Isle of Man. Quayle gained the trust of the al-Qaeda crew who were shipping it back to Ceuta. He travelled with them in a motor launch they acquired in Southern Ireland. The RAF followed them and John Major, rightly, decided to sink the launch in the Bay of Biscay using Nimrod torpedoes. The bomb lies in 20,000 feet of water in the Atlantic.'

'What was al-Qaeda planning to do with it?'

'We never knew, but I would speculate: dismantle it, ship it to New York and reactivate it.'

'So Quayle survived the sinking?'

'Yes, and two of the crew; one of whom we believe was bin Laden himself.'

'My God! We had him in our grasp?'

'Yes, but we didn't know it. Don't forget, those were early days. We knew very little about al-Qaeda. That's why Quayle was valuable as a source of intelligence.'

'Presumably the Irish arms transfers stopped?'

'Yes. The Royal Navy stepped up patrols and worked closely with the Irish Navy. When Quayle returned, he told us there were hard line communists in the Russian Army involved with supplying the terrorists. Douglas Hurd visited Russia soon afterwards and informed Yeltsin. It took a little time, but Yeltsin eventually cleared them out. We believe al-Qaeda now buy their equipment from rogue states such as Iran and North Korea, and on the black market in places such as Turkmenistan.'

'With money from Iraq?'

'No, we think not. Saddam Hussein is financially, as well as morally, bankrupt. Since the Kuwait affair and the imposition of the no-fly zones, he has been strapped for cash. He may have been sympathetic to al-Qaeda in the early years, but for some reason fell out with bin Laden who now relies on dissident Saudi princes, Yemeni businessmen and his own family fortune.'

'But the PM is under the impression that Saddam has restarted a nuclear programme by getting uranium from Niger and is secretly developing, what he calls, weapons of mass destruction.'

'With respect, Minister, that's a load of bollocks. Saddam's nuclear programme ended with the destruction of his Osirak plant by the Israelis in '81. His American sourced biological weapons remain hidden and can't be found.'

'That's not what the PM's been told by President Bush.'

'I firmly believe the Americans are looking for an excuse to invade Iraq to get cheap oil.'

'Are you saying that the Americans have had a hidden agenda of their own?'

'I think they are making a case to invade Iraq by claiming Saddam is manufacturing WMDs. There are still some powerful Texan oil magnates, all Republicans, who lost a lot of money when the Baath Party nationalised the Iraq Petroleum Company in 1972. The IPC, you will remember, was largely owned by Esso. The Texans have the ear of their President. Behind their plan is the vision of again acquiring cheap Iraqi oil. It's true, however, that Saddam has WMDs. Have you ever read The Riegle Report?'

'No. Should I?'

'Donald Riegle is a Senator for Michigan. When American soldiers began returning from Operation Desert Storm in 1991 complaining of Gulf War Syndrome, he took up their cause to get compensation. His investigations took several years, as much of the information was classified secret. What he found was frightening. His report claims that Gulf War Syndrome does exist, and is not a figment of soldiers' imagination. It is the direct result of exposure to chemical weapons in Kuwait. However, the report went further. Riegle discovered that the source of the Iraqi WMDs was America itself. His report lists sixty-five shipments to Iraq of substances such as anthrax, West Nile Fever

Virus, botulinium toxins, clostridium perfingens, and so on. The invoices are all attached to his report. During that time, Bush's father was either Vice-president or President. He effectively approved their export to Iraq thinking they would use them against Iran in the eight-year war.'

'But they did use them against Iran.'

'The chemical weapons – yes, but the biological ones – no.'

'I don't see much difference,' said the Foreign Secretary.

'Largely control. Biologicals can spread on their own accord. Having said that, chemicals can get into water supplies, such as Agent Orange in Vietnam and cause terrible birth defects.'

'Then why are the UN Weapons Inspectors wasting their time searching for something that doesn't exist?'

'I didn't say they don't exist. It's just that they can never be found. Shall I explain?'

The Foreign Secretary filled their coffee cups and nodded.

'When Desert Storm began we rescued an Iraqi double agent who was in charge of their Chemical and Biological Weapons research, development and storage programme. She had been keeping us in the picture of what was going on in Iraq for about ten years. She frequently attended Saddam's Revolutionary Council meetings. She had persuaded the council that the safest way of storing the biological weapons they were acquiring from the Americans – sarin, VX, anthrax and so on – was to bury them in the desert inside thick glass vats within sealed stainless steel containers. She doctored the records of their location by using an infallible method that relied on knowing a secret chess position. Only she could decode the records. We brought her back to Britain fearing the Iraqis would torture her to find out where the weapons were located. You may remember some of our soldiers subsequently suffered Gulf War Syndrome as well as the Americans. If Saddam did manage to spray our troops with chemicals, it would explain GWS. However, if he had used biologicals then the whole of the Middle East could have been wiped-out.'

'So, Saddam has WMDs but doesn't know where they are. Why doesn't he say so?'

'He's too embarrassed and would prefer to play along with the pretence that he has power.'

'But by doing so, he's leaving himself open to being invaded by the Americans.'

'He knows the UN Inspectors will never find the weapons and is hoping that the UN will not, therefore, sanction an invasion as it would be illegal.'

Jack Straw sat quietly, nodding to himself. He was in a deep, pensive train of thought, weighing up pros and cons. He didn't say anything for many minutes. Then he asked, 'What else did Quayle come back with that I should know about?'

'He gave us details on how they organise their madrassas. They have primary and secondary schools like us. Indoctrination and learning English is undertaken first, then students study subjects such as physics and chemistry to gain western qualifications. They infiltrate European countries and the US for further education to become professional pilots, doctors and so on.'

'Doctors?'

'Yes. From now on it's possible that we may have to accept that outbreaks of influenza and similar diseases have been engineered.'

'My God.'

'The madrassas are not only in Afghanistan either. Quayle mentioned they exist in Somalia, Yemen, Sudan and Pakistan.'

'But not Iraq?'

'No.'

'Even Bush can't invade all that lot! Are you certain that Saddam Hussein and Iraq pose no threat whatsoever to the West?'

'Yes. When I showed The Riegle Report to your predecessor, Robin Cook, several years ago, he didn't believe me either.'

'But he believes you now?'

'Yes, I think so.'

Jack Straw sat motionless, his face expressionless. In a world of his own, his head nodded up and down slowly. 'That figures,' he mumbled to himself.

'Pardon?' asked Barbara.

Jack looked up. 'Oh, nothing.'

CHAPTER 50

Thursday 6th September 2001

The four travellers drove north all day. The roads made for an uncomfortable journey. At times Hammed had to negotiate deep ruts and jagged boulders that slowed progress even further. Finally they stopped late afternoon.

'This is it,' declared Mir. 'We can all get out and stretch.'

They were at a remote, isolated hill farm at the end of a steep sided valley. Juan looked around. To the south he could see the road up which they had travelled. To the north there was nothing but scree. Scrawny goats and a flock of skinny sheep seemed to roam wherever they wished. The outbuildings looked like they had been abandoned and were falling down in a random manner. There were no signs to indicate there was anyone living in the farm.

'We will pitch our tents in that barn,' Mir said, pointing to the only one that looked reasonably safe.

'Is Osama staying here, then?' asked Juan incredulously.

'He will arrive sometime this evening. He will conduct the interview inside the farm. The family who live here have gone away.'

The next morning, Juan woke to discover that several 4x4s and half a dozen pack animals had arrived during the night. Seven or eight armed guards sat in a circle around a fire under the shelter of one of the barns making themselves a brew of tea. Mir conducted Juan into the farm, telling Kazim to wait. 'When Osama is ready, we will call for you to take photographs.'

The rooms of the farm were much bigger than Juan expected. They entered the hall and Mir ushered Juan to wait in an empty room. He then left. Two armed guards stood by a second door, from where Juan thought Osama might enter. His heart was pounding, he sat crossed legged on the carpeted floor; there being no furniture. He fiddled with his shoes. *Would the switches work? Would the anthrax escape and be sufficient to kill his enemy – the man responsible for murdering his beautiful Molly and children?* He looked at the two gorillas. He wondered if he could overpower them, grab their AK-47s and shoot bin Laden. *No, be sensible,* he told himself. *This is the moment you have worked so hard to achieve. It's taken six years of planning to kill this bastard. Don't cock it up now. You're doing this for Molly, Peter, Mikey, Sophie and Heather.*

He sat in silence for what seemed hours, but was probably less than 30 minutes. He began to sweat. The nervous tension was getting to him. The guards never moved, and never took their steely eyes off him. Eventually, Mir reappeared through the door they had originally entered.

'Osama will see you now,' he announced.

Juan stood, thinking Osama would enter the room from the second door.

Then Mir swiped Juan with a body blow. 'Take your shoes off,' he said.

Juan looked surprised. Mir read his reaction.

'Osama will see you through there,' he said pointing to the closed door. 'The room is used as the farm's mosque. Osama has been in prayer while you have been waiting. Today is Friday, our holy day. You are honoured that he is willing to see you at all.' He knocked on the door and opened it slightly ajar. He peered inside and nodded to someone. He opened it fully, inviting Juan to enter. 'Your shoes,' he reminded Juan as he began to move towards the room.

God, what do I do now? Juan thought. *All this planning for nothing.* He removed his shoes and placed them next to Mir's.

He entered, followed by Mir and the two guards. He noticed two further guards as well as bin Laden inside. None wore shoes. The room was much larger than the waiting room, but apart from the carpet there was, again, no furniture. In the centre, on the floor, sat Osama facing him. Juan recognised him at once.

Has he recognised me?

There was no glimmer in his eyes. He gestured Juan to sit about ten feet from him. Juan made himself comfortable. Osama had aged, he looked gaunt, and his skin was pallid and yellow. Juan thought he may be suffering from TB or had jaundice. He had lost a lot of weight. *Perhaps his lifestyle – always on the move and not eating properly – is catching up with him.*

'So, you are John Pearson?' he asked.

'Yes,' replied Juan, thinking *how the hell am I going to kill him now?*

'I have read several of your articles. Why are you so sympathetic with our cause and keen to discredit Israel?'

Christ, it's me who's supposed to be asking the questions.

'When I arrived to be *The Telegraph's* correspondent in the Lebanon five years ago, I wasn't. I intended to report dispassionately and be as neutral as possible. However, fate has a way of taking over and running the show. I appointed Kazim as my helper and he was able to show me some of the illegal and awful things the Israelis were doing to the Palestinians: throwing them out of their homes, destroying their olive groves, building the Apartheid Wall and killing them indiscriminately. Unconsciously, he made me realise that the Israelis could only get away with such atrocities because of the Zionists' grip on the world markets; particularly in America. I had to try and do something. Fortunately, my editor in London is sympathetic and usually publishes what I send him without too much alteration.'

'It's as well you don't work for *The Times*, then?' Without waiting for Juan to respond, Osama spat out, 'Murdoch is a Jew.'

Caught off guard, Juan replied, 'I wasn't aware of that, although I have heard that News International is generally pro-Israel.'

Bin Laden nodded slowly, staring at Juan the whole time. His mesmeric eyes were gorgonian; they froze Juan's heart. Momentarily,

Juan was frightened. *He's going to recognise me.* Then it dawned on Juan that he was staring because his eyesight had failed, like the rest of him.

'Where do you want to start?' he asked in a quiet voice.

'Well, since we have brought up the subject of Israel, let's start there. Are there any circumstances under which you would tolerate an Israeli State? If they retreated to their 1947 boundaries, for example.'

He smiled, a sickly, weak smile, as if offered a type of sweet for the first time that revolted him, but he didn't wish to offend the donor. 'Hitler originally planned to ship all the Jews to Madagascar and let them form a State there. A pity he didn't; I could just about have tolerated them that far away.' His smile broadened as he chuckled, expecting Juan to laugh also.

Juan nodded, trying to show approval at the absurd idea, although he knew that Arthur Balfour, when Foreign Secretary in 1917, had tried to persuade Baron Rothschild that the Jewish State of Israel should be set up in Uganda.

'And the 1947 boundaries?'

'Impossible. They will never agree to leave the West Bank, so we will have to drive them out. The best we can hope for is a stalemate. If I could develop a deadly virus that could discriminate between Jews and Arabs, then we might have a chance to drive them all back to America. Then I would die a happy man.'

'Moving on. What has been your greatest achievement to date?'

'Undoubtedly the dual attacks in Tanzania and Kenya. We killed hundreds and wounded thousands. It made Clinton sit up and take notice.'

'But many of the dead were locals?'

'Yes, but the reaction of the arrogant Yankees firing cruise missiles into Sudan and, thereby destroying a pharmaceutical factory that made fifty per cent of their medicines was typical of them. They immediately lost all sympathy and the Sudanese are now queuing to join our cause. Consequently, we have more volunteers than we can cope with. It also proved we can kill Americans worldwide.'

'That brings us onto training. How many madrassas do you have?'

'Let's say we are expanding at the rate of one every year.'

My God, he must have at least a dozen by now. 'And are they structured in any way?'

'By age and talents. Our better pupils are studying to get overseas qualifications.'

Yes, I know, thought Juan. 'What for?'

'They will enter professions in the West and await their time to act. If we are to win this war then we need more than suicide bombers.'

Juan continued asking questions for some time. Many of the replies were the rantings of a madman. He bragged about the bombs in Bali and Jerusalem that killed hundreds. Finally, after almost an hour, bin Laden said, 'I'm getting tired. Just one more question and then I would like to stop.'

'Have you any immediate plans for the near future?'

'A good question and one which you will know the answer to within a few days.' He laughed as he thought about what was about to happen. 'My name will soon be on the tip of everyone's tongue; more famous than Bush and Blair put together. Some years ago we had our hands on a small tactical nuclear weapon. We were betrayed, however, and I never had the chance to use it against the Israelis. This attack, believe me, will be even more spectacular. You understand why I cannot reveal details. You will have to wait and see.'

'I understand you want me to write the report immediately and let you approve it.'

He nodded.

'Can my helper take a photograph of you?'

'When I have approved the article.'

'It may take me about an hour.'

'Do it in the outer room. I will rest here, meantime.'

✶✶✶

That Friday, 7th September, a regular weekly meeting of the British Cabinet was held at No 10 Downing Street. The forthcoming Afghan invasion was discussed and the meeting broke up with members of the government deeply divided between the doves and the hawks. Afterwards, the Foreign Secretary asked Prime Minister Blair, 'Can I have a word in private, Tony?'

They adjourned to Blair's private office and sat down in easy chairs.

'What's the problem, Jack?'

'Barbara Renton, Head of MI6, is taking early retirement.'

'So?'

'She has suggested Phil Jay should be her successor.'

'He's one of us, isn't he? I would be happy to appoint him. He has a good Labour Party pedigree.'

'Fine, I'm glad you said that. I'd already taken the liberty of approaching him to see if he would accept the appointment.'

'And did he?'

'Yes. I'll get on with making it official. It's not the main reason, however, for wanting to see you.'

'Oh?'

'No. I had a long chat with Renton about Saddam Hussein, al-Qaeda, their threat to the West and our going into Afghanistan with the Americans.'

The PM sat upright, suddenly taking notice. 'As we've just been discussing in cabinet, Jack, we're committed to Article 5 of the NATO treaty. We must support the Americans.'

The Foreign Secretary nodded, 'Yes, I'm not disputing the Afghan operation. It's the other possibility that worries me. I know President Bush has been talking to you about regime change in Iraq believing Saddam is behind al-Qaeda.'

Tony Blair nodded, 'The President believes al-Qaeda is financed by Saddam. If Saddam is removed then the threat will be removed also.'

'Does the President also believe al-Qaeda's leader, bin Laden, is alive in Afghanistan or Northern Pakistan?'

'Yes. He thinks he's somewhere in the Tora Bora mountains.'

'There's something you should know that Barbara Renton told me two days ago.'

'What?'

'Five years ago, a year before we came into Government, MI6 mounted an operation to kill bin Laden.'

'No one told me that! Why wasn't I informed?'

'The operation was approved by Malcolm Rifkind. I have checked, and it was mentioned in the handover brief to Robin Cook. Perhaps, in May '97 it didn't seem important.'

'But bin Laden's alive. He's made several broadcasts on Al-Jazeera TV.'

'Renton believes al-Qaeda have made several recordings of bin Laden that can be used for propaganda purposes that don't specifically describe any particular atrocity.'

After a thoughtful pause, during which time Jack Straw stared at his boss thinking how he had aged since becoming PM, Blair asked, 'So, our Head of MI6 is telling us they have managed to kill bin Laden. How?'

'As we speak, the operation is coming to its climax. They set up an agent to pose as *The Daily Telegraph's* Lebanon correspondent. For the past five years he has regularly written articles on Israeli brutality towards the Palestinians. The aim was to gain the confidence of the multitude of Palestinian and anti-Western terrorist groups.'

'Yes, I used to wonder why *The Telegraph* was so anti-Israel. Their correspondent was called Pearson, if I remember correctly? Are you saying it was a put-up job?'

'Yes. A few weeks ago Pearson was invited to interview bin Laden in Northern Pakistan. MI6 had made him special shoes with heels hiding a concentration of anthrax spores that could be released by a hidden button. The spores will be released when Pearson interviews bin Laden.'

'Does Renton think the attack will be successful?'

'Yes. She also told me that the training of suicide bombers to infiltrate western society began at least ten years ago. The terrorists get educated in madrassas all over the Middle East. They then come to the West, integrate into society and become doctors, airline pilots, master mariners, computer scientists and so on. We're facing attacks on an unprecedented scale. I really must insist you support my move to increase recruitment to our security services. If we don't increase our vigilance, God knows what may happen.'

'Gordon will oppose such a move.'

'Maybe, but prudence mustn't be allowed to play with the public's lives.'

'OK. I'm sure David Blunkett will give us full support. What were her views on the danger posed by Saddam Hussein?'

'She assures me he does not sponsor al-Qaeda. He apparently fell out with bin Laden some nine or ten years ago, after the first Gulf War. Al-Qaeda is financed by various dissident Saudi Princes, dubious Yemeni mafia bosses and bin Laden's family fortune. What she tells me makes sense. After all, Iraq is bankrupt. UN weapons inspectors are crawling all over the place and there are restrictions on flying. Saddam couldn't possibly be financing an underground terrorist organisation without us getting wind of it.'

'But he's not so bankrupt that they're not able to have a programme of developing weapons of mass destruction.'

'Tony, from what I understand from Barbara Renton, when President Bush's father was Vice-president, America gave Iraq ten billion dollars worth of aid to help them defeat Iran. Massive amounts of biological and chemical weapons were exported legally through their Department of Commerce. She assures me the chemical weapons were used but the more dangerous biological ones were not. Instead, they were buried in the desert for safe keeping. I've brought along a copy of The Riegle Report for you to read. It's frightening what's been going on.'

'I'm busy, Jack. Who's Riegle and what's his report say?'

'Riegle is the Senator from Michigan who investigated claims of Gulf War Syndrome. His report lists, among other things, the biological weapons America exported to Iraq under licence between 1983 and 1988.'

'So, Saddam has got WMDs.'

'Except he doesn't know where they are.'

'I don't follow.'

'During the 1980-88 war and up to 1991, Iraq's Head of Research, Development and Storage of CB weapons was a woman called Kathab al Jised. She had previously gained a PhD at Cambridge University where she had been approached to keep in touch with us.'

'In other words, join MI6?'

'More or less. She was an ex officio member of Saddam's Revolutionary Council and on an irregular basis kept us in the picture of what was going on. One of our men showed her how to doctor the records of where the weapons were buried in such a way that they could never be found without knowing a secret chess position.'

'Ah, the Shannon number!'

'You know of it?'

'There are more positions on a chess board than there are atoms in the visible universe. I remember our maths teacher telling us at school. None of us believed him. It is, therefore, impossible to guess any particular position using logical processes. What happened to this… al Jised?'

'We brought her back to Britain when Desert Storm began in case the Iraqis tortured her to get the chess position.'

'Where is she now?'

'Living in North West Scotland. She married and has a new identity. When I found out about her, I did some checking. I contacted Renton's predecessor…'

'Sir Peter Stacey?'

'Yes. I went to see him. He's retired near Lechlade.'

'And what did he say?'

'He confirmed everything Renton told me. He had been in Baghdad when al Jised was recruited. He was instrumental in getting her out of Iraq when Desert Storm began. She worked for MI6 as an interpreter in London for a while before going to Scotland. He is totally convinced that the WMDs can never be found.'

'This isn't the woman who was labelled Dr Germ by several of the tabloids, is it?'

'Yes it is. As Peter Stacey said when I met him, it was an unfortunate term because she single-handedly prevented Iraq from using germ warfare. According to Stacey, Iraq has sufficient biological weapons to kill everything on the planet. He gave me details that were not even in the original report.

'What did he tell you?'

'Between 1983 and 1988 America gave Iraq,' he paused as he removed some notes from his briefcase, 'the following: 2,245 gallons of anthrax spores – enough to kill billions of people; 5,125 gallons of botulinium toxin – enough to wipe out Europe's population; 200 tons of VX – a nerve gas that can lead to paralysis and death; 100 tons of Sarin and 600 tons of mustard gas. There were other products too.'

'Do you believe the figures?'

'I've no reason to disbelieve them.'

'That's frightening. We must make sure the figures don't become public knowledge. But why is Saddam leading us to believe he's got WMDs, when he doesn't know where they are?'

'Power, Tony, power. He's tagging along the UN weapons inspectors for the hell of it. He knows they can never find the bloody things and that the UN will not, therefore, sanction an invasion for Bush junior to get his father's biological weapons back.'

The Prime Minister sighed. He rubbed his eyes; he looked tired. He said nothing for several minutes and Jack waited for him to recover.

He put his cheeks in the palms of his hands and slowly raised his eyes to the ceiling.

'So, to summarize, Jack, Saddam has little or nothing to do with al-Qaeda.' He waited for a response.

'Correct.'

'Saddam has WMDs, but hasn't a clue where they are.'

'Correct.'

'Bin Laden could be dead?'

'It's possible and, according to Barbara, probable.'

'But we haven't a body to prove it?'

'No.'

Prime Minister Blair remained staring at the ceiling, deep in thought. The Foreign Secretary knew his colleague well enough to know that their conversation wasn't over.

'Presumably, Jack,' he stopped for a few moments. 'Presumably when Pearson releases the anthrax spores to kill bin Laden he will die also?'

'Possibly, although he has been inoculated against anthrax and took antibiotics with him.'

'So, where is Pearson now?'

'We don't know. According to Renton he could be talking to bin Laden even as we speak.'

CHAPTER 51

Friday 7th September 2001

Juan was given a note pad and pencil. A table and chair had appeared from nowhere and he sat down to write. The guards remained standing at the door to Osama's room; they were still bare-footed, like himself. Mir had left, having put his shoes on. Juan's mind was racing, however. *How the hell am I going to kill him now?* He knew the prose he was writing was amateurish, but he pressed ahead, thinking about the room bin Laden was in. *There weren't any other doors other than the one into this room. He's got to come out this way. I'll have to release the spores in here and hope for the best.*

When Mir reappeared after 45 minutes, Juan looked up, 'Almost finished. You can tell Osama to come and read it if you want. While you're doing that I'll go and get Kazim to come and take a few pictures.'

Mir nodded and took the script. Juan slipped his shoes on and left, walking across the farmyard to fetch Kazim.

'Look, Kazim, when they are ready to let you take a photo of me with bin Laden, can I suggest that you tell them the inner room is too dark? Try and persuade bin Laden to come to the outer room where there is more light from the windows.'

Kazim looked puzzled, 'I have flash on the camera.'

'Yes, I know. But tell him it doesn't make for a flattering picture – red eye and all that.'

'OK.'

They entered the farm's hallway to be met by Mir. 'He wants one or two changes to the script.'

Juan sat down and altered the text as Mir instructed. When finished, Mir said, 'We can go inside now and you may take some photos. Don't forget to remove your shoes.'

Kazim looked at Juan quizzically. 'The inner room is used as the local mosque,' explained his partner.

They entered. Mir handed the amended script to Osama, who put his reading glasses on to read it carefully. The action confirmed Juan's suspicion that his eyesight was failing. After a few minutes, he looked up at Juan, smiled, and said, 'That's much better. Now, take the pictures. They will be worth a fortune to your paper next week.' He laughed – that throaty roar from the bottom of his stomach that Juan had heard so frequently years previously.

'I'm sorry, sir,' said Kazim, 'but this room is too dark for a portrait picture. May I suggest we use the other room where there is much more light.'

Perhaps flattered at being called 'Sir', Osama nodded and they all moved out. The room was fairly full: Osama, Mir, four guards and Kazim as well as Juan who stood to one side, putting his shoes on, whilst Kazim took his time to steady his tripod and angle the camera. Juan pressed the switches under the arches of his shoes, praying that he would not be noticed. Nothing appeared to happen: there was no noise, no smell and no colour from whatever was coming out.

Is anything coming out? Yes, it must be. I feel as if the heels have a puncture. Am I half-an-inch smaller? Please, God, let this work.

Kazim appeared to be unusually nervous, fumbling with the camera more than Juan had seen him do before. It was at least ten minutes before the photo-shoot was finished.

'I will send you copies in the usual way when I have had these developed,' Mir said to bin Laden. He gestured to Kazim for the camera. 'I will keep this,' he said, grinning. 'I am sure *The Telegraph* will buy you another.'

They said their farewells, returned to their overnight barn, packed the truck and departed. It was 1600 hours on Friday 7th September.

As he sat in the back, Juan thought, *He's breathed the spores in that room for at least a quarter of an hour. Let's hope that will be enough.*

That evening they camped early. It was raining heavily and progress was slow. Driving in semi-darkness was tiring and Juan sympathised with Mir when he decided to call it a day. Juan wondered if the guard, still with no name, could drive. He had shown no interest to do so and had not spoken a single word to either Juan or Kazim since leaving Peshawar four days previously.

They broke camp early on Saturday morning. The rain had turned to snow. Even with the Mitsubishi's heater on full, it was cold inside the truck; the windows continually steaming up. All four occupants began to sniff, their noses runny. Juan had taken several of his antibiotic tablets before retiring, and again while washing that morning. He wondered if he too had fallen victim to the anthrax virus he had released. He consoled himself that if Mir, No-Name and Kazim were now suffering from the deadly spores, then so, too, must bin Laden.

The snow storm worsened, the road disappeared. Lights made it worse, they reflected back from the flakes. They were down to a walking pace. Fortunately the 4x4 was doing its work, gripping the slippery surface. By three o'clock the snow had stopped and had begun to melt under a bright blue sky. Visibility suddenly improved. Mir got out of the vehicle to check their whereabouts. He got back in and admitted, 'I think we must have taken a wrong turning in the storm. I haven't a clue where we are. I will turn the truck around and we'll have to retrace our route.'

No-Name said nothing. Several hours passed before Mir proudly announced, 'I think I know where we are.'

'Think or know?' asked Juan.

A scowl was the only reply. As darkness fell, they pitched camp, made a meal and snuggled into their tents. To all intents and purposes, Saturday had been a wasted day. They had made little progress.

The following day they headed south, Juan noticing that their colds seemed to be getting worse. By Sunday afternoon it was 48 hours since he had released the spores. Kazim and Mir were beginning to sneeze frequently and their eyes were streaming constantly. At Mir's suggestion they halted to make camp earlier than usual. It was miserable weather – a damp, cold drizzle that entered the bones. It was getting darker sooner in the evenings – a feeling that the winter was going to be harsh. They made a fire and sat around it. Juan and the minder were suffering the least, although all four were shivering profusely. Juan wondered if his antibiotics were working. He assumed the guard's physical strength was a factor in his apparent resistance. They cooked dinner on their primus stoves. Their supplies were running low; there was one more meal left. 'Tomorrow night we should be in Peshawar,' remarked Mir, but he didn't sound convincing.

Half an hour afterwards, both Kazim and Mir were violently sick. They were spewing up as if they had been poisoned. Juan wrapped Kazim in his sleeping bag and tried to make him as comfortable as possible. When there was no more undigested food to puke, both began uncontrollable shivering – rigors – and spitting green and red clots of slime. Juan felt Kazim's forehead. His temperature was sky high despite the cold night.

'What do we do?' asked the guard.

'We could drive through the night,' replied Juan.

However, it was Mir who managed to gasp, 'These roads are too dangerous in the dark.' And with that he let out a sigh that went right through to Juan's very soul. He was dead. Minutes later, Kazim, too, had similarly expired.

'My God, what's happening to us?' asked No-Name.

'I don't know, I don't know,' replied Juan. 'It wasn't meant to be like this.'

'What wasn't?'

'This, this.' He pointed to Kazim as he sobbed for the loss of his companion.

The guard never pressed any further. He was not the brightest on the block and was clearly clueless as to what Juan had meant.

There was silence – total silence – not a sound. For once there was no wind, no bleating of sheep, no trees to whistle in the wind. The silence was a blanket that had wrapped itself firmly around them.

No-Name gave a loud burp, but didn't offer an apology. Then he asked, 'Do we bury them here or take them back with us?'

'I suggest we load them into the back of the truck, cover them with something, go to bed, get up early and try to get to Peshawar tomorrow afternoon.'

The guard nodded agreement.

The plan would have worked, but for one thing. The following morning Juan found himself alone, except for two dead bodies. The truck and the guard had slipped away in the night, after he had dumped Mir's and Kazim's bodies on the roadside. Juan was feeling weak and realised he had the same symptoms that had inflicted the others; except his were 24 hours later. He swallowed more of his antibiotic tablets hoping against hope that they were working.

He looked around. There was a shallow ditch on one side of the mountain track. He wrapped the bodies in their one-man tents and rolled them into the ditch. He gathered some stones, some as big as a football, others smaller, and covered the nylon shrouds as best he could. The sun was rising and he realised he would have to walk south. He was probably a day's drive away from Peshawar; maybe as much as 100 miles. He had no alternative but to start walking and hope someone would come along, although he had his doubts – they hadn't seen anything since leaving the farm on Friday afternoon. He did his maths. *If I walk at three miles per hour for eleven hours per day then I have at least three days ahead of me.* It was cold and he was hungry. There were several bottles of water left, but plenty of small streams flowed down the hills. *At least I won't die of thirst. It could be worse; it might be raining or even snowing.*

He plodded on. Ahead he could see a precipitation and knew he was going to get wet. He walked into the wall of rain; it was a downpour.

Although his clothing was supposed to be waterproof, he could feel the cold seeping into his body. He imagined he was soaked, but it was only into his shoes that the rain had penetrated. The gentle downhill slope made progress easier, although in places the unmade road was slippery and care had to be taken. His feet were beginning to feel uncomfortable. Prior to discharging the anthrax, his shoes had made Juan feel he was walking on tennis balls. Now the deflated heels were beginning to give him blisters. He realised he would either have to walk barefoot and risk frostbite or improvise and make himself something more comfortable.

He walked on for about another hour and a half when, perhaps two miles away, he saw a spiral of smoke rising. *A smallholding?* As he neared the source of the fire, however, he realised it was their Mitsubishi truck. It had slipped off the road into a shallow ravine and must have burst into flames. He approached with caution, scrambling into the wide ditch to investigate. Inside the cabin were the charred remains of No-Name. *He either went off the road in the dark, or died from the virus before crashing. Unfortunately, the bastard has wrecked the truck.*

He looked to see what could be cannibalised. One of the rear seats was relatively untouched by the fire. The camping kit was intact in the open rear of the truck, possibly because it was soaking wet from the heavy rain. He found a Stanley knife and cut the foam padding from the seat, shaped it roughly to fit his feet and wrapped the padding with strips of nylon sheeting. Then he cut rubber from the spare tyre, also in the open back, and made soles, tying them to his padded slippers. *Excellent! I feel inches taller.*

He packed what food had been left and set off again in high spirits. He noticed that afternoon, however, that he began to sniff and cough. By early evening he was spitting green gunk and his throat was sore. His eyes were running. He made camp, erecting his one-man tent against some bushes that might provide some shelter. He lit the primus and cooked a hot meal. Half an hour later, he was vomiting violently. It reminded him of what had happened to Mir and Kazim. *In 30 minutes, I will die.*

He swallowed the last of his penicillin tables and wrapped himself inside his sleeping bag. The tent kept out the incessant wind, but the howling was intolerable. It sounded like sheep ewes bleating, crying for their lambs. He remembered his flock at Ballajorra. *They wouldn't survive up here.* He raised a weak smile; *a long time ago and a world away.* He began shivering uncontrollably. Rigor had begun. He knew it was nature's way of attempting to raise his body temperature. He shut his eyes. He imagined he heard a noise outside. He thought he saw Molly and the children walking towards him through the mist. She was smiling and the kids were waving at him, skipping along holding hands. He felt cold; his mind began to wander back to his childhood. He remembered getting his first cricket bat – a Slazenger Len Hutton; listening to his mother telling him stories of ancient Egypt; singing in the church choir – *'There is a green hill far away…'* He shut his eyes and began humming to himself *'… he only could unlock the gate of heaven and let us in…'*

Is the zip tent door opening? Can Molly be coming to fetch me?

CHAPTER 52

Tuesday 11th September 2001

By 5pm GMT the phones were red-hot between Downing Street and Air Force One, President Bush's office in the sky. Elsewhere, chaired by Vice-president, Dick Cheney, Washington's clique in The White House was already plotting retribution for the destruction of the Twin Towers and the attack on the Pentagon. The plan to invade Afghanistan had been scheduled for a few months later. It would be brought forward to 7th October. Now right-wingers were openly demanding the President should give the go-ahead to simultaneously invade Iraq. President Bush, having been initially flown to Nebraska for safety reasons, was flying back to his seat of government. He was confused with the alarming amount of contradictory data that was arriving at the bank of computer terminals in his aircraft.

Tony Blair, his best buddy and most trusted ally, was receiving calls every few minutes, or so it seemed. George W Bush secretly wanted his advice on the best way forward.

'Donald Rumsfeld wants me to bomb Baghdad tonight,' he told Tony. 'What do you think?'

'Three things, George. MI6 assure me that Saddam Hussein no longer has any links to al-Qaeda or bin Laden. Secondly, MI6 has been plotting bin Laden's execution for years and believes he may already be dead. Thirdly, Saddam poses no threat whatsoever as he can't access the American WMDs given to him during Reagan's tenure.'

'Are you telling me bin Laden has been successfully assassinated?'

'I can't be certain, but we should know by this time next week.'

'And you're saying he has no WMDs either?'

'No. What we are certain about is that he can't access them because they were hidden in such a way that they can't be found. The records of where they are buried are indecipherable.'

'Ah, rubbish, Tony. I know that bastard Saddam has the weapons. My father gave them to him when he was Vice to Reagan: thousands of gallons of anthrax, sarin, VX, the lot.'

'Yes, we know. We have the details on our files and I've read The Riegle Report. But Saddam never used them, George.'

'And that proves he must still have them and is planning to give them to bin Laden to destroy our cities.'

'George, you know I'll support you whenever you want. However, if you are going to go into Iraq as well as Afghanistan then I'm going to have to keep it secret for as long as possible. I've several pacifists in my cabinet. If they get wind of this, they could make trouble.'

'Sack them.'

'I already have slipped some of them sideways. It's not going to be easy for me, George. The other problem is going to be one of legality. I'll need to take advice from Goldsmith.'

'Who the hell is Goldsmith?'

'My Attorney General. I suspect he'll tell me that Resolution 678 is not sufficient and we'll need a clear mandate from the UN if we're to invade Iraq to implement a regime change.'

'Look, Tony, do what I do with the awkward buggers.'

'What's that?'

'Work around them. Get to know who is with you. Invite them to your private office. Sit them down, give them a drink and make decisions out of cabinet. I do it all the time; life is a whole lot easier.'

'You're suggesting I run a sofa government and keep your invasion plans off the Cabinet agenda?'

'Exactly! My chiefs are already planning Baghdad for March '03.

Meanwhile, we'll soften the place up a bit with the odd cruise missile. By then we'll have cleared up Afghanistan. Resolution 678 is good enough for me.'

'I might have a problem with Barbara Renton. She's the Head of MI6 and is retiring at the end of the month. I don't see how we can gag her when she finds out we are going to war in Iraq to remove a threat that doesn't exist.'

'Look, Tony. I'm not going to be mucked about on this one. As far as I'm concerned Iraq has WMDs that could be launched at a moment's notice and bin Laden is al-Qaeda's chief. That's good enough for me. You leave her to me. What's her name again?' He picked up a pen to scribble the name.

'Your Head of the CIA, Tenet, will know her – Barbara Renton. She is going to retire to somewhere near Carcassonne.'

'Never heard of it. We'll find her and get her to change her mind.'

'That would be a big help, George.'

★★★

Later that night, George Tenet, the Director of the Central Intelligence Agency since 1997, was at the emergency meetings in the White House.

During a coffee break, President Bush took him to one side. 'Before I forget with all this going on, George, I've a job for you that has to be kept strictly under wraps.'

'What is it, Mr President?'

'Now we've all agreed the Pentagon is to begin planning the invasion of Iraq, there may be a problem with the Brits helping us.'

'Why is that?'

'Their Head of MI6 is taking retirement and believes Saddam does not pose a threat.'

'Yes, I know. She told me she is retiring at the end of the month.'

'Prime Minister Blair thinks she could create trouble by going public with the fact that there is no evidence to link Saddam to either al-Qaeda or bin Laden. She's told Blair that Saddam doesn't even know where his own WMDs are.' He laughed, thinking this was funny. 'What a tosser,' he added as an afterthought.

'She is right. All the biological weapons we exported to Iraq were buried in their deserts, and the records doctored in such a way they can never be found. We gave Iraq anything from thousands of gallons of anthrax spores to just two litres of VX-R.'

'VX-R? What the hell is that? And why such a small amount?'

'It is a top secret variant of the nerve agent VX. At the time, about 1984 if I remember rightly, it had recently been developed and we thought we could get Saddam to test it for us.'

'What's it do?'

'We don't know.'

'George, stop pissing me about.'

'Seriously, our scientists are too scared to try it out in case it goes badly wrong.'

'OK. I'll rephrase, what's it supposed to do?'

'The "R" stands for radioactive. Doctors at Berkeley were experimenting with Thorium-90 trying to find ways Beta particles could be used to treat eye cancers. During further experiments minute amounts of the protein drug Botox were infused with Californium-98 to investigate whether the drug could be absorbed through the skin rather than injected. The US Army Medical Command Centre at Fort Detrick picked up on the experiment and went further with various nerve agents. The results with VX were like something from Stephen King.'

'Go on.'

'VX-R emits Gamma rays that are infected with VX. They can be fired like a ray.'

'We have a ray gun? Why didn't I know about this? I'm the Commander-in-Chief.'

'The experiments were stopped because we couldn't be sure of the outcomes. We have the potential of a gun that fires a nerve agent that will penetrate the body. The problem is storage. To confine the VX-R, it has to be kept in a lead jacket, half an inch thick.'

'So why did we give two litres to Saddam?'

'We encouraged him to give it a try. If he killed his own troops, we would learn from the process. After all, we had hundreds of advisers out there watching and training the Iraqis.'

'And did he use it?'

'No. His Head of Research and Development persuaded him all biological weapons were too dangerous and she stored them at secret sites in the deserts, like I've already said.'

'Then we have to retrieve it, George.'

'Not that easy, boss. Iraq is about half the size of Texas. Imagine trying to find a two litre bottle buried somewhere in your home state.'

'I understand she was a British agent and they whisked her away to safety.'

'Correct, Mr President. Saddam Hussein can't find where his former Head of CB Weapons put the damn stuff. She doctored the records so well that they can't be found and will remain hidden forever.'

'I believe that's a load of bollocks. Saddam's a canny bastard and is playing us and the UN Inspectors along.'

'If you say so, sir.'

'MI6 think bin Laden is dead. You're going to tell me you think so too.'

'Ah, the anthrax assassination. Whether it will be a success, or not, I can't say. It has been meticulously planned by MI6. The jury is still out.'

'The former Head of MI6, a Barbara someone...'

'Barbara Renton, Mr President – a fine figure of a woman.'

'She is retiring to the South of France. She knows too much and could pose a threat to our plans. I want you to change her mind.'

'I would advise against that, Mr President.'

'George, do you enjoy your job?'

'Yes, sir.'

'Then if you still want to be in it next year, send two of your best men to France.'

CHAPTER 53

Sunday 7th April 2002

At the bottom of the Grande Rue in the centre of Belveze is *La Chene Verte,* the bar where everyone, who is anyone, meets for an aperitif on Sunday before returning to their wives for lunch.

'Ah, *Monsieur Le Maire,* I'm glad I've caught you.'

'Pardon, *Monsieur Beauchant. Vous avez un probleme?*'

'*Oui,* with my neighbour. She has gone away and her garden is like a jungle. It is ruining the ambiance of our neighbourhood.'

'She is English, *Oui?*'

'She lives permanently in Belveze. Or, at least she did, until five months ago when she disappeared suddenly without telling me. She was an excellent neighbour and had always kept her garden ship-shape.'

'I'm not sure I can do anything.'

'Madame Renton bought the house about five years ago. She used it for holidays while she was having it modernised, but began living permanently here last November. Her sudden departure worries me. At first I thought she may have gone away on holiday, but now I think something may have happened to her. I think you should authorise the gendarme to enter the house to see if he can find her whereabouts.'

'I'm not sure if I can do that. However, Jean is over there. Let's ask him. Jean,' he shouted, 'come here a minute, we have a question to ask you.'

Jean Gallipier, one of the two gendarmes based in Belveze, approached them.

'*Oui, Monsieur Le Maire,* how can I help you?'

'We're not sure. Henri, tell Jean what you have just told me.'

The gendarme listened whilst continuing to sip his pression.

'If you give me the authorisation, *Monsieur Le Maire*, then I will get a locksmith from Limoux tomorrow and we can enter. If I remember, the property has shutters on both the front and back doors and all the ground floor windows.' He looked to Henri Beauchant to confirm. The concerned neighbour nodded.

'What do you hope to find inside,' asked the mayor, 'that will help solve the mystery of her disappearance?'

'Hopefully papers such as the deeds. We will then know who the notaire was that handled the sale. He will have her former address. It may give us a lead to help find her.'

The following morning, the mayor – Jacques Scoffier, the neighbour – Henri Beauchant, the locksmith – Robert Rousseau, and the gendarme – Jean Gallipier, stood in front of the house.

'This is not a run-of-the-mill door shutter, *Monsieur Maire*,' remarked the locksmith.

'Why? What is so special about it?'

'It hasn't a key. It has been closed by a remote control zapper. Furthermore,' he tapped the shutter with his knuckles, 'it is made of high quality steel. It will be a devil to open.'

'But you can open it?'

'I will have to use a diamond tipped drill and my angle grinder to cut through the metal. I will need power.'

'I have a long extension cable and can run it from my house next door,' offered M Beauchant.

It took over half an hour for Robert Rousseau, occasionally swearing at the strength of the shutter, to cut a hole, a little bigger than a football, in the base. Kneeling and shining his torch into the darkness, he peered inside.

'What can you see?' asked the gendarme.

'The front door. What else did you expect?' His patience had begun to wear thin; he was doing all the work while the others hung around doing bugger all. The locksmith put his arm through the hole and tried to undo something inside.

'I think the lock is coming undone,' he said. 'There!'

He pulled and the shutter moved upwards into its recess to reveal the stout oak door. He smiled to himself. 'This will only take a few minutes,' he said, as he fumbled in his tool box for a set of lock picks. In less than a minute, he had opened the door to reveal a corridor, perhaps three metres in length.

All four peered inside and gasped. At the end was a second metal shutter, identical to the first.

'Incredible,' remarked the mayor. 'I've never seen anything like that before.'

'Neither have I,' added Robert, 'and I've been in this trade for twenty years. There would have been an internal door there and it's been replaced. You'll notice it is also operated by a zapper – probably the same remote. I'll bet they came down simultaneously.'

'That's ridiculous,' said the gendarme, 'no one has two shutters.'

'And why?' asked the mayor. 'What's so special about this house?'

'We'll only find out by opening the second shutter,' replied Jean. 'Will it take as long to open as the first?'

'Yes, I guess so,' replied Robert.

'Then, you'd better get on with it.'

The locksmith groaned, knelt down and started his drill. The others adjourned to *La Chene Verte*. Breaking and entering houses on behalf of the Gendarmerie paid well – a good little earner. He had to keep his trap shut or he might lose the contract.

Returning 30 minutes later, the three comrades found the house wide open: all the windows, shutters and the back door too. A draught was blowing through the house.

'It was awful musty in here,' explained Robert, 'I thought I'd better let some air in.'

The gendarme found what he was looking for quickly. 'Here we are,' he shouted. 'Over here, in the desk are the deeds of the house. I see Monsieur Corbiere in Limoux was the notaire.'

'And I've found a photo of her,' said the neighbour. 'This is Mme Renton outside *La Chene Verte*.'

They all peered at the photo. 'A handsome woman,' remarked the locksmith.

'Yes, she must have been quite a cracker in her day,' replied Henri.

'Do you want me to go and see the notaire?' asked the mayor.

'I think not,' replied the gendarme. 'Her disappearance is a police matter; particularly as the house has been left in an immaculate state. It's almost as if the place has been deliberately wiped clean. I will call in to see you later and let you know what I have found out. I will take the photo with me to help with identification. In the meantime,' he turned to Robert, 'can you make the house secure? This could now be a crime scene. I will have to report her disappearance to my inspector in Carcassonne.'

✳✳✳

'Thank you for seeing me so soon, Monsieur Corbiere.'

'Your phone call sounded urgent. How can I help you?'

'I believe you acted as Madame Renton's notaire when she bought a house in Belveze some years ago.' He showed the notaire the photo. He nodded, confirming identification.

'We found these deeds in her house when we forced an entry earlier this morning.'

'*Pourquoi?*'

'Initially her neighbour complained to the mayor about the state of the garden. He hadn't seen Mme Renton for many months. The mayor asked me to investigate. There are certain signs indicating she has disappeared completely. I wondered if you had an alternative address for her.'

'The house is solely in her name. She has no mortgage. She paid for it outright. To answer your question: I have an address on my file. If I remember, she had an apartment in London – Holland Park, I think. Let me have a look.' He called his secretary to bring in Mrs Renton's file.

While they were waiting, he asked the gendarme, 'What are you intending to do?'

'I will ask my divisional inspector in Carcassonne to investigate. There is something fishy about her disappearance, but I can't put my finger on it. Did you know the house had two connecting steel shutters at the front that worked in unison? They effectively created a small cell in the front corridor.'

'No. I've never seen the property. I acted on Mme Renton's behalf. She bought it through the local immobilier: Gaston Fleury & Sons. You could ask them. They may know something about the property's history.' M Corbiere idly continued flicking through his file. 'She left me instructions in case of her death or disappearance.'

'Oh, is that usual?'

'No, but not uncommon when the owner is single. You know what French law is like. Properties can lie empty for generations.'

'What are you to do?'

'Essentially, sell the house. Half the proceeds to go to the local village primary school…'

'Excellent. And the rest?'

'To be transferred to a numbered Swiss Bank account.'

'In the name of?'

'No one, just a numbered account.'

'Untraceable, I suppose?'

'Of course.'

✳✳✳

'New Scotland Yard. How can I help?'

'Can I speak with Detective Chief Inspector Patrick Rice, please?'

'Whom shall I say is calling?'

'Tell him it's Inspector Claude Riou, from the Gendarmerie HQ in Carcassonne.'

There was a moment of silence before a voice replied, 'Claude, good to hear from you! How are you keeping?'

'Well thanks, Pat. When are you coming down to see us again?'

'Mary and I were only talking about you the other day. We were wondering about getting a cheap flight from Stansted next month.'

'Then do it. Lousette and I would love to see you again. Meanwhile, I have a favour to ask.'

'Fire away.'

The French Inspector proceeded to describe the disappearance of Mrs Renton, the immaculate state of the house and the unusual pair of shutters. Pat listened carefully and took the details of Barbara Renton's last known address in London. 'I will get back to you as soon as possible, but there appear to be two possibilities: either she went away for an extended holiday without telling her neighbour, and had an accident, or...'

'Or?'

'Or, her disappearance was carefully planned.'

'Engineered?'

'Yes. She has deliberately flown the nest for some reason or been abducted.'

'Are you suggesting she may have been murdered for some reason and her body hidden?'

'It's a possibility that has to be considered. Although that peculiar hallway you say she had built worries me. I'll do some digging and find out more about her. Now, before you go, let me check I've got the details right... What did you say her full name was?... And her age?'

'I will fax you a photo of her. It may help.'

***

The following day, Detective Chief Inspector Rice, armed with the fax,

411

decided to visit the apartment in Holland Park. He found a retired army officer living at Barbara Renton's former flat.

'She left to live permanently in the South of France when she retired,' he said. 'I have her new address somewhere,' he volunteered.

A quick check confirmed the address in Belveze.

'Did you know her well?' asked the inspector.

'I only met her when I came to live here. Mike, upstairs, knew her better. They were neighbours for almost ten years. He adopted her cat.'

On the floor above, Pat met the long-time resident.

'Do you know what she did?' he asked.

'She was some sort of civil servant. Quite high up, I think. I've no idea what department; she was rather secretive about her work.'

Should be easy to track her down, thought the detective.

Subsequent routine enquiries failed to locate anyone called Barbara Helen Renton, aged about 60 years, as ever having been a civil servant. Puzzled, but sufficiently savvy to realise she could have been in one of the security services, Pat Rice, the following day, decided to go upstairs and see his contact in Special Branch: Superintendent Jack Boulton.

'I'm trying to trace a retired high-powered civil servant, possibly about sixty, by the name of Barbara Helen Renton. This is a picture of her.'

A quizzical look appeared on his colleague's face. 'Why?'

'The French police think she has disappeared under mysterious circumstances.'

'How did you get involved, Pat?'

'An old mate in the local gendarmerie at Carcassonne asked me to do him a favour.'

'You'd better tell me more.'

'Now it's my turn to ask: why?'

'If that's the person who I think it is, then she was the Head of MI6 up to about six months ago.'

'Bloody hell.'

'You may have just opened a can of worms. I think we'd better go upstairs and see the ACC.'

CHAPTER 54

The Assistant Chief Constable and Head of Special Branch, Commissioner Mike Watts, sat passively as Pat Rice regaled the story of his investigations and Barbara Renton's apparent disappearance. The ACC looked at the fax and agreed, 'That's Barbara all right. She was a bright spark. Either something happened in the South of France that frightened her and caused her to run away, or she was taken out by someone. I think the key is the motive. What did she know that was so special?'

Both Rice and Boulton looked blank and said nothing.

Commissioner Watts continued, 'I think the only person who might know is Barbara's successor, don't you?'

They nodded sheepishly, both realising they should have known the answer. He picked up the red phone on his desk, pressed a few numbers, and announced, 'Phil, Mike here. A problem has cropped up that I think needs your immediate attention. Can I come over straight away?'

He paused, listening to the other speaker, then continued, 'I'd like to bring with me Superintendent Jack Boulton from my Special Branch and Detective Chief Inspector Pat Rice, Serious Crime Squad, if that's OK?'

Thirty minutes later, the three police officers were being checked into the SIS building at Vauxhall Cross. They were accompanied to the top floor and into a large office with magnificent views over the Thames.

The usual introductions completed, and a reminder that anything discussed would be subject to the Official Secrets Act, Phil Jay listened intently to the events leading to their meeting.

'I agree with your prognosis, Mike. Either Barbara has done a moonlight flit or she has been murdered for what she knew.'

'What sort of a woman was she?' asked the ACC.

Phil smiled. 'Barbara had, shall we say, an active libido. She and a man called Juan Quayle had been an item, on and off, going back as far as '92.'

'What's special about that?'

'Without wishing to go into too many details, Quayle was groomed for over five years to assassinate Osama bin Laden, al-Qaeda's chief and, of course, the mastermind of 9/11.'

'Bloody hell. So you think she may have been killed by bin Laden's terrorists?'

'No. Let me explain. I'll stick to the salient points to keep it brief. Back in 1990, Quayle was recruited to infiltrate al-Qaeda. He did this successfully for two years. When he came back to us, he was able to give us a vast amount of information about how al-Qaeda operated. At that time the organisation's modus operandi was largely unknown. In 1995 al-Qaeda caught up with him and destroyed his family: a wife and four young children. He was lucky to escape harm, though I suspect he would have given anything for it to have been the other way around. He vowed revenge and we entered into an elaborate plan for him to kill bin Laden.'

'But bin Laden is still alive!' gasped the ACC.

'Not so. The operation took about six years but, in September 2001, a few days before 9/11, Quayle pulled it off in Pakistan.'

'But bin Laden appeared on TV bragging about 9/11 a week or so later. He couldn't have been dead.'

'Believe it or not, he had already been dead for about ten days. What you saw had been recorded previously. There may be a dozen such recordings that are characterised by such vague messages. Bin Laden didn't actually refer to the Twin Towers falling to the ground, only that they had been attacked successfully. Neither did he brag about killing over 3,000 Americans. By such subterfuge, his successors keep the mystique of his charmed life alive for his followers who believe he is indestructible.'

'Then why don't we tell the public that he is dead?'

'Until we find his body, we have no proof.'

'In which case, you can't be certain?'

'No, but take it from me, he is dead. Unfortunately, Quayle died as well; hence no concrete proof.'

The ACC knew better than to press the point. 'So, where does that leave us?'

'The Americans are looking for a scapegoat for the 9/11 attacks. They need bin Laden to be alive. By claiming Iraq has weapons of mass destruction that can be used against the West at a moment's notice is convenient. Preparations are being made to invade Iraq and remove Saddam from power.'

'You said "claiming". Don't they have WMDs?'

'They have them all right. After all, it was the US that gave them to Iraq during their war with Iran. Now America is running scared and wants them back. However, Iraq doesn't know where they are.'

'How come?'

'They were hidden by a former agent of ours when she was in charge of their WMD research and development. She doctored the records so that no one could decipher where they were buried.'

'Surely codes can be broken?'

'Not these ones, unless you happen to know the chess position used to code the lat/longs.'

Mike, not being a chess player, decided to accept Phil's assertion. 'What you are saying is that the US is worried that Mrs Renton may blow the whistle that America's excuse to invade Iraq is wrong on two counts: bin Laden is already dead and there are, effectively, no WMDs.'

'Correct.'

'But if you know this, then the Prime Minister and the Foreign Secretary also know.'

415

'Correct, again.'

'Then why hasn't the PM told President Bush the truth?'

'He has, but Bush won't listen. To make matters worse, Tony Blair has declared his support for the invasion.'

Mike Watts put his face in the palms of his hands and rubbed his eyes, muttering, 'I can't believe it.' The two junior officers sat impassively, knowing full well that this was one conversation that they could never repeat. 'Are you inferring that the CIA has somehow removed Mrs Renton from the scene?'

Phil Jay leant back in his chair and took some time to reply. 'There are only three agencies with the skill to pull this off, apart from ourselves.'

'Go on.'

'The first is the Russian FSB.'

'Why would they want to kill her?'

'Putin is ex-KGB and since replacing Yeltsin there has been a distinct shift in their foreign policy towards the West. When Major Quayle came back from Russia, he claimed a certain General Lutikov, a former associate of Putin, was supplying al-Qaeda with weapons. Subsequently, Yeltsin had a purge after the failed *coup d'état*. Lutikov and several others disappeared to Siberia. A hardliner like Putin would see Helen Renton, effectively Quayle's boss, as an enemy to be eliminated.'

'The second?'

'Mossad.'

'Mossad?!'

'Quayle, during his various times in the wilderness, worked with two Mossad agents who were both killed: the first in Tunis in 1991 and the second helping him last September. They wouldn't take that lightly, especially as, in both cases, we set up their agent, knowing they might not survive the operation.'

'The third?'

'The third, of course, is the CIA who would be acting on behalf of Bush to keep her quiet prior to the Iraq invasion. My guess is it was them.'

'In which case we will never know what happened to her?'

'I wouldn't assume she's dead. Even Quayle was something of a cat with nine lives. We never found his body either; it's probably rotting away somewhere in the Hindu Kush. Barbara had a brilliant brain and would have foreseen the possibility of being targeted.' He turned to Rice, 'Tell me more about this shuttered corridor in her house.'

The inspector told him what little he knew about the co-ordinated steel shutters operated by a zapper.

'You see,' began the Head of MI6, 'CIA hit-men operate in pairs. I can see Barbara trapping them in the hallway and gassing them with something like cyanide. She then disposes of their bodies in the countryside and does a moonlight flit. Brilliant! She is probably ensconced on the Riviera, Turkey, or a Greek island. I know she used a numbered Swiss bank account – untraceable. Good luck to her.'

'But surely the CIA won't let her get away with killing two of their own men?'

'What can they do? They can hardly come to us for help – admitting they tried to silence the former Head of MI6. Nor can they go to the French and admit they tried to kill her on their patch. Furthermore, they haven't a clue where she is hiding. No, I think they will realise they have erred and will continue to prepare for the invasion by putting pressure on the UN weapons inspectors to find the missing WMDs and get a new UN Security Resolution.'

'And if they don't?'

'They'll go ahead anyway.'

***

'It's a lovely evening, shall we go for a walk?'

'Better still, we'll stroll down to the old town and I'll buy you dinner at one of the harbour-side bistros.'

They left their apartment situated on the top floor, took the lift to the ground level, and walked into the warm evening sunshine bedecking

Rue Albert 1st. At the bottom of the boulevard, they walked through the gardens, watched the locals playing petanque and turned east. They strolled past the Picasso museum situated in the Chateau Grimaldi and entered the warren of small streets that make up the old town of Antibes.

'This is paradise,' he said. 'Do you think we'll ever be found here?'

'No, I don't. Those passports and documents I had made up before I left MI6 are genuine. No one will ever find M et Mme Richet. With our money in numbered Swiss banks accounts, how can they?'

EPILOGUE

The following seven-line announcement appeared in the *Gilgit Gazette* on Saturday 15th September 2001:

Moab al Saidenn: In his sleep passed away peacefully surrounded by several of his lieutenants on Wednesday 12th September 2001 at his residence in the Tora Bora. He faced his sudden illness with great dignity and characteristic courage. Although utterly irreplaceable, his fighting spirit will live forever in the inspirational messages he has left for his troops. The events of the previous day will be his permanent memorial.

The *Gazette*, a small local weekly with a circulation of less than 10,000, is rarely read beyond the immediate area of Gilgit.

However, in December 2001, three months after the US led invasion of Afghanistan, a Taliban official unintentionally was overheard by a reporter from the *Pakistan Observer*, admitting that Osama bin Laden had died several months previously in the Tora Bora of unknown lung complications that had not responded to treatment. Subsequently, a speculative report appeared in the Egyptian daily – Al Wafd on Wednesday 26th December 2001:

Moab al Saidenn suffered sudden serious breathing problems and died a natural death last September. His funeral was attended by 30 al-Qaeda fighters and some members of his family. He was buried according to Wahhabi tradition; therefore, no mark has been left on his grave.

The use of Osama's pseudonym was significant. Al-Qaeda desperately wanted to maintain the pretence that he was alive in order to boost their fighters' morale. It also suited the American Intelligence Agencies: they wanted him alive to justify their invasion of Afghanistan.

That December, a massive operation involving US Special Forces and the British SAS had attacked the Tora Bora complex with the specific aim of finding Osama bin Laden. He was never found. With their tail between their legs, the US was prepared to allow speculation of bin Laden's death to become public. Consequently, a few months later, in April 2002, Donald Rumsfeld, US Defence Secretary, hinted at his death when he stated, 'We've heard neither hide nor hair of him for six months, or more.'

On 26 February 2003, during a debate in The House of Commons on Iraq, Peter Kilfoyle, MP for Liverpool Walton, recommended members of The House read The Riegle Report. When Mr Kilfoyle asked the Foreign Secretary if anthrax had been supplied by the United States to Iraq, Mr Straw replied, 'As far as I know, the anthrax did not come from the United States. However, even if it did, *while it would have been wrong of the US to supply it, it would have been even worse of Iraq, in defiance of the United Nations, to continue to hang on to it.*'

On 17th March 2003, two days before the invasion of Iraq began, Robin Cook, then Leader of the House, resigned from the British Government over the impending attack on Iraq. Described by Andrew Marr as the most brilliant resignation speech ever given in the House of Commons, Cook said, 'I can't accept collective responsibility for the decision to commit Britain to military action in Iraq... Iraq probably has no weapons of mass destruction in the commonly understood sense of the term — namely a credible device capable of being delivered against a strategic city target. It probably still has biological toxins and battlefield chemical munitions, but it has had them since the 1980s when US companies sold Saddam anthrax agents and the then British Government approved the building of chemical and munitions factories. Why is it now so urgent that we should take military action to disarm a military capacity that has been there for twenty years, and which we helped to create?'

Three days later the coalition forces, mostly American and British, invaded Iraq. The Weapons of Mass Destruction were never found. There was no response from Osama bin Laden.

Nothing positive was heard about bin Laden until Benazir Bhutto admitted in an interview with David Frost on 2 November 2007 that bin Laden had been murdered. Surprisingly, Frost never followed up the assertion. American TV companies and the BBC removed her reference to the murder when showing extracts of the interview. However, when al Jazeera TV showed the full interview and it subsequently appeared on YouTube, the BBC quietly reinserted the reference. President Musharaf confirmed her assertion to be correct to reporters outside Parliament a few days after the interview.

On 27 December 2007 Benazir was assassinated. The attack had all the hallmarks of al-Qaeda: namely, two simultaneous attacks. Firstly, a gunman fired shots at her passing car; then, secondly, in the confusion, an explosion near the car killed her. An al-Qaeda commander, al-Yazid, claimed responsibility.

In April 2011, President Obama, with his approval rating flagging, needed a boost. Prior to announcing the withdrawal of 30,000 American troops from Afghanistan, he needed an excuse to satisfy his Commanders-in-Chief. An operation was mounted and on 2 May someone purported to be Osama bin Laden was captured. Despite being visibly frail and unarmed, he was shot, his body disposed by dropping it in the ocean and no photographic evidence was released. A few days later, when justifying the withdrawal from Afghanistan, the President mentioned, 'Exhibit A… now that Osama bin Laden is dead… we can begin the withdrawal of troops.' He knew that the cost of keeping troops in Afghanistan was running at a **monthly cost of $6.7 billion** and could not be maintained indefinitely. His popularity jumped ten points. He had learnt a lesson his predecessor, George W Bush, hadn't: *To have a war, you need an enemy. Remove the enemy, and you haven't the need for a war.*

To quote Field-Marshal Montgomery: "*The US… broke the second rule of war. That is, don't go fighting with your land army on the mainland of Asia. Rule one is don't march on Moscow.*"